THE SCARRED KING II

JOURNEY

(1.0)

Rose Foreman and Josh Foreman

Breath of Life Development
P.O. Box 2357
Woodinville, WA 98072-2357

ISBN paperback 978-1-942926-04-7

ebook 978-1-942926-08-5

audio 978-1-942926-09-2

Library of Congress Control Number: 2019900485

Cover art, layout and illustrations by Josh Foreman

To see full color versions of the maps and illustrations
or to sign up for our newsletter, visit

www.BreathOfLifeDev.com

PREVIOUSLY in THE SCARRED KING I:

The Sea Predators, Bowmark's tribe, had fled genocide two hundred years ago. They settled in secret on an undiscovered chain of tropical islands they painstakingly made home: StoneGrove.

The son of the king, Bowmark, feared the day he would have to step onto the Bronze Disc—set over flowing lava—and kill a challenger to prove he was worthy of becoming king.

A conspiracy placed Bowmark's best friend, Sunrise, on the Disc as challenger. There was no escape. Either one or both would die. Sunrise urged Bowmark to kill him and not waste his death.

After Bowmark won his throne, conspirators grew desperate enough to trap the royal family and demand the proving be done again. Wounded and heartsick, Bowmark instead proposed to abdicate and leave the islands to find out if their enemies were still seeking to kill all the Sea Predators. The conspirators gave him an impossible task: He must bring back ten treasures from ten lands.

Bowmark hoped that he would heal and grow stronger and more skilled so he could return, challenge RaiseHim, and kill the usurper.

On his journey, he picked up a magic staffshifter, a lightball, a golden ring in the shape of a coiled snake, and a magician's cord. He also ended up with a tezledek partner against his will. The tezledek, Scolla, looked exactly like the creeping monster that frequented Bowmark's childhood nightmares. The size of a toddler, he resembled a wrinkled black sack covered with spines. He had huge copper eyes framed by large bat wing shaped ears, long arms, and four stubby legs. He promised to help Bowmark obtain a treasure.

In Discoria, Bowmark—ignorant of local culture—was tricked into stealing some politically important jewels and then was denied the promised treasure he could have taken back to StoneGrove. Worried that the people he gave the jewels to would knife him in the back, he dared to trust his uninvited companion's advice and sailed for Bysea with Scolla complaining at his side.

AS TRADE IS THE LIFEBLOOD OF OUR PEOPLE:
SO CRIME, STRIFE AND WAR ARE DISEASES THAT SHALL
BE GIVEN NO MERCY. SWIFT AND SURE SHALL BE THE REMEDY.

~BYSEA CITY CHARTER

Bowmark contemplated his problem. How could he make sure he killed RaiseHim before the lying designate killed him? That RaiseHim would kill him was a given. Bowmark would step on the Bronze Disc set above flowing lava with no weapons and no sandals. The usurping designate would have securely tied sandals to mitigate the heat of the metal and he would have all the weapons he wanted. The thought of killing another person again—even one as vile as RaiseHim—made Bowmark feel ill. But after months of trying to think of a way around it, he had accepted that it was the only option.

Bowmark leaned against the mast of his outrigger canoe and chewed on a twig. Cold sunlight sprinkled gem sparkles on the sea. A brisk wind blew through his short, coiled, red hair. He had not seen land for a day.

Nine more treasures to obtain before he could return home and step on the Disc to save Father, his little brother, and the rest of the Sea Predators from the murderous rule of RaiseHim.

Bowmark gripped the edge of the thwart, rolled to a handstand, and did vertical pushups. If he was strong enough, could he take a spear to the gut, charge RaiseHim, and shove him into the lava before he died? The wind tilted him off-balance. He flipped and straddled the canoe with a foot on each gunwale. He ran through stances.

"Stop thumping." Scolla sounded like a wheezing old man but looked like a monster. Bowmark tried to not hold that against the tezledek. He tried to be grateful the stowaway had given him a magician's cord.

"Stop thumping!"

If he had stayed designate for more than two days, Bowmark would have learned royal-court methods to deal with irritating people. "My canoe, my rules. I need to exercise. Or would you rather I stepped off the canoe to exercise?"

"Quite yes. I need to sleep."

"Perhaps you should step off the canoe to take a nap."

Wheezing, Scolla shifted his baggy skin around. The sunlight revealed shifting iridescent blue as his head emerged from the folds of bumpy skin around his back and shoulders. He squinted as he wobbled on the prow thwart. "Snickering Doom."

What that meant besides that Scolla was unhappy was a mystery to Bowmark. He dropped onto the middle thwart, rummaged through the bags in the prow, deliberately shoved Scolla aside, and found the bottle of fragrant oil he had purchased to use on his hair. Instead he rubbed the oil on his chest over the blistered area Scolla had given him.

Bowmark soaped his Giver's Hand medallion and swished it through the ocean. Again. How his steel, gold and resin medallion could still reek was another mystery to him.

However, why should he care whether or not he learned the answer to either mystery? Somehow, someway, he would find a way to fling out this Scolla.

Now for staffshifter practice. Keeping the weapon in its baton shape, he told the metal, clawed fists on the ends, "Open." Warmth drained from his hand. The exotic metal gently vibrated. Two claws straightened—one more than yesterday. The magic weapon was learning to follow his commands.

The next morning they sailed into the port of Bysea, much smaller than Discoria but much, much larger than Safe Harbor back in StoneGrove. Bowmark hid his magic staffshifter and magic lightball under a pile of net that smelled like rotting fish. He furled the lateen sail, and paddled the rest of the way in. A woman riding high upon the head of a house-sized sea turtle slowly plied the bay. To the east another turtle with ropes attached to its shell tugged the stern of one of the massive box boats, rotating the ship. So that was how such large and cumbersome craft could maneuver into their assigned slots along the docks.

A crowd of rumshas and humans watched Bowmark and his conspicuous canoe pull up to a dock. They speculated about the outrigger floats, spars, trampoline strung between the spars, and the triangular sail. A light drizzle did not dampen enthusiasm for calling out questions about loads, speed, distance, and crafting. They spoke of distance in units called "kilms." Bowmark had yet to determine how a kilm compared to his people's measure of "ropes," which were one hundred strides.

Scolla buzzed near Bowmark's knee, "I go to purchase honey and make arrangements. Do not look for trouble."

Why look for what chased him? Bowmark watched with surprise as Scolla deftly climbed the mooring ladder like a spider. The creature appeared unstable when he walked, but in climbing he rivaled a monkey. Bowmark's brow furrowed as he was reminded of his pet Snatchfast's fiery end. Scolla waddled unnoticed through the crowd.

The day workers asking to unload cargo wandered off, claiming they were looking for more profitable ships. Off-duty sailors detained Bowmark to talk about his outrigger and their adventures in the distant Eastern Islands. Overhead, seabirds squealed. A line of several large, impossibly fast golden insects flew inland from the sea to a warehouse in the center of the docks. One sailor followed his glance and said, "Therein's the hive."

Bowmark nodded as if that meant something to him. As the talk surged and ebbed, he listened for any incidental news about the Southils. When he announced his hunger, a large number of the men took him to the Cauldron Inn. There they talked for candles over a meal of marinated vegetables, hard-shelled fruit, bread, and braised boar loin. Bowmark practiced his improved pronunciation. He also learned some vocabulary he wouldn't repeat to Father if he ever saw him again.

After that, he walked the city for a few candles. Unlike his home and Discoria, Bysea was flat, built on a silty delta. Deep gray skies made the sun difficult to pinpoint, and all the houses and buildings looked alike, with barrel-vaulted roofs, arched doors, reddish-brown plastered walls and round windows filled with a green-tinted, bubbly glass.

Where were the docks? He rotated at one intersection, then another, looking for any landmark he could recognize. He followed a crowd that dispersed one by one into individual houses. How did they know which house was theirs?

The last man turned and pointed a knife at Bowmark. "Robbing me will gain you only hurt."

Bowmark backed up. "Neither money nor hurt do I want from you. Which way are the docks?"

The man snorted and waggled his knife the way they had come from.

Bowmark ran that way until he had to turn a corner or run through someone's home. At the next intersection, a substantial number of male rumshas congregated, gesticulating widely, hooting softly, and wearing tunics and caps that rivaled the flowers of StoneShell in brightness. One of these rumshas was much larger than the rest. This one wore no clothing, only several leather satchels on belts. Where the others stood semi-upright, this giant's body was level with the ground, his heavily muscled tail balancing his large head—a head with a much larger mouth than the tame-sea-pup mouths the others had. This one had large dull fangs jutting from his muzzle. Bowmark leaned against a wall as he grieved that Sunrise was not there to see the rumshas, the strange homes, and the strange humans.

To stave off his pain he visited a weapons shop and marveled at the tiny bows and arrows. How could they aim these toys? His bow, back in StoneShell, was as tall as he was, and the arrows nearly as long as his arm. The shopkeeper let him shoot in a narrow, walled back yard at a target on a bag of rags. A half candle of practice, and he had mastered the tiny bow and arrows. He bought a bow, twenty iron-tipped arrows, and a quiver. Why stop being a pathetic trader now? He handed over his pearls. At least the iron-tipped arrows would be worth more than a couple pearls back home.

Scolla had not returned when he hid the bow near the stern in a bark wrap, so Bowmark ate another meal. As a king's son, he had never paid for anything before, and so he found it fascinating and alarming how fast one's wealth evaporated when every necessity must be purchased. How could he order cheaper meals?

At the Blue Banner Inn, Bowmark found an open seat at a table where sailors, wearing a variety of ship's patches, and a dockworker, whose armless shirt displayed bulky muscles and a delicate flower tattoo, sat trading traveling yarns.

Setting down his mug of hot tea and wishing the rotted juices and yeasty grains that the others were drinking did not smell so noxious, Bowmark sat among them. Had his ancestors dictated that Sea Predators hate what everybody else seemed to drink with relish? With an effort, he smiled. "Might a stranger ask an odd question from simple curiosity?"

"We listen," said a sailor with bright green eyes, blue-black skin, and slate-gray hair curling around his shoulders.

"What do people here in Bysea consider the greatest treasure?"

"Good ale," the dockworker said, hoisting his mug.

"Dead pirates," a sailor with scars that distorted his face said.

"A heavy purse," the sailor with green eyes added.

A full-bodied woman behind him at another table turned, waved a many-ringed hand, and said in a gentle, growly voice, "Nay. Not the heavy purse, but rather what that heavy purse can buy: thick walls and a sound roof."

"A willing woman," said a sallow faced man with a squint eye who looked as though it would take two purses to find such a woman.

"Food and firewood," called a man from a table on the other side of the room.

"A judge," another said. This brought much laughter.

"How do you buy a good husband?" A server laid a platter of bread on the table.

"Aye. There's a rare thing," the many-ringed woman said.

A rumsha at a far table joined in. "A good joke." He and his companions fluttered their long ears, making the bells on them jingle.

"A good laugh."

"A good peace."

A human sailor said, "A good wind and good relations with Discoria."

A mellifluous voice said, "My children. Though they have grown and sail their own ships, I think about them every day."

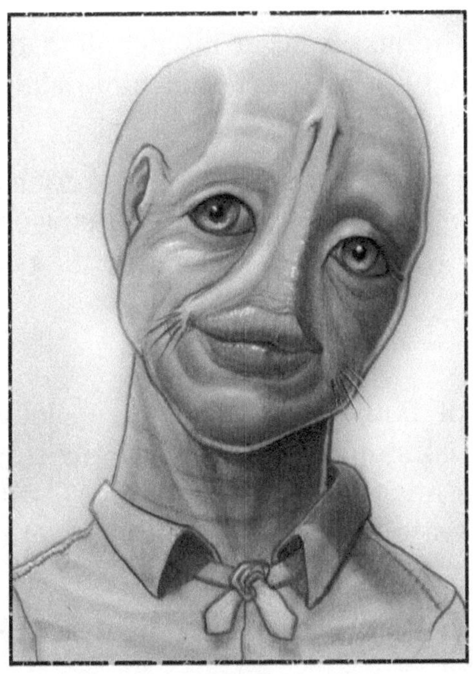

Bowmark looked over. His eyes widened at the sight of a gray-skinned man with webbed fingers and slit nostrils above his large eyes. "Give me pardon." Bowmark rose and ignored the continuing serious and frivolous answers. "I see someone I must speak to."

With opposing emotions tumbling around his chest, Bowmark walked to the gray-skinned man who looked up from his nearly finished meal of marinated sea insects.

"I have—" He thought of Scolla's anger. How could he say it so this seafolk would not explode in anger at how the Sea Predators had murdered seafolks seven years ago? "I have something that belongs—that belonged to one of your people. I thought if I gave this thing to you, you might be able to return it to his family. So they can know what happened."

The seafolk cocked his head and studied Bowmark with large, silvery-blue eyes. "What happened to him?"

How could he justify what his people had done? "There was a storm. A big one. We found him dead on the beach, with two almost adults."

The seafolk shook his head. "We are very hard to drown." He pushed away his plate. "Perhaps they were battered on rocks. Still . . ." He studied Bowmark again. "You're a sunfolk. Am I right?"

"Ah."

"The lack of body hair. The metallic-colored skin. The red hair has... connotations. Those are the clues. Why travel thousands of kilms to deliver this item? Why didn't you give it to the next seafolk in your port? I may not run across his family for decades."

"I, ah. We did not know your people existed until he, ah, showed up."

The seafolk sat up straighter. "Really? How can there be an inhabited island we haven't discovered?"

"I don't know."

The seafolk stood. "By all means, let us see this item. Only first, and you should find this interesting, let me call my traveling companion. Some of the East Islands sunfolks have a custom. Once a decade, they choose a boy about your age to travel the world for a year or two. He looks for Holy Books of some sort. They've been looking for centuries. They're a generous people who overcompensate us. They do all they can to make our lives a joy. We're happy to aid them on their quest."

He turned, then turned back. "Oh, my name is Tosirto. My companion is PledgeKept. You two should truly enjoy one another. Perhaps you could share our room tonight. Wait here." The seafolk rushed up the stairs.

Bowmark gasped. A tsunami of hospitality had smashed over him. How could his people have murdered such a one? He was sorry to give up the Atlas, his guide to the world, but to give it to one such as this would ease the loss. But why was he giving up the Atlas? After all, he was planning to dump Scolla and his disapproval of Bowmark owning an Atlas.

He sank into the chair vacated by Tosirto and rubbed his wrist across his forehead. He had fallen into a game with unknown and indecipherable rules. Stupidity and shame sat on either shoulder.

Behind him, Tosirto said, "And here he is, a lad from an unknown island."

Bowmark turned in the chair and looked up at a young man who looked like Sunrise's cousin from Vertical Drop. He looked into PledgeKept's golden brown eyes and at the three horizontal tattooed lines under his right eye. He should know what that meant.

PledgeKept frowned and looked at Bowmark's large spearhead tattoo on his left shoulder and then the arrowheads tattooed above his right eyebrow.

PledgeKept stepped back and pulled a knife the same time Bowmark knocked over the chair in his haste to grab his own knife and assume a defensive posture. "My enemy!" they exclaimed together.

Other people stood and backed away.

"What is this?" Tosirto cried.

PledgeKept's knife gently arced as he sought an opening.

"Not here," Bowmark said. "Innocent people could be hurt." Some men shouted, but what they said, Bowmark did not know. He kept his gaze on the Southil's eyes as he slowly, carefully backed toward the door.

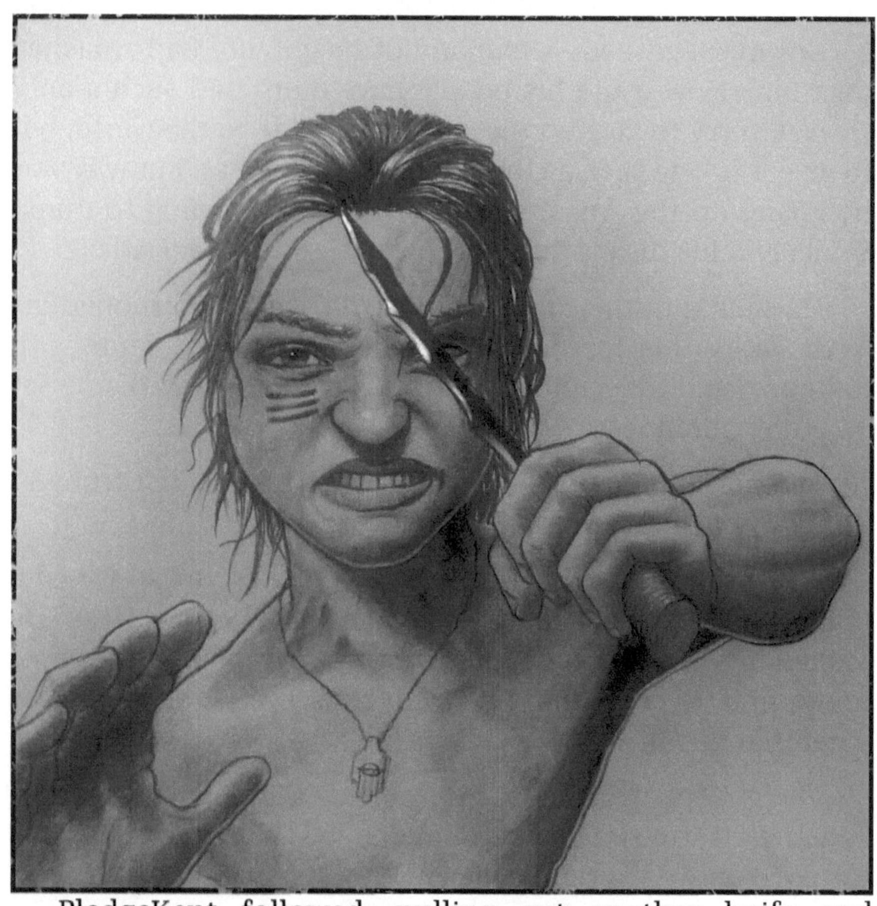

PledgeKept followed, pulling out another knife and ignoring Tosirto who clapped his hands in distress, saying, "Lads! Lads! This is unneedful. Stop!"

Bowmark's heel touched the closed door and he dared not drop his defense long enough to open it. The two crouched, their arms out, knives gleaming in their hands.

The patrons of the inn jammed against the walls.

"Lads! Listen! We can discuss this over a tankard. This is some misunderstanding."

"No misunderstanding," PledgeKept said as he kept every bit of attention on Bowmark's face. "Before you stands a cruel murderer. His people slaughter other people like animals. They tear out the hearts of their victims and stack them as offerings to the god of war, Vanquish All."

"Lies," Bowmark said. "We would never worship that Hag of Murder. It is your people who have pursued mine from island to island, staining the seas with our blood. It is you who wear capes of human skin."

"I beg you, lads, stop! PledgeKept's people are peaceful. PledgeKept! Put the knives away!"

"Not while this man breathes."

The seafolk man twisted. "Someone! Help me stop this!"

PledgeKept darted forward and swung his blade. Bowmark ducked, blocked, and slammed into the door.

The many-ringed woman screamed.

The rusting hinges of the door gave way. Bowmark stumbled backward.

PledgeKept slashed forward.

Men rushed and grappled the two from behind.

PledgeKept struggled against two men gripping each arm and one with an arm around his neck.

Bowmark stood with hands clutching him all over, and not once did he cease watching PledgeKept and looking for an opening. Men wrenched his arms, but he did not let go of the knives. If PledgeKept's people learned that his still lived, they would scour the seas until they found StoneGrove and slaughtered everyone. Bowmark must not let PledgeKept return to the Southils. He had been training his whole life for this moment: this need to protect his people from the enemy.

Guards rushed in and tied their forearms behind their backs, hobbled their feet, set nooses about their necks, and pried the knives from their hands.

Tosirto pushed himself in front of PledgeKept. "I will not have this violence brought aboard my ship. Find your own way home." He marched away.

PledgeKept made no reply and only made sure to keep Bowmark in view as they were prodded down the street accompanied by a growing crowd and then forced into a large black building with polished stone walls, and into a room that smelled strongly of wax, perfume, and sweat. They were shoved down an aisle to a wooden wall that reached to their shoulders. Atop the wall, a metal grid rose to the ceiling.

Behind PledgeKept and Bowmark, people from the inn and street filled up benches and chattered loudly and excitedly with each other. Some captains with tassels of authority on their shoulders walked in and moved up front against a side wall and eyed the young men.

Guards palpated the islanders' clothing and pulled out knives of varying sizes from their boots, pants and shirts.

A corpulent man of pale hue, wearing a red robe and scarlet cylindrical cap, entered the room from a door behind the wall and mounted a raised chair where he could look down upon the men. "This disarming is taking too long," he growled. "Strip them."

When PledgeKept's arms were untied, he lashed out at the guards who were tugging off his shirt. They knocked him down, tightened his noose, and kicked him until he curled into an unresisting ball. They finished pulling off his clothes and jerked him upright.

Bowmark did not resist even though humiliation and rage heated his face and chest. The goal was killing PledgeKept, so he could not let himself be damaged by these guards.

Both had their hands retied together in the front and then tethered to their waists. Behind them, a woman cried, "Oh, Larinna, look at those beauties." Then followed a discourse of their various body parts. Bowmark clenched his teeth and kept his gaze steadfastly on PledgeKept.

The judge raised his hand, and a boy in the back of the room blew a strange curling metal trumpet. The people quieted. The man in red harrumphed. "I have a bed. I have a table. Why, I don't know. When I lie on one or sit at the other, I am called to come here. Once, I would like to finish a meal that is still warm. Strangers, I suppose you think you had a good reason to disturb the peace of Bysea. You with the black hair, what happened?"

PledgeKept said, "Master, this man is a spy for a blood-drinking people who will gladly steal all that is in Bysea and kill everyone here."

Bowmark could not restrain himself. "Lies! His people have sought mine for centuries in their quest to obliterate us."

"Quiet!" roared the judge. "I need three witnesses." A number of people in the room stood. "You, you, and you." Three stayed up while the rest sat. "Sailor, what did you see?"

The squint-eyed man said, "There I was in the Blue Banner, minding my own business and drinking fine rotgut, when this fellow with the black hair comes down the stairs with a seafolk captain. They walk over to this fellow with the red hair. They take one look at each other and shout, 'You're my enemy!' Next thing they're waving knives and throwing furniture."

"Hold a moment. A seafolk was also in this fight?"

"No, your judgeship. He were trying to stop the fight."

"Go on."

"The redhead says he's innocent. They try to cut each other. The guards come and grab the redhead. Me and some of the others grab the black-haired one. Oh, and afore that, the red hair says he wants the treasure of Bysea."

"Enough. You."

The blue-black man fiddled with his shirt buttons as he said, "The red-haired boy seemed friendly enough until he saw the black-haired one. They shouted something about enemies. The red-haired one said he was going to hurt some innocent people. The black-haired boy talked about tearing out people's hearts. They both had a knife in each hand. There was a lot of talk about my people this, your people that. I don't think they live in Bysea."

"Hold. You two. Are either of you a resident of Bysea?"

"No," they replied in unison, both staring at each other.

"All right. You."

A dark brown man with yellow eyes and yellow hair said, "'Tis as the others said. Before the fight the red-haired one was asking about the valuables of Bysea. Looks to fit the description of eastern pirates I've heard of. When they fought I think one said something about using the other one's skin as a cape. It did not look like a scuffle for fun. I think they would have killed whoever got between them."

"Hold. Sergeant."

"A serving girl came running to us about a fight in the Blue Banner. We heard a scream. When we opened the door, that one fell into our arms. This one tried to stab him, but the patrons were able to grab him. They resisted arrest."

"Hold." The judge scowled down at the young men, who ignored him and only stared at each other. He raised his hand and the boy blew his trumpet again. "Here is my judgment. Bysea does not need, does not want, and will not have your wars brought here. We don't care if you kill each other in some wasteland, but we will not allow you to disturb our peace and endanger our citizens and trade. Your sentence: a flogging of ten strokes each, a night in captivity, and exile. Should you return and renew this feud within our borders, you shall be weighted with stones and thrown into the sea. Ship captains, I need one going north, one south."

The captains conferred with each other briefly and two stepped forward.

The judge thumped his desk. "You with the black hair, have you pay or ability?"

PledgeKept said in a quavering voice, "I know how to run the riggings on a two- or three-masted ship."

The judge said, "You'll sail south with that captain. You are indentured to him for six months. If you attempt to desert, he has the right to kill you." He shifted in his chair. "You with the big tattoo, have you any pay or ability to sail?"

Bowmark snorted. "I have some gems. I can sail my outrigger."

"Right. I don't trust you to enforce your own banishment. Instead you'll pay this captain for a six-month tour north. Sergeant, check his belongings."

The guard squeezed the last of Bowmark's gems from the waistband and handed them to the ship's captain. The portly gentleman examined the gems and cleared his throat.

The judge raised an eyebrow. "Is this payment insufficient for the travel?" His tone becoming as short as his patience.

"Tis… close. Mayhap we give some chores to clear the difference."

The judge slapped his hands on the arms of his chair. "So be it at your discretion. Now. Everybody go home." He climbed down and left.

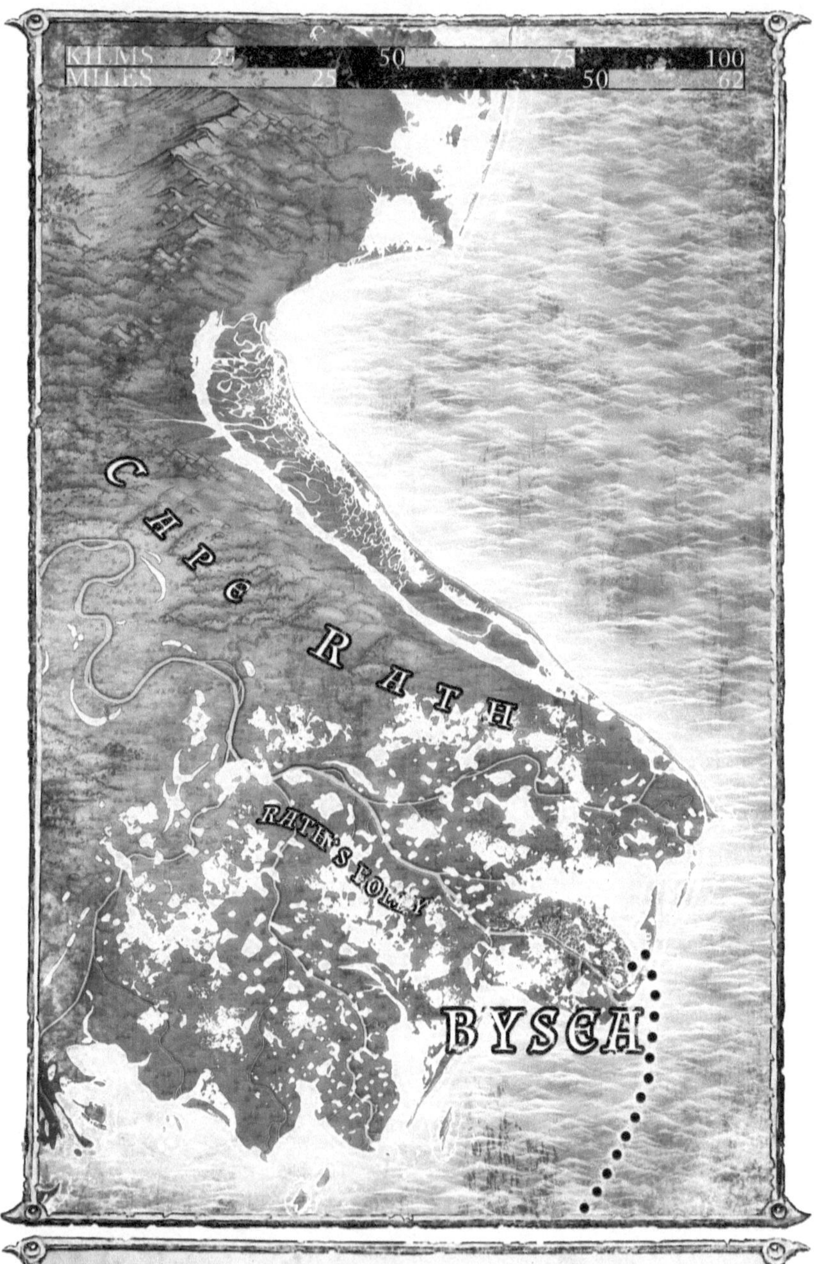

BLESSED BY FAVORABLE WINDS.

— FORAGER SHIP MOTTO

The guards grabbed the young men and shoved them through another door into a dim room with three tall posts, rings affixed to them at different heights, and walls with a variety of ropes and tools hanging on hooks. As their names, description, crime, and punishments were recorded, guards stretched their arms above their heads and tied their hands to metal rings on separate posts facing each other.

PledgeKept had a swollen eye and he favored one hip. Bowmark's enemy also wore a Giver's Hand medallion. A crude wooden version, like a commoner's, but a Giver's Hand none the less.

Two of the guards uncoiled whips and positioned themselves behind the young men.

PledgeKept snarled. "How dare you wear the Hand?"

"How dare you? He would not accept anything from your blood—" The first stroke hit. "Uh!" Bowmark breathed through clenched teeth as he glared at PledgeKept. He would swim through lava before he showed weakness to his enemy.

PledgeKept seemed to be trying to ignore his pain also, but he hissed through his clenched teeth and winced strongly with each stroke. When one stroke sliced through the skin of his lower back above the kidney, he shuddered and turned his face away from Bowmark to press his forehead against the post. On the ninth stroke, he fainted.

Each lash left a line of fire on Bowmark's back and sides. When they released his hands from the ring, he needed to hang onto the post a few breaths. Blood trickled down his legs.

Two guards dragged PledgeKept, and two pushed Bowmark.

Bowmark hissed through clenched teeth, "I will go where you say. You don't need to shove me."

They shoved him anyway, shoved him through a hallway, hurried him down dark stairs, and pushed him into a cage, a room with a frigid stone floor and back wall, and three sides of rusty iron bars. They dropped PledgeKept into the next cage.

As they locked the doors, Bowmark said, "I need my clothes, or a blanket."

One of the guards laughed. "You don't like our inn, don't pay for a room." He set an oil lamp on the floor against the far wall from the cells. "May all your dreams be, ha, peaceful." The guards left. A few moments later, the thudding of heavy doors echoed in the damp stone basement.

Bowmark sank to his knees and watched PledgeKept in the dim light.

The Southil opened his eyes, then slowly sat up. After a quick glance around, he said, "Tomorrow then." His breath caught at every move.

They sat, shivering, staring at each other.

Some candles later, someone made a small noise behind Bowmark. He tried to turn, but stiffness held him in place.

Scolla waddled in front of him holding several bags. He mosquito-whined quietly, "I should have tested you for intelligence before committing to you. I have our goods. I have a mount. What have you done, what?"

Bowmark rasped, "You go where you wish, yes? Get my clothes, some knives. I can end this now."

"No."

"That is my enemy. The enemy of my people. My duty, my life, is protecting my people. If I fail in this—get me some weapons."

Scolla pulled a wide-mouth jar from a sack. "My people do not interfere in human affairs. Do you care which boar is the leader in your herd, do you?" He waddled behind Bowmark.

PledgeKept crawled closer to the bars and opened the eye not swollen like a purple fist.

Bowmark whispered, "The people of this city care nothing for justice either."

"How would they know what justice is, how? They do not know you or your people." Scolla rubbed icy lotion on Bowmark's back.

Bowmark gasped. "I'm cold enough!"

"Be still." Scolla spread some higher.

"I didn't know those things could talk," PledgeKept said.

Bowmark returned his attention to the Southil.

PledgeKept tried to pull himself to a stand but settled for kneeling. His teeth clicked as his shivering intensified. "Did

I hear you say the word justice? How can your mouth utter that word? How can you mock the Hand?"

Bowmark touched his medallion. "I worship the Giver of sun and world, of sea and sky, of food and drink, of day and night; the Hand that strengthens our sinews to work, our minds to thought, and our hearts to love." He stopped when he realized PledgeKept was reciting word for word with him.

Scolla slathered some more cold lotion across his shoulder blades as Bowmark studied the Southil.

Why would he worship the Giver? Bowmark said, "You slaughtered us as sacrifices to the Hag of Murder."

"Lies. That is why you killed us!"

Bowmark's back warmed and the pain lessened from excruciating to merely bad. "Tell me then why your people pursue us."

"What, you don't have songs about the rape and killing of our saints? You don't have feast days celebrating the theft of our Holy Books? You don't dance about the day you stole an entire village of children?"

"So those are the lies your people are told."

"Not lies. We want our books and children back."

Bowmark still shivered, but nothing like his enemy did with teeth-clicking tremors. He gazed at the man's swollen eye and hunched posture and trembling, blue-tinged lips. He remembered Father's words about an injured bird, "Leave it alone or kill it; do not *torment* it!"

"Scolla. Put medicine on his back also."

Scolla moved into his view and tapped his clawed fingertips together while looking from one to the other. Then he waddled to a place where the bars were wider apart—though not large enough for a human—and slipped through.

Why did all the human buildings have built in access for Scolla's people?

PledgeKept jerked away and fell over. "Keep your filthy paws away from me!"

"Fool," Bowmark said. "He's putting on medicine. It will ease the pain."

PledgeKept flinched every time Scolla touched him, but he lay still. "Why do you do this?"

Would not wanting PledgeKept to be tormented be construed as weakness? "It will be difficult to rest if I listen to you whimper all night."

PledgeKept turned his face away and covered it with one hand.

Bowmark hung his head. Had he forgotten that words torment as well? He hated saying this to his enemy, but he could almost feel Father's hand squeezing his nape, "Give me pardon. I should not mock you."

PledgeKept peered at him with a bruise-distorted face.

Bowmark whispered, "When I kill you, it will be quick. Unlike your people, we do not torture."

Fury mottled PledgeKept's face. He choked on several words before he finally ground out, "You dung-sucker! We're peaceful people! Tosirto can tell you. We had to defend ourselves."

"You're so peaceful you tried to kill me the moment you saw me."

The muscles of PledgeKept's cheeks twitched as he glared at Bowmark.

Scolla returned to Bowmark and whispered, "If you could escape on your fifth evening, you should have a one to three kilm swim to the Sharp Point Lighthouse. I will meet you there. Then we will go to Central Place."

The cold seeped from the stones into Bowmark's legs and up his body. He tried to convert the foreign measure of kilms to his people's lengths of rope, but fatigue clouded his mind. "I can't do that until I have killed my enemy. He must not return to his people to tell them we still live. Help me find a way to do this."

"There will be time to visit Central Place and Megaloth, and then to return before the ship he is on comes back."

Bowmark ground his teeth. "He could escape."

"That he shall not. He shall be chained to an oar."

"No!" PledgeKept cried. "I said I could work the riggings."

"Good ears for being so stubby." Scolla turned to face the Southil. "You are considered an unwilling worker, so you shall be chained for six months."

"There's no air in the rowing pits. That's where they put the criminals!"

Scolla tapped one of the iron bars. *Klink. Klink.*

PledgeKept huddled on the floor and said in a sorrow-etched voice, "Sweet TruthLove, dear TruthSay, I have failed you."

Bowmark bowed his head and closed his eyes. "Will I be chained like an animal also?"

"No. You are a paying passenger." Scolla picked up his bag and waddled through the bars, crossed the hall, and entered a hole cut into the stone wall opposite the cells.

What about his duty and the history he had memorized? He had known of the enemy's three lines tattooed under their right eyes. He had known about their brutality. He had known they were searching for his people. What he had not known was that they resembled exactly the people he had sworn to protect when he became a Noble Warrior. Killing PledgeKept would feel like killing Sunrise's family.

Several frigid, dank candles passed. When the guards finally came back and tossed the sunfolks' clothes to them, Bowmark moved slower than the protocol officer's oldest friends. His knives, magic items and Atlas were not returned. His body and mind were too numb to panic. His stiff fingers could not maneuver the buttons on his shirt at all.

The guards led Bowmark away while other guards jammed PledgeKept into his clothes, giving Bowmark no chance to get to his enemy.

Bowmark was escorted onto a ship, shoved into a storage room and left in the dark when they barred the door.

But he was warm. Hungry, but warm. And he had a plan. A *stupid* plan.

Obviously Scolla had no idea what it would take to swim to shore in these cold waters. He curled up, felt something in one of his belt satchels, and pulled out biscuits stuffed with honey, oil, and something gritty that soon made him feel very good indeed. And there, in a coat pocket was his lightball along with a small emerald. This last item was a mystery, but it gave Bowmark an idea. Warm, full, grateful to Scolla, and in the dark, he dropped into sleep.

When he woke, sailors released Bowmark from the storage room. Immediately, he volunteered to help clean the ship, for Father had often said in exasperation over the royal family's lack of privacy, "From my mouth to the maid's ear." Cleaning both endeared him to the crew and let him learn where things were on the ship. He also learned, as had the maids in Father's palace, a host of secrets he kept behind his lips. Over the course of four days Bowmark had made himself useful enough that no one watched him closely anymore.

One afternoon he replaced a rotting board that should have been replaced in port but had been overlooked. He carved a chip design on the old plank, giving him the excuse to carry around the long piece of wood.

By the next evening, Bowmark leaned on the railing, staring at the smear of land to the west, the blare of sunset above it, and the gold-and-orange-streaked sea below. The old board leaned against the gunwale beside him. He chewed on a spicy twig. The weight of the bag holding his coat and boots pressed against his thigh. The overturned bucket that one of his feet rested on should be able to carry that weight.

The dark man with the bright green eyes nodded at Bowmark as he strolled past. He still watched Bowmark a lot but grew less concerned as Bowmark cheerfully moved from one task to another. He was called a quartermaster; similar to a protocol officer, keeping all the sailors reminded of all the rules.

Bowmark watched for the light that guided ships along this shore. Farther aft on deck, two men sang while another played a bellows type of instrument. On the other side of the deck sat a sailor, humming quietly to himself as he worked on a carving of a sea dragon, a four-stride-long, twelve-legged sea-dwelling version of a snake. Two men concentrated over a game of Jump and Hold on a checked cloth. Dusk deepened.

A light appeared on the darkening horizon: Sharp Point Lighthouse. The tower lay a little to their north, but the current would tug Bowmark past that point by the time he reached land—if he reached land. He had no time to hesitate.

Leaving his plank and bucket at the taffrail he trotted past the captain's quarters. He dropped a paper he had folded around the emerald Scolla had secreted away for him. On the page was his best attempt at a formal royal receipt.

In the name of My King, I hereby thank you for hosting me upon this voyage and pray the Giver's Hand of blessing on your future endeavors. Please accept the enclosed gem as payment for the loss of my service for the remaining contract you purchased from the government of Bysea.

~Bowmark

With his foot he nudged the envelope under the door, then jogged back to the aft deck, swept up board and bucket and vaulted over the railing.

SLEET AND DARK AND FOG AND STORM. HER EYE PIERCES THEM ALL. LOOK TO HER AND BE SAVED.

~ CARVED AROUND THE FOUNDATION OF SHARP POINT LIGHTHOUSE

Bowmark pulled on the handle of the huge brass-plated wooden door, but the door would not budge. He sagged, leaned his forehead against the door, and then jerked back from the frigid metal. The cold night air soughed past as he raised anew the magic lightball to read the plaque, Sharp Point Lighthouse. The ball fell out of his shaking hands, rolled off, and winked out. He could not summon the energy to search for it, but he had already seen the bell beside the door with a sign in three languages: *Please ring bell for admittance.* He groped for the striker, then hewed at the bell savagely. What felt like a candle later, the sound of bars being drawn through brackets startled him.

A man with sienna skin, violet eyes, and gray, curled hair opened the door and grabbed Bowmark. "Ah, no! Where be your ship going down?"

"Not, not down." His frozen jaw refused to help him speak. "Work, for warm, please. I will work."

The man pulled him in. "Come in, come in. You be too wet to be roaming out here. Can you be climbing stairs? I must needs tend to the light. This way. Come. I be having some hot soup the wife just be bringing me."

Bowmark nodded numbly, and his feet followed the man through a cluttered home, then up endless curving stairs. At the top of the stairs his body folded into a chair at a small table set beside a pillar with a huge flame atop.

Walls of glass pent in the round room. Curved mirrors slid on a track around the flame as the gray-haired man turned a massive handle before he stepped to an iron-enclosed fire with a pot on the shelf above the fire.

The man noted Bowmark's gaze on the windows. "Aye, impressive. The Merchants and Seamen's Guild well considers it worth the massive expense." He set before Bowmark an iron pot filled with a meaty stew of exquisite aroma.

Bowmark needed to use both hands to wrap his fingers around the spoon. "Master," he stuttered, "which way must one travel to find warmer places? I'm so tired of cold." A bite of stew reached his mouth. No feast had ever tasted this good. He shoveled in several more mouthfuls, ignoring the trickle of gravy on his chin.

The man sat on the other side of the table. "South. The more south you be, the warmer. Where be you from that you be not knowing that?"

His knotted muscles refused to loosen. "South. Island in the ocean. I didn't know that sailing north would be so cold."

The man chuckled. "You southerners. Now be late spring here."

"What is spring?"

"Spring be the time of year much warmer than winter. Oh hold on now… today's eleven-four. We're actually in early summer, though I've seen not a trace."

If this wasn't cold weather now, Bowmark did not want to see winter. He applied himself to the soup and wondered why his hands still shook and his vision sometimes blurred. Every joint ached. "Can you increase the heat in here?"

The man raised his eyebrows but went to the wall oven and threw in some black rocks from a bucket. Were rocks here magic, that they could burn?

Warmer air wafted over Bowmark, but the gentle heat did not help. If anything, he felt colder. "I hate volcanoes," he said. "My life was good until a volcano erupted and we had flowing lava to fight over. My people had a safe home until a volcano blew it up and killed most of us."

The man wrinkled his forehead. "You don't say. And when be that?"

Why had he brought that bit of history up? The room tilted. After the last mouthful of stew, he said, "About two hundred and fifty years ago. We wandered, searching for a home. We were attacked everywhere we went." His bones had transmuted into cold stones.

The man rose and walked behind Bowmark. "That be the time the seafolk say a tsunami destroyed their marsh. They think that be a sign from their gods." A trickle of water echoed metallically and then the man placed a mug beside Bowmark. "Most of them not be living on land since."

It took great effort for Bowmark to raise the mug. One swallow and a cold line of a metal knife pressed under his jaw. *Not again.*

"Now you be telling me why you be here, and you will not be lying."

Father had talked bravely to the protocol officer. Bowmark's shaking hand lowered the mug. *Use calm language. Find out what your opponent wants. If you can give it to him, he becomes a friend.* He concentrated on moving tongue and lips with precision. "You are right to be careful. I am so aware of my goodwill, that I forget it is not obvious to everyone else."

"I be waiting for an explanation."

"I swam away from a ship that was carrying me against my will away from my partner in Bysea."

"And your crime?"

"I . . . irritated a judge during his supper by defending myself against a man who wanted to stab me. The judge wished me to gain the attitude that I never want to irritate him again. This I have gained." His collar was jerked back as he heard the spluttery sound of a man unsuccessfully suppressing laughter.

"Not branded. A point in your favor." The man moved in front of him while tucking in his knife. "Who be starting the fight?"

"My enemy."

"Business rival?"

"No. An old enemy of my people."

"So, an overseas feud?"

Bowmark laid his aching head on his cold arm. It probably was, though feud seemed too small a word for genocide.

The man said softly, "We can't be having war in our streets with disrupting of peace and safety and trade. Someone else's fight could be causing our poverty. Can you be seeing the judge's point?"

"No." His teeth clicked together. Why wouldn't the fire warm him?

The man patted his chest. "Oh, to be young, strong, and stupid again. 'Tis more fun to be knowing you are always right."

Bowmark's eyes would not focus together, so he closed one and used the other to peer at the man. "Is my partner here? We were . . ." He closed both eyes and concentrated on the sentence. "We were . . . we were supposed to meet here. Then go . . ." He was going someplace. "Go west. Central Place." Suddenly, the aching head and joints; the lassitude; the deep chill; all made hideous sense. "You poisoned me!" He tried to reach for a knife but slid off the table and thumped onto the floor.

"I did no such thing." The man's fingers probed his muscles and face. "You be a-roaring with fever."

Bowmark was left alone, moaning, "I'm so cold," while the man ran downstairs. He came back with a look-alike teenage son.

With their support, Bowmark stumbled down to a lower room to a great copper tub. He almost dove in; he wanted a hot bath so badly. "I'll put my throne in a hot spring. Never leave."

When they took off his clothes, he heard behind him a woman with a Bysea accent. "Oh! The poor boy! That judge is a brute!"

The man tugged off Bowmark's boot. "Brute, mayhaps. Efficient, I be saying."

"And you're a brute, too. There's no reason to tear up a boy's back like that."

The man put his arms under Bowmark's armpits, the son his feet. They lifted Bowmark and laid him into the tub of frigid water.

"Hiii!" Bowmark screamed. His breath failed as he whimpered, "Not cold! What did I do to you?"

The man took Bowmark's head and dipped most of it under the water. "I be not drowning you. Your brain'll be boiled like an egg if we don't do this."

Several boys came and looked in at Bowmark while the father directed one to go upstairs and tend the light, two to prepare a pallet in their bedroom, one to fetch rags, and two more to get out of the way and go back to bed.

"Here's some willow-bark tea for the pain and fever," the woman said. She held the cup for him.

Bowmark finished the nasty brew, but his head still throbbed, and his eyes would not cooperate. "Is my partner, Scolla, here?"

The woman said gently, "No one has been by the last week. There is no one named Scolla here."

Bowmark fought tears. When you're eighteen and a man, you don't cry just because you've been deserted and you've lost everything and you hurt everywhere and RaiseHim is going to rule your little brother and you let your people's worst enemy escape. Tears splashed in the water, completing his humiliation.

He was pulled out of the tub, dried, wrapped in a sheet, and laid on a bed in a tiny stone room with slit windows. Sleep claimed him.

Bowmark awoke with a piercing headache and a dehydrated-down-to-his-toes thirst. He slowly turned his rigid neck to observe his surroundings. Strips of moonlight lay across his bed, ribboned across two brothers in a tangled sprawl on the pallet on the floor, and strobed over a short, dark creature with a wobbly gait. Three efforts, and finally he rasped, "Scolla? Is that you?"

The creature turned to face him, its shining copper eyes large and its pointed ears flipped up. Its ears were larger than Scolla's, and the eyes closer together.

Bowmark cleared his throat. "My partner is a person like you. His name is Scolla. Have you seen him?"

The room filled with the snickering of delighted little boys. The small, black tezledek turned and waddled rapidly toward the door.

"If you see him, tell Scolla I'm here."

The door opened, showing the mother with her hair awry and wrinkles pressed into her face.

The creature scuttled past her, using its long arms like crutches.

"What is so amusing?" the mother asked, with sleepiness and anger roughening her voice.

The boys hooted and laughed harder. "He was talking to—to—" The younger boy pointed past his mother, and fell over, laughing, unable to complete his sentence.

"Hmm. Since you boys are so awake and jolly while our poor guest is hallucinating from fever, you can lay a fresh cold rag on his head every half hour."

"Ma!" chorused the boys.

"I'm too cranky to say this twice."

In subdued tones they said, "Yes, Ma."

Several moments later, a cold, wet rag was laid on Bowmark's forehead. The headache eased enough that he could return to sleep.

THOUGH EXCEEDINGLY SLOW, NO LAND
MOUNT CAN MATCH THE MULIG
FOR STAMINA, PLACIDITY
OR CARRYING CAPACITY.
~SEAFOLK ATLAS

Bowmark sat in the glass-enclosed room, wrapped in a blanket, sipping willow bark tea, gazing at the sun rising from the sea. In lucid moments over the past two days he had had enough conversations with his hosts to learn their names and get his bearings, but what should he do now? Try to find PledgeKept? Keep trying to obtain ten treasures? Try to go home and warn his people? How? He could not even pay back the kind lighthouse keeper and his wife. His gems, his magic things except for the lightball, even the Atlas were gone. Should he stay here and tutor their six boys in archery? He drained his cup. A blue and gray seabird hovered outside one of the massive glass windows and regarded Bowmark with a bright eye.

Bowmark rose and, dragging the blanket behind him, shuffled toward the stairs. One slow step at a time, he descended with his hand on the wall for balance. He concentrated on the cup so he would not drop and break this one. A wave of dizziness forced him to sit on a step.

The lighthouse keeper, with his heavy tread, came onto the porch and pushed open the door. He entered his home, dropped something weighty on the floor with a thump, and announced, "Wife! News and more news!"

The wife's light step tapped across the floor. "I thought I saw something gold streaking over the field. Come, sit here, and tell me."

Furniture scraped across the floor. "Biggest dractil swarm in a century. A queen took the temple of the rumshas."

"Oh no! Surely the mazies will do something about the dractils now. Oh, my. This will mean rationing come winter."

"Mayhaps. I'll talk to the trappers about procuring more meat up north."

"My brother could be summoned with more seed for the planting end of month." The clink of a cup against a dish. "What else?"

"A coup in Discoria be completed nine days ago. Jeeto Brakor rules now."

"I'll need to remember to wear blue beads the next time I'm there."

"Can't you be persuading your mother to move back to Bysea?" After a silence, the lighthouse keeper cleared his throat and resumed, "They claim a magician stole the jewels for Jeeto Brakor."

"Why would a magician bother?"

"They say that he flew off the cliff and disappeared. But a few saw him. He be having a tattoo of a black spear head on his right shoulder, and red hair."

A much longer silence. "No. Bowmark does not resemble a magician. Perhaps his partner, the missing Scolla?"

"What magician be tolerating a flogging? Still. Be watchful."

Bowmark leaned his head against the cool stone wall. What did a magician look like?

"I be sitting on two chairs here." The lighthouse keeper's voice boomed up the stairwell. "Do I be sending the garrison upstairs to watch our polite and well-spoken guest, or out patrolling for dractils?"

"If you had the sense of slugs, you would know the answer. I'll talk to Bowmark. Oh, he mentioned he had a throne during his fever. Do you suppose his kingdom is influencing politics for gain here?"

The lighthouse keeper scoffed. "So what if he be king of some rock in the ocean? We be having larger, closer neighbors to worry about. I expect Ironia to invade within the year. Then Megaloth be pushing Ironia back. Bysea be trampled under the feet of Empires that be wanting all the world to be subject to them."

"Ma! Da!" Smaller feet pounded through the front door. "A driver arrived with a mulig and a letter for Bowmark!"

Bowmark pushed himself up and slowly stepped down the stairs until he met the family coming up. The lighthouse keeper pulled Bowmark's arm over his shoulder. With the man carrying much of his weight, Bowmark walked outside.

In the clearing in front of the lighthouse, a large animal snuffled the grass. Brown fur, long muzzle, six legs. The back four legs appeared like two giant fingers on each side of the animal, joined at the spine to form a flat, broad back on which rested a wooden platform, stretched hide canopy, and some webbed packages. Atop the luggage lay a black bundle that was either Scolla or a person exactly his size. The mulig eyed the humans placidly as they approached.

South, a human and two laden muligs plodded away toward the garrison.

The lighthouse keeper strode up to the creature and slapped it on the neck. "Well she's a fine mare for ya." The beast chewed on a weed.

If a lighthouse keeper could approach the animal without fear, then surely Bowmark, a warrior, could. He tottered over to it and leaned against its powerful foreleg.

The lighthouse keeper grunted. "A spitter hitchhiker. Good baggage protection."

Bowmark was about to ask Scolla about the goods and his lateness, but the boy handed him a paper and glanced from Bowmark to Scolla. The boy's lips were wiggling in an effort to keep from laughing. What did little boys find so hilarious about Scolla's people?

Bowmark opened the paper: *Here are the supplies, goods, and mount. Take the road to Central Place.*

Central Place was a rumshane city. Rumshas were also called mazies. The Atlas said they were fair traders, though they would never commit to a delivery date. Was this the same place he had heard was being invaded? He wanted to check the Atlas. Fumes, he was going to miss having that book to tell him where he was. The magic items, too, unless . . . Had Scolla brought his belongings?

Bowmark folded the paper into a flying bird shape and tossed it for the boy to run shouting after. He searched through the dew-covered bags, baskets and boxes that littered the platform until he found a packet of loose diamonds. He looked at the wife, Glorin, a one-time food server in Discoria, and the lighthouse keeper, Fal, an ex-sailor from the small island northeast of Discoria. "I can never repay you adequately for your kindness." He pressed a diamond into Glorin's hand.

She squealed at the bright stone glinting in the morning sun, and the lighthouse keeper looked over. "What is it?"

Bowmark swiveled his gaze to the lighthouse keeper. "I must leave, and you deserve some reward for saving my life."

Glorin said, "You can't leave. You're not well."

"Don't be standing in a man's way, wife," the lighthouse keeper said.

"But—" She frowned, then nodded, backed away, and ran toward the lighthouse.

Bowmark's gaze followed her before he looked back at the lighthouse keeper. "If I was rude, please give me pardon. I don't know your customs."

"No. Not at all. The pay be beyond extravagant." The lighthouse keeper patted the mulig between its eyes. Diffidently, as though discussing the weather, he said, "Be you having anything to do with the coup in Ironia?"

"Accidentally." He had earlier overheard the couple discussing the tariff situation between Discoria and Bysea. He must tread carefully. "Irritating a judge was not my first mistake. I was fortunate to escape alive."

"Hmm." The lighthouse keeper stroked the mulig's neck. "Be magicians involved in Ironia's politics?"

"I wouldn't know. I'm not a magician. Nor do I know the local politics. If I had, perhaps I would not have been so easily tricked by Jeeto."

"Tricked." The lighthouse keeper patted Bowmark on the shoulder, avoiding the still-healing stripes, and smiled. "A good lad. Safe journey to you. Watch out for road robbers."

"Thank you." Bowmark tugged on the harness fitted over the mulig's head and, hanging onto its neck for support, shuffled down the path to the fitted stone road. *Giver!* He was going to miss their family stories and good food. Bowmark kept looking back. Was he leaving a safe, warm shelter to wander into a violent storm?

The lighthouse keeper watched him for a while, then walked to the small garrison down the hill from the lighthouse.

By the time Bowmark reached the road, he was panting from the exertion. Perhaps he should have stayed another day, but who knew if those garrisoned soldiers were searching for him? He could not think why they should be, but he understood nothing about this place, except that Ironia and the Megaloth Empire were willing to waste their wealth and people on warfare. What if Discoria or Bysea was willing to waste some wealth on hunting him down? He was still unclear about what political entity truly controlled this region.

He was not surprised to hear a familiar whine, "You idiot. From now on I tell you what to pay for things."

Bowmark sighed. "You tell me whatever you want."

"Why aren't you riding, why?"

Bowmark stopped. His legs trembled. "Ride what? You didn't bring a wagon."

"Szz. The mulig."

The smell of mulig, grass, and dust tickled Bowmark's nose. No animals large enough to ride or use for pulling lived in Stone Grove, except for the sea-chariot beast. "Where do I sit?"

Scolla grumbled something in his language, then said, "Directly behind the shoulders on the bench that is clearly designed to be sat upon."

Mulig and man gazed at each other. The mulig's back was even with Bowmark's chest. Any other time, he could have easily leaped astride that, but now he was as limp as seaweed. As if sensing his difficulty, the mulig ponderously knelt until Bowmark could drag himself on. He stroked the mulig's neck as the beast rose. "You're a fine animal. Yes, you are. A fine one." Somebody had said something like that within his hearing. What did you say to tell them where to go?

The mulig twitched her ears and set off with a pleasant rolling gait.

Bowmark found the reins. They were almost identical to the ones used on the muntee that pulled his sea-chariot. He could handle this. A mild breeze soothed the burning stripes on his back. The air carried the scents of unknown trees, unfamiliar flowers, and the very familiar sea. In the late afternoon, Scolla pointed to a side trail that split off westward from the well-paved road they had been following south. They entered a forest and trod on a narrow track overhung with branches from which the mulig grabbed leaves with her long tongue. The ground gently rose more than it dipped, and the leaves rustled softly in the slight breeze. Every bend and rise showed more empty road with only the rare bird flitting across it.

He closed his eyes and slipped off the bench.

Thud!

Bowmark looked up at branch, sky, and mulig nose from where he lay on the ground. He could not breathe. An anvil was crushing his chest.

Through ears filled with indistinct sound, he heard Scolla quavering, "You fool! You fell asleep! Why are you alive when you are so stupid, why?"

The muscle spasm released, and air rushed into Bowmark's lungs. He leaped up, snatched Scolla, flung him to the ground, grabbed and squeezed Scolla's tongue before he could spit, pressed his knee onto the bug's belly, and poised a knife, point first, on Scolla's throat.

The smell of ginger deepened as Bowmark gazed straight into the Scolla's large copper eyes. "I am saturated with you calling me stupid. Saturated and drowned. I got these wounds on my back because I was trying to return the Atlas to a seafolk, just like you wanted. How could I know he was going to thrust my enemy into my face? I am sick, Scolla. For all I know, you made me sick. I didn't ask you to join me. You forced yourself on me like a tick on a dog. But even a tick knows better than to call the dog stupid every ten breaths."

Scolla gargled incoherently.

Bowmark let go of his tongue.

After several labored breaths Scolla said, "You need me."

"I can find a hu—" Money. Food. Resources. Where would he find a human happy to drop their life and follow Bowmark around and give him advice? "I don't need you to insult me continuously. If you hate humans so much, why do you keep following me?" His hand holding the knife trembled. He willed the trembling to stop.

Scolla wiped both eyes, flick, flick, with his tongue and sucked it back in before Bowmark could grab the tube.

"My people consider me odd because I like humans. I write books about you and your interactions with other peoples, such as the rumshas. I wrote a well-liked book about the misconceptions the two of you have of each other."

Bowmark touched the back of his fingers to his lips. Dizziness threatened to topple him. "Wait. Back up. You like humans?"

"Quite yes."

"Then I don't want to know what the rest of your people think about humans."

"Quite no."

"And nobody but you talks to us."

"I am the only one I am aware of. I think humans may yet be trainable."

A keening began in Bowmark's ears. He was on an impossible mission with an insane creature stuck on him like a tick. Sweat oozed down his face. His head floated away. "Give heed. If you call me stupid one more time, I will . . ." His eyes closed. "I will . . ." He fainted and collapsed atop Scolla.

TRUE POWER IS UNSEEN.
THE ESSENCE OF FORCE IS UNFELT.

~TEZLEDEK PROVERB

When he awoke, he thought at first he was lying in his canoe, wrapped in his cape, at sea. The odors of beast and trees told him the rolling motion was the mulig, and the perceived cape was instead thin cording that held him curled on the flat platform on the mulig's back, with his head under the small, curved roof. He could not move, for the cords that held him secure were stronger than they should be, given how fine they were. No thicker than the twine they used to tie podvines to lattices back in High Harbor. A different kind of magic rope? His gaze followed the black cords until he saw Scolla perched on the driver's bench.

Scolla wore metal discs pierced with tiny holes and sewn onto black cloth covering his eyes. He seemed to be watching Bowmark.

Bowmark licked his dry lips. "Am I a prisoner?"

Scolla shifted. "Why do you think evil of me so easily, why?"

"Maybe because I threatened you. And then I *stupidly* fainted. And now I am tied up better than a boar before the feast."

"Zzz zzz zzz. You are held so that you will not fall off. The next time you fall, you might break your neck. Or fall off that cliff into the ocean."

Scolla gestured toward Bowmark's right. Bowmark strained to see, but the awning hid the view. The smell of the cold sea wafted over him and water broke on rocks far below. Was it morning or late afternoon? How long had he been unconscious?

Scolla continued, "If you die, how will I reach your island, how?"

"You're not going—"

Father's words came to Bowmark. "If the argument does not benefit, do not argue."

Dad, Sunrise's father, had put it another way. "I don't care who's wrong. Both of you get to clean out the boar pen, now!"

This was becoming tedious. He whispered, "I need a privy. Can you loosen my bindings?"

Scolla crawled off the bench, clutching the rail, almost tumbling twice. He moved stiffly—more awkwardly than usual—as if afraid or hurt. Scolla's sharp teeth severed the cord that lashed Bowmark's chest and arms. The person who the lighthouse family called a spitter chewed and swallowed the cord like noodles.

Bowmark tried a nibble, but his teeth made no impression on the stretchy fibrous material, and the burning, putrid taste almost made him vomit. He spit several times, trying to rid his mouth of the foul taste. He sniffed the cord which had no odor. Neat trick. "How can you—?" He waved vaguely at the remnants of cord that Scolla was slurping up. Scolla ignored him.

Bowmark sat up, but quickly lay down again on his other side. Sparkles filled his vision. "I have never been this sick before."

Scolla said calmly, "Travelers often sicken when they go to a far land for the first time. Fortunately, tezledeks never sicken."

Bowmark slowly rolled off the side of the platform and hobbled behind a tree to relieve himself. It was a great relief. He must have been asleep for over a day. As he carefully climbed back on the platform, he tried to get his bearings. With the heat and the angle of the sun, it must be late afternoon. With the sun in his eyes, they were headed west.

Scolla, still stiff and pensive gestured toward Bowmark. "Shall I secure you again, shall I?"

Bowmark considered the ground lurching below him and the steep cliff overlooking a large bay to his right. "Do it. But let me sit up a bit, and maybe, not so tightly."

Bowmark pushed a woven basket behind him while Scolla gripped one of the strands attached to a side rail, then pulled away with black webbing trailing from his hand and reached over Bowmark to grab some webbing behind him.

"How are you doing that?" Bowmark grabbed one of Scolla's hands and turned it over. There, in the groove of his divided palm with three opposing fingers on each side, in the middle of the groove, a pore protruded. He touched the pore. "You can extrude your own cord like a spider? That's incredible." He studied the perforated disks covering Scolla's eyes.

Scolla's voice quivered. "You are the first human to have so touched one of us. Let go."

Bowmark let go. "Give me pardon. Is that offensive?"

Scolla's tongue whapped one of the disks and knocked them askew. With shaking hands, he reset his eye shades. "I do not know. It has never happened before. Why are you crying, why?"

"I'm not." Bowmark wiped his eyes. "I wish Sunrise, the brother of my heart, could have met you." Bowmark took a deep breath of the warm, still air. "How long will it take us to reach Central Place?"

"About two weeks."

Bowmark practiced the math that the sailors had taught him. Rather than the two seasons that Sea Predators recognized, these people divided the year into ten segments they called months. And each month was further divided into six segments called weeks. And each week had six days. Therefore, two weeks would be twelve days. Beyond this division that they decided that a day would be cut into twenty segments called hours. The quartermaster had shown him a device called an hourglass which had sand that drained from one glass bubble to another. It took about a candle to drain, so it seemed that Bowmark's people had a similar sense of timing, though back home, he never knew anyone who felt it necessary to track every hour of the day like these people did. But the quartermaster assured him that keeping the ship running smoothly meant always being aware of which of the twenty hours of the day they were in. And even more pedantic, he could always tell Bowmark what… what was the word? Minute. One hundred of them in each hour, and the man could call out the hour and minute, and that was what he called "the time." Everything about this new country was strange and overly complicated.

After all the recent events, Bowmark didn't mind the idea of a twelve day vacation on this gently swaying platform. He laid his head back on the soft basket and watched tree branches slide by. "What happened to my outrigger?"

Scolla resumed webbing. "My people have hidden your vessel. When we have what you need we can order it sent to any port."

"The things in it?"

"I brought everything of value, save for the Atlas. That you will not need, as I am here to guide you.

"But it is my duty to return it to a seafolk!"

Scolla waved a hand dismissively. "I have a far better network than you. I can have it transferred without a knife fight."

Bowmark's face heated. He forced three long breaths.

"And my magic things?"

"The bailiff thought to keep them for himself, but we did not let that happen."

Bowmark relaxed. "Why were you late? I thought—I don't know what I thought."

"It takes much longer to travel by land than sea. Surely you understand this. Additionally I had to hire a driver."

"Why? Obviously you can drive a mulig."

"I can. But humans have never seen us do so. We prefer they not see us do so. Any human seeing a mulig alone with me would assume that the mount was lost and would try to take the animal."

"I see. But if humans think your people are no more than animals, how did you hire a human driver?"

"Intermediaries. I told you, we control the ebb and flow of human activity."

Bowmark watched the late afternoon sunlight dapple and dazzle through branches and leaves. What Scolla said sounded foolish. Ah, truth, Scolla was insane. What advice could he believe? His hope staggered. "Scolla. Humans don't look at you, and you're afraid to be seen riding a mulig alone. How is it your people rule the world?"

"Quietly."

Bowmark laughed weakly. "So quietly, no one knows it but you."

"It is best that way." Scolla finished the webbing and crawled forward.

"Scolla, that seems uncomfortable for you."

"Yes. I prefer underground to rocking far above the ground with bruised ribs."

"I am sorry for that. I think I was delirious with fatigue. Here. There's enough room for both of us. You can curl up next to me and feel more secure."

"Zzt!"

"What?"

"You are unusual. Do your people call you odd, do they?"

"No. What's the problem?"

Scolla scooted back and settled in front of Bowmark. "There is no problem. You do the unexpected."

"I just thought of something. How did you get me onto the mulig?"

"I called for help and some tezledeks came."

"You called. Amid these empty cliffs and woods your people showed up in enough numbers to pull me onto a mulig. I don't understand, ah, anything." How would he come to understand with an insane teacher? "Will you teach me your language?"

Scolla sputtered. "Humans cannot speak our language."

"Maybe not. But I could learn to hear it. And read it. You said you brought books. Teach me how to read them." Maybe the books could tell him what Scolla wouldn't.

Scolla tapped his fingers rapidly. "What a fascinating experiment that would be. Why do you want to do this, why?"

"I came to get more than treasure. I also came to learn about the world. Why not start with you?" *So I can better discern how dangerous you may be for me and my people.*

Scolla curled into his black-bundle shape. "I need to consider this."

"Could I visit one of your homes or wherever it is you stay in the daytime? Maybe only my head will fit, but I want to see."

"Very unusual. No one will believe me. No one."

"Why?"

Scolla peeked at him through the slits of his bat-wing ears. The mulig snorted. Mottled tree trunks slid by. "Despite all the benefits we give humans, they do not want us to touch them. They do not want to think about us. You are almost the first in all our millennia of living together who recognizes that we are people."

"Maybe it would help if tezledeks talked to humans."

Scolla buzzed laughter.

Bowmark scratched his leg. "Besides hitchhike, what is it your people do?"

"We seek knowledge. We build. We raise families."

"I meant to humans. Every human structure I've seen so far has openings for your people."

Scolla uncurled and clasped his hands together. "Zzzzz." He surveyed the forest on their left. A yellowed leaf detached and twirled down to land between them. They passed a small arch of undressed stones just off the road beside the sea cliff. "What will you do, what, if you discover that we have been herding humans toward the ungols for the last two centuries?"

Ungol. The same mysterious invaders who demanded treasure from his new friends in Rolocton. Bowmark still had no idea what they were. But then he was struck by the image of tiny Scollas herding humans around the way he and Sunrise herded pigs. Bowmark strove to keep a straight face. What a fantasy. "Herd humans? How? Why?"

"How is our secret and sacred duty. If humans knew, they would fight against us, even though our guidance is to their benefit."

Bowmark said slowly, "But you just told me, and I'm a human."

"What will you do, what?"

Two weeks. Two weeks of living with whatever Scolla did if he gave the wrong answer. Two weeks to Central Place with a madman. The idea of a vacation slowly evaporated. "I am practiced in keeping government secrets."

"Swear. Swear by that Hand." Scolla pointed at Bowmark's chest.

Bowmark pulled the Giver's Hand medallion from under his shirt. What was the harm in promising to never reveal a madman's fantasy? "I promise, lest Giver deal me disaster and death, that I will never reveal any of the secrets of the tezledeks."

"Good." Scolla curled up again.

"Scolla. How does it benefit humans to be herded toward ungols? I understand ungols are nasty. The people I met in Rolocton said they were raided by them every two years, but never described the ungols themselves."

Scolla uncurled. "Humans are nasty. Ungols are evil intensified. They kill people on a whim. They take. They don't create. We withdrew from them, and they did not care. They ruin and waste all they touch. We were patient with them for centuries, but they never changed. We decided to send humans to exterminate the ungols. Our hope was that two or three hundred years from now, the last ungol would die." Scolla's tongue knocked awry his eye shades. "The destruction of Rolocton was a setback. Now it may be four hundred years before the ungols are extinct."

Bowmark tried to quell his anger. There were madmen in StoneGrove as well. One claimed to be king, and when he tried to kill Father, claiming him an impostor, he had been subdued and moved to Rice Island, not punished. "Tough luck for the human herded onto an ungol spear."

"Quite yes. For the individual victim, life is not so good. However, for humans as a whole, ungol extinction will be a benefit. Ungol lands have many resources. Once the danger from ungol raids is over, the humans can return to killing each other."

Bowmark listened to the step, step, step of the mulig. "Your concern for us touches me. Is there nothing your people gain from this?"

"We gain territory and resources as humans do. We continue to gain in knowledge. Furthermore, there is satisfaction in accomplishing our duty."

"Duty? To whom?"

"The wardens. We are their agents."

"Wait. You said you rule—it's not important." Wardens, wardens—the people who oversee animals that are outside of pens? Scolla had said the tezledeks were herding humans. So . . . no, he also said they had no king. So who gave them that duty? Bowmark's eyes closed. Another nap beckoned.

When Bowmark opened his eyes again, moonlight dimly silvered the surrounding tree trunks. He could no longer hear the sea. The mulig chewed noisily. Bowmark's cape covered him and one of Scolla's strands about his waist loosely tethered him to the platform. He slid under the strand and off the mulig who was staked and nosing in a basket. Where was Scolla? Thirst compelled him to find a water skin, but the stowage around the edge of the platform was disorganized. A basket of firewood strapped next to a net with fruit, all jumbled over a bundle of walking sticks and blankets. His short bow and quiver of arrows lay against the rail. A wooden chest with metal corners and latch was secured next to a basket full of rags and a blanket. A leather bag with loops attached to one side seemed like it could be worn over the shoulders and back, keeping both hands free. That could be useful. Finally, he found a water skin dangling from a hook on the other side of the platform, along with miscellaneous cookware. Bowmark tried not to guzzle the whole thing. He wondered if he'd ever get used the strange taste of water in these lands. The frigid night air prompted a quick return to the platform that was warmed by the back of the mulig. He thought about Father and Spearmark before sleep claimed him.

Scolla woke him while dawn was still gray, one bird hummed monotonously, and dew beaded the mulig's coat. "Will you be able to drive today, will you?"

Bowmark yawned. "I can tell you after breakfast. Is there more water?"

Scolla waved toward the right side of the road. Bowmark followed the direction until he heard running water. The cold creek water he poured over himself woke him thoroughly. Indeed, it woke him a great deal more than he wanted. Shivering, he brought back the refilled water skin and pulled on fresh clothes over his back. Scolla searched the mounds draped over the platform rails for the provision sack and passed it over to him.

The sack held great disappointment. "This bread is mostly mold."

"Finally ripe!" Scolla said, taking the bread from him and licking the gray fuzz.

Bowmark looked away and tried not to gag. Half the dried fruit had spoiled and some of the dried fish. The spoiled food he quietly tossed behind a bush lest Scolla claim that also. Only a little untainted food remained. He tried to fill the rest of his belly with more water from the skin. Hunger made the food delicious.

He was still hungry when he finished. "That's the last of my stores. What did you buy me for food? Where is it?" He laid his hand on one of the webbed mounds.

Scolla stopped licking the moldy crumbs from his fingers and stared at Bowmark. "I have never been responsible for feeding a human before. I forgot to buy you food."

Bowmark kneaded his biceps. "You forgot to buy me food? You expect me to fast for the next two weeks?"

Scolla licked his eyes. "I did not plan for you to fast."

"I'm not going to." He pulled out a familiar lumpy package that had grown larger since the last time he had seen it. "You are going to share some of your eggs with me."

"Sssss!" Scolla swelled to twice his size and his normally floppy spines stuck out like rigid nails.

Bowmark lunged and hid behind a tree. "Now what!?"

"Put those down carefully!"

Bowmark complied. "Is it a crime to share?"

With a quiet hiss, Scolla slowly deflated. "I also forgot how ignorant you are. Those eggs are children."

Bowmark looked from the sack of small black, leathery eggs to Scolla. "Whose—your children?"

"They are not mine specifically. I have no wife to lay me any. Every place I stop has parents willing to donate a child to a new colony and the advance of civilization."

"No! No! No! No!" Bowmark marched over to Scolla and glared down at him. "Are you insane? What are we going to do when they hatch? You can't travel hither and thither with, with," he glanced at the bag, "with nine babies hanging on you! And you call *me* stupid?"

"You fret overmuch."

How dared he sound like Sunrise? Ha, he had just asked a madman if he was insane.

"Our eggs don't hatch until they have been incubated at a certain temperature for five months under a slurry of a particular fungus. Until then, they rest, neither growing nor dying."

"I hate this," Bowmark said. "And I'm beginning to hate you. So many demands and rules… and you forget I need to eat! I want to dump you headfirst into a privy." When had he gotten so short-tempered?

"Zzz zzz zzz."

Bowmark jabbed a finger toward him. "And I really, really hate how you are always laughing at me!"

Scolla looked past Bowmark and screeched. "Kill it! Kill it now!"

A ONE HANDED GRASP
IS NO GRASP AT ALL

~TEZLEPEK PROVERB

Bowmark spun and looked up. In an opening in the trees hovered a nightmare, thin enough to be a child's stick drawing, bristling with orange hairs. It was man-high, gaunt, and twisted like old roots, with mottled green insect wings and iridescent green insect eyes. Bowmark gaped, and then his training kicked in. He rolled under the mulig, came up the other side, and threw aside baggage in a search for the staffshifter.

"Arrows!" Scolla squealed as he scooted under the canopy and rolled into a ball.

There! Bowmark grabbed the bow and threw himself under the mulig again as the nightmare swooped toward them with a whirr. The thing touched ground with a large scythe-shaped toe, then shot straight up. Bowmark rolled out from under the mulig and fumbled as he tried to quickly string the bow. The monster flitted behind a stand of trees. After some skinned knuckles and a bruised thigh, Bowmark had the bow strung, then realized the quiver dangled from the platform rail on the other side of the mulig.

"Scolla, get me arrows!"

Scolla tentatively poked his head out of cover.

Bowmark gestured aggressively at the quiver. "There! Arrows!"

The flying monster appeared above the trees again and streaked toward him. Scolla retracted under the canopy. Bowmark rolled back under the mulig. The monster crashed down onto the platform.

The mulig tucked in her head, stretched her four ears over her eyes, and lowered herself, compressing Bowmark.

He squeezed out the other side, procured an arrow and stood. The winged monster spread its arms and unfolded a scythe of a finger as long as its forearm. It began tearing at the stowage.

Scolla! Bowmark shouted at the monster as he nocked the arrow. "Burn you!" Its head jerked up, distracted. Scolla took the opportunity to scuttle out of the pile of blankets, and between the monster's legs to hide behind the driver's bench.

Bowmark raised the bow and loosed the arrow, missing his target as it sprang up and away. This was no dumb beast. It understood the threat. Hovering on the other side of the mulig it emitted a rasping hollow moan.

Bowmark quickly grabbed another arrow. The monster lunged and swung a scythe at him. Bowmark deftly rolled backward into a kneel and drew the arrow just as he had practiced countless times as a child. The creature darted back to the other side of the mulig again. Scolla was now exposed, and ran, screeching, back toward the cover of the jumbled stowage.

The hovering nightmare tracked Scolla. Bowmark tracked the nightmare, sweeping the point over the mulig's back, until he had a clear shot, and released the arrow.

The creature folded around the projectile and was propelled backward until it thudded into a tree several strides away. It twitched, then shook violently. One leg began to swell rapidly, then an arm, then the other leg. Bowmark slowly stood as he watched in dumbstruck horror. CRACK! A leg burst and a cloud of dark orange hairs erupted from its chitin.

Several spots on Bowmark began to burn.

"Down!" Scolla squealed. He had climbed off the platform and was cowering next to Bowmark's feet.

Down he went and reached for his burning face. Bristles protruded from his skin. *CRACK! CRACK! CRACK!* Bowmark heard what must have been the other limbs exploding— sending more venomous hairs in every direction— but the mulig was between the monster and them, taking the brunt of the stinging hairs.

"On your back! Don't move!" Scolla commanded.

Bowmark rolled over and held still. The burning grew and spread. His closed eyes watered. He smelled mulig, ginger, and something acrid as Scolla scuttled to his head and commanded again, "Don't move."

Scolla's nimble fingers plucked bristles with a gentle haste as burning sensation strengthened to pain. He then moved to the back of Bowmark's hands. A few moments later, he said, "Sit up."

As Bowmark did, he breathed slowly through his teeth, concentrating on mental exercises to lessen the pain. Scolla pawed through the luggage and stumped back. Cold water poured over his face and hands.

"Keep your eyes closed."

Bowmark's skin swelled as Scolla dribbled slime on his face, soap perhaps, and rubbed vigorously. Air hissed through Bowmark's teeth as he withstood the explosion of pain.

Scolla rubbed Bowmark's hands, rinsed his face and hands with cold water, and then announced, "I removed all the hairs."

Bowmark opened his swelling eyelids. Scolla opened the jar he had used in prison.

"We do not yet have the antidote for the poison, but this lotion will ease the pain and help keep the wounds from inflammation."

Bowmark welcomed the cool dabbing on his face, though having Scolla's claws so close to his eyes made him nervous.

Then Scolla picked a few hairs from his own skin and rubbed on lotion.

Bowmark rose and walked over to what now appeared like a broken puppet pinned to a tree. Dark ichor dripped from the mangled remains. There were clawed hands—one with the scythe-finger—similar feet, and a skull-like head with huge, protruding insectile eyes. Its torso looked like a collapsed jellyfish in a ribcage. There was no discernable lower jaw, but a gaping hole in its chest served as a mouth. "What did I kill?"

"A dractil. Be cautious. You should sit far away while I brush the venomous hairs off the mulig."

"You're short, and I can help."

"You have already taken hurt. The dose you received should not kill you, but had there been four or five dractil, you might now be dead. Zzz. Change your clothes." Scolla wheezed. "I cannot imagine why a scout was so far east."

Bowmark plucked off all the bristles he could see before he pulled off his shirt. "I remember now. The lighthouse keeper told his wife that this is the largest swarm of dractils in a century and a queen had taken a temple."

Scolla hissed like water dropped on a hot stone. "We tell them, and tell them, but our dear friends cannot think strategically."

"I'm sure what you said meant something."

Scolla raked his claws through the mulig's short matted fur. The animal moaned mournfully. "From now on you must always have the bow on ready. Ssss!" A bristle stuck in his hand. "May they wallow in their filth and die of disease!" He pulled out the bristle and resumed raking. "Dractils are a people whose stronghold is much farther north and higher in the mountains."

"A people?" Bowmark stepped back. "Like tezledeks?" He placed his palm against his chest. "Like humans?"

"We think so of the ones on the far coast who trade hides to humans for piglets. Those dractils produce what we suppose is art. Zz zz. They stand around making noise at each other which we presume to be language. They sing. Humans cannot hear their singing, but we can. They leave marks in clay that appear to be script. But in everything else, they behave like animals, animals with an army. The ones on this side of Akinda trade with no one. They act only like animals."

Bowmark remembered more of what the lighthouse keeper had said. "What does it mean that a queen took the temple of the . . . mazies? Is that a nickname for rumshas?"

Scolla picked carefully over the mulig's ears. "Szz. Our poor allies. You will never meet a braver or kinder people. However, rumshas fight only if directly attacked or if their children are endangered. If we thought herding humans over the rumshane lands would leave the rumshas unscathed, we would do it. Humans would destroy the dractils."

That brought up so many questions that Bowmark had no idea which to ask first. "Why did the scout attack us?"

Scolla snarled, startling Bowmark, and semi-inflated. "You are food. I am an incubator." He sputtered and hissed in his own tongue for a few moments. "If there had been a troop of them, the mulig would have been food, too."

Bowmark gathered up their scattered goods and puzzled over the word Scolla had used. Birds incubated eggs, and so, apparently, did Scolla's people. Scolla could not have meant that he tended the monster's eggs until they hatched. Or could he? What were those black eggs, really? "I don't know what you mean by incubate."

"People or animals too big to fit in dractil tunnels are killed, dismembered, and eaten. Tezledeks and small human children are paralyzed and dragged into one of their dens. Dractils lay eggs on us. We are piled in the dark surrounded by their stench as the eggs grow tendrils under our skin. They use our blood for food until we starve to death. Then the eggs hatch and the larvae eat what is left of us."

Bowmark swallowed several times. *Please let this be the ravings of a lunatic. Please.* "Why haven't your people destroyed them?"

"How can we, how? We have no skill with bow and arrow. If we approach near enough to cause damage, they shoot their bristles at us. One bristle or three is only an irritation, but hundreds or thousands will either paralyze or kill us. And hurt. A great deal." He hissed some more.

Bowmark was almost sorry that Scolla was teaching him. He slipped the loose white shirt Scolla had brought over his head. How had Scolla managed to acquire additional clothing for him but not food? He stuffed his dirty green shirt into one of the cargo nets on the edge of the mulig's platform. "Food. You didn't pack any for yourself either."

Scolla said distantly, "There is always food for me wherever I go."

"Of course. The forest is full of moldy bread."

"My eyes hurt." Scolla tapped the mulig between her floppy ears. The animal snorted and raised her head. Sunlight shone through thousands of leaves, but even with the light diluted, Scolla squinted. His bat wing shaped ears folded over his eyes and his head was retracted so deeply into his shoulders that the rolls of flesh on his hump swallowed all but his face. "We need to leave."

"Here are your eyeshades." Bowmark picked Scolla up, though the fellow stiffened, and put him on the platform as the mulig rose. "Do we start with a language lesson or a culture lesson?"

"Tonight." Scolla curled up tighter.

"Culture it is. Tell me about these allies, the rumshas. They seem strong to me, stronger than humans." He pulled himself onto the mulig. "I saw one in Bysea that was as large as this mulig."

After shaking her head, flopping her ears, and shivering all over, the mulig ambled down the trail. The animal seemed to need no direction to continue down the road, so Bowmark wrapped the reins around the knob that appeared to be designed for it, and moved to the platform.

He settled next to Scolla. "Tell me why it is they don't kill every cursed dractil? They don't think strategically?"

Scolla wheezed, then uncoiled enough to speak clearly. "They worship the Unfathomable Jester."

"I remember. Rumshas like a good joke."

"Laughter is an act of devotion."

"What happens to a gloomy rumsha?"

"He pretends to be jolly. They believe in a concept you will not comprehend."

"Stop calling me stupid."

"I am not. Turn around. Give me your hand."

Bowmark scooted backward, then turned around. The mulig continued plodding. He extended his hand.

Scolla sat up and placed his hand beside Bowmark's. "Had we the training, both of us could play flutes. But your flute must be shaped differently from mine."

Bowmark examined their disparate palms. Although he had not brought one with him, he did know how to play the flute.

"Think of language or concepts as types of flutes. You could not play a rumshane flute."

"And this has what to do with their letting a dractil queen take their temple?"

"Zzz. They do not believe in the future. There is only this moment, this pleasure, this acceptance of the ridiculous. Zzz. There is seeing behind the appearance, zzz, understanding the joke. None of these words are correct. Common cannot carry the meaning."

"Why are they your allies, and humans are not?"

"They appreciate us. They live underground in tunnels as we do and help us on many projects. They do not fight among themselves."

Bowmark touched the itching welts on his forehead and concentrated on not scratching. "And now they are surrounded by hundreds—or thousands—of dractils?"

Scolla's ears drooped. "That is so. Zzz. But now you know about dractils and you have a bow. You can kill them at a distance without their bristles touching you."

Bowmark laid his hands flat on the mulig's platform. "And so I am herded."

Scolla's ears flipped upright and rigid.

Bowmark reached behind himself and pulled on the reins. When the mulig stopped, he swung off, strode to the bifurcated back legs, and with a steel knife severed the net that held most of his belongings on the mulig.

Scolla stood and wobbled from foot to foot. "What are you doing, what?"

Bowmark pulled his laundry from another net and stuffed it in his new backpack. "I am not your dog to be sicced on the dractils. A Bysea judge taught me that. My fights are not yours, and yours are not mine." He slipped his arms through the loops of the backpack. He reached for the water skin then paused, noticing it had been pierced by several dractil hairs and was slowly leaking. Bowmark paused at the sight. *He* was leaking. Time. Health. Patience. Sanity. *Drip, drip drip.* He left the waterskin and began walking back towards the east.

"Where are you going, where?"

"Back to Sharp Point to earn some food, and then . . . ." Where *was* he going to go? "We'll see."

"You misunderstand! I am not asking you to kill dractils for our allies!"

Bowmark kept walking.

"The goal is to get you home safely!" screamed the spitter, his voice pitched higher than usual. His head now fully extended from his body on a neck Bowmark had never seen before.

Bowmark winced from the hurt his ears took, turned, and walked backward. "Then we'll both go back to Sharp Point and travel north along the coast."

"A bay blocks the way. The only way north on the coast is to continue this direction. On a mulig it will take six weeks to reach the next coastal town." Scolla tried to slide off the mulig, tripped over one of his ropes, and flopped onto the ground. "Dismuld Point is a poor town. Then you need to cross a barren mountain chain to reach the next poor town. My itinerary gives you the greatest chance in the shortest time to obtain your treasures before we return to Bysea." He staggered to his feet and waddled after Bowmark.

"And accidentally herding me through a swarm of dractils you want me to kill since the rumsha won't do it for you. Goodbye Scolla."

"I did not know about the swarm."

Bowmark turned his back on Scolla.

Scolla's scream followed him. "I did not know about the swarm!"

As Bowmark walked, he examined the growth near the ground. Would he recognize what was edible?

Scolla screeched, then screamed, "You will kill me!"

Bowmark stopped. What difference would another quarter candle make? He returned to Scolla, sank to his knees and then sat on his legs so he could see Scolla eye to eye, or rather, eye to eyeshade. "How will I kill you when I am taking nothing away from you?"

Scolla licked his shades. "We do not discuss our ways, not even with our allies."

"And humans aren't allies."

Scolla sat, which shortened him very little. "That diamond you so blithely threw away at Sharp Point is but a small part of my ruin."

"Those people saved my life."

"So I shall argue. I must give account of absolutely everything that is spent on this mission."

"Your mission, not mine."

"They are the same mission."

Bowmark wanted to strangle the spitter. "You don't care which boar leads the herd. You don't care that RaiseHim will step on my subject's heads. You don't care that I have a blood-spilt oath to defend my people."

"You should rejoice that once I get you safely home, I will not interfere in your politics."

Bowmark touched his forehead, then deliberately lowered his hand lest he scratch and make his face sting more than it already did. "I grant you that. How do I kill you by leaving you?"

"I should not have said that. I was distressed."

"I'm about to distress you more by walking away again. If you can't answer every question I ask you, then we are not on the same mission and we are not partners. I swore to keep your secrets. Give me some to keep."

Scolla patted his palms together. "I now complete my ruin. I put my name on record. I would be the first to expand the tezledek's territory in over one hundred-seventy years. I did not know how many resources I would need to take. I did not know how complex your needs were. Already there are complaints about the multitude of my requests. The reward would be worth it, but many question whether or not you can possibly meet your self-imposed conditions."

Bowmark held up a hand. "What is your reward?"

"More land. More knowledge. We bring civilization to your people. We hope in two or three thousand years to create a civilized world at peace."

For a while there, Bowmark had forgotten that Scolla was insane. Or was it that all his people were insane? "Does that peaceful world include humans?"

Scolla clicked his teeth together. "It is possible."

"I do hope so. I interrupted your story." A bug crawled over his ankle. "How do I kill you by leaving?"

"The greater the undertaking, the more severe the penalty if there is failure and waste of resources."

"The spitters will execute you?"

"No. Quite no. Tezkedeks are not so crude as that."

"What are tezledeks so crude as?"

Scolla wheezed. "Understand, we have social duty that all must do. Those who will not fulfill their duty are exiled to live as ferals in wilderness away from libraries, schools, and experiment stations."

"So you'll be exiled?"

"Let me finish. Then there is special duty for those who would be great. That is what I am doing now. If I fail, I will be given shame duty. In this locale, the shame duty is to spend each night of an entire year killing dractils. No one who has been given such duty has lived more than seven weeks." He picked up a fallen leaf and poked holes in it with his talons.

"So then." Bowmark shifted away from a twig indenting itself in his knee. "You can't lay guilt upon my head for that. I didn't ask you to do this."

Scolla picked up another leaf to poke.

Bowmark watched him for a moment. "What happens if I get killed?"

"I am called a fool for the rest of my life. I return all the resources I can return. I work extra social duty for years to pay back what I cannot return." Scolla poked multiple holes in a large leaf.

"So then. Why can't you run away and make a new life for yourself elsewhere?"

Scolla jumped to his four stubby feet and swelled. "I shall the day you shall! You and I, we are the same. We are more than bellies to be fed, more than ears to hear gossip, more than eyes to gaze upon beautiful women! We choose duty to our people and we do not throw that duty away."

Bowmark studied him, wishing he could see through the creature's sunshades. And, even though the answers were weird, Scolla had answered his questions. "So then. If we are the same, we can be partners."

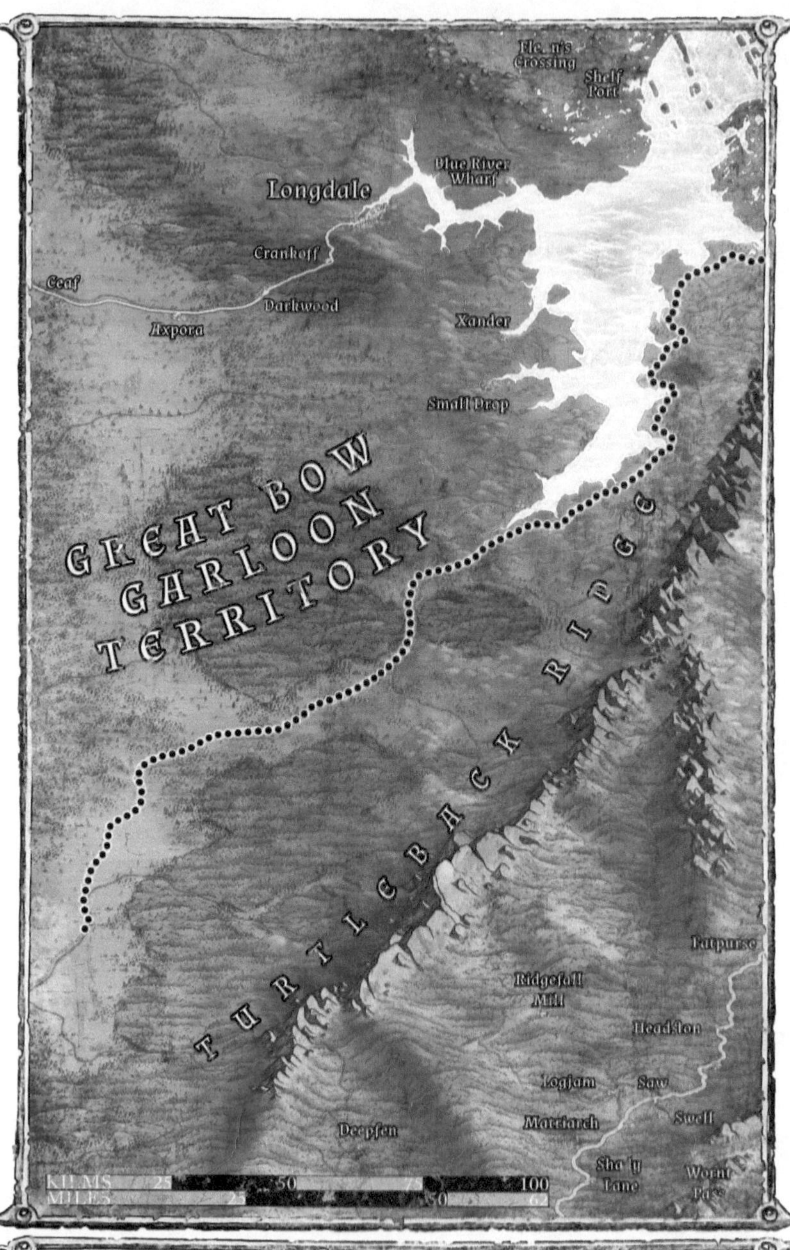

SUNDOWN ROAD CUTS THROUGH DENSE WOODLAND 200 KILOMETERS INLAND AND IS KNOWN TO HARBOR ROAD BANDITS. CARAVANS ARE RECOMMENDED A 20% SOLDIER COMPLEMENT.

~SEAFOLK ATLAS

Bowmark awoke with a start and grabbed his bow, scanning the early morning sky. It had been four days since the dractil had ambushed them, and he had not been sleeping well. Every bird call, insect chirp and lizard song had jolted him to full alert. Since the path had been following a river for the past day Bowmark had been able to catch a few small fish, but despite this his stomach felt continually empty, and his nerves were frayed. He could not see what had startled him awake, so he set the bow down.

Scolla sat on the bench as the mulig trundled along. At least they were making steady progress towards a goal. Scolla said that muligs were content to walk all day and most of the night as long as brush and tall grass was abundant. So while their speed was only that of a brisk walk, the beast made up for it with endurance and a placid temperament. Scolla claimed that they were traveling at least fifty kilms every day. Bowmark estimated that a kilm was around ten ropes, and he found himself counting off every hundred strides while he walked beside the mulig. But hunger and distraction continually ruined his attempts at math.

Scolla rotated his head almost completely around to look at him. Bowmark shivered at the sight. He didn't know if he'd ever get used to that. Scolla wrapped the reins around the bench horn. "Good, you're awake. It is getting too bright for me."

Bowmark nodded. "I think I'll walk for a while. You can go to bed." Bowmark hopped off the platform and stretched.

Scolla was burrowing under the bedding when they approached a small clearing in the forest. Rocks pulled from the ground were set in a ring with branches balanced on them. In the center of the stone ring rose a tower of rocks set one upon another. All the rocks wore mud on one side.

Bowmark picked up a pebble and reached toward the tower.

"Do not touch!" screamed Scolla.

Bowmark pulled back. The tower of rocks collapsed. "I didn't touch it. I was only going to add another rock."

"That is a garloon construction. You must never touch a pile of rocks or woven twigs in the forest. The garloons do not care if wind or wild animals break their constructions, but humans and tezledeks are forbidden to interfere with the works of the garloons."

The drawings of garloons in the Atlas had intrigued him.. They appeared somewhat like upright elk with antlers, three-fingered hands and long, long toes. "I hope we will meet with some garloons."

Scolla wheezed. "If you see a single garloon, do not look him in the eye, or else you will set him off into a murderous rage."

Bowmark dropped the pebble and vaulted onto the driver's bench and flicked the reins. "So then, I hope we do not meet with some garloons."

"Zzz zzz zzz. If we meet with a group of garloons, we should be safe enough."

Bowmark rubbed his face. Life on Akinda seemed unnecessarily complex.

Three days later, the small trail intersected a larger road at a town called Doublecross composed of several clusters of low boxy buildings with colorful plastered walls and sod roofs covered in swaying grass. A handful of people were sweeping or carrying water. Bowmark realized he had not seen a human face in so long that even these strangely pallid people gave him solace. But more so the chance to purchase real food.

As he directed the mulig onto the road heading west, they passed a line of human travelers, a family, walking with a laden mulig behind them down the wide road towards the east. Their skin was yellow-beige, their eyes brown, their hair a rippled gray.

As it was mid-day Scolla was sleeping, but the sound of voices roused him. He extended his head from the pile of bedding to survey the town.

"This is the Sundown Road. It stretches from the western coast of Akinda all the way to Fairenwell in the east. We should have no trouble procuring food for you now that we are on this road. Look for a building with large windows and supplies inside."

Bowmark looked around for such a building. "When I was on the boat from Bysea we stopped at the port of Fairenwell briefly."

"Yes, many goods travel from this region overland to the east in order to avoid Megaloth's sea route taxes."

Three buildings west, just before a wooden bridge, he found the windowed building. A small bell tinkled as he opened the door. A middle-aged man with pink skin and blue-gray hair nodded at him from behind a waist-high counter. Assuming this was a greeting, Bowmark nodded back. He eyed their many shelves full of goods. "Please, tell me you would be willing to sell me some food. And a water skin. I've been living off berries, rodents, and small fish for many days."

The man smiled. "Certainly, stranger. I'm guessing you came through the northern Garloon territory, eh? Did you run in to any dractil? We've heard word of them flying as far east as Wellingree, not but two days west of here. Been thinking we may need to board the place up and evacuate if we don't get a garrison here soon."

"I encountered and slew three of them."

The petite man pursed his lips. "Oooh, not good news that they come in from the north as well. I thank you for the news. Now to your needs. We have shortbread, honey and hardtack we can sell you. And perhaps you would like some smoked lizard?" He riffled through large barrel next to him and pulled out a jug. "How about some good brew? I can imagine after your journey you could use it!" He pulled out the cork.

A yeasty smell assailed Bowmark's nostrils. "No. I can't drink that rotted stuff."

The man raised his eyebrows. "Ah ... I have met your kind of variant before. Sunfolk, eh? I can understand why they made you sparkly. But I cannot understand the kind of addleheaded ancestor that would decree that none of his descendants would be able to enjoy the fruit of the vine or hops. But what can you do? None of us gets to choose our ancestors."

Bowmark chuckled. "I don't know that I am missing so much. What I have seen is that the fruit of the vine first makes you stupid, and then makes you vomit. And then you have a headache all the next morning."

A woman he had not noticed earlier laughed from the other side of the room.She "Got you there, Drue."

Drue shook his head. "You don't need to drink so much at a time. A mug a day won't hurt you. Mm, I take that back, it might hurt *you*. Let's get to that hardtack, shall we? And I'm sure we have a spare skin."

"Thank you so much. Oh, I need payment. Excuse me for a moment." When Bowmark returned to the Mulig platform he remembered he also needed another bow. He had kept his short bow strung for days, never knowing when it would be needed for a dractil ambush, and it was beginning to wear.

"How much should I pay for food and a bow if they have one they can sell?" Bowmark whispered to Scolla who had re-covered himself in the blankets.

"Try to barter with this." Scolla's hand emerged from the jumble and deposited a silver coin on the platform. "If they seem pleased, ask for them to add more food to the order until they stop smiling."

Bowmark sighed, and followed Scolla's directions just enough to say he tried.

Late the next afternoon, they passed a small town that seemed completely abandoned. The doors had wooden planks nailed over them. The planks were painted with bright yellow markings that Bowmark did not recognize. He looked for signs of struggle but saw nothing that indicated such. They continued out of town and crossed a stone bridge over a slow winding river.

Bowmark took a deep breath. "Zmmssoshinim."

"Zzz zzz zzz."

"What did I say this time?"

"It was so garbled, I cannot even guess what you meant to say. Perhaps you were speaking about dogs swimming in this river, perhaps?"

"Doesn't ssoshi mean hope?"

"No. Ssoshi does."

Bowmark clenched his teeth and tried to vibrate his tongue against them to say the syllable he might have mispronounced. "Sso."

"No. Sso."

Bowmark picked a leathery leaf from a shrub and used a fish bone to poke holes in a pattern. "This sso."

"Right spelling. Wrong pronunciation. Your teeth are too large and blunt to produce this sound."

Bowmark rubbed his face. "I still think you're making it up."

Scolla held up three fingers and waggled each in turn. "Sso, sso, sso. Which one is the root for hope?"

The three syllables sounded exactly the same. "The second?"

"Sso means dog."

"I knew that. Shall we set up camp next to this river?"

Scolla lifted up his shades and squinted. "Not yet. This area is open to the dractils."

"We haven't been attacked anywhere near a settlement before." Bowmark gestured to the village on the other side of the river to their left.

"Nor have we been attacked at night. Nor have we been attacked when there were red flowers nearby, four clouds in the sky, or next to a pothole."

Bowmark blinked quickly as he tried to make sense of Scolla's statement. Did Scolla believe that flowers, clouds and potholes were magical wards that kept the dractil at bay? Then it dawned on him.

"You are being facetious. Calling me a fool for thinking I understand the rules that dractil follow when I have so little experience. This is not the kind of relationship I require of a partner."

Scolla made a dismissive buzz.

Bowmark flicked the mulig's reins and muttered sso to himself repeatedly. Then he remembered to look up. He needed to look up every hundred breaths. So far he had killed three dractils. Three times Scolla had rolled into a screeching ball. The dractils' brittle chitin cracked easily. What was all the fuss about?

Bowmark took the leaf and punched in the other two letters that stood for sso. His ear could not yet tell the difference, but his eye could. He turned around to face the rear of the mulig.

Scolla dipped his finger into a small vial of honey and then partially unwrapped sections of a long tube to drop the honey in.

"What are you doing with my breakfast?"

"Feeding the messenger flies."

"What about feeding me?"

"You will not starve to death. They might."

"So. What do these bugs taste like?"

"Zzz zzz zzz. Is food all you ever think about, is it?"

"Only when I haven't eaten or slept well in over a week. What do you do with the bugs if they aren't emergency rations?"

Scolla suddenly rolled up.

Bowmark surveyed the sky in case Scolla was reacting to another dractil. Nothing. But a group of human travelers approached them on the road ahead. They rode on a lorglin, a green serpent shaped multi-legged furry beast, pulling a heavily laden wagon. Bowmark raised his hand with fingers spread wide. "Safe travel to you."

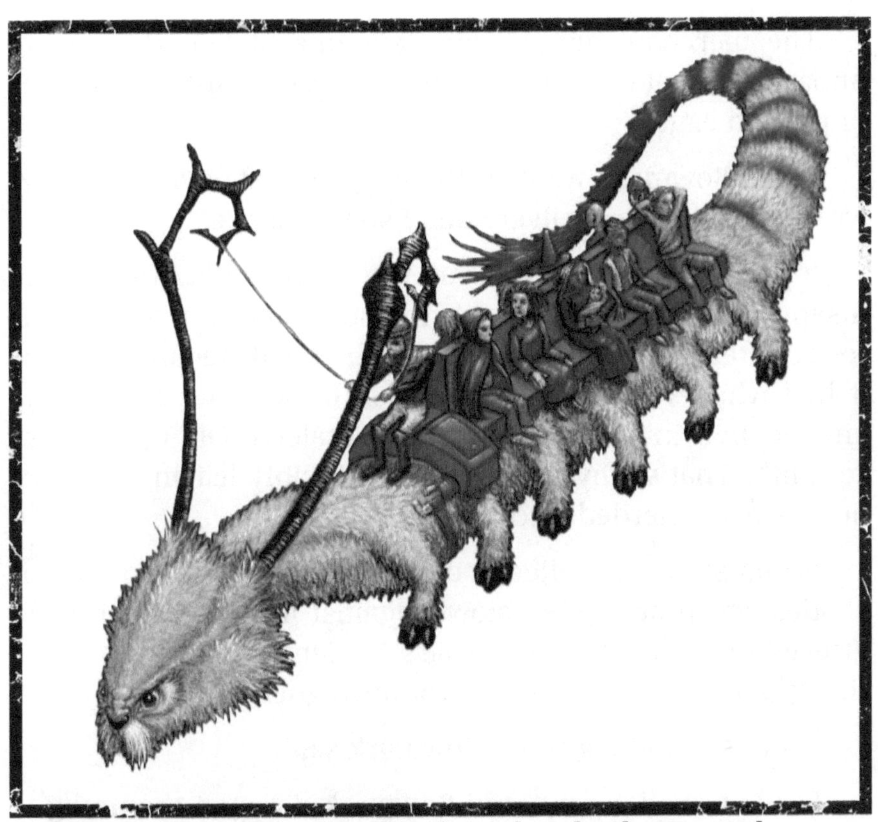

When they reached each other, they both stopped.

The woman in front, dressed in green with a puffed and slashed merchant's hat with tassels, said, "I would wish ye the same, but ye are going the wrong way."

"Is this not the way to Central Place?"

"Indeed 'tis, but swarming as 'tis with dractil scouts, 'tis no safe place to be. When the queens in the temple start hatching their eggs, 'twill be even worse. I'm moving my business elsewhere, New Renan perhaps."

Bowmark considered before speaking formally, "I am convinced to stay there only a short while." He smiled in what he hoped was a disarming way. "Perhaps you would agree to a business transaction. I would like to buy some food."

The merchant agreed and sent one of her servants to unpack a box of crackers, two bags of dried fruit, and a crock of pickled eggs.

When Bowmark went to the baggage for payment, Scolla whispered, "A small silver coin. Expect change."

It was hard to wait until the merchant's wagon had disappeared behind a hillock for Bowmark to tear into the food. After a few bites his stomach roiled, feeling the way it had whenever the volcano shook back home. How could anyone live in a state of constant alert? Oh right. They couldn't. That's why they were all sensibly leaving the area he was being herded into.

Scolla slowly unrolled. Dusk allowed him to take off his shades which he tapped slowly against his foot. "Such news grieves me. I lived twenty years in Central Place. To see it thus polluted. . . " He gazed around vaguely.

"Yon is a walking tree," Bowmark said.

Scolla waved assent, and Bowmark directed the mulig to a massive tree with huge roots arching out in all directions. They stopped under one of the arches. On the other side of the tree, a rocky ravine opened like a mouth in the ground.

Bowmark stuffed another egg in his mouth before sliding off the gentle mulig and tying the animal next to a bitterberry bush. "What did you do in Central Place?"

"The same thing I did in Jukalog, New Renan, Bysea, and Discoria. I taught."

Bowmark reached up for Scolla and carried him to the ground.

"Ho!" came a jeering male voice. "Now there's a fastidious traveler."

Scolla instantly rolled up as Bowmark turned. Under another root arch on the other side of the wide trunk, three human men had dismounted and were stretching out a picket line for their loaded muligs.

The man with a black beard laughed again and pointed at Bowmark. "He brings his own dungman and carries him with his own hands." The other men laughed. "What kind of person keeps a dung-sucker for a pet?"

"A wretchedly lonely one," said the slight man with a striped hat.

Bowmark was glad for the weight of the staffshifter and the knives about his waist. In the dim light he marched straight to the black-bearded brute and glared down at his face. "You don't mock my friend with dirty names. If you need to bully, try bullying me."

The man's eyes widened. He held up both hands with fingers spread wide and he backed a few paces. "I meant no harm."

"You mean that you thought someone that small could not harm *you*."

The three men shifted uneasily. The man in the striped hat muttered, "Why don't we move on?" They mounted their muligs, drove them outside the tree's root area and clopped down the road toward another walking tree with more muligs and people under its canopy. One of the men looked back, scowling. "You never win a fight with a madman."

Bowmark returned to the mulig and unloaded his baggage. Munching a fistful of dried fruit, he loosened the ropes holding the tiny cabin on the mulig's back. Since the animal did not seem to mind wearing the combination saddle and cabin all night long, he left the structure on its back. That way he could pack faster and get away from those men in the morning. He contemplated the root arch he stood under. Could he convert his blanket into a hammock? How could everyone in this land could sleep on hard flat surfaces every night?

A hiss and twig-snap made him turn and clutch his staff-shifter at his waist.

The black-bearded man held the leashes of two enormous lizards. Their scaled skin drooped in folds under their necks. Their heads reached Bowmark's thighs. Their lengths equaled his height. The man said, "Do you want to threaten me again?"

Bowmark huffed. "No, I don't want to threaten you. I want you to leave my partner and me alone."

The man pointed at Bowmark and commanded, "Take."

The lizards leapt toward Bowmark.

He backed into the mulig then pulled out the staffshifter and swung the baton form into the muzzle of the lizard snapping at his face. The mulig squealed and shied away. The other lizard clamped his teeth around Bowmark's leg. He pointed. *Zip!* The metal snake fist crashed into the lizard's skull. It let go of his leg and slumped. The first lizard scrabbled at Bowmark's chest with its claws and bit the staffshifter.

Bowmark backed up again and bumped into the mulig's neck. He wrestled with the lizard for the staffshifter. The mulig groaned and side-stepped out of the way. The man shouted. The lizard would not let go. Its enormous weight dragged on the weapon. Bowmark shortened the staff until the

snake claws were inside the lizard's mouth. The beast shook its head, twisting violently. Bowmark's fingers lost their grip. The lizard closed its lips around the staffshifter. Bowmark stumbled backward. He slapped the end of the staffshifter. "Open!" he urged. The lizard hissed as the staff expanded, puncturing its bottom jaw and palate. Bowmark lunged and grabbed his weapon, dislodging it from the monster's jaw. The lizard dropped away, splattering orange blood.

The man commanded, "Come!" The lizard raced to his side.

Bowmark shook his staffshifter. "This is a magic weapon. Do you want me to kill both your lizards?"

The man turned and ran, waving his arms and shouting, "Go! Go!"

Bowmark's mulig screamed. Her hind legs fell over the edge of the ravine. The middle legs scrabbled at the edge.

Bowmark retrieved his magic rope from the loop on his belt and pushed it into the staffshifter's claw. His practice was paying off, the snake claw accepted the rope, gripping it like a vise. He tossed one end of the magic rope at a nearby root arch which it instantly wrapped, then carried the other end that was attached to the staff to the ravine edge. He jumped over, gripping the staffshifter and the rope tightened. His feet found a boulder. He caught a mulig hind foot and pressed the foot into the cliff to give the struggling beast purchase.

The platform groaned and slowly slid backward, threatening to topple off the mulig's back. A spray of dirt and gravel was kicked in his face.

The mulig kicked again, grazing Bowmark's ear. He caught it with a free hand and shoved the hoof upward. The boulder under his feet began to roll. In a last ditch effort, Bowmark threw the staffshifter at another large arching root on the other side of the animal and yelled, "Rope stick!" Though he could not see it, the staff or rope must have found purchase as the cord pulled tight against the back of the mulig under her broad tail Bowmark quickly scrambled up the ravine and dashed to the head of the mulig where he coaxed and tugged on the reins.

After a tense few moments she pulled up and over the edge.

Bowmark sprawled on the ground and panted. Then, remembering the unpredictable gang that was still nearby he quickly retrieved his magic items that were wrapped from one root to another like a bannister next to the rim of the ravine. Bowmark was amazed at the versatility of these tools. They had never listened to his commands so well before.

As the excitement waned the pains from the encounter began to exert themselves on his senses. All he had wanted was to eat his own weight in food and to sleep for a week. What was *wrong* with people? "Fumes!"

Scolla uncurled. "Why did you do that, why?"

Bowmark watched Scolla, a tezledek, who still appeared more animal than person to him, who *still* resembled a kratchnak. He propped himself with shaking arms on the mulig. "Don't you castigate me for defending you." He stuffed a handful of dried fruit in his mouth and began tightening the platform straps.

"What do you think you were defending me from?"

"That bully! I hate bullies. I've watched them all my life. Name-calling is how it begins. If you don't stop it there, they move on to physical violence, as that man just demonstrated."

"That human was not violent until you frightened him."

"No, Scolla, no. With your big ears you didn't hear him call you a dungsucker?"

"What nasty names, what? I heard none. He merely called me what I am."

Bowmark almost choked on his food. "What? You don't—you—"

Scolla said levelly, "All that live must eat something."

Bowmark stared. "You eat—You eat our—" He jumped up. "No! That's *disgusting!*"

"How human." Scolla flipped an ear dismissively.

Bowmark's stomach tried to evert. He spat out the remaining fruit pulp he hadn't swallowed yet. He gulped some air, turned and walked away. So that's why there were never any mulig droppings in the camp when he woke up. And he had touched him! No wonder the men laughed!

As he stumbled through the brush, he concentrated on not losing the largest meal he had eaten in days. The filthy kratchnak had touched everything Bowmark owned.

Bowmark sat on the trunk of a fallen tree. He winced at the memory of grabbing Scolla's tongue. His hand felt filthy. How was he supposed to travel the world with a dungsucker? The lizard bite on his leg throbbed. Scolla had rubbed ointment on all his wounds!

Bowmark sat up straighter as other memories came. Rolocton, Discoria, Bysea, Sharp Point; everywhere he had traveled, the streets smelled clean. No cesspits. No night soil fertilizer. If the tezledeks did for Stoneshell what they did here in Akinda, his people need never face the wrath of the shlaks for polluting the sea.

The maids would rejoice in losing the chore of emptying the slop jars. The king would have one less disgusting thing to worry about. There would be no more contamination of cisterns. That's what Scolla had meant about bringing civilization. Humans could not gather in such great numbers without stench and sickness unless tezledeks were also there.

In the growing dark, Bowmark pushed through the brush until he reached the camp site and found Scolla unrolling a blanket. "Scolla! *You* are the treasure from Discoria."

Scolla's ears fluttered.

Bowmark picked him up and hugged him.

Dismuld
Covert
DISMULD GARLOON
TERRITORY
GREAT BOW
GARLOON
TERRITORY
LAKEWIND
PRARIE
Doublecross
STREWN
STEPPES
TURTLEBACK RIDGE
KILMS 100   200   300
MILES   100   186

HE SHALL STAY. AT THE FORE POSITION AT ALL TIMES.
HE SHALL HAVE NO MORE THAN 2 THIMBLES OF RUM PER DAY.
HE SHALL BE SUMMARILY DISMISSED UPON ANY SUSPICION.
HE SHALL BE DISMISSED WITH FULL PAY AT
THE MEGOLOTH BORDER."
                              ~CARAVAN MASTER CORTH

Bowmark shook his head to dislodge the drop of sweat dangling from his nose. He pushed up, arms trembling slightly, into this set's twentieth handstand on the back of the six-legged mulig. The mount continued at an easy gait through the dappled wood, flicking her four ears occasionally at an insect or reaching with her long tongue to pull up a weed.

"You tire me by the watching of you," Scolla whined.

Bowmark flipped to a seated position to face the tezledek, who peered at him through the gaps in his folded bat wing-shaped ears. Imitating the dung-eater's mosquito whine, Bowmark said, "And you tire me by the hearing of you. What of it, what?"

"Why do you do this and disturb my sleep every moment you are not eating, why?" The copper shine of his large eyes disappeared when he blinked.

Bowmark clenched his fists. "I need to become stronger."

"How strong do you need to be, how?"

Bowmark wriggled his fingers as he swept them across his chest. "The current flows like this: We Sea Predators live and die by the Protocol. Our ancestors chose to make it difficult to overthrow a king. I have no choice but to kill the man who is usurping the throne. I do not wish it, but there is no other way. And I cannot kill RaiseHim until we meet on the Bronze Disc set over lava. When we fight, I will have no weapons. He will have all the weapons he wants. I must have fasted for the three days before. He will be as well fed as he wants. Unless I learn how to fight an armed man with my bare hands, I expect to be killed."

Scolla stirred and his spines straightened. His ginger scent intensified. "More new information! You will be killed by this, who?"

"RaiseHim. He took my throne. If I can take him with me, then I am satisfied."

"I am not, quite no. If this RaiseHim lives, how will he treat tezledeks, how?"

Bowmark grimaced and glanced up into the leafy canopy. No man-tall, insectile dractils to deal with—for the moment. "RaiseHim enjoys tormenting animals."

"Ssss."

"So think I."

Scolla rewrapped himself in his blanket and burrowed deeper into the luggage. "Doom," he whispered.

Bowmark's lips twisted as he thought of the multiple names he now knew Scolla's people went by: tezledeks, spitters, cleaners. "I would tell you to let him know that you are not animals, but RaiseHim enjoys tormenting people, too."

No response followed that statement. Bowmark reached for the water skin. His eye caught movement with his peripheral vision. With practiced ease, he rolled off the mulig and rose with bow and arrow on the ready.

No killer dractil hovered in the tree canopy, but rather a huge beastly head, ridden by a human who waved at him.

Bowmark stowed the weapon and stood, staring, as his mount and the beast slowly approached one another. "Scolla?"

Scolla shifted. "A well-funded caravan. Nothing to worry about."

How could something that big not be something to worry about?

After the mulig rounded a slight curve in the trail, the beast with an elongated neck, massive chest, tree-trunk-like front legs, steeply sloped back, smaller hind legs, and a brightly colored fin tail appeared in glory. The beast extended a purple tongue twice as long as Bowmark was tall, stripped the leaves from the top half of a tree, and stuffed the resulting bundle into its mouth. The beast pulled a wagon overtopped with bags.

Behind the majestic creature stretched a long line of lorglins, the cargo-carriers Bowmark wanted to call centipede-elk, all laden with many boxes and people. A human riding the last lorglin rubbed a bow over a box covered with strings, making musical tones. Someone sang in a language Bowmark did not know.

The human atop the tree-tall silvery-gray beast was in a large basket that reminded Bowmark of the crow's nest on the large ship he had been imprisoned on. The man beckoned, then twirled a rope down to Bowmark. After his last encounter with strangers, he was wary of the invitation, but Scolla's nonchalance convinced Bowmark's curious side to prevail. Several moments later, he had pulled himself to the top and stood in the basket, shoulder to shoulder with a lanky man whose skin was the color of old ivory and hair as dark as the underside of rain clouds.

Bowmark scanned over the trees and saw the forest ended abruptly several ropes to the west. Flat, irregular fields divided by meandering paths spread out to the horizon. A straight road cut through the fields and paths, leading to a distant, brown smudge.

The ivory-colored man spoke slowly, as though he had all day and tomorrow to deliver his sentence. "Yonder is Central Place, and humans are fast leaving it. We are the last large caravan. Have you met many dractils?"

"Three. I killed them."

The man twisted some rope in his hands. "All solitary?"

"Yes."

"Good. We trek to Bysea. Perhaps you would join us for safety from robbers while you keep us safe from dractils?" With an open hand, the man pointed to the caravan of lorglins.

"I am to go to Central Place first."

The man snorted. "Safe travel to you then."

Bowmark stroked a horn of the beast he stood on. "I want one of these."

The man chuckled. "So do I. But only merchant guilds and dictators of large countries can afford these beauties. The feed bill of a koigence is enormous. And my driving skills command a hefty salary."

Bowmark stroked the horn again as the head swung to another tree and stripped it. "How expensive can it be when it eats passing trees?"

The man chuckled again. "Leaves are good fillage, but low in nutrients. We provide more substantial fare at all stops. You are good on your feet. Few can ride the koigence without nausea. Maychance you could even handle a peek through my spyglass."

He proffered the arm-long leather tube he had been holding, pride beaming from his sly smile. Bowmark hefted it curiously. "I'm afraid I don't know how to… peek through this."

"Never seen a spyglass, eh? Suppose I shouldn't be surprised. Quality lenses are rare these days, what with the sabotage of Megaloth's glassworks back in Joapin's reign."

Bowmark scrunched his brows as he tried to parse what the man was saying. Recognizing the confusion, the man demonstrated how to hold the spyglass to look through it.

Like magic, Bowmark could see the boarded-up tavern he had passed several candles ago. The sway of the koigence and the unnatural effect of the magical tool suddenly flipped his stomach. Bowmark flinched back, blinking rapidly. The man gently chortled. Bowmark offered it back to him.

"I've been warned about magic items."

The man chuckled and pushed the spyglass back to Bowmark. "Tis not magic, son. Just two finely polished glass domes in a tube."

"Glass? That's what the lens is made of? We have glass at home. But all you can see through ours is faint light and distortions."

"Indeed. The art and craft of lens making is now only kept by one nation, and its secrets are so well guarded no other nation has been able to replicate it. More valuable than diamonds, these lenses here." The man was clearly enjoying talk of his status.

"May I try again?" This kind of treasure could mean the Sea Predators could patrol for intruders without being seen!

"Aye. Try something closer this time. Look down at the caravan." Bowmark leaned precariously over the edge of the basket and peered through the glass."

"Everything is a blur, as though my eyes were squinted against the sun."

The man showed him how to telescope the body of the spyglass, bringing the images below into crystal clarity.

Bowmark looked down upon the caravan. Humans held reins attached to the lorglins' antlers except on the lead lorglin. On that one, a small, patchy, yellow-furred creature sat between the antlers, yellow ears flopped down and four arms holding the horns. Its long-toed feet extended over the lorglin's muzzle. Spatulate toe-tips hooked into the nostrils.

Bowmark pointed with an elbow, and then remembered to use his finger. "What is that?"

The man frowned and stuck out his tongue, as though tasting something nasty. "Ungol."

The same ungols that terrorized the island of Rolocton? "What? Give me pardon. I learnt the word ungol as meaning a vicious race that harries the coast of Discoria."

"So they sail, now, do they? Clever monsters, they, though they usually act so stupid."

Bowmark's face scrunched. "People fear ungols. What can that do but bite your knee?"

"Heed me, lad. Don't anger an ungol, not even a loser as yon. His needle teeth are the least of your problems. He can direct an animal to gore, trample, or bite you."

"Truth? Why do you allow so dangerous a person in your caravan?"

The man shrugged. "Not my idea. Losers work cheap. We hired this one just outside the Megaloth border. Ungols and anyone who lets them into Megaloth territory are killed on sight. The Empire is at war with the ungols on the southern border." He paused, spit, and said, "Ah, ungols south of us, sidj to the west, and now wild dractils in the middle. I think I'll move to South Akinda. The few dractils there leave people alone. Why our ancestors came here, I'll never know."

Bowmark mentally worked through the accented speech and the new words. "It seems every day my ignorance of these lands ambushes me. Pardon me if this is rude, but… how could one acquire a spyglass?"

The man's easy-going nature evaporated. He took back the spyglass and scanned the horizon, his face gone stony. "I'm sorry I haven't time to correct your ignorance. Go back to school, lad. We must move on. Safe travel."

"And to you," Bowmark said. *I can't expect to bring home every treasure.* He rappelled down the rope and led his mulig into the forest so the caravan could pass.

All the humans who had scattered throughout the forest to water the shrubs dashed back to the caravan.

Bowmark watched the workings of the multiple legs of the lorglins as he whispered to Scolla, "There is an ungol in the caravan."

Scolla did not reply. Bowmark leaned back on the luggage, poked Scolla with his elbow, and said, "Evil personified is in the caravan."

"A dispirited loser is no danger," Scolla growled.

"The caravan leader said it could kill me."

"Therefore do not provoke the ungol."

Bowmark raised his eyebrows. "How do I keep from doing that?"

"Sss! Do not poke him with your elbow!"

Bowmark leaned forward and stretched to hide his grin. "But why do you say that ungol is no danger when it can kill people?"

Scolla sighed theatrically. "He will soon die of grief or from injuries when he meets and fights another loser. He is not reproducing. He is not an army. If he kills a stupid human, the world is better off."

Bowmark stopped grinning. "What about stupid spitters?"

"Should one show up, we hope he pokes an ungol. Leave me alone."

Scanning for dractils, Bowmark took some deep breaths. Scolla was Scolla, and he would say what he would say. A load of finely carved chairs with the fragrance of resin passed by. "I would guess tezledeks have a real feast when that longneck dumps."

"Sss. I do not mock the nasty raw food you eat."

The last of the caravan passed and Bowmark led the mulig back to the road, now caked with mud, manure, and compost. "Truth. Give me pardon." He rolled off the mulig and circled it with great strides, exercising himself to become strong enough to fulfill his duty to kill RaiseHim.

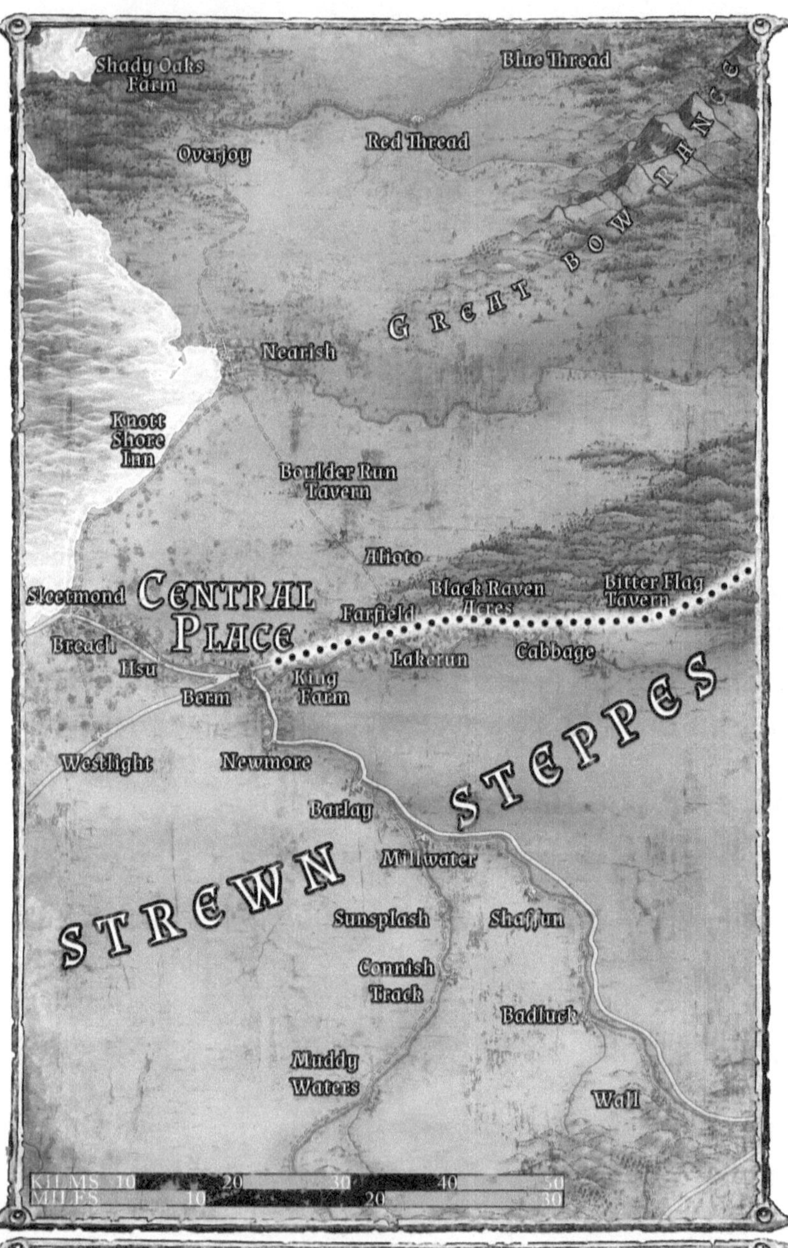

THIS ANIMAL ASKS TO SPEAK AS THOUGH IT WAS A PERSON. FURTHER, DEMANDS TO BE TAUGHT. NEVER IN HISTORY HAS THIS OCCURRED.

~SCOLLA THE PIONEER

Two days later the land had relaxed from rolling hills to a flat sea of plains and fields surrounding small houses and barns. Every door he could see had the boards with yellow marks covering them. If any people remained they were well hidden. The forest had faded to small copses dotting the landscape. As they wended through fields of mixed vegetation, sleek, brown and yellow, hard-shelled, chirping creatures a bit smaller than tezledek rambled on the meandering paths between plants. As soon as any of the creatures saw him, each snapped itself into its spiral shell and rested silently on the mossy path.

Bowmark stood upon the mulig's platform to gain a better view. He practiced commanding the metal clawed snake fists on the ends of his staffshifter to open and close, attempting to whisper as quietly as possible. He was finding the limits of the weapon. After about ten full expansions and retractions the magic became sluggish. He hands ached with stinging cold. Scolla advised him to leave the staffshifter in sunlight whenever possible, implying that it gained energy from the light like a plant. And indeed, after a day of basking in the sun, it lasted longer and sapped less warmth from his hands.

When the sun was near the horizon, he laid down the weapon and gently, not poking, patted the rolled up Scolla with his foot. "These fields are filled with shelled animals, or people, or I don't know what. You tell me."

When Scolla shifted and peered over the luggage, all that could be seen were stalks and leaves and flitting birds. "Zzzzzzz. If they roll into balls, they are farmers. They are somewhat smarter than dogs and a lot more agreeable. Rumshas teach them to eat the weeds and pests. At night they sleep in rumshane burrows. Zzz. They are no danger to you. Now leave me alone."

Bowmark thought about the furry dogs that lived in Akinda that were like the leathery, quilled seadogs he knew from Stone Grove. He could think of no similar creatures to these farmers. Annoyed that he needed Scolla to tell him what he was encountering, he jiggled the reins. "If you wish. I shall ride into Central Place without your counsel to guide me."

Scolla unfolded, refolded with a squeak, and unfolded again, this time wearing his eye shields.

Bright irregular forms in the distance resolved into fantastical giant creatures covered in mesmerizing patterns and every color Bowmark had ever seen. Smaller creatures walked around the giant shapes. Ah, those were people of some kind. The giants were buildings, covered in shiny tiles. As they got closer the paving stones were brighter, reflecting the setting sun. Agate and quartz, Scolla noted. Large unnaturally colorful rocks flanked the road. Some had funny faces illustrated with chips of tile cemented to them.

They entered a stone plaza, an apron a good quarter-rope wide that skirted an extensive cluster of buildings that Bowmark could now see were composed of piles of boulders with vibrantly colored tiles cemented around them in stripes and patterns. Some buildings seemed to have been carved to resemble animals, but only in a vague impression that left much to the imagination. Some of these dwellings were almost as large as his Bamboo Palace, but impossibly balanced on smaller boulders underneath. Most of the buildings had bright ribbons fluttering from metal rods on their tops. Paved paths meandered in seemingly random waving and spiraling patterns. Only a few people, none of them human, walked among the haphazardly placed towers and buildings. Their hunched-over gait and tails held straight behind told Bowmark they were rumshas.

Scolla stretched, then crawled through Bowmark's legs to reach the mulig's shoulders. A happiness that Bowmark had not heard before animated Scolla. "Go to the western part of town and search for a building with green and yellow ribbons. That represents a restaurant. Purple and orange are trade rooms. Red and blue are storage facilities. White and magenta are banks. Zzz. Black and gray are places to sleep. Zzz. Brown and teal are stables."

Scolla continued, "Rust ribbons indicate a repair shop. Light blue shows where rafts and boats are sold, and pink where provisions are sold. This is the code when no mismatch jokes are being played."

A faint cloud of smoke wafted over them, bearing the smells of burning wood and savory breads. Bowmark's mouth watered. Lights appeared in slit windows, each slit in its own length and shape.

They passed openings in the pavement that accommodated fruit trees, nut bushes, or basins of water with pumps and stabling rings beside them. Central Place stretched to the limit of Bowmark's vision.

"How does anybody find anything in this place?"

Scolla slid off his eye shields as the last bit of orange sun slipped below the horizon. "Those who are scent-blind like humans must memorize their routes."

They passed a forge where a human-sized rumsha, limned by red fire, hammered on a glowing piece of iron. Next to him, another rumsha worker, this one the size of a human child, was fitting a delicate metal hoop around a device Bowmark did not recognize. He rehearsed the colors and institutions. Until he had those firmly memorized, he dared not ask for the colors of healers, temples, and public baths.

"Zzz. You will be amazed when you see the great train yards."

"I'm not sure what that means."

"Trains are like this mulig platform, but instead of an animal, they ride on wheels that are set on a track. Many of them in rows. That way, several large animals can pull many such platforms with less effort."

"I see nothing large enough. Are the temples also large boulders?"

"Zzz zzz zzz. What you see on top will not tell you how many levels are below. The Temple of the Unfathomable Jester is on the north side of Central Place and far underground. The walls and columns are carved from white marble. Mirrors shine sunlight to the central altar, a massive block of quartz streaked with pyrite. Golden incense burners, bowls, candlesticks, and statues nearly cover the altar. It hurts to look upon, yet one desires to do so because of its beauty."

Bowmark was about to ask what marble and pyrite were, but as he scanned north he noted a faraway cloud of moving particles that funneled down below the skyline.

Scolla also looked. "Ssss! Those must be the dractils in the Temple. It makes one weep."

They rode silently in the gathering dark. The moons rose and lit their way with a pale light.

Scolla pointed. "We'll leave the mulig there. And that building over there with the triangular door is a place with human-sized beds. When I lived here, that place was free of parasites. I need to speak with the tezledeks here before I can tell you if that is still true."

"Just show me the baths."

As they bedded down their mulig in a nearly empty stable, a spitter waddled up to them. Scolla rummaged through a bag he had slung over one shoulder and pulled out an oblong disc-shaped metallic object. Bowmark had often noticed Scolla fidgeting with it at night when he was trying to sleep. He had always forgotten to ask Scolla about the device by morning.

Without a word, the spitter took the small package and scuttled away.

Bowmark pulled off a tick from the mulig's hindleg. "If that's an account of our expenditures, I want a budget increase for my food."

Scolla wheezed. "I deliver the account to the Council later tonight. What you saw was another chapter of my book."

Bowmark's entire nation held five books, six briefly, until he took the seafolk Atlas with him. "You're writing a book? I've never met anyone who has written a book before. What is it about?"

"Our travels. Zzz. I am accumulating much social capital and status with it."

"And no doubt saying wonderful things about me. I want to read this book."

"Your skills are not adequate."

"And I want to meet with the Accountability Council. I might ask for another guide, one who isn't hiding everything from me."

"You would not fit in the Council Hall."

"Ah. I *forgot* I was bigger than a tezledek. I *forgot* you live in tiny tunnels underground. Scolla, *maybe* the Council could meet out *here* with me."

Scolla regarded Bowmark a long time, gently hissing between his sharp teeth. He licked an eye with his tube tongue. "You are obnoxious." He tossed a coin that flickered in the dim light of an oil-lamp flame. "Wash off your foul odor. Then meet me at the restaurant called the Cavern Tavern just to the north."

Bowmark caught the coin and clenched his teeth. "Thank you."

By the time Bowmark washed, dried, oiled, dressed, and had reached the restaurant door, he had decided what he would do. He paused in the massive doorway, wondering at the yawning entrance, when a giant rumsha ambled by him. Like the other he had seen in Bysea, this one wore no clothing, but carried an impractical looking axe with a face etched onto the serrated head. The warrior's massive talons scraped the rock floor, fangs jutting from hislower jaw, and curved claws on his hands delicately folded together. Leathery armored skin covered his back like scales with studs. His powerfully muscled tail floated by Bowmark at eye level. The heavy knobbed end of it bobbed past.

Bowmark gaped when a human-sized rumsha in a glittery green vest rushed forward to bow at the giant. The huge rumsha settled on the floor as the host rolled out a vat with a pipe in it. The giant rumsha carefully set down his battle axe and took the vat with his knuckles so there was no chance of his impaling the host and sucked blissfully on the pipe.

The smell of whatever liquid was in the vat did not make Bowmark think of bliss, but other smells in the room did. Scolla sat at a table in the far back corner, oddly enough, like any customer at a table. The room had a tumbled, dispro-portionate appearance with a sloped ceiling. Colorful fabric hung in haphazard draping shapes. There were several stone tables of differing sizes with an eclectic mix of wooden and iron stools surrounding them. The smallest and shortest table fit Scolla perfectly. His ears fluttered as he poked at another of his metal book devices. Lamps cast a yellow glow through corrugated metal, projecting fantastical shapes across every surface. Bowmark was the only human.

He joined Scolla at the small table, sitting with his legs crossed on the ground. Scolla ignored him, continuing his poking motions. Now Bowmark could make out how this tezledek book device worked. The metal case was the size of a small hand. It held a ribbon of paper that was exposed through a rectangular window on one side, and was pulled through when Scolla rotated one of the emblems on top. He wrote by jabbing his claws through the paper which left little punctured words.

Soon they were joined by the host who boomed merrily in Common, "So this is the human male I have heard so much about." Bells and jeweled hoops pierced the host's ears. Purple and red ribbons draped his vest and wreathed his neck.

Bowmark glanced at Scolla. "No doubt you have."

Scolla put his book down and made an unknown gesture to their host. Then the rumsha handed Bowmark a triangular four-sided object.

Bowmark studied it. The size of a baby's fist, it had ornately carved rumsha heads on each side, with tiny round bells on the corners; two silver, one blackened iron, and one gold. He looked back to the host. "Give me pardon. I don't know your customs. What do I do with this?"

The host chortled. "Roll for your supper. Silver bell up, you pay normal price. Iron bell up, you pay twice the price for your meal. Gold bell up, you eat for free."

Bowmark slid the die toward Scolla. "Perhaps he should roll."

Scolla pushed it back. "Roll it."

Bowmark did. The tiny bells tinkled, and the rumsha host smiled widely. The topmost bell was iron.

"Ho ho hoo. Pay me, good Scolla. For the hulking human, a mash of brownroot, and for yourself a chamber pot freshly filled."

Bowmark's throat constricted. "Here? I mean—ah—I—" He rose. "I don't think—Pardon." He bolted for the door.

The buzz of Scolla's laughter and the hooting of the host filled the room. He turned at the doorway. Everyone in the restaurant watched him with amusement on their faces.

Scolla waggled his black fingers. "Fret not. Tezledeks never eat in front of other peoples."

Bowmark's lips imitated a smile. "A joke. Truth. Please tell me dinner is not a joke. My stomach will eat itself if I don't get food soon." Whatever strength held his joints together left as soon as he had dragged himself back to the table. He sagged onto the colorful tile-covered floor.

The host brought a variety of sweetened baked roots, seasoned eggs, steamed grains, tri-leaf tea, and chopped fruits. Bowmark could not eat as fast as his body demanded, but he strove to do so.

The host sat with them, stroking his unbound whiskers, which radiated like sun rays around his muzzle. He absent-mindedly licked his fingers and said something to Scolla in Rumshese.

Scolla clacked his claw tips in irritation and replied in Common. "No river can overflow his ocean. He will bury me in social debt."

"Hmmmm. Hoo, you did not stay forever in Discoria. Your ambitions surpass all."

"My ambitions will ruin me."

"An odd thing to know. Do you own time?"

Scolla hissed in simple Zledek to Bowmark, "Student, listen and learn."

Bowmark looked up, straightened, and swallowed. He replied in thickly accented Zledek, "I listen and dog, no, hope to learn."

The host's eyes widened. "Here is true amusement. No one knows that slithery tongue, save you cleaners. What are you up to now, Friend Scolla?"

Scolla said in Common, "Friend Host, tell what has happened to the Great Temple of the Unfathomable Jester."

The host snuffed and wrinkled his muzzle. "Dractils have moved new queens into the Temple. Huurazzmatum, they are called in my tongue. I have not seen, but I have been told that they have knocked all the treasure off the altar and lie there themselves. Dractils attack all who try to enter to worship. The hallways are lined with animals, eggs, and dractil stench."

"Why do you not attack and cleanse your temple, why?"

The host flicked an ear, jingling a bell on its tip. "If the Unfathomable Jester does not care that dractils stink up Its temple, why should we care?"

Scolla tapped the table with a claw. "You should care because when those eggs hatch, the dractils will swarm over Central Place. Your mothers and children will be killed to line the temple hallways."

The host flicked his ear again. "Tomorrow comes when we come to it."

Scolla tapped loudly on the stone table. "True Friend, must tezledeks be slaughtered at the entrance to the Merry Library before you will defend us?"

"You offend me. Of course, if we see you attacked, we defend you. We defend all true friends. Scolla, do you not laugh and enjoy tonight?"

Scolla turned to Bowmark and said in Zledek, "What have you learned, what?"

Bowmark ate more of his meal as he thought about the conversation and what he could say about it in his limited vocabulary of Zledek. A sudden thought caused him to turn to the host. "Good host, what is your name?"

"My name? Hooo, let me think. Oom, yes, Umbanoo. Umbanoo is my name. I do not understand why you ask."

Bowmark sat back. "Give me pardon. If I was rude, I am sorry. I do not know your ways."

"Zzz zzz zzz. Calm down, human. Rumshas only use their names when they are on teams performing complex tasks that require a differentiation between who does what. Many have never named themselves."

Bowmark took a deep breath. "So then."

"Ho, ho," boomed the rumsha. "I had forgotten that humans have an obsession with names."

Bowmark rubbed the back of his neck. Was his plan going to work? Why not? Dractils were ridiculously easy to kill. "Umbanoo, will your people reward me if I kill the dractil queens?"

"Nooo!" Scolla screeched as he erupted in spikes.

The host considered. "The queens sit on the altar. You sit here eating and, we hope, enjoying life. Please do not upset my dear friend." He gestured at the spiny ball that Scolla had become.

Some spitters entered the room through a small hole in the back wall. A few of the rumshas, who had been leaving, stopped to watch Scolla swelling.

Clenching his hands together, Scolla deflated. "You will not do this. A night's rest, and tomorrow we start for Megaloth."

Bowmark shoved aside his plates to lean on his forearms and look eye-to-eye at Scolla. "When did you buy me? Every coin you spend on me puts me deeper in your debt. I intend to earn my own way so that you can never think you are my king again."

"You try this and you shall die."

"So you think."

Scolla hissed. "Do not do this."

Bowmark straightened up slowly. "Umbanoo, ah, Host. Could you please give me more of these eggs? Whoever cooked them should be told how delicious they are."

"With pleasure." The host hurried off.

Bowmark pulled back the plates and scraped them clean.

Scolla hissed like a teakettle about to go dry and melt.

Bowmark licked his knife. "You aren't planning to call me stupid, are you?" And what would he do if Scolla did?

"Human. This is not the time to disobey me."

Bowmark glanced at the spitters watching him. "Maybe not." What if they all decided to spit at him at the same time?

The host returned with a bowl.

"Thank you, Umbanoo." Bowmark took the proffered bowl.

The host left to carry a heavy, laden tray to the giant warrior. They hooted gently at each other.

Scolla licked his eyes and whispered, "I *ask* you not to do this."

"Hmm? Can't hear you."

Scolla glowered.

Bowmark chewed blissfully on his eggs until he saw a human female enter the dining area from the kitchen. He inhaled a bit of egg and choked.

She glanced up from the table she had begun to wash. Smiling, she sashayed over and kneeled next to the low table across from Bowmark.

He tried to swallow as she leaned forward. His eyes greedily studied her: sandy hair, sandy eyes, skin the earthworm color he had finally grown used to, ears that, instead of smoothly attaching to the head, hung in fleshy lobes that were stretched even longer by heavy earrings, tiny mouth with big, crooked teeth, and the rest of her a shape that everything in him responded to. She was at that moment the most beautiful woman in the world.

Scolla dropped off his chair to waddle to the back wall.

"Hello," the worm-colored woman said. "Wherever you're going, may I go with you?"

Bowmark choked again.

She said, "I can cook and clean. I have a small amount of money, too, to pay my way." She leaned over and slapped him on the back. "Should I get you some water?"

"No," he croaked.

"Look. I slept in and missed the last caravan. I loved living and working here, but it's time to go, and you're my only chance."

"But—I—I go to danger." He shot up from the floor and rushed out the door, leaving the woman open-mouthed.

Outside, his feet pounded on the colorful fitted stones as he ran a straight line. Moongleam. Sunrise. Moongleam hated him. Sunrise should have been in that restaurant. Moongleam. Women. Moongleam. What was he going to do? A cavity the size of Moongleam and Sunrise together opened inside him, and no amount of tears in the world could fill that hole. Moongleam plaiting rope and casting lighthearted jibes at him while he wrestled her brother. Him accidentally knocking her off a log into a stream. She rising up laughing to knock him off, too. Precious memories like daggers in his heart.

A plaza tree intersected with his shoulder in the dark and spun him to the pavement. He lay there, shivering, staring up at the blurry stars.

Inside the restaurant, the host leaned down to Scolla. "You warned me about his reaction to charred meat. You did not tell me about this reaction to a female of his own kind."

Scolla glared at the open doorway and said flatly, "He surprises me each day."

"Hoo. What a wonderful companion, then. I like him." The rumsha moved away to gather the last dishes.

One of the spitters standing at the back wall clicked his teeth. "I do not like him. He came close to committing a capital offense. Will you be able to control your herd animal, will you?"

Scolla said nothing as he fingered the scar from Bowmark's knife on his neck. Bowmark had already done that which would earn him the death penalty. Sometimes, justice was not what was wanted in life.

Whiskers tickling his scalp startled Bowmark as he lay supine on the cold pavers. A child-sized rumsha snuffed around his face, hooting gently. Blinking away his dark thoughts, Bowmark sat up and nodded at the rumsha. "Good evening to you. Can you direct me to a weaponsmith?"

After a dizzying trek around spiral roads, needless stairs, and a dead end or two, Bowmark was led to a forge. The tables were covered with beautifully crafted items that he had to assume were weapons. But most of them seemed so impractical that he could not be sure. Many were as big as he, and had grinning faces painted or etched into the metal. Most were painted garish colors, even over the blades. Bowmark wondered if the rumsha proclivity for pranks could extend to something as important as their defense. But then he imagined fighting one of the giant Rumsha and realized it really would not matter much what kind of weapon they held. One rumsha warrior could probably destroy every guard in the Bamboo Palace without *any* weapon. Perhaps these arms were more symbolic or decorative for the rumsha.

Bowmark addressed the human-sized rumsha who was painting a wicked grin a giant axe. "Hello friend. Are there any weapons that one of my size could use?"

The artisan hooted a small laugh, then rummaged through a pile of goods, emerging with a snarl of rope and rocks. It resembled the tangle snares he and Sunrise played with as children, hunting birds and rodents. But this had larger rocks and stronger, tightly braided rope. Each of the three rocks had a different funny face carved on it.

"A bolas" the rumsha announced. "Small, but still full of potential surprises!"

Central Place
Great Temple
of the
Unfathomable Jester
Merry Library
Wayward Tailor
Cavern Tavern
Caved Inn
Able Stable
Rainbow Plaza
Blessed Weapons
Triple Tree Embassy
Lulay River
KILMS
MILES
1
2
3
4
5
1
2
THE JOKE THAT BLINDS US BINDS US
~INSCRIPTION ON RUMSHA ALTER

Bowmark woke huddled next to the mulig, relieved that Scolla had not wrapped and strapped him to the animal. He breathed in frigid air laden with the smells of hay and mulig. This was the hardest part of every day: leaving warm sleep and greeting cold morning.

"I would have paid for a bed," Scolla buzzed.

Bowmark pulled back his blanket. Scolla sat on the drowsing mulig. She snorted and raised her head. Bowmark stretched. "I need to eat. I don't need a bed. Your Accountability Council should be happy I'm saving them money."

"Examine this." Scolla held out a bit of shaped metal. "I have a talisman of the Unfathomable Jester to add to your collection of treasures. And the council informed me of a place where you can learn how to fight an armed enemy without any weapon but your body. The school is on the way to Megaloth City."

There was a way to survive fighting RaiseHim? Could he find this school on his own? "Good." Bowmark unrolled from his blanket. "Now, what's the quickest way to the temple?"

"Ssss. Why do you want to kill me, why?"

"I don't want to kill you. I want to kill a dractil queen. The rumshas are nice people. They need help, since they can't think strategically. And I need an independent income. Our needs meet and kiss." Especially if it involved the easy killing of dractils.

"Ssss. I hope you are killed. I will be called foolish for the rest of my miserable life, but I would be rid of you."

"Happy partners, we." Bowmark slid knives into their compartments in his clothes and took up his bow, new arrows, and bolas he had paid double price for after rolling iron-bell-up on the merchant's four-sided die.

Defying Scolla didn't feel good anymore, but he wasn't going to back down now. He grabbed the bag of leather clothing and gloves he had won with a luckier roll against a shop owner with insomnia. Heavy boots on, an ironsmith's leather apron, staffshifter stuck in its sheath, some pocket pies to eat on the way, and he was ready to go.

The sun pinked the sky in the east. Bowmark headed north, wending easily around the irregular pile-of-boulder homes and shops, solitary fruit trees spangled with blossoms, and public fountains shaped like fanciful animals.

After nearly three rope-lengths, a giant rumsha lumbered toward him and then marched beside him. Bowmark studied him out of the corner of his eye. No, he was not the same giant he had seen last night. This one had a thick leather hood crested with spikes the length of Bomark's hand. "Sir, do you go also to the Temple?"

The giant rumsha rumbled, "I go with you. I am told that you provide amusement."

Bowmark thought about that as they walked down a purposelessly winding road and a straighter thoroughfare lined with flower boxes. "It is good to be good for something."

"Indeed."

"How did you get to be so big, I mean, compared to—that grocer there?"

Bees buzzed around the flower boxes set around cartons of fruit. A small rumsha arranged the bright blue fruit into pyramids.

The giant rumsha said, "I am born a warrior. He is born an outsider."

"Outsider?"

"Those who work outside the tunnels: the merchants, the ambassadors, the harvest-gatherers, the smiths, the hosts, some of the engineers and artificers."

Bowmark did not think that truly answered his question about the disparate sizes, but he was sure he did not want to press anyone with such teeth. "So that one is not a child? And I have not seen a single woman since I arrived. Are they hiding from the—"

A deep rumble crawled up his bones, and Bowmark turned his head. The warrior's lips pulled back from his many teeth.

Bowmark slid his hand to a knife hilt. "Because I do not know this place, would you help me stay far away from your women and children?"

The rumble became a low laugh. "Hoo, hoo. You do provide amusement." The warrior's tusks disappeared into his cheeks as a smile emerged.

Bowmark let out a long low breath. A drop of sweat trickled down his temple.

His voice squeaked. "Apparently this is a gift I did not know I possessed."

They continued in silence. If this giant was to be his fighting companion, Bowmark needed his name. "Hey you" or "sir" in the heat of battle would not suffice. "I have met a host named Umbanoo, and my partner tells me that rumshas build their names. Have you built a name?"

"Hooo I do love the way you pronounce that name. But no. I have no name right now."

"What do others call you?"

"There has never been a need."

Bowmark was stymied. "May I call you 'friend'?"

"Hoo. That is not how such things work. But that makes it all the funnier!"

"Friend it is."

Some ropes later,another warrior joined them, this one wielding a spiked club the length of Bowmark. The club, he realized, was shaped like a rumsha, the spikes were stylized whiskers. Another rope, and three more warriors holding polearms emerged from an underground entrance to walk beside them, their steps loud on the colorful stone pavement.

In the north, dractils swirled into the sky and streaked away to the east and west. They did not come toward the city.

Breakfast fires wreathed the rumshas and human with pungent and savory smells.

Several ropes and several warriors later, they came to the edge of the city. No more giant boulders, but a vast plain of yellow grass and patches of the stony ground, with one curving road leading to a large lump on the horizon. They were now close enough to distinguish individual dractils flitting in and out of holes beyond the distant shape. Some carried small objects in. Bowmark swallowed. This was feeling like a ridiculous plan. But before he could falter, he saw Scolla's raised finger of admonition. Heard his arrogant tone. No. He would not subject himself to that. Besides, he now had a small army with him.

A quarter candle later, the group arrived at an entrance built of stone carved into the distorted shape of a warrior's head. Bowmark saw no door. Several of his new companions circled to the back of the head and climbed onto tree trunk levers. It took eight of them before their weight began to tilt the giant stone head. It groaned as the mouth opened. Fang-shaped stones ringed the opening, a ramp that descended steeply into darkness.

"This doorway," rumbled one of the giants, "begins a passage to the Temple of the Unfathomable Jester."

Bowmark studied the assembly behind him. "Are you coming to help me kill the queens?"

They flicked their ears and tilted their heads this way and that as they studied him with eyes shaded by their brow ridges. Finally, one said, "We meet tomorrow when tomorrow meets us."

Bowmark waited, but no other comment was made. "So then."

They still stood, watching him, with the occasional whisker twitching.

"So then," he said again. "I will—ah—I do not refuse help." He turned and entered the gaping maw, descending the sloping tunnel.

The smooth stone glittered with a spattering of mica flakes. Every ten steps, a stone bracket bore a glowing fungal mass that emitted only enough light to show where the intricately sculpted walls were. A breeze carrying unfamiliar musty and sweet scents cooled Bowmark's damp scalp. Footsteps and hooting echoed and re-echoed down the long tunnel. Most of the floor was flat smooth stone, but in places where the descent was particularly steep there were stairs carved off to the side, just wide enough for one person. The rumshas had no trouble walking at any angle.

They came to an intersection where every surface was covered with sparkling faceted tiles. "This way," rumbled one giant, and turned; and two ropes later turned at another cross tunnel. Bowmark tried to memorize every intersection and turn but arbitrary angles, slopes and dim lighting left him completely baffled. Nothing he had read or seen of the rumshas gave him cause to fear they would betray him, so he moved with the crowd and hoped his eyesight would adapt to the darkness. The turns and lack of light made it impossible for Bowmark to gauge the time or distance. It was a long time before all halted at a five-way intersection. A large ball of glowing moss hung from an intricate scaffolding of polished metal and crystals. It illuminated fanciful figures of all sizes and shapes sculpted into the walls and ceiling. Bowmark ran his fingers over the smiling face of whale with strange fins.

"Blind human," said one of the warriors, "if you desire to enter the once-beautiful Temple, the hall on your right leads there."

A faint, acrid odor emanated from the tunnel discernible only by a retreating double line of green blobs. The crowd shuffled around him and sniffed as he opened his bag. "I'm trying out one of your weapons today," he said. "This bolas, oops—" One stone of the three clunked on the floor.

He pulled on a new leather coat over what he already wore. "My thinking is this. These leather pants and hooded shirt should withstand those dractil poisonous hairs. So, too, these gloves. I practiced last night, and I think I can still fight wearing them. This was a smith's apron." Surely a double layer of leather across his front would be enough. The hairs did not have the projectile power of arrows.

Bowmark wrapped a scarf around his head. "A scarf across the front of this hood protects my face. I borrowed a spitter's day shields for more eye protection." Scolla had said the temple itself was lighted. He hoped so or he would be fighting blind. He peered through a layer of fabric and the tiny holes in the metal discs. "You warriors, is this adequate protection?"

After some murmuring and gentle hooting, a voice in the darkness said, "Maybe." Another chimed in, "We all agree that you look very funny, and this is excellent since you are entering the Unfathomable Jester's home. The Jester grants the mirth-causing blessings."

Bowmark repositioned his weapons into pockets and loops of his leather coat. All he could hear was the breathing of warriors about him. He shifted his shoulders. "If you go with me, welcome. If you stay, farewell." He followed the glowing line of green globs.

The passage turned and curved more often than a split-fin's tail. The acrid odor strengthened. The fungi on brackets allowed him to see, dimly, ceiling and floor as well as walls.

He stepped in a gushy pile of excrement. Weren't the spitters supposed to take care of this? And then he came upon his first incubator. A small, furry animal of some sort he did not recognize lay stiffly on its side. A dirty white leathery egg, about the size of a child's head, clutched the creature's abdomen with hooked finger-like talons. It pulsated slowly.

In response to Bowmark's agitation, the claws on the ends of his staffshifter opened and closed, scraping the inside of the sheath he had tied to his belt.

Bowmark knelt and slashed the egg with one of his boot knives. A glistening gel oozed out of the egg, and then a dark stream of blood. The animal it was attached to gasped once and died.

He turned at the sound of rustling ahead of him. A thin shadow from beyond the turn moved on the wall. Bowmark jumped up and swung the bolo in such a way that the cord caught the inside corner of the turn, and the stones swung in an arc from that point. One stone ball crashed into a wall, another into something that crunched.

The shadow dropped. Screeching bounced off the walls. Dractils, multitudes of them, scuttled around the corner and thronged him. Warriors' bolos and spears flew past him and crunched into many dractils.

Bowmark pulled out his staffshifter, extended it, and swung it forcefully, knocking most of the surviving dractils down. Twitching spastically, the fallen bodies began their multi-stage destruction. The dim light grew hazier with flying hairs. Dractil pincers grabbed his sleeves as he punched into their chests with the snake fist ends of the staff. Some of the broken dractils crawled toward him despite their guts dragging on the floor behind them. Bowmark smashed their heads to end their miseries and leapt over the tangled bodies.

A little digging had retrieved his bolas. He charged up the stone hall. Rumsha warriors sounded like an avalanche behind him.

More animals lay on the floor with eggs attached to their abdomens. His disgust opened the claws on the ends of the staffshifter. He swung the lengthened staff, this side, that side, bashing eggs apart. Gore puddled on the floor.

Another corner, more advancing shadows, and he used the bolas again, but this time, he missed every one of the dractils. Fair enough, it had taken more than a night's practiceto master archery, knives and staff. His staffshifter pierced and bashed as dractils threw themselves upon him.

He advanced up the passage, stepping on broken bodies, limbs crunching under his feet, the smell of bowels gagging him. Acrid sweat ran down his sides, back, and arms. Leather was so stifling hot!

He turned another corner and faltered. *Giver, no!* There lay Scolla, eyes open, an egg clutching his abdomen. No, no, it was a different spitter, but at that moment, all pity for the brave dractil warriors dying to protect their eggs flamed out. Bowmark shouted, "Murderers!" and ran into the next group, scattering them and their parts like a tearjaw in a school of fish.

Around another bend, a straight passage led to a sprawling lighted room half a rope in circumference. White granite speckled with dractil filth lined the walls. Around the massive altar rose pillars of white marble covered with quartz carvings of smiling rumshas. A wide ledge five strides up connected the pillars. It was covered in incense burners, trinkets, and lanterns long burnt out. Portable mirrors reflected light that had been funneled into the room through-mirrored light shafts in the high, domed ceiling. Those must have been the holes through which the invaders had entered.

Dractils stepped around the things on the ledge, dropped off, and flew up from the ledge, joining a hovering swarm.

And on the other side of the room at the long altar itself— *Oh, Giver!*—stood five dractils five times taller than those he had been fighting. They stood on a raised dais on massive tripod feet. These giant Dractils were hairless and had much thicker arms that bifurcated at the elbow. Tiny vestigial wings fluttered. Monstrous holes in their chests pulsated.

Between the altar and the back wall lay mounds of unattached eggs.

Rumshane warriors lined up beside him. His Friend with the spiked hood lowered his head and nodded; his facial expression unreadable to Bowmark.

Bowmark had stared too long. Swarms of flying dractils attacked him. He mowed the dractils before him with his staffshifter, like he had whacked flowers off their stalks when he was a boy.

They packed thicker and thicker in front of him. So many of their poisonous hairs stuck in the scarf he could barely see. One stuck though the perforated metal disks covering his eyes, stinging his brow.

It became sheer butchery in bedlam and stench. His eyes watered. More and more grabbed hold of his leather clothes as he beat them down and advanced step by step towards the queens.

Pincers crept up his hood and stabbed his nape. He turned and smashed a dractil in its face.

The monster jerked his hood half round, nearly covering Bowmark's face with leather.

Bowmark had only a tiny strip of vision. *Fumes and ashes!* He swung his staffshifter blindly and pushed forward as blood mingled with sweat trickled down his neck.

More pincers snatched his hood. He grabbed its edges and shoved himself forward as he pulled the scarf to the front. Part of the scarf ripped off. His cheek burned from poisonous hairs. He slammed his staffshifter into chests and limbs. He stumbled on another pile of loose eggs and bounced off a rumshane warrior's thigh.

A dractil threw himself onto Bowmark's back and pulled on the hood again. They were not as mindless as he had assumed. Bowmark fell back and smashed the monster into a wall.

A rumshane warrior threw a bolas into the crowd and Bowmark followed with a barrage of staffshifter strikes that opened a path before him.

Like water through a breaking dam, he burst onto the lighted dais upon which sat the altar and five looming queen dractils. The bright light, bouncing from white pillars and golden brackets and treasures and mirrors, blinded him. He swung his staffshifter, sure he would hit a dractil whether he saw it or not. He struck a pillar so hard the shock nearly broke his wrist.

The staffshifter dropped from his nerveless hand. A mountain of dractils fell on him. He staggered a few steps, then folded to his knees. He fumbled for a knife, but countless pincers held his arms.

The chamber reverberated with the bone-shaking roars of dozens of rumshane warriors who waded into the melee, squashing dractils underfoot, flinging cracked dractils into walls with their iron-plated tails, stabbing with spears, slashing with blades, and smashing with bolos and clubs.

Swarms of dractils rose into the hazy air.

In his struggle to rise, Bowmark's hood was wrenched off. He screamed as more poisonous hairs penetrated his face and scalp.

Huge claws swept dractils off him.

Through the tiny holes of Scolla's metal eye shields, Bowmark could see the warriors, some now wearing mica eye shields, swatting dractils out of the air with their massive claws and armored tails.

A rumshane warrior grabbed his arm and pulled him free from the pile of crushed and smothered dractils. The warrior snagged the staffshifter from the jumble of bodies and skeleton shards, then tossed the weapon to Bowmark, giving a bow as roars and screeches echoed in that gore-smeared stone chamber.

A huge club swung from above and crashed into the warrior, crumpling him to the floor.

Where had that come from?

The club was in fact a thick forearm of a giant queen, a forearm encased in an exoskeleton and as long as Bowmark was tall.

He batted dractils aside to clear a space, sheathed his staffshifter, grabbed his bow, and fitted an arrow. The queen nearest him screamed loud enough to hurt his ears. Bowmark shot.

The arrow skittered across her carapace and broke against the back wall. Her exoskeleton was like iron.

A rumshane warrior on his right threw a spear, which nicked a joint of the queen's arm before falling off to clatter on the altar.

A dractil collided with Bowmark's head. His face flamed as more hairs pierced his skin. He grabbed the dractil's head and twisted until the thin neck snapped. A dractil snatched an egg and flew up a light shaft.

He nocked his arrow. Three more dractils snatched eggs and flew toward the shaft. His arrow shattered one dractil, but the other two escaped.

A queen's arm crashed into him and flung him against a pillar knocking out his breath. A dractil's pincers snapped on his ear. He seized the dractil's arm, jerked and broke it, then threw his enemy to the floor.

More rumshane spears arced toward the queens, but most skittered off their hard exoskeletons.

If only he could breathe! Black specks swirled across his vision as he attempted to writhe out of the way of multiple threats.

Breath rushed in, but his chest muscles still spasmed. Hairs stung his lips. He wasn't going to live through this. That queen would. He had a weapon that could chip stone, but how could he reach any vulnerable area on her bulk?

He snatched out his shortened staffshifter and hit the head of the dractil reaching for him. Its skull cracked, and the monster fell back.

Bowmark labored over bodies still twitching and popping, the pain in his side keeping him bent double. He tried to hide his face in the crook of his elbow whenever he saw a body begin its self-destruction, but stray hairs still found their way to his neck and head.

In the chaotic mass a queen swung her arm toward him.

He knelt, pointed the staffshifter—*Zip!*—and punched her arm in the elbow joint. She screamed as the arm folded back on itself and swung uselessly over Bowmark's head. Yellow-green ichor from the wound sprayed over him. He stood, braced himself, and used his staff to punch her kneecap. The blow was deflected by her armored skin.

More dractils dropped on him.

Roaring rumshane warriors soon scrunched their way through to rip the dractils off him.

One of these rescuers pulled Bowmark closer to the altar.

Bowmark punched a descending queen's arm with his staff, deflecting the blow to the warrior's head.

The warrior staggered. Blood spurted from his nostrils. He grabbed Bowmark and flung him up onto the altar.

Pain sparkled Bowmark's vision as he tumbled over candle holders, statues and other religious accoutrements that covered the raised altar. Blindly, he punched about himself frantically. Dractils were crushed against him when another queen swatted at him. He was at chest level to the queens now. He slipped to the edge of the altar. With one hand he gripped the torn and oozing carapace of a battered queen, and with the other he punched randomly. The staff-shifter froze his hand as it shortened and lengthened like lightning. He needed to conserve his magic or the staff would stop responding. The queen backed away from his violence, turning towards two warriors who were jabbing at her legs.

Pain, light, and roaring receded from him. He was in the eye of a storm. Chaos and shrieking all around, but no dractil was actively attacking him. Shaking his head, he dropped to one knee and brushed stinging hairs off his face and head. He needed to get higher, closer to the queens' heads. And there, nearby, he saw Friend with the spiked helmet attempting to bite the nearest ueen's leg.

"Friend! Friend, I need your help to get higher!"

Somehow, through the din, his Friend heard him and was quickly climbing onto the altar with Bowmark. "Then up you shall go." Friend picked him up the same way Bowmark picked up Scolla. Stretching onto his tip toes, Friend got Bowmark close enough that he could scramble up the ledge onto a huge slab of stone that bridged two of the pillars. From this vantage, he had a much better perception of the battle.

The giant rumshane warriors, those still standing, swung and stomped, and lashed their tails at the vortex of dractils that crashed around them. The warriors toppled the queen he had disarmed. Friend leapt onto the collapsed body and bashed her head into pulp.

Bowmark stood almost level with the remaining three queens, who were attempting to squash the rumshane warriors with their forearms or stomp them with their sharp tripod feet. He ran as far as he could on the ledge toward the nearest queen and punched his staffshifter through the back of her head.

The two remaining queens turned their fury toward him.

He rolled out of the way as an arm smashed through the stone slab he occupied, crumbling the smiling face of a rumsha carved on a buttress. Bowmark leapt to the next ledge and spun to smash her pincers.

His maneuvering left him blind to a queen behind him. She grabbed him around the waist and lifted him while opening the maw in her chest. *Zip!* His staff retracted as he was helplessly drawn towards the dark hole. Instinctively, he jammed the metal rod in her mouth-like orifice as her head descended to shove him down. *Zip!* The staffshifter's snake-fist burst out of the top of her head. His hand ached.

Her limp pincers released Bowmark, but his staffshifter wedged in her chest-mouth, and he dangled from his weapon.

The last queen's hand grasped his shoulders and pulled his body away from the staff. He squeezed with all his might, but his hand was weak and the ichor-drenched staff was too slippery. His hands slid off. He was yanked backwards, slamming into the queen's chest, and knocking her off-balance.

She held him as she tripped backward over altar, rubble, and carcasses, wailing like storm wind.

As she crashed, his jaws cramped. His tongue swelled.

Dimly, he perceived a queen's thorax in front of his face, and the neck above him. He reached up, grabbing the shovel-

like lower jaw appendage as she righted. She steadied herself with one hand on a ledge and used the other to claw Bowmark off her body.

His strength faded.

Her chest came towards him preparing to scoop him into her maw. Summoning the last of his strength, he hoisted himself towards her face. He grabbed his boot knife and plunged it into a huge, blank eye.

She bucked. The knife was wrenched from his hand.

He fell onto the body of a rumsha on the floor.

The corpse of the queen toppled forward, landing on Bowmark. His ribs bent. His sight narrowed to one of the pinholes in his eye shields. In that pinhole, he saw a small, blood-and-hair-coated, gold figurine of a laughing rumsha on a cylindrical base, lying on the marble floor. His hand crept toward the figurine, grasped it, and slowly pulled the tiny statue back into a pocket.

A rhythmic pounding started. Confused, Bowmark craned his neck to see the warriors who could still stand stamping their feet in unison. All of the surviving dractils had retreated with as many eggs as they could carry. Was this a victory dance? Friend's spiked helmet vibrated with every stomp. *POUND POUND.* A cacophonous shout. *POUND POUND.* Each warrior shouted a different word. Were they names? *POUND POUND.* With every repetition the shout became more unified. *POUND POUND.* Friend participated in the stomping, but not the shouting. *POUND POUND.* Now each warrior shouted the same sounds, an amalgam of all the previous words: Uutoor. The pounding stopped as they chanted the word again and again, standing nearly upright, heads held high. Suddenly the dispersed group rushed towards a central point, crashing into each other, forming a writhing, hooting, laughing pile.

Bowmark's vision became dim and blurry. Emerging from the pile of warriors, Friend took notice of Bowmark's limp body and approached. The giant tilted, lowering his head.

"You live! What a wonderful surprise! You helped me build a name. I suppose you have this name as well. We are Uutoor. Uutoor!"

A chorus of warriors echoed: "Uutoor!"

Bowmark's pinhole of vision and consciousness disappeared.

Grating pain jolted Bowmark awake. He gasped as Friend—Uutoor—carried him through a dim tunnel and rumble-hummed.

The rumsha said, "Human Uutoor is a True Friend, the diggers clean the temple, and we are grateful. However, we do not understand. Why does a human do this?"

Bowmark built up breath. "I hate the dractils. They slaughter innocents. I like you. You hurt no one until you are attacked."

"Hmmmmmm. Hoo. Worms fear us."

Bowmark laughed weakly until pain shoved him back into unconsciousness.

THE RUMSHA LACK OF FUTURE AND PAST TENSE
CREATES UNIQUE CHALLENGES IN TRANSLATING
THEIR THEOLOGICAL TEXTS, AS WELL A FORMALIZING
BINDING AGREEMENTS.

~SHEENO THE LINGUIST

A faint, irregular *tick, tick, tick*, and nausea greeted Bowmark's return to awareness Only one hand could move. Feeling around, he discovered he was naked under an exceedingly warm blanket, and spitter ropes bound one arm to his chest. What had the kratchnak tied him to now?

The smells of mulig, straw, sour sweat, and pungent herbs competed for his attention. Sticky goo covered his face under a loose swaddling that surrounded most of his head. Gently, he pushed the material back until he could see a stone ceiling in shadowed daylight.

His tongue scraped across his dry mouth. Heat raced over his face. He blinked gummy eyes as he turned his head. Scolla sat on the reclining mulig, poking letters with his claws into his book.

"Dry," Bowmark croaked.

Scolla looked up from the book and scanned the stall. "No one else is here, therefore, again, I am your nurse." He slid off the mulig and waddled out of Bowmark's sight. The echoing metallic sound of water-filled pots being knocked against each other ensued. Scolla waddled back with a steaming tin cup. He knelt and lifted Bowmark's head with one hand and with the other trickled medicinal tea into Bowmark's mouth.

"Ssst!" said someone behind them.

In Zledek, Scolla said, "It is at your left. I have nearly finished the next scroll. Come back in an hour."

Small feet scurried away.

In Common, Scolla said as he took away the empty cup, "What small dignity I had left is now gone."

Bowmark cleared his throat. "How odd that both humans and Tezledeks find dignity in not touching each other."

"Zzz." Scolla brought a bowl of soaked bread chunks and fed Bowmark. "Your head looks like a nematode-infested borton root."

Bowmark tried not to think about where Scolla's hands had been. "Why am I tied up?"

"You are not tied, you are bound. Two bruised ribs must heal. You stink because we are sweating toxins out of you."

"Odd that you should notice stink." The nausea abated slightly as his headache grew worse.

"Zzz zzz zzz. You needed the skills of the best physician in Central Place. I was required to pay him double because he was offended that I asked him to work on a herd animal."

Bowmark closed his aching eyes. "That's it. If I need to crawl the rest of the way, I'm not going anywhere with you."

Scolla sat on the edge of the blanket. "What do you want from me, what?"

Bowmark opened his eyes to gaze into Scolla's large, polished-copper eyes. "Respect. The same respect you give tezledeks."

Scolla stared back. "But you are human."

"I have always been."

Scolla crawled up to the back of the mulig and took up the book. *Tick. Tick. Tick. Tick.* His talons pierced the paper.

Bowmark wanted the cleanliness they could bring to Stone Grove. He didn't want this. "Are you disappointed that I survived?" The words scraped over Bowmark's sore throat.

"No. Surprised. I could have let you die. You came close, for you were extremely poisoned. It has been four days since your battle." *Tick. Tick.* "We sewed up your ear and the back of your neck. We purged you and cleaned you." He wound more of the paper scroll with the dial.

"It seems I must choke with gratitude. No, not so. You were only protecting your investment."

"Zzz zzz zzz. Your anger is unwarranted." Scolla held up the metal book. "This is the Rumshese translation of the book I wrote about your battle with the dractils. A useless battle, however—"

"Why useless? We killed the queens."

"So you did. But the dractils are expanding their territory, and there shall be another queen here next year."

"Hot lava, but you know how to cheer me up." His grimace stretched the swollen skin on his face. "I need more water."

"Let me finish telling of good events. The story of your battle is so intriguing that all the tezledeks and all the rumshas want a copy. I am gaining so much social capital that I may be able to repay all I have spent on the journey so far. You are the first human to have built a rumshane name. Bowmark Uutoor. Very unusual."

"Scolla, would you please go away?" Bowmark must not, absolutely must not, scratch his face, but the burning and itching were driving him to distraction. Maybe if he gently rubbed. He reached up and explored the multiple stitches on his neck and a few on his ear. "Where are my clothes?"

Scolla tipped some blessedly cold water into his mouth. "They were unsalvageable. Your clothes and the slain were burnt in a far field."

"I saw one of your people in a hallway near the Temple."

"Sontila died."

"I'm sorry."

"You did not kill him."

Bowmark drained the cup. "More, please." Four cups later the host Umbanoo entered, arms laden with blankets.

The bells on the host's ears tinkled as he leaned down, touched his nose to Bowmark's, and snuffed loudly. "Human Bowmark Uutoor True Friend, it is good to have you rejoin us. I bathe you and change your bedding." He shoved aside the warming rocks, pulled off the blanket, and poured a basin of herb-scented water over Bowmark.

More rumshas came in to rake away the wet straw and replace the sodden blankets while the host toweled off Bowmark, wiped off the goo, and smeared on new goo.

"Human Bowmark Uutoor True Friend," said the host after Bowmark had been rebundled in dry blankets, "we found this in your pocket." He displayed the golden figurine from the Temple of the Unfathomable Jester, cleansed and shiny. "Did you hope to steal this?"

Bowmark touched the figurine. "I am no thief. My plan was to ask your leader if I could claim it as my reward for helping to kill the queens."

The host's stiff whiskers quivered. "*This* is what you want? Then surely you may have it."

Bowmark licked his oiled lips. "Will it offend you if I remove the figure and melt down the base to gain some coins?"

The host snorted. "I am not offended, but how many coins do you think you gain for lead?"

"Lead? What?"

"Is it not a fine joke? If anyone steals our gold-painted lead, the thief wins only a sore back. Hoo hoo hoo."

Unwanted tears filmed Bowmark's eyes. "A joke. Fumes and ash. My life is a joke."

"Who could have expected a human to understand theology so well? Hoo hoo. True Friend, we thank you." The host bowed and backed away.

Bowmark gloomily studied the heavy figurine he had picked up from the Temple of The Unfathomable Jester. If he had been strong enough, he would have thrown it against the wall.

Scolla waddled back into view. "Do you still want it, do you?"

Bowmark sighed. "Yes. Not the heavy base. The small statue, yes. It perfectly exemplifies what rumshas value most." He sighed again. "You're right, Scolla. I am stupid. If I had taken a little longer to study the situation, I could have had a decent helmet with better eye shields. Or I might have left things alone. Or . . . I don't know. I was in a hurry to rid myself of debt to you so I wouldn't need to listen to you mock humans anymore. I see now that mockery is all I deserve. You're right. Let's just buy eight more treasures. I want to go home, kill RaiseHim, and die."

"The poison is making you despondent. Here, swallow this. It will help you sleep through the discomfort of healing."

Bowmark drank the sweetened, but still foul-tasting medicine, lay back, and lost his pains.

Bowmark ran through trackless tunnels, ran from something dark and formless, until he jerked awake with a huge, leathery nose pressed against his.

The nose moved back until Bowmark could see the face of a rumsha.

The rumsha blinked. "Hoo, I did not mean to wake you, flat-face Uutoor True Friend."

"I'm not angry," Bowmark stammered. He could not move under a crushing weight. How many blankets had they put on him?

The rumsha stepped back and bowed. He was nearly the same height as an outsider, but with a much broader chest, thicker neck, and thicker arms. The fingers had fused together. The claws of each finger were as broad as shovels.

Memory clicked into place. "Are you a digger?"

The rumsha laughed. "Not many flat-faces see diggers. You are the first flat-face I have seen. How do you breathe with such a small nose?"

"I've never thought about it."

The digger bowed again. "I thank you, dractil-killer." From his huge hand dropped a tiny, bright red bag tied with a purple ribbon.

Bowmark looked down. Hundreds of tiny bags and their contrasting bright ribbons covered his blanket. No flower necklace had as many colors. When he looked up again, the rumsha had left. He slowly worked an arm out and pushed off the bags.

Scolla appeared with a bowl of hot broth, which Bowmark sucked down in a few heartbeats.

"Scolla, what are all these?" Bowmark gestured with his elbow toward the bags.

"Gifts from grateful rumshas. I have not opened them, so I do not know what the bags contain."

"How long was I asleep this time? Hunger is biting me."

"Two days. Here. Eat these slowly." Scolla set a plate of thinly sliced fruit before him.

Pushing himself up to a seated position, Bowmark discovered this time both arms were free and his chest was bound with wide bandages. "My teeth have grown skin on them. May I have a twig to brush them? And water. Buckets of water. And a mirror?"

Scolla wheezed as he moved about. "You are healing quickly."

"Scolla, did any warriors die?"

"Five. Two more are crippled."

"What happens to their wives and children now?"

"Warriors are not breeders."

"Oh, so, no children. Or wives?" Bowmark sucked on the fruit and concentrated on not bolting down the entire plateful. An abdominal pain made him lift his blanket. "If I have not eaten in six days, why is my stomach distended?"

"Not your stomach, your liver."

Bowmark prodded and gasped from the pain. "Why my liver?"

"That organ destroys poison."

"Truth? The physician on my island told me the liver stores extra blood to replace what we lose when we are cut."

"Zzzz. Ignorance." He handed Bowmark a polished metal mirror.

"Hot lava! When did my eyes turn yellow? Is this permanent?" He pointed to his face.

"No. Yellow eyes show your liver has worked too hard. Zzz. Most humans who get as much poison as you did, die. A few survive and are forever after sickly."

"My face looks like a tortoise shell. I look absurd!"

"Zzz. All humans look absurd."

Bowmark lowered the mirror. "The digger called me a flat-face. What do they call you? Flatter-face?"

"They call us cleaners. They appreciate our work."

"I never heard of eating being called work before." Bowmark handed the empty plate to Scolla. "Please give me some more work before I die of starvation."

Scolla studied him before taking the plate. "With health comes impudence."

Bowmark stirred the enormous pile of bags with his hand. He took a midnight blue bag and pulled off its maroon ribbon. Two tiny bells fell onto his lap. He laughed, abruptly stopped, and winced. Bruised ribs don't like laughter. Neither do inflamed livers. He opened another bag. "Ho, I am given another gold-painted piece of lead to enjoy." He held up a heavy coin.

Scolla took the coin from him and replaced the heavy metal with a bowl of crumbled bread and mashed vegetables in broth. He took the coin to a gas flame that was simmering a pot of herbal water and thrust its thread hole into the hottest part of the flame and examined the metal for a few moments. "You err. This is real gold."

Bowmark swallowed the disgusting bread mush. "Truth?" He opened a saffron orange bag. He knew glass, and he knew gems. This was a gem: a faceted and polished ruby. The next bag held carved coral earrings, and the next an oblong sapphire. A copper brooch with inset agate, two more gold coins, some triangular glazed tiles, and a lustrous silver pearl joined them. A chartreuse bag gave him a four-sided die. He held it up. "Someone made barter die with all four bells of gold. I wonder what this one does?"

Scolla glared, his ears stiff and vibrating. He slowly waddled closer and inspected the die. After a long silence he whispered, "Tezledeks have allied themselves with rumshas for over twenty-three hundred years. Only once have one of us been given the Gold Die. Only once in twenty-three hundred years."

"Is this important?"

Scolla faced away from Bowmark. "Any rumsha you meet, should he have something you need or want, must freely give whatever you ask when you show him the Gold Die."

Bowmark rolled the glistening die in his palm. "Nobody should trust someone else that much. My father would call this a fool's promise. Which of your people received this unbelievable, generous gift?"

"Sheeno. She was the first to study the rumshas long enough to learn their language. Then she taught us how and what we should joke about with them. She became our first ambassador to the rumshas."

Interest piqued, Bowmark asked, "What are you not supposed to joke about with them?"

Scolla turned, squinting at the die. He answered distractedly, "Children, the future, and structural integrity."

"I…" Scolla's gaze was so intent it unsettled Bowmark. "Is there something I need to do with this gift? Something I'm not understanding?"

Scolla closed his eyes for a long moment and turned away again. "It is yours to do with… as you please." The strain in his voice made the last words quaver.

This was worse than being designate. "Scolla. Talk to them. I can't take this. If they expect me to become an ambassador, they need to know that once I have returned home, I can never venture forth again."

"The Merchant's Guild already has a human ambassador to the rumsha."

"Why did they give this to me?"

"I do not know. Sss. Perhaps you amuse them."

Perhaps he could read those lowered ears and hissing. "Are you angry?"

"No!" Scolla waddled stiffly out of the stall.

Liar.

The mulig snorted.

Bowmark set aside the die and emptied out the rest of the bright tiny gift bags. He made separate piles of loose gems, jewelry, gold coins, bells, ribbons, glass blades, castanets, tiles, and combs.

By the time Scolla came back through deepening shadows, Bowmark had oiled and combed his hair—now almost finger length—dressed, eaten all the food, and maybe some things that weren't food, and leaned against the warm mulig. "Scolla. Come here and hold out your hands."

"Why do I do this, why?"

Bowmark pressed several gold pieces into the spitter's hands. "With this, I pay you for the mulig." He gave him a small bag of gems. "With this I replace the diamond I gave to Glorin, and pay for the physicians, medicines, and food. And now I dissolve our partnership."

Scolla bristled with spikes. "Tezledeks do not give up partnerships so easily. Have you forgotten the penalty, have you?"

"But you won't owe anybody anything anymore. I thought this would make you happy."

"Sss. Debt does not make nor unmake this partnership nor this quest I made public. I searched forty years for someone like you."

"Scolla, I am tired of your partnership. And you clearly don't like me. I am not your mulig. If you cannot respect me, then I am leaving without you."

"Ssss."

"I respected you as my equal," Bowmark said.

"That was presumptuous. I am your superior. You need me."

"That is so. I do need you. I do not need your continual mockery of me or my people. Will you accept me as your equal if I promise to consult you about every big decision?

Will you stop ordering me around like your mulig? Will you start asking me as your equal?"

"Sss." The spines lay back down. Scolla peered about carefully. No witnesses. "I accept you as . . . I accept you as . . ." His words wanted to stay behind his teeth.

"My equal," prompted Bowmark.

"But you are not. You are not as intelligent as I am. Nor does your body have as many defenses as I have."

"That is so. But I am still a man. I use reason, logic, and emotions as you do. Did your speech about how both of us are more than bellies mean anything?"

Scolla wheezed. "You discomfit me. Yes. You are… my equal."

"I promise to use your wisdom more often." Bowmark brought his hands together. "Now. Is it advisable to depart tomorrow?"

"It is not. You have been damaged in many ways. And I have been informed that as the patrols along the roads in this region have been withdrawn due to the dractils, the banditry has increased proportionately. Do you want to succeed in your mission, do you?"

Bowmark fought back irritation. "Truth."

"Then you must minimize risk by venturing into unknown danger when you are at your strongest, not enfeebled as you are now. This is obvious. Even for a human."

It *was* obvious. "I don't want to leave my kingdom in peril any longer than necessary. Every day RaiseHim grows stronger and better trained. But I see the wisdom in what you say. We'll stay until I can do my full routine without pain."

Scolla turned and waddled away without reply. Why had he expected a thank you? Digging through the pile of treasures and trinkets Bowmark found a croshet needle. His hair was just about long enough now. Sitting back against the mulig he began the process of drawing out his hair, jabbing the needle through, and forming new locks. Looking in one of his new mirrors he felt embarrassed by the stubby dreadlocks. He looked like his baby brother when Spearmark had first started his locks.

Sighing with frustration, Bowmark collapsed onto his blanket and tried not to think of home.

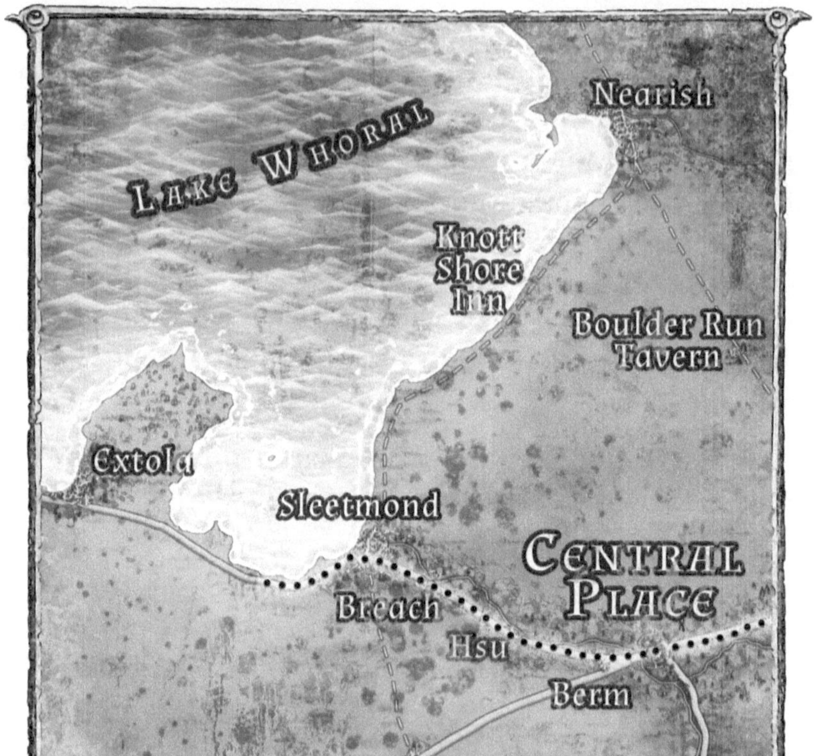

SEVERAL CHEESES FROM JUNKALOG PROVIDE
EXCELLENT PROTEIN IN HARD RINDS THAT KEEP
WELL PRESERVED FOR LONG VOYAGES.

~SEAFOLK ATLAS

Bowmark stretched as he scanned the canopy and sky. The mulig flicked her dangling ears. The sunlight massaged his back as they entered a meadow of granite boulders breaking the soil like great whales surfacing for breath. It had been nineteen grueling days of recovery before he could run thorough his entire workout session without wincing. During the last week, the better his body felt, the worse his anxiety grew over what could be happening at home. *Are father and Spearmark safe? Are RaiseHim and the other usurpers honoring their vows?*

Being well enough to face more dractils and other unknown dangers comforted him. The fresh breeze and forward movement made him happier than he had felt in a long time.

Humming quietly, he poked the Zledek alphabet into leaves. He had felt discouraged when he first discovered that one of the letters was beyond his range of hearing, but he had learned to recognize that sound in what seemed a slight pause in a word. He carried on simple conversations with Scolla that did not *always* cause the spitter to convulse with buzzing laughter.

Bowmark glanced back at Scolla sleeping on the baggage. A flock of ribbon birds wheeled overhead.

He adjusted the staffshifter sheath strap that looped around his right thigh. The new blue linen clothing he had commissioned from a surface-dwelling rumsha tailor were incredibly comfortable. Unfortunately the smooth fabric didn't grip the leather straps of his sheath like the course cotton trousers from Discoria had. After fussing with the sheath unsuccessfully, Bowmark removed it and stuffed it in the leather backpack that rested behind him on the platform. He made a mental note to have adjustments made at the next town that was not abandoned. They had recently passed through a city by a massive lake. It had a few people hurrying about, and a garrison of soldiers; one or two posted on most street corners.

"To stop looters," a passing merchant told him.

The soldiers watched Bowmark more intently than they watched the sky for dractil.

Bowmark was stunned that any country had people who would steal from abandoned homes during an emergency.

The road met the lake and they had turned left following the coast. Scolla insisted it was a freshwater lake, but Bowmark could not see the other side and found this idea preposterous. But his nose confirmed Scolla's claim. A couple of candles later the road passed into a copse of thumbnut trees. White petals drifted lazily in the sweet air and speckled the broad road before them. As they approached a dense-brush area, Bowmark said, "Scolla, I think I'll go feed some of your relatives."

Scolla sighed.

"Halt, good mulig." Their mount stopped and twisted her head to forage on softleaf bushes. Bowmark hopped off the driver's bench, relieved that his liver no longer stabbed him with pain at the jostling. Scolla clambered down to the ground as well.

Bowmark walked off the track to a small clearing in the brush with an old firepit. As he began unbuttoning his trousers he noticed the burnt end of a log crumble and fall. This camp fire was used recently. Simultaneous twig-litter crunching on both sides alerted Bowmark, but not in time to prevent two humans from grabbing his arms. He lifted his legs to drag them down with his weight, but a third man rushed up and kicked his belly.

Bowmark felt like he had burst open. All his senses contracted to that fierce pain. He could not see; he could not breathe. This was intolerable. Why couldn't he faint? He retched and writhed on the ground where they dropped him.

When he could stagger upright, the mulig and men had gone.

Gone.

His two treasures to prove where he had been. All the gifts from the rumshas. He leaned against a thumbnut tree and tried to swallow a sour taste. Water gone. Food gone. Weapons gone. No, he still had all the knives he wore and the magician's cord. He slid to the ground and struggled with breathing around the monstrous pain.

"Thieves!" hissed Scolla. "They took my children!"

Bowmark opened his eyes a slit and watched Scolla pace. He practiced breathing before brushing his fingers over his stomach. No blood. "Why didn't you?" He struggled to take a breath. "Stop them?"

"You could not stop them. I could not."

"I was—" Both breath and speech were impossible tasks. "Caught by surprise. You. You took me out. Easily enough. When you saw the Atlas."

Scolla crawled under a softleaf bush and curled into his black-sack shape.

"You could. Have tried!" Tears leaked from Bowmark's eyes.

"Zzz. We do not interfere in human affairs."

"I'm not asking you. To interfere in human affairs. I'm asking you to interfere for *me*. It's what friends do for each other." Bowmark wrapped his arms around his stomach.

Scolla sighed several times. "We must be partners. We must be equals. Now we must be friends, must we?"

"I thought we *were* friends."

"Do you know what a friend is, do you? Have you had a friend before, have you, that you could think proximity creates a friend?"

Bowmark's throat ached and tears overran his lids. "Truth! I had a brother of my heart. I loved him. And mine, mine was the hand that slew him!" He saw again his spear piercing Sunrise's heart.

"Zzz. That kind of friendship I do not need."

With an inarticulate cry, Bowmark pushed himself to his feet and tottered away from the spitter and his annoying whine of a voice.

"Where do you go, where?"

"I am retrieving my mulig and belongings. Which way?"

Scolla unfolded and pointed back the way they had come. "You are too weak yet. Your liver must not have completely healed as you claimed. They will kill you. If you will but wait, all shall be returned to you."

Bowmark ignored him and staggered up the gentle rise and out of the trees. Gradually his legs remembered how to walk and his lungs to breathe. He pondered many things as he put one foot before the other. He tried to resist thinking about killing the cursed spitter.

He came to a whale-shaped boulder that the road curved around, and while resting on the mottled stone he thought he heard screams far off. Pray Giver it wasn't those thieves killing innocent travelers. His hands trembled. Pray Giver he was not bleeding inside.

He rounded the boulder and followed the road up and over a rise. In the depression between the grassy swells of terrain was a jumble of boulders he remembered traveling through earlier. Thick black smoke wafted from the tumble of rocks, the smell of burnt flesh assailed him.

He backpedaled and tripped over a stone root, falling onto a bitterberry bush. Something inside felt like it had torn loose. He struggled out of the bush and pushed himself back around a boulder. This time when he smelled burnt flesh, he stopped and concentrated. *This is not Sunrise. This is something else. I can walk toward whatever this is. Move, foot.*

He forced himself forward one step. The next step, sweat beaded on his forehead. His gorge rose and he kept swallowing. *Keep going.* With clenched teeth, he concentrated on the next boulder, trying not to see Sunrise, speared, falling off the Disc, the smoke of Sunrise when he fell onto the lava. He crept around a pile of three man-sized rocks. What was wrong with him? Bowmark deliberately took another step forward.

A blackened space in the grassy clearing between boulders opened before him. The stench made Bowmark's eyes water, and he knelt to vomit. Then he shuffled into the burnt place and stopped in shock.

A charred skeleton lay near the center of the circle of smoldering grass, bushes and clothing. White ash drifted over the detritus. Bowmark traced the black scorch marks to a central object on the ground. A disembodied hand, mostly blacked bubbled flesh with some exposed bone. Gleaming on an ashy finger bone was the golden snake-shaped ring from Flaming Bird Island. Next to the charred skeleton lay a totally burnt corpse, and close to that a badly burned body. The third body was the man who had kicked him.

His belongings, some burned, were strewn across ashes and the bodies. If only he could tell his servants back home to come salvage everything for him. His heart was beating so fast, dizziness made him sway.

He backed away. Where was the mulig? He tried to whistle but his lips and tongue were parched. With concentrated effort he wetted his lips and whistled.

Far down the road, the mulig peeked over the ridge. Breathing easier, Bowmark left the burnt sphere of grass and stone.

The mulig came willingly, still carrying most of the gear, her tail hairs scorched. The animal pulled against him when he tried to enter the fire zone. Bowmark mounted, rode around the blackened boulders, and finally reached Scolla in the woods as dusk approached.

Scolla hissed as he climbed the mulig's leg. "I told you to wait. Tezledeks would have retrieved our mulig and baggage in the night."

"I don't see any tezledeks."

"Fool. We live underground."

They did. Bowmark hung his head and focused on breathing. "How would tezledeks have persuaded the robbers to return our belongings?"

"That is our business. Did you retrieve everything, did you?"

"Not the clothes, jewelry, or gems. I couldn't get close to the burned bodies."

They returned to the scene of destruction with Bowmark holding himself still on the mulig's platform. Scolla left to rummage through the remains, then returned with a sack full of the valuables Bowmark failed to retrieve. Bowmark said, "So, we have discovered what the magician's ring does."

"Nasty. Zzz. Other rings would possess other properties. Regardless, it is very valuable and should be carefully kept."

"I would bury it, but I might not like how it gets back to me." The brighter stars appeared in the darkening sky. "Scolla, please give me pardon. I keep asking you to be what you're not. You're not human. You don't want to be." He sighed. "I can't figure out what to expect from you."

"You can expect me to be reasonable. You can expect me to be irritated every time you ask for pardon. You think that takes away what you have done."

"No. I don't think that. But listen, my father taught me: Fear will make people obey you; affection will make them follow you. Arrogance can create allies; humility will create friends."

"Zzz."

Overhead, small bats swooped after moths. More stars dotted the dark sky. Scolla was not taking his hints.

"Scolla, I'm lonely."

Scolla flicked one ear but said nothing. The mulig continued plodding.

"I miss Father. I miss Mom and Dad. I miss my little brother. I miss—oh, Giver, I miss Sunrise. I even miss my monkey. Scolla, are tezledeks ever lonely?"

Scolla wheezed. "I have been lonely for forty years, indeed, for seventy. You will survive."

Bowmark stopped the mulig and slid off to picket the exhausted animal near some softleaf bushes next to the road. She chose to lie down instead of browse. Bowmark pulled a striped blanket crocheted from soft hair out of the baggage— another present from an outsider rumsha-- wrapped it around himself, and lay against the warm mulig. "I wish I could have a friend on this journey. I wish I knew that somebody would try to protect me as much as I protect him."

"You need sleep, not useless wishing. Rest while I search for someone to tell me if there are more thieves about."

"Scolla, if I die of internal bleeding tonight, what are you going to do?"

"Tch, tch, tch. That is unpleasant to contemplate. I would call for some of us to help me drag you some distance off the road and leave you. I would report to an Accountability Council and turn in the treasures. Zzz. I would seek a place to teach."

Bowmark gripped his Giver's Hand medallion. "Would you miss me, for even one moment?"

"Go to sleep. Zzz. Please." Scolla used his long arms like crutches and swung into the underbrush.

Bowmark pulled the blanket over his head. He was a pathetic warrior begging for somebody to care about him. How was he going to survive long enough to kill RaiseHim? Sleep overtook him as he lay, Giver's Hand medallion in hand, remembering in as much detail as he could the day he taught his baby brother to swim.

Bowmark inwardly fumed at the top of every rise as the mulig climbed an endless sea of foothills. How far did this land stretch? A lake that must be larger than his home archipelago spread out on his right, and an endless sea of grass and shrubs on his left. The vastness was surreal. Bowmark could traverse any land on Stoneshell in under a day. Most of the islands in his home could be circumnavigated in under a candle. And he had never feared that bad men hiding around over the next ridge would randomly attack him.

On the fourth day they entered a city that rivaled Bysea in size. Surrounding it were tall stone walls patrolled by many soldiers. While some doors were boarded up, it seemed as if the city were waking from a slumber, with storefronts being cleaned, merchants carrying goods, and beasts of burden passing frequently. Some surface rumsha were loading a cart with barrels. And he was surprised by the sound of children playing nearby. Bowmark asked a woman selling large blue fish if the dractil threat was over.

"We'll not know for certain 'till comes a complete survey, but word has it that some human foreigners helped the rumsha clear their temple of ten queens. We've heard only of stragglers about Lake Whoral, so braver folks are coming back."

Bowmark was tempted to correct her errors about the events at the temple, but reconsidered, remembering that some might still consider him a criminal. The less attention he drew to himself the better. Instead he bought a fish that would make for an interesting dinner.

A half-candle later they crossed a water-filled stone chute straighter than a street gutter and as broad as a river. It was made by the wardens also known as deep-dwellers, Scolla told him, part of a channel to the sea.

"No." Bowmark shook his head. "That's not possible. Unless your deep dwellers are different from our deep dwellers. Ours are like bags of soupy water. They live on the bottom of the ocean."

"The same," Scolla said. "They can surface if the need is sufficient. They exude an acid to erode the rock."

Erosion, Bowmark understood well. Cropland and terraces were an ongoing concern for his people. Acid was a new word he would ask about later. As far as Bowmark could see on either side, water rushed unimpeded, sparkling orange in the light of the setting sun. "Why would they make this?"

"That you will see when we go to Megaloth. The Empire requires many large modes of transport. There are so many different peoples there that you could obtain three, maybe four treasures in one place."

He studied the deep groove in the ground. Dissolved rock. Amazing. What did the deep dwellers do with the glass blocks StoneGrove sold to them through the intermediary shlaks; the crab-like people who threatened his home?

A week later, they huddled under Bowmark's singed cape, while the rain pelted them with drops like stones as if it meant to wash them down the mountain. Bowmark studied a regional map Scolla had procured in Central Place and traced the various roads that eventually led to Megaloth City.

"Give me pardon, Scolla." Bowmark laid his hand with care on Scolla's back. "You said at the next junction we would turn right. That takes us to a town called Jukalog and takes us far out of our way, around this huge lake. It would be faster to continue straight."

Scolla grumbled in his old man's voice as he unrolled, "Zzz. We can restock in Jukalog."

"We can restock in HeadWater. It's closer."

"Jukalog is more convenient."

"Why?"

Scolla did not answer.

"Is there something special there for me to pick up as a treasure? I'm not sure it would count. It still lies within this region of Feggralind according to the map. I'm supposed to go to ten different nations." Too bad all he had from Bysea were the scars on his back. He considered counting Scolla as a treasure from Discoria. But handing the protocol officer a kratchnak the monster threat that every child on Stone Grove feared would not give him the results he wanted. "Who lives in Jukalog?

"Humans and rumshas. Zzz."

"Tell me again why we're going there?"

"Let me, zzz, please sleep. I do not, please, wake you at night."

"Truth, you do. Do you think I don't notice when you bring strangers over to ogle at me? What does so't'zta mean?"

"I did not use that word."

"I know. It was somebody fat and slow who said that. So what does it mean?"

"Lesson later. Please."

"If you insist. So then, since you will be sleeping when we reach the junction, I will go straight and continue to HeadWater."

"Zzz." Wheeze. "Jukalog is famous for its cheeses."

"What are cheeses?"

"It is the, zzz, firm, white food you never eat. You say it stinks. It is made from the milk of goats."

"Animal milk? Rotted hard? What are goats?"

"Goats are herd animals that humans brought to this world."

Which meaning of "world" did Scolla intend? A pooling of water in one of the folds of his cape emptied itself on the map, splattering cold water in Bowmark's face. "Augh!" He wiped his eyes and surveyed the rain-streaked landscape before him. Muddy water purled over the mulig's feet. "I don't want to go to a town famous for rotted milk."

"Nonetheless, there is where we will go. Zzz. Please."

The spitter was working on politeness. Bowmark should give him credit for that. "Give me a good reason. Please."

Scolla squirmed. "Zzz. It is a private matter."

"But I seem to be going with you. I don't think I have time to waste on a side trip."

Much wheezing. Scolla peeked at Bowmark through the space between his divided ears. "It has been forty-five years since I have been with my parents. I wish to visit them one last time before I leave for a new country where we cannot correspond."

"So then! Of course, we must go to Jukalog. Please teach me something polite to say to your parents."

Scolla's ears flicked like the mulig's in a cloud of gnats. "You will not see them."

"Why not?"

"You are human."

"I think we had this discussion before. I am not your mulig. If you lead me into your home, I won't poop on the floor. Oh wait. That might be considered gift-giving."

Scolla's teeth clicked.

"Tell me how to behave and I'll endeavor to not embarrass you in front of your family. I truly want to meet them. I'd like to know what sort of parents produce a Scolla."

Scolla sizzled. Rain beat and soaked into blankets and clothes with cold discomfort. "I do not want you to threaten them. I do not want a marred visit for a last memory."

"Why would I threaten them?" Water splashed off the mulig's hide as Bowmark patted her. "Ah. Comprehension trickles in. I could promise not to grab their tongues. You could promise simply to ask them if they would like to visit with me."

Scolla buried his head. "I could ask. However, they shall say no."

Bowmark settled back and watched the rain. If there was anything he could tell Sunrise now, it would be that long journeys involve a lot of boredom and discomfort.

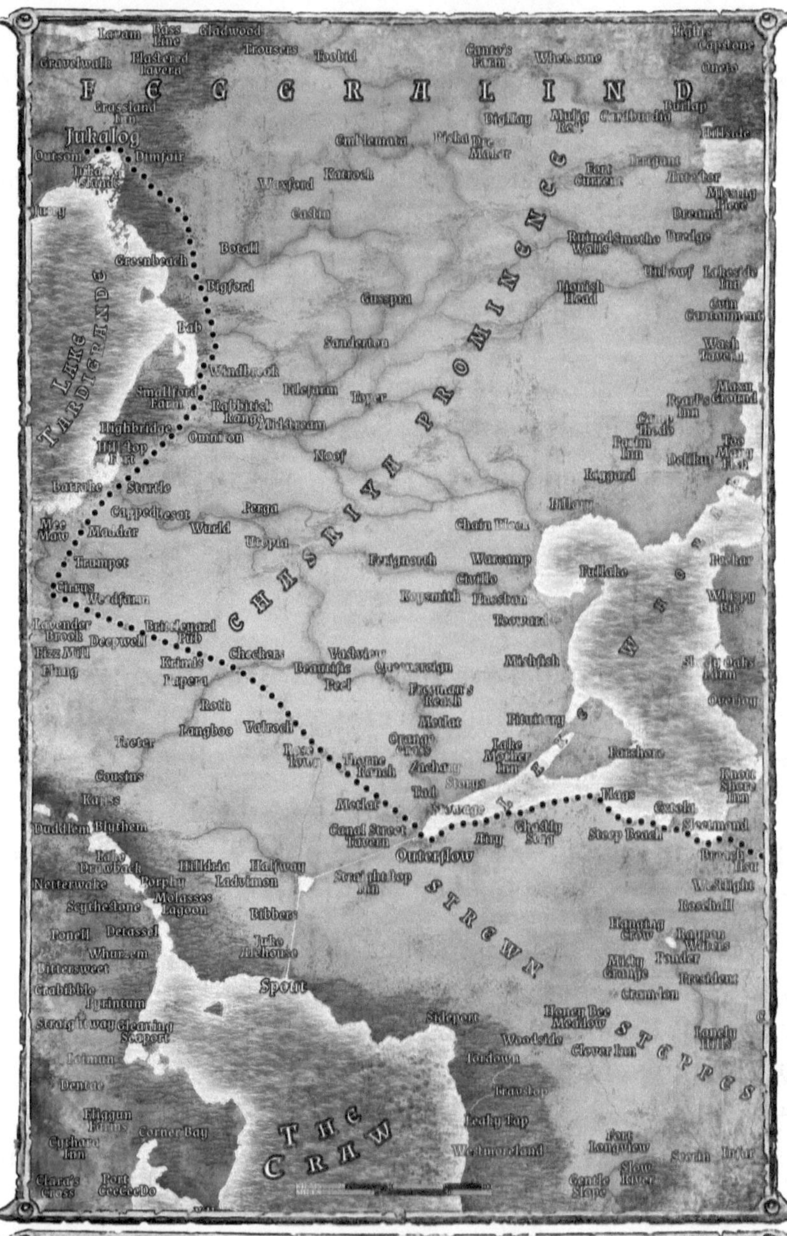

MY HUMAN BOWMARK RALLIED 23 RUMSHANE
WARRIORS AND THUS DID KILL HUURAZZMATUM
THE GREAT MATRIARCHS

~ SCOLLA THE PIONEER

Bowmark sat in a barn with a coal brazier next to him and a damp blanket around him. Many small feet shuffled and dozens of dark eyes in dark bodies in a dark night reflected the embers. Sipping ramchew tea, he watched the gleams appear and disappear as the spitters blinked or turned to whisper to a neighbor. He could understand a word here or there, but not enough to comprehend a sentence. Nonetheless, he kept his face motionless so they would not know he was trying to overhear. Their ginger smell made his bitter drink taste better.

If Scolla did not return by the time he had finished his tea, Bowmark planned to give up and retreat to the small inn for a warm and dry place to sleep. Still, it would be a shame to disappoint all these waiting spitters. Maybe he could juggle or do handstands before he left for a warm, dry bed.

A tiny black ball waddled into the wavering light. Round, black hands grabbed the tiny spitter and pulled it back into the darkness where the toddler squeaked sadly.

An escalation in whispering caught his attention. He set aside the cup as a corridor opened in the vaguely-seen crowd. Three spitters walked toward him.

Bowmark bowed to them with his forehead and knees on the packed dirt. He sat back and suddenly decided that now was not the time to use the Zledek he had been practicing all day. This was Scolla's hometown. This was where Scolla should shine. "Good evening," he said quietly in Common.

The simple statement elicited much excited conversation.

Scolla drew nearer with two fatter, slower replicas of himself. One of them seemed to have a green sheen to his or her black skin. Both had drooping skin around the jowls and moved with exaggerated care.

Scolla said, "Human, these are my parents, the Honorable Scossa and the Honorable Illas."

One stepped closer and studied Bowmark's blue-gray eyes and scabbed face. The spitter said in Zledek, "So this is what my youngest drags home as a prize for a life's work. Foolish son, this herd animal is diseased!"

"Honorable Father." Scolla looked neither at his father nor at Bowmark, "When you read the book I have written, you will understand what this animal has done and what he is healing from."

Bowmark's ears felt hot enough to burn off, but he kept his face passive. He cleared his throat, startling some of the spitters. His days in court had taught him that flattery eased tension. "Honorable Scossa, I appreciate your son. I live today because of his help. He gives me hope to return to my homeland, where the tezledeks will bring us civilization." He waited.

The only sounds heard in the barn were that of the mulig eating and pigs grousing at each other in their sleep. Bowmark could almost feel the weight of dozens of people's astonished gazes at him. Scolla continued to study the ground between his feet. *I need some help here. Scolla, a hint, a word, anything.* His thoughts stayed inside his skull. Scolla gave no hints.

Bowmark hazarded another sentence. "Your son has taught me much, which I also appreciate."

The barn filled with sibilant Zledek. Scossa whined in Common, "My son was meant to teach tezledeks. Not humans."

Inspiration struck. "Anyone can teach a good student. It takes a master to teach an inept student."

The barn filled with buzzing laughter. Illas, the one with a green sheen on her skin, stepped forward. "Is this a new shape of rumsha, is this? But no. It smells like a human. Would that all humans were as well taught as this. I thought my youngest to be foolhardy, yet he brings home a wonder and gives proof of possible success in a great risk. I see we have much to read and discuss this night. After meal, let us all meet outside my home."

Bowmark quickly bowed with his face to the ground so that they would not see how hard he was suppressing laughter. The tezledeks receded from him with whisper-soft shuffles. After waiting one hundred breaths, he looked up. Alone. So then. He stroked the mulig's muzzle, picked up his wet clothes and blankets, and trudged through the rain to the nearest inn.

They had finished the day's cooking, so he did not need to smell the roasting of goat meat. A handful of people -some human, some rumsha sat at tables. They were smoking and chatting quietly. A couple hunched over a contraption that clicked and clacked as they rolled a small metal ball through a wooden maze by tilting it this way and that. Bowmark strode up to the hearth. A small man who moved as jerkily as a feathered bird watched Bowmark drop his things before the fire. "Good sir, I wish to buy the use of your warmest and driest room. I will pay extra to have my clothes washed and dried."

"Hold, hold, young man. Boono says to me that he saw you talking to spitters."

"Truth. They said—"

"Per-perhaps it would be best if you stayed in the barn."

The revulsion on the man's face told Bowmark all he needed to know. Bowmark caught himself rolling his eyes and stopped. "I promise not to steal your slops."

The man's face hardened. Bowmark had erred in not carefully guarding each word. "Give me pardon. I—I study animals. Truth. And then I write books about them." That was exactly what he should have been doing all along. If he did not survive, a book could yet tell the Sea Predators about peoples of the world who bore them no animosity. "Then I give these books to schools."

The revulsion was replaced by blank incomprehension.

Bowmark brought out a silver coin worth twice what he should be paying. "I understand there are no public baths, so—"

"No, no, we don't traffic in such goings on."

"What? In bathing?"

"In doing it publicly!"

"Ah. Just so. It is good to finally find some privacy." He pressed the coin into the man's hand. "If you could bring the largest basin of boiling water to my room, I will forever owe you gratitude."

The man hefted the coin. "Eh. It's off-season, as you can tell by the tomb quiet. Pick any room you wish. For another silver, my daughter, who is flashing quick with a needle, can repair your clothes."

Bowmark agreed and handed him the coin. "Truth, I would appreciate a loop sewn onto my trousers here to help my sheath stay in place. I will leave them outside my door." Within one hundred breaths he had washed all travel and care from his body and crawled into a stone-heated bed.

In the morning he was wakened by claws gripping his hand. Bowmark yawned. "May the sun rise with goodness for you, Scolla. Please tell me that I did not embarrass you too much in front of your parents."

"I had thought you would enjoy embarrassing me."

"No. Hear me. I have decided that even if you are not my friend, I am yet your friend. What good is pride to me if it gets me killed before I can free my people?"

"Precisely."

"I found groveling a new experience. I'm still thinking about what I learned from that. I think that were I not royal, I could easily hate royals and nobles. Ah. There are some that I do hate."

Scolla watched him as Bowmark sat up and shivered. Bowmark pushed himself out of bed and dashed over the frigid floor to his stiff, dry clothes by the fireplace. He cracked the door enough to grab his altered trousers.

After dressing and arming himself, Bowmark was still watched by Scolla. "Do you wish to tell me something? I promise to behave properly."

"Zzz." Scolla closed his eyes and said quickly, as though if he did not release the words now, he never would, "I owe you gratitude."

Bowmark stamped his heel into his boot and waited for the world to end.

Scolla approached and gave him a small waterproof gut bag with a metal tezledek book in it. "The tezledeks here hope to speed your journey by gifting you with a treasure of ours. While we possess most nations rather than living in a separate nation by ourselves, we thought this would add to your treasures."

Bowmark thought. An empty box from Rolocton to demonstrate friendship, a lead figurine of a rumsha. Not much to put in a storeroom. And now this. If he brought this to Stone Grove, would the protocol officer accept the odd device as a treasure? "What is this book about?"

"A history of the coming of the humans."

Bowmark pressed it against his heart. He could not speak.

At a breakfast of bread, poached eggs, braised vegetable stalks, toasted nuts, and untouched disgusting cheese spreads, the innkeeper's wife lingered after being paid. "My Boono says to me that you speak with spitters."

Bowmark considered. Scolla had already packed the mulig. He had nearly finished eating. The likelihood of ever seeing these people again was small. "Truth, I do. They can tell you interesting things."

"I do not wish to know about my neighbor's intestinal products."

Bowmark laughed, then tapped his plate. "These eggs, as delicious as they are, good lady, do not make me what I am. I can yet discuss weather and wagons."

The woman frowned in confusion. "Um." She wiped the coin that Bowmark had given her with a soapy rag. "You do know this is a clean town. We are proud that our cheeses are never fouled."

Cheese could smell worse than this? "Your hard work and that of the spitters make it so."

The woman turned away, shaking her head and muttering to herself. "May the ship return soon."

Back on the road, under wind and low clouds that hugged their rain to themselves, Scolla said, "I am remembering why I left on the first cheese wagon I was allowed to board."

Bowmark adjusted his new leather jacket. It was fitted well, but still supple, allowing for free movement. "How old were you?"

"Twenty-five. We do not consider our children fit to make judgments until then. We are allowed only to do what we are told. At twenty we are apprenticed, I to a teacher. I sat silently for five years watching my master teach. After the lessons, he would explain his methodology. After the five years came my Coming of Age Day. Our people say that if one has not learned how to behave properly by then, he never shall. The following morning, I left."

Scolla had never said so much before about the tezledeks. Bowmark turned around to face him. "Scolla, is the word "foolish" a term of endearment among tezledeks?"

"Sss. No." Scolla curled into a tight ball.

Bowmark turned back around to face where they were going. A ribbon bird bawked at him. "You remind me of the brother of my heart, Sunrise. It is forbidden to leave our island lest our enemies, the Southils, discover where we live, yet Sunrise determined to travel the wider world."

"Is that why you killed him, is it?"

"No! Yes. No! It was that which brought him to the attention of my enemy, RaiseHim."

Bowmark swallowed several times and wiped his eyes. "As Presumed, I had to prove before I could become designate and, like you, apprentice for five years, after which I would have become king." He sniffed. "Sunrise was chosen, because, because—" Bowmark wailed, "Like you, like you, he was smarter than I, and he didn't need to take my advice! And so he was chosen. I—I would have let him be king. I would have! But he refused! And Giver, he feared burning. I had to kill him before he hit the lava. I had to. Because he wouldn't listen to me! The *one* thing I ever commanded him to do, he refused to do, and so I live the rest of my days with a ripped heart! That cursed, arrogant, dirt-eater!"

Bowmark stopped, appalled. His breath jerked in his chest. He couldn't have said that about his best friend, the best man on the island, save Father. "If our positions had been reversed, he would have found a way. He—He would have stabbed me in the foot when I wasn't looking. I could have done that if only I had been brave enough. I could have saved him. I could have. I could have."

Bowmark leaned forward and laid his face on the mulig's neck. Every organ in his body tried to twist away from the others. Bowmark groaned.

The mulig slowed, perhaps trying to understand if Bowmark was giving it an order. As Bowmark continued to groan, the animal could not discern any commands, so she kept slogging up the road.

Bowmark must have fallen asleep, for he awoke with a blanket on him and Scolla draped over his lap, asleep. The spitter had voluntarily touched him? "Scolla? Are you all right? '"

Scolla slowly righted himself and crawled to the platform, dragging the blanket behind him. He buzzed and wheezed as he rerolled into a ball with the blanket over him.

Bowmark rubbed his thighs. "You have never done that before."

"Zzz. It seems humans need to be touched when they are sad."

"Huh. Sad." Bowmark turned away as new tears filled his raw eyes. "So then, now you know what happened."

"No. Zzz. Nothing you said made sense."

Bowmark almost laughed. "That's humans for you." He rubbed his face. He sighed shakily and pulled out the metal book to practice reading Zledek and to learn of human history. He could only comprehend a few of the words. But remembering his progress learning the Atlas as a child, he studiously applied himself.

Four crossroads and eight days later the flat horizon was broken by a jagged mountain range. The gentle undulations of the grassland gave way to rocky ground with occasional angular stone protrusions. Late one afternoon as the road meandered through sparse forest of needled trees, Scolla crawled out from under the blanket and stood in the cold breeze. When he did not say anything after a few moments, Bowmark put away his book and said, "You're up early. Are you having trouble sleeping?"

"I am trying to smell a rock goatish."

Bowmark thought a while. "So then, I have two questions. What is a rock goatish? What do I need to do about it?"

"It is a pack animal we need to travel to the Gathering where you will learn new fighting techniques." Scolla glanced around and rubbed his shoulders with his palms. "My thoughts are colliding."

Bowmark mentally noted Scolla's movements as indicators of indecision or worry. He himself raised his eyebrows and waited. Scolla said nothing. Perhaps Scolla could not read that facial expression. "Yes, I recall the plan. I must learn to fight while unarmed so that I can defeat RaiseHim. I wait to hear about the collisions in your head."

"I did not know this when I learned of the place from the council at Central Place, but I discovered more facts about it at Jukalog. This Gathering is not a good place, for it is centered on a magical stone. Should we go, you must never touch that stone. Danger surrounds the school, for I do not know the nature of the artifact. The educated tezledeks have left, save one who stays as an observer. A few ferals live close."

"Ferals?"

"Tezledeks who do not fulfill social duty in favor of a life of indolence. Our libraries and laboratories are barred to them."

Bowmark contemplated. The value of learning to survive his fight with RaiseHim balanced against the unknown risks of going to a school of fighters wielding magic. "What else do you know about this place?"

"Nothing more yet. Though, if we approach carefully, it may be possible to observe unseen from a distance in order to ascertain more. This is where my thoughts collide. For I do need you to live after your confrontation with your usurper cousin. If I could trust you not to be impulsive, this would be an easier decision."

Bowmark diverted all his energy to keeping his mouth shut lest he prove Scolla's point. Pushups would help. He hopped off the bench and flattened on the ground. The mulig had become used to this behavior and continued on without him. After a hundred pushups, Bowmark jogged to catch up with the mount.

"So then," he panted between breaths. "It's settled. We go to surveil this school, and will deliberate further when we know…"

The ground shook. Bowmark suddenly felt like a ten-year-old, afraid that the Proving was about to happen.

"This is strange," Scolla whined. "Earthquakes are rare in this region."

Bowmark closed his eyes and focused on breathing. The quake passed and he clucked to the mulig who had slowed down, confused by the sensation.

Scolla retrieved his journal to record the event.

Later in the afternoon the road led them through a sparse woodland. Crooked gray trees wound around boulders speckled with white and pink lichen. The road became winding and narrowed in places as it conformed to increasingly rugged terrain. Bowmark was wondering about how edible the blue-colored berries he was seeing might be, when he noticed a tick on the mulig where neck and foreleg met.

He bent low to pull off the bloodsucker, sat up, and turned to throw the crushed arachnid. A flicker in his peripheral vision caused him to turn more and an arrow skittered across his chest, tearing a red line along his skin. He continued the turn into a roll off the mulig.

Crouching under the slow-moving animal, he reached up blindly to snatch his bow. That weapon was on the other side of the platform. He rolled behind a cracked boulder with a twisted tree growing out of it. By the Giver's Hand, who was after him now?

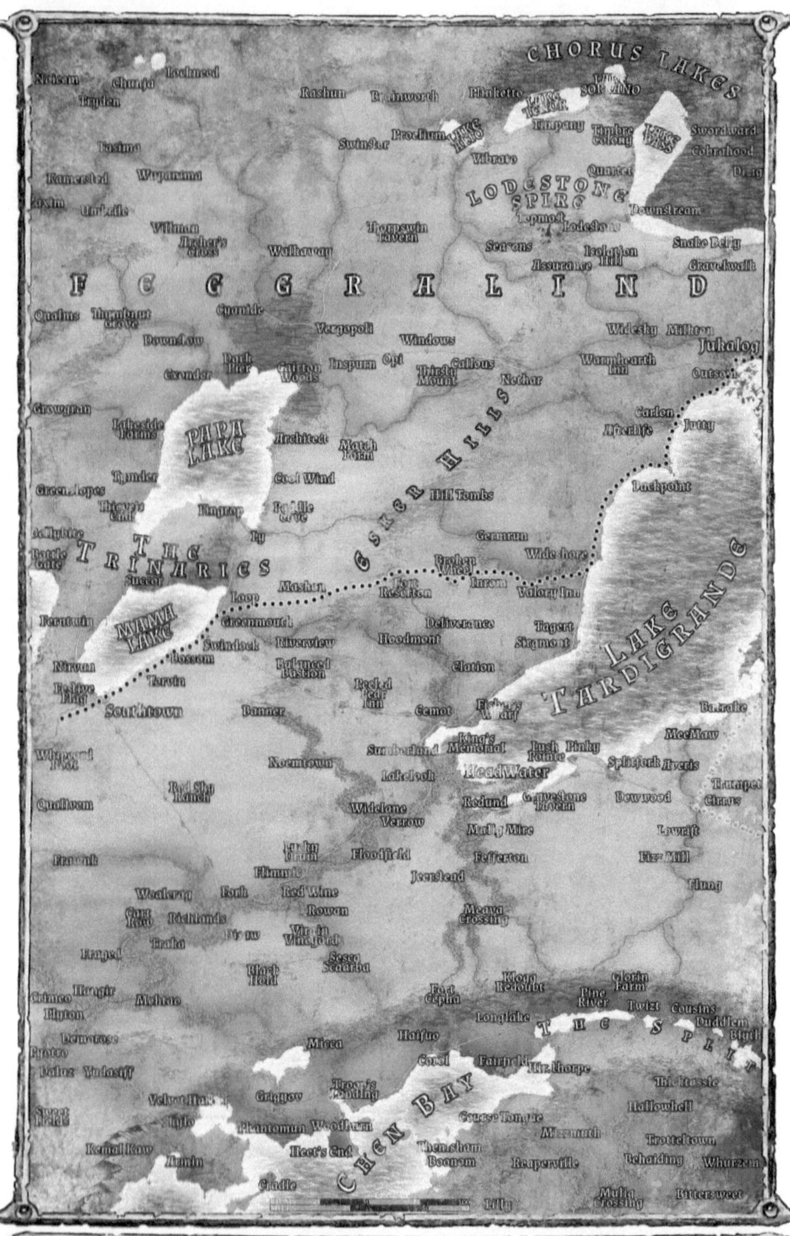

CHORUS LAKES
LAKE SOPRANO
LAKE TENOR
LODESTONE SPIRE
LAKE ALTO
LAKE BASS
FOGGRALIND
ESKER HILLS
THE TRINARICS
PAPA LAKE
MAMA LAKE
LAKE TARDIGRANDE
CHEN BAY
THE SPLIT
Nriem
Chnja
Lockwood
Rashun
Brainworth
Pinketto
Tipiden
Tinbre
Celong
Swordward
Cobrahood
Drag
Fastina
Swinster
Proclum
Vibrato
Quartet
Downstream
Ramested
Wryanna
Thompswin Tavern
Lepnost
Lodeston
Snake Belly
Zaxin
Un'exile
Villnun
Archer's Cross
Walkaway
Searons
Isolation Hill
Gravelwalk
Assurance
Qualms
Thumbnut Grove
Cyanide
Vergopoli
Windows
Opi
Callous
Widesky
Milton
Jukalog
Downflow
Inspurn
Thirsty Mount
Nethar
Warmhearth Inn
Outset
Ecander
Park Pier
Cutton Woods
Carlon
Growgran
Lakeside Foults
PAPA LAKE
Architect
Match Point
Afterlife
Jutty
Thunder
Cool Wind
Hill Tombs
Backpoint
Green Slopes
Thorns Gathe
Tingrep
Egg'lle Cove
Ely
Germrun
Widewhere
Hobble
Battle Gate
THE TRINARICS
Succor
Loop
Mashun
Fort Resolute
Inron
Valory Inn
Ferntain
MAMA LAKE
Greenmouth
Riverview
Deliverance
Tagert
Sigmont
Burrake
Nirvan
Bossom
Hoodmont
MeeMaw
Festive Cliff
Tervin
Pecked Pear Hill
Elation
Fisher's Wharf
Splatfork
Averis
Southtown
Banner
Cemot
King's Memorial
Lush Pointe
Pinky
Whispered Fleet
Noemtown
Sunderland
HeadWater
Trumpet Crnrs
Bad Sky Ranch
Lakelock
Redund
Gravestone Tavern
Dewwood
Qualiven
Widelane
Verrow
Muddy Mire
Lowrift
Franvik
Lucky Frain
Floodfield
Fefferton
Fizz Hill
Flimnig
Jeerstead
Flung
Wealery
Fork
Red Wine
Weald Crossing
Gut Row
Fieldlands
Rowan
Draw
Virgin Vineyard
Fraha
Erahu
Sescu Sciarba
Fraged
Black Fold
Klogg Redoubt
Glorin Farm
Crimeo
Hrugir
Mahno
Fat Cepha
Pine River
Twizt
Cousins
Flipton
Longlake
Duddlem
Lewrose
Micca
Hatsuo
Carol
Fairfield
Blyth
Pyotto
Dalnz
Yudasiff
Frosr's Landing
Fitzthorpe
Thickassle
Velvet Hall
Griggor
Course Tongue
Hallowhell
Shilo
Phantomun
Woodturn
Thensham
Mizzmuch
Trottletown
Remal Kaw
Tumin
Heer's End
Boanam
Reaperville
Behaiding
Whurzen
Cradle
Lily
Mula Crossing
Bittersweet

NO LONGER VISIBLE, THOSE LOVED STILL
WHISPER THROUGH THE MARROW.

~ SOUTHIL PROVERB

The riderless mulig placidly continued up the road.

Listening intently, Bowmark assessed his options as blood from his shallow wound trickled down his stomach and soaked warmly into his nice blue shirt. The smell of blood and thumbnut blossom and bark and duff enveloped him. A slight breeze soughed through branches. The mulig snorted. A lizard peeped. Bowmark had his knives and magic things, not much against bow and arrow at a distance.

The massive crooked tree in the boulder grew straight once the trunk had reached three strides high. Roots like rivulets meandered over the stone and forest floor.

Bowmark took his staffshifter and pointed to a branch higher than he could reach. "Slowly," he whispered. Practice had attuned the staffshifter to his desires. The claw hand opened as the staffshifter gradually lengthened. The metal snake claws nudged the branch. "Grip." The little claws tightened on the wood. "Lift slowly."

He held one-handed onto the closed-fist end of the magic weapon and rose gently to that branch. Scars pulled on his skin. Hanging from the branch, he disentangled the staff-shifter and pointed his magic weapon to a higher branch. He rose farther, hoping that his assailant could not see him ascending behind the trunk. *He'll steal my mulig, won't he?*

From experience, Bowmark knew how hard it was to shoot upward accurately at anything in a tree. He felt safer when he had risen ten strides. Balancing on a branch, he listened for his attacker. If they had not seen him rise, the likelihood was low that they would glance up and see him.

Keeping his body in line with the tree trunk, he watched the road. The sound of a rotten log imploding below and behind him startled Bowmark. He turned smoothly. The attacker had the wit not to follow the road, but not enough to keep from stepping on a rot-hollowed, fallen tree.

The attacker crouched over the log, holding his bow ready as his head swiveled. Slower than a worm, he rose and extricated his foot. His muddy, brown shirt showed golden-brown skin through multiple tears. His straight black hair was only partly held in a greasy braid. He moved forward incrementally.

Bowmark held his breath while he scanned the forest for any other movement. He pressed his thumb against a knuckle as he saw the attacker was not going to pass directly under his tree. Too many branches blocked a clear throw for the magician's cord. The cord always stuck to whatever it hit first. *What do I do?*

Bowmark took a deep breath and pulled the magic cord out. He brought looped cord and staff claws together and whispered to them. The claws opened and then closed on the coil of cord. "Good," he breathed. "Now slowly extend." *Please, let something work today.*

The staffshifter extended. The attacker was still too far away.

Bowmark dropped his lightball into a softleaf bush growing at the base of the tree.

The attacker stopped and jerked his face toward the sound. He crept toward the bush.

When he passed under the fist of the staffshifter, Bowmark said, "Open! Cord, stick!"

The attacker turned part-way before the cord fell on him. His arrow drilled into the ground. He flailed, then tripped. His head thunked on the tree-hugged boulder as he fell.

Bowmark winced. He swung down, pulled out a knife, and turned over the unconscious man. He almost dropped his knife. "PledgeKept!"

Bowmark stirred the broth of dried vegetables and fresh-caught lizard in the small iron kettle seated on coals and hot rocks.

"Why do I do this, why?" whined Scolla as he tied the last stitch on the gash on the side of PledgeKept's face. He daubed a brown salve along the puffed, purpling wound. "In Bysea you said you need to kill him. Then asked me to heal him."

Bowmark crumbled some stale bread into the broth to thicken it. "I can't kill him when he is helpless and hurt like that."

"That is the easiest time to kill him."

Bowmark sighed as he tipped in salt and ground seed spice into the stew. "I need to talk to him."

"You have bad ideas. It is much easier to slit his throat and keep traveling. We waste time."

"I did not think tezledeks were so bloodthirsty. Here." He extended a knife. "Do you want to do it?"

Scolla waddled to the other side of the mulig.

Bowmark pocketed the knife and gazed gloomily at his attacker lying on the forest duff, Bowmark's bloody shirt bundled under his head. "Ashes." He leaned against a boulder and bit a pemmican stick. The arrow wound on his chest stung with a sticky ointment that Scolla claimed would clean it and hold it closed. A strip of cloth wound around his shoulder and under an armpit. He wore his second loose fitting white shirt. How long before all his clothes were tatters agai? At least they were in better shape than his adversary's.

PledgeKept's face was marred by patches of red oozy skin that indicated a fracas with a dractil, and a split in his lower lip that Scolla had sewn together. His ankles were scarred. His skin stretched over prominent ribs and a hollowed-out stomach.

"Fumes and ashes." Bowmark rubbed salve along the furrow across his own chest.

Scolla waddled back with the brass book he had been working on and sat beside Bowmark. His talons pierced words into the strip of paper. "Do you want to kill your enemy, do you?"

Bowmark scooped up a handful of dead leaves and dry needles from the forest floor. He crushed them and let the fragments dribble through his fingers. "It isn't a matter of want to. It is my duty. Not to do so is treason."

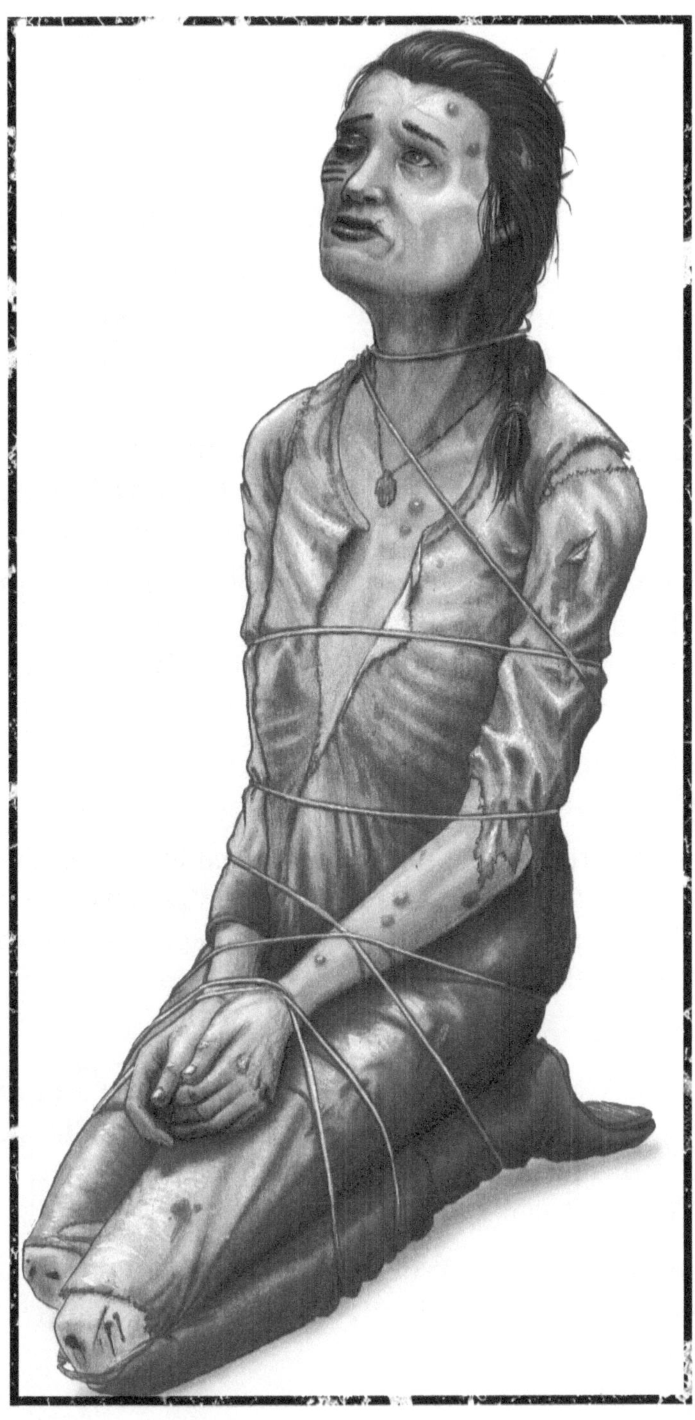

Scolla's discs gleamed, his claws still imbedded in the scroll. "Why do you totter on the top of a wall, why? Decide and do."

"Scolla. I can kill him anytime. What I cannot do is unkill him. What I cannot do is forget." *Giver, I don't know what to do.*

Scolla resumed punching letters and Bowmark watched the coals turning to ash as the smell of stew permeated their clearing. The mulig cropped the new leaves from the bushes concealing them from the road.

Presently, PledgeKept twitched and tried to raise a hand. The rope tightened, firmly jerking the hand back to his side. His face twisted with pain as he blinked open his eyes.

Bowmark moved to crouch before PledgeKept and showed him a metal cup. "You must be thirsty. This water has something like bitefinger liver venom, but it comes from a plant. It has a noxious taste but should abate the pain."

PledgeKept licked his lips, his tongue stopping to feel the stitches. He said hoarsely, "Poison."

Bowmark drank from the cup and made a face. "I've been guzzling the stuff the last few weeks, but it never tastes any better." Then he propped up his enemy and pressed the cup against PledgeKept's mouth.

Warily, the man drank.

Bowmark gazed into his golden-brown eyes and tried to swallow an ache in his throat. He took the cup, dipped stew into it, and returned to PledgeKept. "What happened to your ankles to scar them like that?"

"Nothing a paying passenger would know anything about." His gaze never left the cup of stew.

"If you promise you won't fight me, I'll release you from the cord so you can eat this."

PledgeKept nodded jerkily.

"Cord, come." The cord slithered off.

PledgeKept snatched the cup and gulped the stew.

"I know from experience that you'll make yourself sick. You must not eat quickly after a long fast."

But the cup was empty, and PledgeKept licked its sides noisily. When there was not even flavor left, only then did he study his legs tied together with natural rope from knee to ankle. Expressions of fright, rage, and despair flickered across his face as he reached up and fingertip-explored the swelling side of his face.

Bowmark pulled the cup away from him. "I am trying hard not to be stupid." He filled the cup with only broth. "I wish I succeeded more often."

With shaking hands, PledgeKept gulped the broth, spilling some on his chin.

Bowmark knelt to look him straight in the face. "Understand this: I don't want to kill you. It would be too much like—like killing—like—"

"Not again," whined Scolla.

Bowmark turned. "Go away!"

"You cannot tell me that. I am observing."

"So observe quietly!" He turned back.

PledgeKept's voice wavered. "You take orders from your pet spitter?"

Scolla bristled.

"Not pet. We are equal partners. You can discern that by noting we annoy each other equally."

PledgeKept breathed raggedly.

Bowmark rubbed his face and swallowed. The pain stayed in his throat. "It would be hard to see humor when you expect at any moment to be eviscerated."

PledgeKept gagged.

"No. I would not do that to you. When the time comes, I will untie you and give you any knife you choose. We will have a fair fight."

"Stu—Zzz. Reckless." Scolla ticked holes in his scroll.

"Fair," sobbed PledgeKept. "Fair!"

Embarrassed, Bowmark rose and walked into the sparce forest. Warriors do not cry. He leaned against a tree. Unless they're exhausted and hungry and hurt and hopeless. How was he going to do this?

When he returned, PledgeKept was wiping his face with Bowmark's discarded, torn, and bloody shirt.

Bowmark brought him another cup of stew. "Eat. Let's discuss some matters."

PledgeKept sniffed and cleared his throat. "With good will. I can talk. I can sing. I can tell stories for hours. Days. A month. Two months. However long you want."

"Begging demeans you."

"I wasn't. I'm saying that I can do those things. I'm not a warrior. I'm a musician. I tell jokes. I recite poetry."

"Stop. What am I to do? If I don't kill you, you'll kill me."

"No, no. I wasn't trying to kill you."

"If I hadn't turned when I did, your arrow would have gone through my heart. I call that killing."

"I was aiming for your shoulder. I wanted to disable you long enough to talk without *you* killing *me.*"

Bowmark stood and walked back to Scolla. "I don't like liars."

"I told the matriarchs I was the wrong person to send on this mission. But the innocent child chose me and so I had to go. They didn't care that I had an intended, that I was trained in music, not war. At the inn, I did the wrong thing. I was startled. When you pulled your knife, I lost my sense. I've ruined everything. My mission isn't to kill you. My mission is to find out where the Sea Predators live."

"So you can slaughter all of us instead of only one."

"No. You have not committed the crimes of your ancestors. No. All we want are our Holy Books and our children."

Surely the Holy Books of Stone Grove did not belong to the Southils. Bowmark shook his head. "We fled from you over two hundred years ago. If we had taken your children, which we did not, but if we had, they are long dead."

"We know that. But we want their descendants to know that we will always welcome them home. We want them to know that we have never forgotten them."

"So you hoped to torture me into revealing where we live."

"No. I was desperate. I don't have a magic cord. I don't have food. I don't have a mulig. I don't have the riches you have. I don't have the gratitude of thousands of rumshas. And you were going farther and farther from the ocean. What good will it do me to learn where your people live, and then die of starvation before I get home?"

Bowmark scraped a cup of stew for him. "I respect your dedication and the arduous journey it took to follow me this far. Eat."

PledgeKept ate his food faster than a pig in competition with his littermates.

Bowmark watched Scolla pricking the paper. Now what? Now what? He set down his cup, walked to PledgeKept's pack, and retrieved a bone flute. He walked back and handed it to PledgeKept. "Explain this. This is human bone, is it not?"

PledgeKept wiped his mouth. "Yes. My flute is the most important thing I own."

"What else do you do with the bones of your enemies? Drink from our skulls, perhaps?"

Fear gave way to indignation. "We would never play the bones of our enemies. This is my grandfather. We play our ancestor's bones at festivals to remind ourselves that, alive or dead, they are always a part of us."

"You *eat* each other?"

Indignation gave way to disgust. "Never! We go back a year after burial and pack the bones into a special basket which we place in a burial cave. If the flute we make ever gets broken, we put it back respectfully with the other bones. My grandfather was a good man. Whenever two men disputed, he would do all he could to bring peace between the two. I remember as a boy how safe I felt when he held me. It is my honor to play his flute."

There was nowhere soil deep enough to bury a body in all of Stone Grove. "We eat fish until we die. And then we feed the fish." Bowmark closed his eyes, remembering the tapestry his mother had been wrapped in, the wailing during the long trip far out to sea, the attachments of stones and cords to the tapestry, the despair on Father's face, the tapestry growing dimmer as it slipped farther under the flower-strewn surface of the water. "Play something."

PledgeKept licked his lips and slowly brought up the flute. The first few notes were ruined by fright-driven breathing. He deliberately calmed himself, and sweet notes filled the clearing.

Bowmark recognized the song and, translating the words into Common, somberly sang:*Come play with me in the surf.*

Come play, come play in the surging surf.

Come dance, come swim in the sea.

Too soon our prints are washed away.

Come dance, come swim, come dance, come swim,

And Splash!

PledgeKept stopped. "You know the song. We use different words with the same meaning."

"I sang that song to my little brother while I taught him how to swim. PledgeKept, why are we enemies?"

The young man said, "I won't be yours anymore."

"Until I untie your legs."

"What would you do in my place?"

"You mean lying on the ground bleeding to death with a shattered shoulder?"

PledgeKept touched his wound and winced. "I was wrong. I lost my sense again. We only know Sea Predators as monsters. You frighten us."

"We only know you as enemies who have scoured the seas seeking our destruction."

"We're Southils. My village is Hovahill. We have never attacked anybody."

"Except Sea Predators who were only searching for a place to live."

PledgeKept rubbed the polished metal that ornamented his flute. "We know different histories."

Bowmark grasped his Giver's Hand medallion. Could he commit treason if it meant the salvation of his people? "What would it entail to make a peace with the Southils so they cease pursuing us?"

"Give us back our books. Let the children free."

"Will shedding our blood to obtain our Holy Books make you holy?

"Why do you keep them when you worship Vanquish All?"

"We don't."

PledgeKept shifted with evident discomfort. "I see a twig with a charcoal end. Please give it to me."

Bowmark did and bent to undo the ropes around the Southil's legs. "Your promise."

PledgeKept nodded, and when freed, shakily rose to sit on the boulder next to an almost flat surface on the rock. He brushed away dried leaves. "The Holy Books are written thusly." With charcoal, he traced a loopy lettered word.

"No surprise. That's our alphabet."

PledgeKept's grip on the stick snapped it in three. "No. Absolutely not. I spent five years learning your ugly language and alphabet."

"You know better than me what my alphabet is?"

"Here is Vanquish All in your alphabet." Now he traced straight lines at various angles and positions with dots near some of the joins.

Scolla waddled over. Bowmark set him on the boulder opposite PledgeKept.

"The Southils have misunderstood. That is merely a decorative design."

"Not possible. See. A design is a series of curves, or a series of circles. Or a series of alternating lines and circles, thusly. *This* is a word." PledgeKept's index finger stabbed the charcoal lines.

"I see how you came by your error." Bowmark touched the design. "This is carved on the pillars of our Temple. We employ more complex designs than you do.

PledgeKept tapped his stub of charcoal on the boulder while he thought. He pointed to the word of looped letters. "What is this?"

"Giver."

"In your language."

"Khortsoch."

PledgeKept paused. "We say Lee-ohben. Mmm. We have one alphabet and two languages. No. That works with pictographs. It wouldn't work for an alphabet." He rubbed the unhurt side of his face, smearing charcoal on it. "How can you read our books written in our language?"

"I don't read the books you call yours. Only the King and confirmed priests are allowed to read the Holy Books."

"Oh ho."

"Oh ho what? I have memorized the two books."

"How would you know?"

Bowmark clenched his jaw to keep from speaking in anger.

PledgeKept scrawled three more words on the rock. "Can you read these?"

Bowmark touched each word in turn. "Nonsense word, nonsense word, tresik, which in Common is 'rice'.

"Mmm. We read it as besal, tree. Maybe the only word we read the same is Giver. Maybe you should join the priesthood when you get back."

"Why? Oh. So I would have permission to read the Holy Books."

"If you can't read the writing, then you'll know they are written in South. You'll know they do belong to us. Then maybe you could persuade your leadership to return them."

His unease, already high, jumped. Bowmark crossed his arms and kneaded his biceps. He needed to dive into the clean sea and swim for ropes. "Pressing for that course of action could earn me an execution."

"By the Hand, but your people are bloodthirsty."

Bowmark hissed through tight teeth. "What happens to you if the Southils discover you met me, and you let me live?"

"Without discovering where you live? Without regaining our books?" PledgeKept lowered himself to the ground and leaned against the boulder. "Not good. My parents and teachers would wither in shame. I would never get another job at a wedding or festival. My intended would likely disintend me. Most Matriarch would take my flute away and give it to someone more worthy." He sighed, then looked up. "Unless you bring the Books to us. Then I would be a hero, the finder."

"My people want peace."

"You could have it. Return the Holy Books and free our children."

"How do I free what I don't have?"

"Unless you ate them on—"

"We don't eat people!"

"Then there should be descendants. You. You are obviously a Sea Predator with your red, curly hair and blueish eyes. I don't remember hearing about your shoulder tattoo, but everything else is what the histories say. Our children would appear like me; straight black hair and light brown eyes. You do have people like me in your midst, don't you?"

Bowmark ran.

PledgeKept stared at the quivering foliage left behind. "Where is he going?"

"Zzz zzz zzz. My guess is he will run five kilms, chop down a tree, and drag it back. Then he shall beg me to heat water for a bath." Scolla twisted the mechanism on his metal book to advance the paper strip and wrote rapidly. *Tick, tick, tick.* He returned his book to a bag dangling from the Mulig platform and glanced around. A moment later he picked a large leaf off a waxleaf bush and pieced several holes in it, then stuck an end through a twig, and drove the twig into the dirt near the smoldering campfire.

PledgeKept sagged against the boulder and closed his eyes.

"Up, human. I leave a note for Bowmark to meet us at Warble River."

"My head hurts."

"You need to wash. You reek."

"Of course, I reek. The Predator frightened me. May the Hand hold me, that Cutfish still frightens me. Two hundred years we search, and it must be me who finds him. Why me?"

"I do not enjoy your whimpering. Get on the mulig, and I shall give you more medicine." Scolla scattered the fire and gathered the cooking utensils.

PledgeKept stumbled to the mulig and mounted. "I can't believe I'm taking orders from a spitter. Buzzards, my head hurts. Ho, I could steal this mulig."

"Zzz. You could," whined Scolla directly behind PledgeKept, startling him. "The last three humans who tried ended up cinders."

"Cinders?" PledgeKept said weakly. "How did my ancestors ever drive his off? Do you think it would anger him if I ate more of his food?"

"No. He is stupidly—no, not that—recklessly generous. You will find boiled eggs and dried fruit in the red basket." Scolla pulled on the stake's rope until the stake popped out of the ground. "Point the mulig west. If you get sick, do not do it on me. I am going to sleep for the rest of the day. You have bothered me enough. Do not do so again." Scolla struggled to the platform since PledgeKept did not think to lift him to the structure, dragged a blanket over himself, and curled into a ball.

PledgeKept stuffed an egg into his mouth and mumbled around it, "If I live, this is going to be some song."

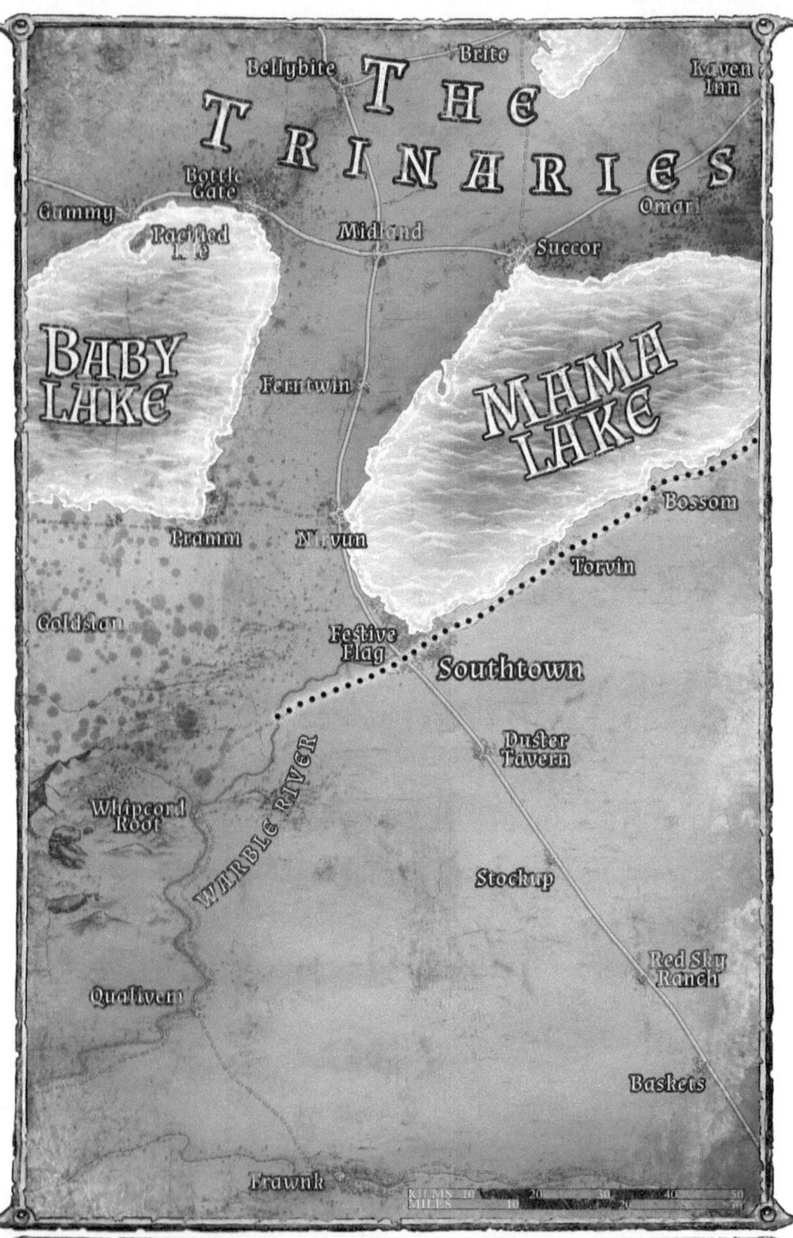

Bellybite
Brite
Raven Inn
THE TRINARIES
Bottle Gate
Omari
Gummy
Midland
Succor
Pacified L.
BABY LAKE
Ferntwin
MAMA LAKE
Bossom
Pramm
Nirvun
Torvin
Goldslan
Festive Flag
Southtown
Duster Tavern
Whipcord Root
WARBLE RIVER
Stockup
Red Sky Ranch
Qualivern
Baskets
Frawnk
KILMS
MILES

10 TARO LEAVES. 10 PORK BUTT CUBED TO THUMB WIDTH.
5 BLUE FLEET-FISH FILLETS. 1 PALM OF SALT.
SALT AND WRAP MEATS IN LEAVES AND TIE 5 BUNDLES.
STEAM FOR HALF A DAY.
~ STARSHINE'S RECIPE BOOK

Near sundown, Bowmark staggered into the camp under a huge load of dead branches.

PledgeKept jumped up from the blanket next to the mulig where he had been dozing. His left eye had swollen and turned purple, like the first time they met. "I fixed you a fish stew. I would have roasted them, but Scolla says you only eat boiled meat. Scolla gave me a fish from your stores. What did you use to cut down the tree?

Bowmark's sweat-and-dirt-streaked face turned toward the Southil. "What?"

"The tree. The branches. Did you use magic?"

Bowmark dropped the wood next to the main fire. "I used my teeth."

PledgeKept gaped and turned his eyes toward the sky.

"Don't they have jokes where you…" Bowmark trailed off, turned to follow the young man's gaze, and was struck silent by amazement. Near the horizon a whale swam. Or something like a whale. In the air. It was too far to see details. Both young men stood, saying nothing as the thing ponderously floated towards the west.

Scolla waddled up behind them and gingerly pulled a shade off one eye to observe. "This is glorious news."

Bowmark could not tear his gaze away until the thing was a spot on the horizon. "What *was* that?"

"That explains the earthquake. It must have been caused by a caveshroom collapse."

"A caveshroom?" Bowmark and PledgeKept repeated in unison.

"Yes, quite. It is a cave. A living cave. It creates the food for majismontem. They must populate their travel routes with these food sources because walking is very energy intensive for people of such magnitude. They must eat even more than you do."

Bowmark blinked rapidly as he tried to make sense of these statements.

"What does food for giants and caves have to do with flying whales? And HOW did that fly? I saw no wings."

"That was a zephyrean animal called a nisporean. Some call them sky whales despite the fact that they live underground in caveshrooms. If one is in the open air, it means a caveshroom has collapsed. That must have been the tremor we experienced. Zephyrean animals cannot live long outside a caveshroom. Though they are very difficult to study in their habitat, so this one will hopefully be found by quality researchers before it dies. As to how it flies, it is filled with thousands of pockets of a gas that is lighter than air."

"What is a gas?"

"Air is a gas."

PledgeKept jumped in, "What could be lighter than air?"

Scolla turned and waddled back to the mulig. "I don't have time for science lessons now. The nisporean was headed west, I need to alert the others. Maybe we will be lucky enough to find it."

The two young men looked at each other, still confused, full of questions that neither could answer, full of strange words neither of them could remember.

"So then," Bowmark finally broke the silence. "I'm tired of being filthy."

The Warble River gleamed under long streamers of sunlight and rippled darkly under the stretched shadow of a stone bridge. Bowmark waded through the young grasses and shallow water, and then dove. He came up splashing and shouting, "Cold! Cold!" Shivering, he stood, took off his clothes and swished them in the water. After wringing them out, he walked back to camp and laid them on a branch overhanging the second fire.

PledgeKept watched every move and hovered near with towels and gourds of warm water.

Bowmark opened a jar of soap and lathered himself. He tried to stay patient while he rinsed with water from a gourd and checked for ticks, stickims, and land leeches, but he finally said, "You're worse than my little brother. Move away so I can breathe my own air."

With alacrity, PledgeKept retreated to the mulig.

Bowmark dried, dressed, and rubbed aromatic oil on his hair.

PledgeKept called, "Might I use some of that oil?"

"Your scalp and hair don't need it," Bowmark said. He swiped at a trickle behind his ear, then began poking his crochet hook through his embarrassingly short dreadlocks.

"How do you know that, unless my people live with yours?"

Bowmark stopped. Slowly he lowered his hands, and then rubbed them clean on his arms. He dipped himself a bowl of fish stew. "They are *my* people. Some of us have red hair. Some of us have black. My duty is to protect both from *your* people. Cease pursuing us and there will be peace."

"We will, as soon as—"

"I know." Bowmark took a big swallow of the soup. "Gah! This is nasty!"

"I know."

"You didn't even cut up the fish."

"Scolla wouldn't let me have any knives." He swatted away a buzzer.

"So then. Let's see what we can do about this before it gets too dark."

PledgeKept followed Bowmark at a respectful distance to a bush bright orange with new leaves. Bowmark plucked buds and said, "These buds add a nice flavor. Never take more than a tenth so the plant can recover. This grass here," he pulled up a tuft, "has small bulbs. Take some twigs off this tree, peel off the bark, and the underside, these white fibers, will thicken the soup."

"How do you know all this?"

Bowmark rolled his eyes. "I ask questions."

"Must be nice to have someone to ask."

Dusk deepened. They returned to the fire, added the forage to the soup, set out smudge pots which stung the eyes but kept away the worst of the insects, and set up blankets and insect netting.

They squatted next to the fire to eat, resting on their heels. Bowmark watched the firelight play across the bruised face of the Southil and remembered when he and Sunrise would sit around such a fire and roast crustaceans. The smell of river was so different from the smell of ocean, and the smell of this smoke was also not the same, but the gleam in the golden eyes of the man across from him evoked memory after memory. He needed to think of something else. "Is your dractil rash feeling better?"

PledgeKept touched his face with broken fingernails. "Yes. Thank you."

"How did that happen?"

"I was following you and this dractil carrying a white bag of some sort, landed on the trail in front of me. I never heard of one carrying anything before, so I thought maybe it was the kind that trade with humans. I said "Hi." The putrid monster laid down its bag and attacked me."

"A bag? What was in it?"

"I don't know. After I killed the dractil, I was too busy trying to get those hairs off me to look. I remember. There was something like a cluster of hooks or claws on one spot. On the outside. And something like blisters. After that, all I remember is agony."

"No bag, that," whined Scolla behind him.

PledgeKept dropped his bowl as he wavered off-balance.

"That was an egg, ready to be attached."

"To what?" PledgeKept asked. He scooped up his bowl.

"The dractil scout must have been desperate to seek you as an incubator."

PledgeKept turned to Bowmark. "What is he talking about?"

"I'm not sure. I've seen their eggs attached to small animals and a tezledek. Scolla, I thought the dractils caught small prey—"

"Such as me," Scolla said.

"—and dragged them back to their tunnels. To take an egg out and then drag egg and incubator back does not make sense."

"Zzz." Scolla's ears flicked. "You have forgotten the dractils that escaped your slaughter."

Bowmark set down his dinner with deliberation. "I did not think—I have not—I thought—" He passed his hand down his face. "I have not been watching for dractils."

"Ssss!"

"Truth! I know!"

In the brittle pause, PledgeKept interrupted, "Would now be a bad time to talk about peace?"

Bowmark sighed. "It is easy enough to promise 'I will do this,' or 'I will do that,' but the current flows like this. I don't know if I will live long enough to return home. I don't know if I will have a chance to examine the Holy Books. If I got the chance, it would be at least five years after returning home. I don't know if you've told me the truth about them."

An unknown creature grunted nearby as Bowmark stood. "Only this can I promise you. My people want peace. If I live long enough to examine the Holy Books, and if I determine that they do belong to your people, then I shall do what is in my power to return them to you."

"And the children?"

Bowmark slapped an insect that had wobbled through the smudge smoke and landed on his neck. "When there is peace, and I know that you will not harm my people, then whoever thinks they belong to you may go anywhere they wish. My fear is this: since merely going home could take over a year, and getting to your island could take more years, and my access to the Holy Books would be at least five years after arriving home, how can I determine if your people become impatient? How do I keep Southils from attacking us while we consider the books?"

"That long a time?" PledgeKept scratched carefully around his stitches as he stared into the fire. Then excitement animated his gaunt face. "The Sea Predators have moved inland! You must have settled in South Akinda! No wonder we can't find you!" The animation was replaced by fear as he realized too late he had just said the stupidest thing he possibly could have.

In the cold silence, a log popped in the fire.

Bowmark saw an opportunity to misdirect the Southils. He whipped out a knife.

PledgeKept rose and stumbled back a step. He flung his arms out wide as Bowmark's knife slid under his chin and rested its point against his neck.

Bowmark stepped close and searched his eyes. "Give me a reason to let you live."

PledgeKept's breath and voice shook. "You want peace. You said you did. How will people know if I don't deliver that message? I won't—I swear I won't tell anyone where your people live. I swear!"

An evil memory tore at Bowmark as he said, "A man might promise anything with a knife at his throat. How do I know you will keep your oath?"

"You could take the knife away?"

Bowmark held his position.

PledgeKept gradually brought up his hands and eased his necklace over his head and onto Bowmark's wrist. He clasped the medallion and said tearfully, "May His Hand deliver me disaster, disease, and death if I betray your people to mine."

Bowmark waited until PledgeKept's fear dissolved into despair. He moved back. "I accept that." Now, even if PledgeKept was a lying snake, the Southils would search the wrong place in the world.

PledgeKept fiddled with the front of his shirt where the Giver's Hand medallion had lain. "I will tell my people that whoever carries that is safe to travel through our lands."

"You can do that?"

"The seeker can. But what can I take back as proof I found you, besides, besides scars? How will people believe me?" His gaze vacillated between Bowmark's eyes and his medallion.

Bowmark did not like this, but the Southil was making a reasonable request. He touched his Giver's Hand medallion and paused. He had worn his every day of his life since his adult name day, only taking the symbol of Giver off long enough to clean it, and on the day of proving. Reluctantly, he took his off and handed the medallion to PledgeKept. Together, they put on each other's Hand. There were differences: the Southil's was hand-shaped, Bowmark's oval, with the Hand covered by a dome of polished resin. The fingers were longer on the Southil's, and in the palm lay a black circle. Bowmark traced the circle with a fingertip. "What is this?"

"A hair from my intended. I glued it on before I began the search. When you come to Hovahill to give back my Hand, you can meet Starshine. She is beautiful, with a voice sweeter than any lizard's song. I will ask her to make clamcakes for you. They thrill the tongue so much you may never go home. What I would not give to have some now. Every night I think about all the good food she can make. I see her hands kneading the rice dough and pressing it flat to spread sweet root on it and then sprinkle on nuts and dried fruit and oil. She rolls it up and cuts it into thin slices."

As PledgeKept blathered, Bowmark rubbed the black circle with his fingertip. Would the hair were Moongleam's. The hollow ache within him gnawed on his stomach. Sunrise was dead, and Moongleam hated him.

Bowmark let go of the medallion. He needed again to think of something else, so he interrupted PledgeKept's recitation of recipes and said, "PledgeKept, you are a brave man seeking to serve your people. I admire that."

PledgeKept gulped, smiled weakly, and said in a breaking voice, "Tell that to my pants."

Bowmark remembered his little brother wetting his skirt. What was Spearmark doing now? Another surge of homesickness gripped his stomach.

Bowmark handed his jar of soap to the Southil. "The body does what it does. You lather here and I'll get you some water."

"You don't need to bother. I can bathe in the river if you'll allow it. Scolla told me not to until you came back."

"Fish don't like soap. Stay here."

A quarter candle later he brought back buckets of water and took hot stones from under the fire, dropping them into a large gourd to heat the water.

He then went to the mulig, wrapped himself in his blanket and lay against the warm beast. The smell of ginger told him the spitter was near. "Scolla? Why are you still here?"

"Watching you two humans is fascinating."

Bowmark said in Zledek, "Why didn't he run away, why? I gave him ample time."

"Any stray dog will follow the one who feeds him."

"He is not that."

"Without his knives and bow, he will die."

"Truth." He concentrated as he continued in Zledek. "Tomorrow we'll return cracks. Could you—"

"You meant 'them,' not 'cracks,' if indeed you meant his weapons."

Impatiently, Bowmark said, "Could you watch a little gangly to ensure he does not bash me toward the head, could you?"

"You meant 'longer' and 'on'."

"What did I say, what?"

"Amazing!" broke in PledgeKept as he walked toward them. "I had no idea there were so many ways to say 's' and 'sh'."

"You can hear the differences?" asked Bowmark.

"Of course. Can't you?" PledgeKept said.

Bowmark pulled the blanket over his head.

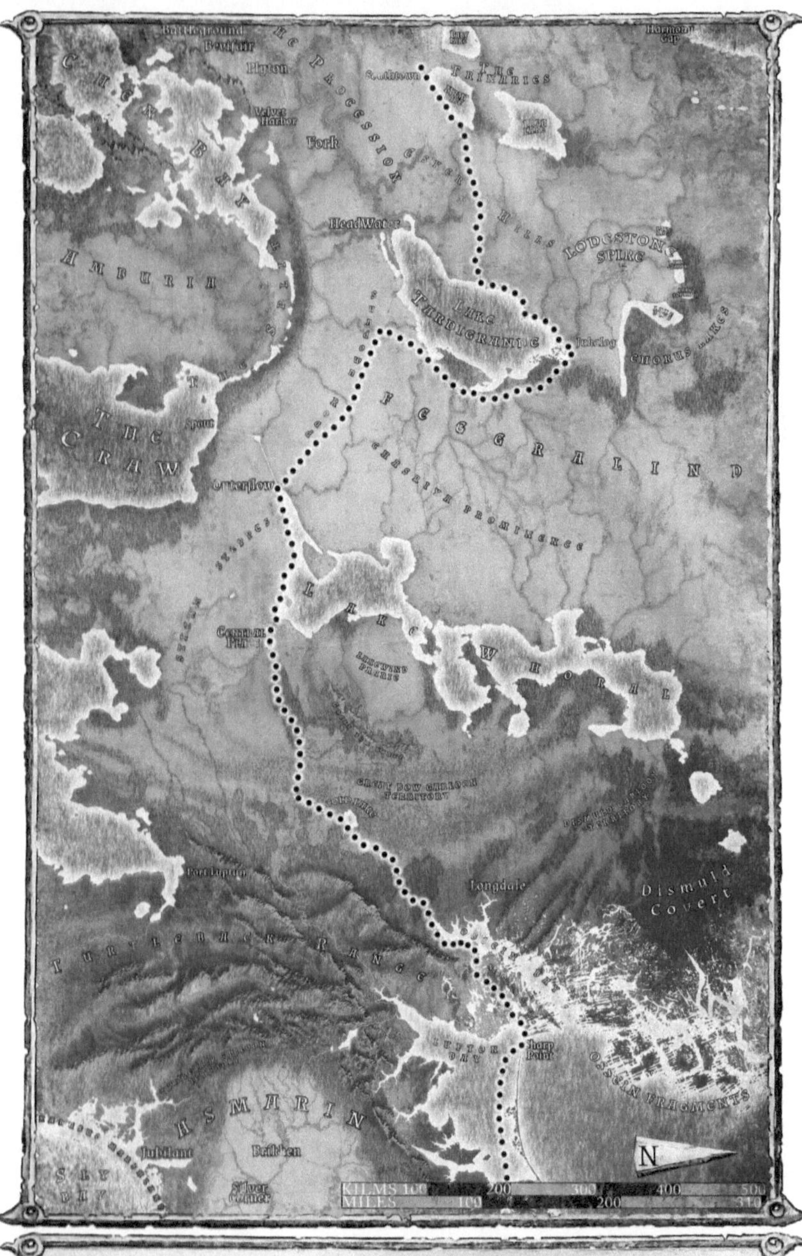

FROM ONE MOTHER TO THE NEXT,
WISDOM IS CONTINUALLY REBORN.

~ SOUTHILL PROVERB

16

In the still, cold night, Bowmark awoke with claws on his lips and Scolla whispering in his ear, "No move. No open eye." The awkward wording omitted any sibilants that might carry farther than his ear. Bowmark listened intently. Was PledgeKept up to something?

There were quiet footsteps, a spicy, musky odor, and a snort from something that was not the mulig.

Bowmark disobeyed and opened his eyes the merest crack. Beyond the huddled form of PledgeKept, the low fire barely illuminated an upright creature with brown feathery fur, long horns, and incredibly elongated legs and toes. Hands with two long, muscular fingers and a fat thumb held onto a stick as it bent to sniff around the fire. Padded three-toed feet stepped gently on the forest duff. Large, tufted ears swiveled this way and that. The creature turned its head to look at the travelers.

Bowmark forced himself to breathe deeply and slowly, as though he were still asleep, and he held that position even when it turned its head and appeared to be staring up into the canopy. The Atlas said garloons had excellent sight and hearing.

The garloon whuffed gently to itself and moved on.

When Scolla finally took his hand off his mouth, Bowmark whispered, "I thought you said garloons were friendly."

"Indeed, they are—in a group. Usually. A single one might be on a quest. Such a one will not suffer being seen. He will kill whoever looks upon him. If you should ever see a single one at a distance, you must develop a desperate itch that requires all your attention, or start reading a book. No, I misspoke. Do not read a book. They consider writing to be evil."

"Why?"

"They say that writing captures thought and kills it." Scolla crept to the high road near the bridge and looked around. Garloons should not be this close to a human settlement. The dractil invasion has thrown much planning into chaos."

"So." Bowmark yawned, then peered over at the sleeping Southil. "Scolla, were it not for you, I could easily be in his state, or worse. I see that I have not been properly grateful. I would say that I am sorry, but I know those words mean nothing to you. So I say this: Thank you. Thank you for guarding and guiding me."

"Zzz. Good." Scolla waddled into the darkness.

That morning as they were loading the mulig, Bowmark was astonished to see PledgeKept's face freeze in fear when Bowmark handed him his knives.

The Southil squeaked, "Now? But—I thought—why are we going to have a fair fight now?"

"You misunderstand. We are at peace. I am restoring your possessions."

PledgeKept sat abruptly. "Peace. Easy for you. I don't know if, thirty breaths from now or thirty hours, you might slide a knife into me. Have you ever had a knife indent your throat? Have you?"

"I have." That brought memories of RaiseHim and the protocol officer that heated Bowmark's ears.

"You have? What did you do?"

"Nothing I'm going to tell you." Bowmark clasped the Southil Giver's Hand medallion on his chest. "Be at peace, PledgeKept. Unless you attack me or my people, I shall never harm you again." He could almost see the fear drain out of PledgeKept. Was he a monster to have such an effect on PledgeKept?

The next day and a half was entertaining. Whenever PledgeKept wasn't eating or sleeping, he was talking, or singing, or playing his flute. While Bowmark did stretches and handstand pushups, PledgeKept told him the life history of everyone in Hovahill. When he told of his six-year-old cousin who glued soona bird feathers on his arms and then "flew" out of a tree to land on his grandfather who was carrying a bowl of fish guts to bury in the garden, Bowmark laughed so hard he lost his balance and almost fell off the mulig.

While Bowmark jogged around the plodding mulig, PledgeKept acted out fables. As Bowmark thrust his staff-shifter and paced through his forms, PledgeKept sang satirical fishing songs.

After nine candles of this, Bowmark increased his giving of food to PledgeKept so his ears could have some rest.

When they had stopped for supper and Bowmark was honing his knives, PledgeKept's eyes shone in the firelight. "From old we have been told that you choose your kings by having candidates fight over a pit of knives. Is that truth?"

"We don't do that anymore."

"Good. With the worship of the Giver, your people have become more civilized."

The smells of smoke and soup danced around them. "Now we fight over a river of lava. The loser falls in."

PledgeKept's mouth gaped. "Doesn't that seem to you to be a nasty way to pick a king?"

"It's supposed to be. That's why there are decades between provings." He saw again Sunrise, looking surprised, clutching Bowmark's spear through his heart. Hastily, Bowmark asked, "How do the Southils pick a king?"

PledgeKept tossed a twig into the fire. "We don't have one. Every woman over the age of sixty has a chance to be a matriarch. All the old women take one year turns as village matriarch. The village matriarchs get together and decide who will be the Southil most matriarch, also for a year.

"Every year you get a new most matriarch?"

"Truth. We don't need a lot of governing. Our lands are rich. Sometimes we need to repel pirate raids. If a typhoon destroys a village, then the most matriarch must organize the other villages into repair teams. That's about it."

"There are no taxes? No crime?"

"Wherever there are people, there are taxes and crime."

"What do the men do while the women manage everything?"

"We lie on the beach and suckle our babies. What do you think we do? Some fish, some farm, some build."

"Some never stop talking."

"That's my job. I shall be invited everywhere to tell of how I met you. I've been thinking about what sort of song to write about you. And Scolla. Do you think he will let me learn Zledek? I want to surprise my household spitters. What kind of songs do they have? Do you know?"

"No."

PledgeKept slapped his sunken stomach. "I'm still hungry. May I—"

"Please."

That night Scolla complained that Bowmark should have killed PledgeKept because then he would have had a better day's rest. PledgeKept could not go to sleep and wanted to talk all night. Bowmark began to pity Starshine. He wrapped his head with a towel and snored through PledgeKept's ghost stories.

The following morning Bowmark fed and groomed the mulig in blessed silence, letting PledgeKept sleep in. After breakfast, PledgeKept brought out his flute, hesitated, and said, "Would you sing the *Come Play with Me* song in your language?"

Bowmark looked up from scouring the kettle and complied.

He had sung only two lines when PledgeKept clapped his hands over his ears. "Stop! Stop!"

"I didn't know I sang so badly." Ha! Who would say that to a king's son?

"Your voice is fine. Untrained, but fine. The language is the problem. I assumed Predator couldn't be sung. You proved me wrong. It can be sung, but it shouldn't be. Your language is made for chanting." PledgeKept chanted in archaic Predator:

We will rape you,

We will raze you,

We will kill you,

We will eat you.

"You stop. I've never heard anything like that."

"It's what your ancestors chanted as they raided our villages."

"Your matriarchs are lying to you."

PledgeKept thrust his flute into his pack and gathered things to put on the mulig. "I wish I could see your history books."

"We don't have any. We memorize our history."

PledgeKept frowned. "Without a reference to check against, how do you know you're memorizing correctly?"

"The historian listens to us recite."

"No. How do you know he has it correct?"

Bowmark loaded the cooking supplies. "One can lie on paper."

"Truth. But if there are many copies to contradict one man's version, you can have a better idea which version is correct." He gazed at a lizard gliding from one branch to another. "Do your people have poetry?"

"Of course."

"When you come to Hovahill, would you bring a poetry book for me?"

"We have no books of poetry."

PledgeKept's jaw dropped. "What books do you have?"

"The two Holy Books, the Protocol, the dictionary, and the king's records." He did not mention the Atlas they had kept temporarily.

Scolla peeped out from under his blanket and whined, "How many copies of each are there, how many?"

Bowmark waved a fly away from his face. "We have no copies. That's why we treat our books so carefully."

"No copies," echoed PledgeKept. He stood speechless while Bowmark tightened the straps. Finally, he burst out, "Five books for all of you? Only five?"

Bowmark mounted and held out his hand to help PledgeKept onto the mulig.

Once seated, PledgeKept said, "My people will not consider anyone an adult until they have written their own copy of the Holy Books. We have thousands upon thousands of the Holy Books."

Bowmark turned around to face the Southil. "Doesn't that make the Holy Books common?"

"They are supposed to be."

"That seems disrespectful."

"No. That shows the utmost respect."

Bowmark rotated to face the mulig's head and urged it onto the road. Commoners would like things to be common. Common rulers. Common books. "If you have thousands, why do you insist on taking the only ones we have?"

"Because *those* are the ones written by the hands of our Holy People that you raped and killed! Why can't you copy them and give us the originals?"

Bowmark snapped, "I have told you what I will attempt!"

PledgeKept ducked his head and fingered his flute. They traveled the rest of the morning and afternoon in silence.

As dusk dimmed the road, dull thunder rumbled in the distance, a harbinger of another downpour. Bowmark stood and surveyed the plain they were crossing. Nothing larger than small scrub brush as far as he could see in the twilight. No. There—just on the horizon to the southwest of the road— was a low stone outcropping. Perhaps they could shelter there. He clicked his tongue and tapped the mulig on its left shoulder. The beast adjusted her heading without complaint. Occasional drops became a torrent as they reached the rock formation, now a dark outline against a dark gray sky completely covered with clouds trailing vertical walls of rain.

Bowmark leaped down, jogged to the side of the mulig platform and pulled a handful of firewood from a net. "PledgeKept, there are stakes on the other side. Hammer one into the ground and lash the reins to it." PledgeKept fumbled through the stowage. The noise and jostling roused Scolla who waddled over and directed the clueless young man.

Large, cold drops fell, splashing on Bowmark's head and shoulders as he kindled a fire between the mulig and the rocks. The stone wall did not overhang the fire, so Bowmark pulled a blanket from the side of the mulig platform, tied one side to the platform, and staked the other side into the ground near the fire. The slanted shelter would be cramped, but still larger than the mulig platform. Both men could wait out the rain and gain some warmth from the fire.

PledgeKept joined him under the shelter just as the rain became a torrent. The fire sputtered. Bowmark sighed. "We will suffer either cold or smoke. Which do you prefer?"

PledgeKept stammered as if the question were a test. "I, I, whatever you wish."

Every day cold or colder. Bowmark pulled a walking stick from the stowage and propped up a corner of the blanket to protect the fire. Laying back to avoid inhaling the smoke, Bowmark studied the stone wall which was carved with intricate maze-like patterns over the whole sandy-colored surface. "Hey Scolla! Is this more garloon art?"

Scolla, still on the mulig platform, made a non-committal buzzing sound. Clearly he did not want to venture from his dry nest of blankets and nets.

The wind shifted, blowing the rain through the back of their shelter and kicking a burst of embers from the fire. One ember stuck to the rock wall, and rather than winking out like the rest, swelled like a crab newly emerged from its carapace. Bowmark leaned as close as he could without leaving the shelter to gaze at the odd sight.

POP!

Bowmark's head jerked back. A fist-sized chunk of the wall exploded outward, like a bubble of sap on log. A small gush of orange flame shot out of the rock and dissipated, leaving behind a vile smell. PledgeKept bolted upright. "Did you catch the stone on fire?"

Several glowing lines radiating from the pockmark slowly tracing paths through the carvings. As one line faded another swelled. Dread seized Bowmark. "Scolla! We need your advice."

Scolla unrolled and emerged from the platform shelter, his large copper eyes reflecting the firelight. As he surveyed the scene his eyes got even bigger. "What have you done, what?" he screamed.

"We're leaving now." Bowmark yanked the blanket shelter, tearing it free from the stakes, and tossed it onto the mulig platform.

POP! POP!

"You have doomed us!" Scolla wailed.

Bowmark fumbled with the wet reins trying to unleash the twitching mulig. More and more fiery lines traced the popping rock wall.

POP! A chunk of rock whizzed by his face. Then another piece hit his leg with a stinging smack. It felt like he had been hit with a fish, not stone. No time for fumbling. Bowmark whipped a knife through the reins and pulled the mulig away from the rock face that was now spotted with gaping holes and glowing patterns. PledgeKept had mounted the bench, so Bowmark tossed the shortened reins to him, slapped the mulig's flank, urging her to speed, and jogged beside the mount.

Scolla frantically pulled the baggage over himself. "Out of all the millions of kilms of empty prairie on Akinda, only *you* would find a nisporean carcass and then ignite it!"

"Nisporean? The, the sky whale thing? Full of explosive gas?"

Though they were now half a rope from the carcass, the popping was only growing louder. Bowmark ventured a glance over his shoulder. Gouts of fire shot out of the lumpy form in multiple directions, clearly illuminating the carcass of the sky whale they had seen two days earlier. Then a chunk the size of a mulig exploded half the whale's head into a fireball and a heavy pelting of rubbery chunks joined the rain.

POP! POP! BOOOOM!

A force like an ocean wave threw Bowmark face down into the wet grass. The shelter on the mulig platform blew away along with several sacks and baskets. PledgeKept collided with the mulig's neck, and the beast stumbled forward.

Bowmark groaned as he regained shaky footing. The mulig had sprinted ahead. Behind, a few small fires winked out in the rain amid piles of destroyed carcass. The putrid odor made his nose and throat hurt.

Perhaps the worst was over. Bowmark hobbled, walked, jogged—and when he felt confident enough in his legs—ran to catch up. He tripped over a bag in the dark, and plowed into the mulig.

She had stopped running, though her legs and ears still twitched. PledgeKept dug through the pile of upset supplies on the platform between bouts of gagging. As Bowmark approached. he breathed a sigh of relief to see the dim outline of Scolla unrolling from the detritus. Scolla's makeshift barrier had protected him.

They faced a long, cold, wet night, hunting down their lost supplies in the dark and salvaging what they could. Why did anyone live here where whales exploded? Bowmark's teeth clenched. "So then."

After a blessedly uneventful day and a half they arrived at a goatish master's stables on a sunny afternoon. Several corrals cloistered around a low log cabin with a sod roof. Bowmark felt sorry that he would say goodbye so soon to a man he wanted to call friend. He had learned so much. Some comforting. Some confusing. And much of it disturbing. But PledgeKept's sincerity was evident.

Following Scolla's prior instructions, he spoke slowly to the mountainfolk. He had not seen a mountainfolk before, a human all covered with fur and wearing only an embroidered leather breechcloth. Shorter even than the worm-colored men of this land, yet he was thicker in the limbs. Dark gray fur did not obscure the keen, blue eyes of the trader. Bowmark learned there was no negotiation, for he charged the same fair price to all for renting a goatish. "I need to travel mountainward. My friend here needs a way to the coast. I thought I might trade my mulig for two goatishes."

"Nae, ye may not," rumbled the barrel-chested man. "I have just rented me whole lot to a group of mazies seeking new veins of coal. Ye may speak to the caretaker left behind, but I doubt me he'll be selling."

Bowmark scratched his chin. "Well, I'm told we can't take our mulig over the mountain paths, so I suppose PledgeKept can take her south to the sea. I'll see if I can bargain with this rumsha caretaker."

"He's 'round the side." The mountain man gestured to a crooked log fence that enclosed some of the surrounding evergreen trees and several more animals. Leaving the goatish master, Bowmark walked to n outside rumsha who was brushing one of the four-legged, brown and tan goatishes. Tall and gangly, the animal had a single horn in the center of its large forehead.

PledgeKept walked stiffly behind, eating pemmican.

Bowmark bent to be eye to eye with the rumsha and pitched his voice low, "Good day to you, friend caretaker." He blew gently toward the rumsha's nose.

"Hoo." The rumsha sounded pleased. He straightened his orange, silver, and dark-green vest and flapped his ears, jingling bells. "Good day, friend human." He snuffed. "You have a desire."

"Quite yes. Yonder store has provisions I am allowed to buy for this human here who must go to the coast. He is taking my mulig, but I am in need of a goatish as I travel towards the mountains. Might I buy one of your goatishes?"

"Hoo. This grieves me, friend, for I cannot help you. Each of these already has a rider."

"I am willing to give you enough gold to buy two goatishes from the next caravan."

"No, I cannot."

Bowmark pulled out a bag and everted it into his hand. "Gold is heavy. These gems are light."

The rumsha's eyes widened. His thick claw pushed aside the gems to reveal the Gold Die. "You call me friend, and yet you seek to dishonor me. Take the goatish of your choice. What a fine joke on the one who walks home."

"No. I don't want to cheat you."

"Will you cheat me of honor? You pick the goatish. I will gather provisions that a human may eat. That human must eat much, else he blows off your mulig. Hoom." He turned and darted into a tent on the other side of the fence.

Embarrassed, Bowmark turned to PledgeKept. "As soon as you reach the coast, you give the mulig to the first rumsha you meet. Do you have enough money for passage home?"

PledgeKept swallowed the last of the pemmican. "Once I find a seafolk, I don't need any money. They know my people will pay them whatever they ask when they return the seeker. But I think I'll stay at the lodging here for the night. I'm not the unstoppable warrior that you are. I need to recover from things like exploding whales."

They both chuckled, then worked in silence to unload the supplies that Bowmark and Scolla would take with them. Scolla's eggs, Bowmark's weapons, a sleeping roll, pan, and medicines. Having only one water gourd and little food, Bowmark purchased additional supplies from the goatish master. He placed these in a strong chest that had remained intact after the explosion. Turning to PledgeKept, he grasped the young man's forearms.

"PledgeKept, I hope you get safely home."

The Southil smiled. With his swelling and bruising abated, he seemed like a completely different person from the attacker Bowmark had tied up not so long ago. "We agree on something." Then he pleaded. "Please, make me a hero."

Bowmark glanced away. "I cannot promise to succeed."

PledgeKept held the Giver's Hand. "Now I know that not all Sea Predators are rapists and child-eaters. I thank you for that knowledge."

Not knowing how to respond to that, Bowmark nodded toward the goatish enclosure. "Looks like I need to learn to ride one of these things now." He walked away as one emotion after another wrestled within.

He needed stirrups to get atop the long-legged goatish. This animal had four shaggy legs with split hooves, and a bad odor. It grumbled and blinked both the clear and the furred sets of eyelids. Its prehensile tail curled as it began a swaying walk that reminded Bowmark of a choppy sea. The goatish master gave him pointers on controlling the animal and advice on food to avoid. PledgeKept sat in the shade of tree and shouted encouragement.

The goatish master chuckled when he saw the pile of luggage Bowmark planned to take. "Ye'll be wanting the passenger saddle if ye want to take all that. Plus yer spitter."

Bowmark noted the mountainfolk's lack of disdain at the last comment. "Yes, a larger saddle would be very helpful, thank you."

The goatish master nodded, ducked into a shed, and moments later returned, hefting a sprawling padded saddle almost as long as the man himself. The dark leather saddle had a carved wooden back section that reminded Bowmark of a shallow dugout canoe. The bag of eggs and Scolla would fit comfortably back there. Additional saddle bags stowed foodstuffs for himself and for trade, camping gear, the treasure collection, medicine and his torn blue shirt.

It took the goatish master and Bowmark half a candle to get the bulky saddle and bags securely strapped and loaded on the unhappy beast. To both men's surprise Scolla effortlessly scrambled up the goatish's haunches and settled into the stowage.

PledgeKept approached them. "I pray the Giver speeds you and protects you." His words were a variation of a commoner blessing that Bowmark was familiar with.

He wanted to reply with grace, but awkwardly said, "I need to leave now." He felt too many emotions to know what to do with them. Part of his mind screamed, "Traitor!" while another part worried that PledgeKept would be hurt or killed on the journey. One part was glad the noise, noise, noise would go away. Another part was sorry not to hear any more tales of the folk of Hovahill, who were no different from the people of StoneShell. It had been good to have a friend again. He mounted the goatish.

"Well, then I guess ye'r all set." The gruff mountainfolk rubbed the goatish's neck with his furry hands. "Keep'em safe. Been seeing more dractils about recently."

Bowmark nodded to the goatish keeper, then looked down at PledgeKept. "Do you have a song of farewell?"

PledgeKept's eyes lit up, and the flute was brought to his lips with effortless grace.

Bowmark gently dug his heels into the goatish's flanks and the steed set off towards the mountains in the west.

Behind them floated the sweet notes of a bone flute.

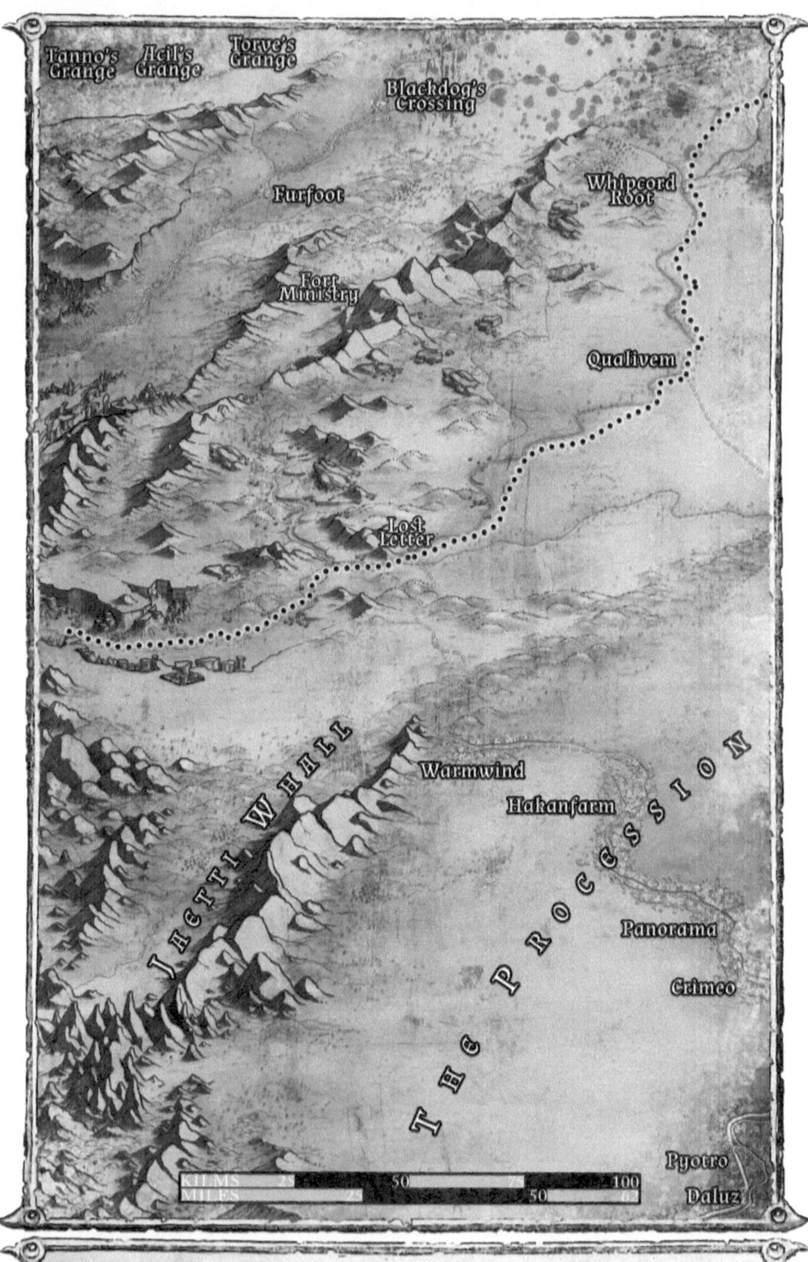

SEMI-DOMESTICATED, GOATISH DISPLAY STARTLING
DEXTERITY, SPEED AND GRACE,
EXCEPT WHEN REQUIRED BY THE RIDER.

~ SEAFOLK ATLAS

"This is a path?" The goatish Bowmark rode on stepped from one tumbled boulder to another. It had taken only one day of travel for Bowmark to come to love the sweet-tempered mulig he had left behind and to hate the easily irritated goatish. The animal had definite ideas about how the reins should be held, and when Bowmark deviated in the slightest, the goatish would arch its head around trying to whack Bowmark with its long horn or bite him with its flat grass-grinding teeth. The goatish's only saving grace was the ability to leap over terrain that would have trapped the mulig, and to scale steep hills with incredible speed. Bowmark glanced back at the spitter, rolled into his black-bag shape on the extended back end of the saddle. Semi-rigid rods held the boxy rear in place but allowed the structure to bend and bounce slightly as the goatish tilted forward and back. Bowmark had no such luxury. He had to strain in every direction as the animal jumped, pivoted, stopped suddenly, and leapt again. Bowmark's lower muscles and core were burning with the effort after the first day.

Muffled by a blanket draped over half of him, Scolla whined, "This smells right."

"How can you tell? All I can smell is goatish. Gah."

"We mark paths with a pungent odor. Do not bother me until we reach the limestone karst."

"The what?" Bowmark gritted his teeth. He had asked without thinking. Now he would have to endure a long lecture on geology and how smart spitters—or, rather—tezledeks— were and how stupid humans were. He rubbed the last of the peeling scab from the shallow arrow score across his chest.

When no lecture came, Bowmark relaxed and wondered what the humans appeared like at this school he was going to. His ancestors had decreed that Bowmark would have curly red hair only on his scalp and brows, and that he would be unable to consume fermented food or drink. His copper brown skin would have a sheen no other humans had. Other peoples' ancestors had decreed that they would have hair on their faces and, strangely, in their armpits. What kind of person would make that decision?

What kind of ancestors did Scolla have who would have decreed that he should have a tube tongue, triangular teeth, divided ears like bat wings he could wrap over his huge copper eyes, arms that hung nearly to the ground, and the ability to extrude rope from his divided palms? He had too many features for one creature. Perhaps his ancestors had been two types of people that merged to make tezledeks. They might have been fools, too, to grant to their descendants such stubby legs and no ability to swim despite their ability to swell up with air like a puffer fish. Bowmark smirked. Scolla had assured him that swelling meant only they sank more slowly.

After rubbing his chest, Bowmark kneaded his stomach. His abdominal muscles twinged occasionally. His thighs and buttocks alternated pain and numbness. Did Scolla have similar muscle fatigue?

Someone screamed. Scolla erupted from his wrappings. "Weapons! Go!"

"Where?" Bowmark pulled on the reins and looked back. The goatish curvetted angrily.

Scolla pointed left. "Hurry!"

The scream had cut off suddenly, and because of echoes, Bowmark did not know precisely where the scream had come from.

"Go!" squealed Scolla.

Bowmark punched the goatish on the muzzle—before the animal bit his knee—and urged it to the left. The goatish leaped with uncanny accuracy from rock to rock into a grove of drop trees. The animal scooted under every low branch as if trying to dislodge Bowmark. Dead leaves and twigs shot up from the flashing hooves. Bowmark clung to the saddle handle with his free hand and tried to see through the leaves slapping his face.

"There!"

Bowmark pulled hard on the reins. The goatish slid to a stop. Bowmark almost went over its head, but his shoulder caught on the beast's single horn. He grabbed his metal staff-shifter the same moment he saw the stick-insect-like dractil on the ground. The staffshifter flicked to full length and flexed the metal snake fists at both ends in response to Bowmark's anger. He jumped off the goatish and threw the elongated staffshifter with a single, sharp claw erect like a javelin. The goatish nipped his ankle while his back was turned.

Bowmark snatched his arrows and ducked behind a small, twisted tree. The staffshifter struck where the dractil's neck joined the chest and crushed the monster against a boulder. An arrow through the head finished the job. He backed away before the dractil's cast-off poisonous hairs reached him. The goatish glared at him, and he glared back.

Where was Scolla?

When the poisonous, orange hairs had settled to the ground, Bowmark looked around the tree. Scolla bent over something black near the dead dractil, ignoring the few orange hairs stuck in his black hide.

Bowmark yanked his staffshifter from the remnants of the dractil's body, and the snake claws curled back into fists. He wiped ichor and hair off it with a large, pale green leaf and crouched beside Scolla. The dractil egg had sunk its claws into the abdomen of another spitter. *Giver! Eggs with claws! Why? Why did You give us that?*

Scolla rubbed his shoulders and rocked from side to side. When Bowmark, remembering that shoulder rubbing indicated indecision, reached for the other spitter, Scolla snapped, "Don't touch her! Give me the smallest, sharpest knife you have."

Bowmark hesitated. The sharpest would be the obsidian; the smallest would be the steel alloy. He pulled the small steel knife from a seam in his boot. "Do you want me to pluck the hairs from your skin?"

"Later. Get a towel, get two, and tear one into strips."

The goatish sidled away from Bowmark. He grabbed the reins and jerked the beast's head over until he could glare into one ochre eye from a thumb-width away. "You vex me one more time, and you're goatish stew!"

Did the beast understand? The animal stood still as Bowmark searched the camp bag for the towels. Ah, His ruined blue shirt could be put to use. He quickly tore it into strips.

When he returned, Scolla had turned the downed spitter onto her side. He slit the egg. Clear fluid gushed out. The tiny embryo inside twitched.

"Won't she bleed to death?"

"The egg has not had time to grow into her veins. Do not bother me." Scolla sliced away the rest of the egg from its claws. He shook egg goo from his hands. "Lay down a blanket and lift her onto it. Fetch my bag of medicines."

Where in this rocky tumble would Bowmark find a flat place to lay her? Of course, where the goatish was standing. Shoving persuaded the beast to move elsewhere, and then he draped a blanket over the flat-topped boulder. The spitter weighed less than Bowmark's little brother Spearmark. Bowmark fearfully but easily raised her and laid her beside Scolla's bag of medicines.

Scolla smeared painkiller paste on the knife and around each claw's puckered penetration area. He whined in Zledek, "This is sad, sweet one, but I cannot simply pull these claws out. They have barbs that would tear you to shreds. Better is a clean cut that I can stitch."

"You don't have much thread after stitching PledgeKept."

"Sss! Unravel your old bandages."

Bowmark pulled out threads from a strip and laid them beside the curved needle on the blanket.

"Have courage, beautiful one." Scolla cut swiftly. He pulled out the claws and threw them against a boulder.

Bowmark held strips of his torn shirt against the bleeding wounds as Scolla stitched them one by one. Then Scolla rubbed a variety of salves on the stitches. He ordered Bowmark to wash her carefully while he pulled some of the hairs from his skin. When all that was done, they secured her to the saddle box with spitter-extruded rope and gently covered her with Bowmark's clean blanket. With the camp supply bag, medicine pouch, egg bag, Scolla, and now an unconscious tezledek, the saddle would be so full that Bowmark would need to wear his backpack and the bag with foodstuffs they brought for trade in front of him, which would make dealing with the stubborn goatish even more difficult as they rode.

As they were reshuffling the stowage Bowmark asked in a low voice. "What happens with her now?"

"Zzz. That depends on how much paralyzing toxin has been injected into her, and our care of her. Zzz. I'll need to keep her fed so she won't starve to death. We need to keep her clean, shift her position several times a day, and exercise her limbs."

Bowmark pointed at the dractil hairs still stuck in Scolla. "Is your liver going to swell up now?" With huge copper-colored eyes, who would know if his eyes turned yellow?

"I may feel ill for a day. My needs are nothing compared to hers."

Bowmark prodded the goatish's sides and they began moving down the ravine again.

"Are you a teacher of medicine to know all this?"

"I teach reading and history to little ones. I prepared myself to move to a land where we would have no doctors." Scolla gingerly picked the remaining hairs from his arm and belly.

"Um, Scolla. Can I ask a stupid question?"

"You generally do."

Bowmark clenched his teeth a moment before taking a slow breath. "How can you discern she's female?"

"Zzz zzz zzz. She looks like one."

"She looks like you."

"Sss. Pay attention. Our heat patterns are completely different."

Bowmark fumbled with the bag of foodstuffs trying to keep it balanced as the goatish bounded up a small rock formation. "So then. What is a heat pattern?"

Scolla pointed with a bronze-colored claw to various points on his wrinkled, blue-black skin. "You can see that I am warmer here and here than I am there and there."

Bowmark twisted to see what Scolla was pointing at. "You appear black to me. I do not see variations of heat, only some iridescent blue and purple on your... smooth skin. Your bumpy skin looks almost completely black to me."

"Sszz. It has been so speculated. That would explain your night blindness as well as how you could not tell a nisporean from a rock." Scolla turned around to show his back. His head swiveled almost all the way around, pulling his saggy skin taut around the neck that was usually not visible. His arms were so long that he easily traced places on his back. "Also, I have manly stripes; whereas she has interrupted stripes, lines of spots. Beautiful spots."

"All I see is black and maybe some iridescent purple. And wrinkles. And little spikes."

"So you cannot see the color ulavi. Bad eyes, bad nose, bad ears, no claws, dull teeth, not large enough to best a garloon or rumsha, not small enough to hide effectively—how is it that humans have survived, how?"

"Guess we're too stupid to know we should die from that. I'm ready to go. Is there anything else we need to do?"

"I did not say you were stupid."

"Truth. You merely thought it very loudly." Bowmark hoisted the food bag as it threatened to slide away again. "This won't work. We need to leave something behind. Which of these foods is largest and least valuable for trade?"

"Zz, if they have messenger flies, they will want the honey. Keep as much of the fine flour as you can, and some dried fruit. We can dump the bread loaves and pears. Though because you have an insatiable appetite I think you should simply eat the rest."

"Now that you speak of it, I *am* hungry." Bowmark had a pleasant afternoon and evening reducing the size of the foodstuff bag until it could be jammed into his bulging backpack.

WE SHALL BE THE FULCRUM UPON WHICH THE MEGOLOTHI EMPIRE WILL HELPLESSLY TWIST BEFORE CRUMBLING AT OUR FEET.

~ THE GATHERING RECRUITMENT PAMPHLET

The next morning their path skirted another long lake.
The land twisted itself into pinnacles, caves, towers, cenotes,
ravines and ridges made of a light stone riddled with cracks
and round holes. In places, water could be heard running
underground. Wiry vines crept over and through the stone.
Bugs the size of Bowmark's palm scuttled into crevices as
they passed. He asked again, "Are you certain these rocks
haven't been carved by anyone?"

Scolla had finished exercising the limbs of the paralyzed
spitter, laid her in a new position, and draped a blanket over
her. "Carved, yes. By water, wind and time."

Bowmark gaped at a stone the size of a mulig precariously
perched on a thin column of lighter-colored rock. Stoneshell
had some rock formations that resembled faces, and there
were three arches scattered along the coasts. But nothing like
these hundreds or thousands of pillars with balanced rocks
on top. "I see no water, and I have never seen wind strong

enough to scratch stone, let alone place a giant boulder on top of a pillar."

Scolla sighed as he sat back, leaning against Bowmark's backpack, apparently unwilling to explain.

Bowmark glanced up at wavy rows of thin white clouds. "If you don't get some sleep, you're going to fall on your head and break it."

"Szz. She requires constant care lest fluid fill her lungs and drown her, lest her muscles wither to such flaccidity that they cannot work even after the toxin wears off, lest ulcers eat into her skin, lest she starve or dehydrate to death, lest deathwhim steal her spirit."

"I understand that. I also worry about you. Why don't you leave her with some local sp—cleaners?"

"Leave her with ignorant ferals, leave her? I am not so cruel."

The goatish swerved around a tangled bush covered with stinging insects that protected the plant in exchange for exuded sap globules. Scolla jerked to the side, but the female was held securely by strands.

"If she's paralyzed, how do you feed her?"

"You do not want to know. Zhh."

It took less than a heartbeat for Bowmark to form a mental image he wished he hadn't. "That's so. I wonder what she was doing out in the day."

"Tch. Tch. A mystery. My guess is this: Since she appears not a season over twenty-five, she may have left a city far from human transport on her age migration. At sunrise she could not find a safe crevice or tunnel and kept searching for a safe spot. She did not succeed."

"Ah, like when you jumped on the cheese wagon. Do all of you do that?"

"No." Scolla wrapped himself with spitter string and then attached himself to the wooden saddle. A few moments later, his small buzz vibrated in the hot, still air.

Bowmark resisted the urge to pat him affectionately as he would have his little brother. Although Scolla had long ago given up resistance to being touched while Bowmark assisted him, he still fussed about Bowmark's friendly touches. But then, Scolla fussed about everything. These were the moments when Bowmark would catch himself thinking of him as a kratchnak, the monster that ate bad children.

A day later they followed a meandering river that Scolla claimed had dug the canyon they were in. The canyon was many kilms wider than the river, so this made little sense to Bowmark. He could not decide what information Scolla gave him should be trusted. What was simply tezledek mythology? Scolla's advice about day-to-day survival had all been correct so far, but Bowmark could not forget his preposterous claim that tezledeks secretly ruled the world. His thoughts were interrupted by Scolla's whine. "Sometime today you will see a waterfall pouring out of a cliff wall. Wake me then. We must find the secret path at that point."

"Very well." How did water flow through rocks in this strange land that Sunrise would have loved to see?

Bowmark tried to push that thought away by focusing on the enjoyable heat and sunlight on his skin. He liked wearing his skirt again instead of all the wrappings the people of this continent wore. The Sea Predators generally wore only skirts. The women often added tunics, but the men wore tunics only for ceremonies. The people here wore underclothes and overclothes with sleeves for arms and legs and clunky boots and socks to keep the boots from rubbing their feet raw. Why would people inhabit a land so often cold that it required so much clothing?

The goatish was finally doing, usually, what it was told to do. The smell of hot stone and aromatic plant oils suffused the quiet air.

Following the canyon wall, they entered a shadowed, narrow defile. The vertical, rough walls undulated into a tighter pass, and then fell away on the left into a rough circle. Stone slabs the size of houses tilted against the walls of the circle and on the flat ground. Shadows under the slabs darkened the shapes of goatishes underneath chewing languidly with eyes half-closed.

His goatish sniffed and suddenly turned into the circle. The beast walked straight to a basin of lukewarm water. The smells of dust and stone, manure and beasts filled the hollow.

Why are there no caretakers here? Then Bowmark saw someone's bare feet protruding from a dark crevice in the surrounding wall of light stone. They shifted slightly.

"Can this be the Gathering?" Bowmark murmured.

"Zzz." Scolla's head wobbled. "No. Zzz. The Gathering live on a pillar. Keep going."

Bowmark twisted around. "A pillar?"

"Offer them food instead of your gems or money. Some of the humans there have killed or damaged other humans to steal their gems."

"Oh right. I almost forgot you're leading me to a gang of robbers." Bowmark wrapped his arm around his stomach. He still had the ring safely wrapped in a rumsha bag. If he was kicked again, should he offer the robber the ring?

The spitter had returned to sleep. Bowmark let the goatish drink until its belly swelled, then urged it back to the trail.

A candle and a half later Bowmark saw a small trickle of water running out of a hand-sized hole and down the rock wall just off the path. He pulled back on the reins and gently jostled Scolla.

"Could this be the waterfall?"

Scolla unrolled and surveyed the area, swiveling his head at angles that would break a human neck. "Do you see an orange cloth, do you?"

Bowmark examined the rock walls, scrub brush, gravel and the rivulet that dampened the path. "No."

"Keep going." Scolla whined.

Following the undulating wall for a while longer led them to a true waterfall. It issued from a hole that was bigger than Bowmark and had hollowed out a bowl of tumbled boulders where it hit the river below. The path turned sharply to follow the river to the left and eastward. On the right, the rock wall was crisscrossed with small ledges at steep angles. Bowmark could easily climb the wall but he ould see no way for a fully loaded goatish to do so. There, twenty strides up, was a thin strip of orange cloth tied around the base of a scraggly bush that tenaciously clung to the rock. Bowmark stood as high as he could in the saddle and strained to see an alternate path.

Scolla's voice startled him. "We must ascend, we must."

Bowmark's heart sank. "It's too steep. Maybe if we unhook the saddle then the goatish might be able make it, and if we had rope I could pull the saddle up. But we don't have a rope that long... unless your extruded string could... no, that's way too far."

Scolla rocked from side to side, rubbing his shoulders. He looked up, up the hundred strides to the top, down to the unconscious tezledek female, up the cliff, back to her. Finally he asked, "Can you climb that with the saddle tied to your back, can you?"

A pit was forming in Bowmark's stomach. "Maybe. But what about the goatish? I don't think it will wait for us if we let it free."

Scolla's breathing intensified and turned to a whining buzz. Then he stopped rocking and said, "I will ride the goatish. You carry the saddle and the female."

Bowmark tried to block the thoughts of all the ways this plan could go wrong. *I made a promise. I won't waste your death, Sunrise.*

Half a candle later Bowmark stood at the base of the cliff with weight equivalent to a full-grown man lashed to his back. He watched with dread as the goatish slowly picked its way up the cliff. The animal used its bifurcated horn as a hook to steady itself as it repositioned its pliable hooves. Scolla stuck to the base of its neck like a tick, his ears straight up and quivering.

Stones occasionally gave way, skittering and clattering down near Bowmark. With one final grand leap the goatish disappeared over the top of the cliff and Bowmark sighed, realizing he had been holding his breath. Flexing his fingers, he breathed deeply, and began his climb. The unwieldy weight on his back made what would have been a fun climb into a nightmare of near topples, bloody fingers, and scraped knees.

Panting as if he had just run a full obstacle course, Bowmark pulled himself over the edge where he found Scolla still splayed out over the goatish's neck. The steed was content, chewing on a thorny bush. Bowmark slowly severed the sticky strands that held the saddle to his back with a small obsidian blade, then rolled over, trembling. "We make . . . camp here."

The next morning Bowmark took a little extra time stretching. His legs were getting used to riding, but the previous day's climb had engaged many muscles to near exhaustion. After an unusually large breakfast of dried meat and fruit, they set off again. There was no discernible trail now, but there was an occasional strip of orange cloth tangled among brush and rocks. The terrain here did not have the strange carved rock forms, but instead innumerable small ravines wrinkling the rocky ground, most no deeper than Bowmark. Some ravines were narrow enough for the goatish to leap. But most had to be navigated around. They continued to find markers which they followed southwestward for another four days.

A pleasant afternoon heat radiated from the orange rocks around them when they found another cliff wall. Following it south they discovered a crack covered with yellow vines. Pushing through the tangled foliage revealed the final path they were looking for.

The cliffs on both sides pressed in so that Bowmark's legs nearly brushed against them. Some instinct caused him to glance up.

A man clothed entirely in loose tan attire perched on the edge of the right-hand cliff, ten strides above him holding a large stone in his hands. When he saw Bowmark's face, he set the stone down and motioned for Bowmark to continue.

More warning than threat, he hoped.

Prodding Scolla, Bowmark whispered. "Is that man a part of the school? If so, I fear we lost our chance to surveil the place before we decide if I should attend."

Scolla held his shades to his eyes as he peered up. "It is likely so, for he wears a uniform."

Two ropes later the trail took them through a bowl-shaped area where a young goatish keeper tended to six goatishes. Passing the natural corral, they squeezed through another narrow passage where the path ended abruptly at the edge of a deep canyon. A single, huge reed acted as a bridge, swooping to a ridge that had eroded to an undulating line of several spires, all with flat tops ranging from a few steps across to large enough to build houses on. The spires that stood one step apart had no connections. Those stone columns farther apart were connected by bridges of thick reeds. The seven largest spires led to a mountainous column of vertical stone capped by a mesa.

Far below, nets hung between the rock spires. Below the nets, a few irrigated farms on the valley floor grew strips of greens and grays that stood out sharply against the pale ochre, yellow, and orange striated walls and spires. More rows of stone spires jutted out from the canyon walls, but none of them led to a mesa, as the spires in front of Bowmark did.

He gazed across to where the stepping-stone spires led: a mesa two ropes wide and enclosed by a rock wall. A hefty reed rested on the last spire and on the mesa. A bracket in front of a carved hole in the side of a wall supported the other end of the reed. Thick doors made from layers of reed blocked the hole. The wall of fitted stones surrounded the mesa, hiding whoever lived on the flat-topped rock.

He looked up and behind him again. Three men, shrouded in dirty tan loose-fitting uniforms, on the right-hand cliff above him, motioned for him to continue.

Bowmark studied the flimsy reed bridges. "Scolla, I don't like this." The only reply he got was a soft buzz.

Somehow supplies got to that fortressed mesa. This appeared to be the only route. Bowmark took one more moment to admire how defensible that massive rock pillar was. Where the cliffs weren't sheer vertical, they were undercut. The reed bridges along the line of spires could be easily lifted from their brackets. Ah, and there, on the side of the middle spire, a man rested in a hammock above fifty strides of air.

"So then," Bowmark muttered and urged on the reluctant goatish. The animal set one foot on the thick reed and stopped, moaning and twisting its neck. Bowmark snapped the reins. "I can do this. So can you. Go on." The goatish backed up a step.

Fighting with the stupid animal would likely earn them a swift fall. He slid off, took the reins, walked to the middle of the reed, and held out a lump of sweetened grain. "You know you want this," he crooned.

The goatish stretched out its long neck, stretched out its tongue, and rolled its eyes, looking from lump to empty air to reed to the cliff it stood on the edge of.

Bowmark tapped the lump on the tip of the goatish's tongue. "Come on."

The goatish took a hesitant step forward.

A man, with hair the color of the rocks around them, wearing the same dirty, tan outfit, walked up behind the goatish. "Did you know most men can't do what you're doing?" His voice sounded neither friendly nor hostile.

Bowmark shrugged. "You can die as easily falling five strides as you can falling five ropes."

The man looked at him quizzically.

"Ah ,truth. I mean you can die from falling five meters as easily as you can falling..." Bowmark tried to puzzle out the ratio of ropes to kilms. "Ah, half a kilm. Never mind."

The bright haired man grunted dismissively.

The goatish kept stepping. Bowmark walked backward, occasionally tapping the goatish's nose or tongue. When the goatish reached the middle of the reed, their bridge dipped. Bowmark studied both ends and calculated. As long as the weight of them did not bend the reed so far that the ends slipped from their supports, they should be safe. He knew how far bamboo and logs could bend. How far could this reed bend before breaking? The thought of the similarly situated ironwood log that held the bronze Disc in its stanchions perturbed his concentration. Bowmark looked down at the canyon floor and across to the man standing with folded arms watching him. Somehow supplies got to that fortress. There was no other route.

But suppose this was a trap for uninvited visitors?

Sweat popped out on Bowmark's forehead. Tugging lightly on the reins so the goatish wouldn't fight back, he continued backing up until he reached the top of the first spire.

The three men watching from the higher cliff and the one man watching at the end of the reed clapped slowly. The goatish joined him on the small platform of rock. Bowmark rewarded the animal with his treat.

As the animal chewed noisily, Bowmark rubbed his mouth and patted his satchels. Four more reeds to go. Did he have four more treats?

The hot, still air evaporated the sweat on his face.

The light-haired man jogged across the reed. "Go on."

The other choices were unsavory. The goatish and Bowmark crept from spire top to spire top. When he walked across the last reed and past the opening doors, the tension between his shoulder blades eased.

Before him stretched an immense open area of pale stone carved into multiple levels, as though he was in the bottom of a huge serving tray. Many doorways perforated the fortress walls ringing the mesa. Two buildings were situated near the center on the topmost level. Rows of vegetable crops crowded against the walls and paths that wove through the complex. He was led up a ramp towards a central plaza.

In the center of the open space stood a pylon of bound reeds holding a faceted, triangular white stone bracelet that glinted fiercely.

A bald man in a clean tan tunic and trousers marched toward him.

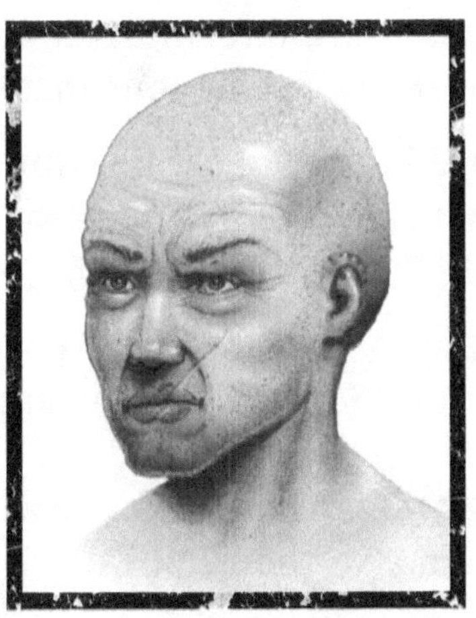

Bowmark tugged the goatish onto the plaza. He held the reins and studied the man who was nearly as tall as he was.

The man's left ear was notched so many times it seemed fringed. A scar from cheekbone to chin crossed his lips and puckered them crooked. When he had walked within a step from Bowmark, the man pressed his fists onto his chest. "Ho, the traveler. What brings you to our hidden home?"

Bowmark forced himself not to step back into a more comfortable distance. "I desire training in unarmed combat against those with weapons."

The man studied him, bringing his fists to his mouth. Tan-uniformed men gathered near the two, enveloping them with the smell of fresh sweat.

The goatish urinated noisily on the stone.

The man spoke through his fists. "You have not the appearance of a Megalothi, and certainly not the… dress." His gaze paused at Bowmark's skirt. "How did you hear of us?"

None of the men surrounding Bowmark had his copper skin and red hair. They were even paler than the earthworm-colored people of the island of Rolocton. "I come from a southern island. I travel the world to fulfill a vow. When I return, I must fight a formidable enemy. He will have weapons. I will not. Thus, I seek your instruction."

The man bounced his fists off his chin for a few breaths. "You did not answer my second question. Who told you of our hidden location?"

Bowmark hesitated. The spitters purposefully did not speak in front of men. Scolla would be angered by Bowmark talking about him. With the other paddle, these men deserved an answer, and their response to what he would do next would tell a lot about them. "So then." Bowmark stepped back and lifted the blanket covering the spitters. Scolla lay as still as a rock. Bowmark gently laid the blanket back. "My partner informed me. From whom he heard, I do not know." Was his face impassive as it should be? Or could they read the fear stabbing his heart? Would they rob him now?

A few of the men surrounding them snickered. Their leader frowned.

A mountainfolk clad only in his lustrous black fur and a small breechcloth stepped through the other men to stand near the leader. "Spitters can speak. They generally choose not to."

The leader glanced from mountainfolk to Bowmark. "What does your nose tell you?"

The mountainfolk leaned forward and inhaled noisily. His violet eyes gleamed as he considered. Everyone stared intently at the short hairy man. "Mayhaps he is an accomplished liar. Mayhaps he tells the truth."

The leader dropped his fists. "A spy would be a skillful liar."

"I travel for my own purposes, and for no one else." Bowmark tightened his fist around the reins. "I have been to Discoria, Bysea, and Central Place of the rumshas. I am on my way to Megaloth City before I return to—"

Everyone tensed.

Bowmark scanned the frowning men, then used his most courtly voice, "I do not know how I have given offense."

The leader spat on the ground. "Megaloth searches for us to murder us all."

Redstone
LITHSPEEN MOUNTAINS
SEVERE VALLEY
KILMS 25 50 100
MILES 50
NONE HAVE CHARTED THE MAZE OF UNDERGROUND
LAKES AND RIVERS IN THE SEVERE VALLEY REGION.
MANY WATERFALLS POUR FROM MYSTERIOUS
HOLES IN THE CLIFFSIDES
~ THE OUTER TERRITORIES
OF THE MEGOLOTHI EMPIRE
BY CALUS THE CARTOGRAPHER

"So." Bowmark laid his hand on Scolla's back and grimaced. "I don't know what I can say that will prove I mean you no harm. I didn't know you were hiding. I was told only that there was a school *en route* that could teach me the skills I need." He looked directly into the leader's eyes, willing him to believe.

"I don't know who your enemies are, but I understand hiding. My people, too, hide from an enemy. We—" He took a deep breath as sweat filmed his hands and sides. "We kill strangers. Is that what you will do to me?"

The leader quirked an eyebrow as he glanced around the group. "Your story is far too ridiculous to be that of a spy." He laughed. "Can you keep a secret?"

"I keep many."

"Why should we take you in?"

Bowmark blinked and rubbed the back of his neck. "I don't know why you should take me in. I only know why I should join you." He lifted his deflated food bag from 's backpack. "I brought dried fruit, flour, and honey for trade. Though, sadly, I have little left because I needed to make room on my mount..." Bowmark trailed off because he had no idea how to explain the rescue of a comatose tezledek.

The leader grinned. "That *is* sad. But, I see you brought a spitter too. I wish you had brought a dozen. All ours left a month or so ago as if we'd offended. However, what we really need is a reservoir full of water. If you are strong enough to get us water, if you will follow my every instruction, if you will live in harmony with us—then you can start on the path to perfection. Eventually you'll desire to join our cause and overthrow the tyrant." He motioned to one of the men. "Hirat, take that stinking beast to the shed after this young man stows his belongings."

"Sir, my name is Bowmark. My partner is Scolla. How should we address you?"

"Mm? Ha. My name's Larkum. We'll talk again after you've spent two hours on the buckets with Montee." He turned and strode away.

"Ha, got my shift again, furballs," said one of the men, feigning a blow to the mountainfolk's head.

Montee ignored the jibe and spoke to Bowmark, "There's an empty cell next to mine ye may have. Right over there."

Bowmark, and Hirat pulling on the goatish reins, followed Montee to a rock room with a rolled leather flap above the door. A clay ewer and basin sat in the corner on a small shelf of rock. As the men unloaded Bowmark's supplies and dodged teeth, horn and hooves, Bowmark gently laid Scolla on a blanket. When he brought in the female, Bowmark muttered, "Let me think. She was on her right side, so now I should place her on her left, or her back?" He was fairly sure he shouldn't lay her on her stomach and stitches.

"She?" Hirat asked. "They come in male and female?"

One corner of Bowmark's lips lifted. "Unless they are immortal, there must be some way to make more spitters."

"Me mam told me most maggots turn to flies, but some maggots what get special treatment turn to spitters."

Bowmark pressed his lips together to keep from laughing.

Hirat set down a bag of powdered beans. "How's it you're partners?"

"Our needs met and kissed."

Hirat backed against the door frame. "That's vile!" Montee had the same revulsion on his furred face.

"What did I say?"

Hirat choked. "You have sex with a—"

"No!" Bowmark's revulsion matched theirs. "No! Scolla needs to find a place where spitters don't yet live so he can expand their civilization. I need a guide. Together, we both get what we need."

Montee laughed. "Interesting figure of speech. I would not use it again."

Hirat relaxed and laughed also.

Montee combed the fur of his neck with his pointed fingernails. "Do ye understand the phrase: a little spitter told me?"

Bowmark shrugged. "Does it mean that I'm not the only human who speaks to spitters?"

"Mm. I'm a human. Ye're a degenerate."

Hirat snorted and strode off with the unloaded goatish.

Montee continued, "It means that ye are not about to reveal who told you something."

Bowmark lifted his eyebrows. "So then. I insulted Larkum when I told him that Scolla informed me of this place."

Montee laughed. "That ye did. Ye are a stranger here. I can tell by smell and mannerisms. Also, ye are only the second degenerate that has not tried to hit me after I told the truth."

Bowmark shrugged again. "Scolla calls me worse." He paused a moment. "Now that you know I don't, um, with spitters, why do you think I'm degenerate?"

"Ye're naked."

Bowmark glanced at his skirt and then at Montee's small flap of tooled leather. "I have on more clothing than you do."

"Yer skin is naked, like a worm's. The first humans were not naked."

Bowmark wasn't sure that hairless skin was the stupidest reason he would ever hear used to determine degeneracy, but he would not be surprised if it were. Still, he was here, and he needed to get along. "So. Montee, I am a stranger. I have already offended twice—"

"Thrice."

"Thrice then. Will you help me to not do so again?"

"Perhaps. Let's see how useful ye are on the buckets. I'll be honest with ye. As long as Larkum thinks ye be contributing to the cause, ye be worth keeping about."

Bowmark wondered what would happen if Larkum decided he wasn't contributing enough, but he decided to keep the question to himself until he understood the social dynamics better. They reentered the dazzling sunlight and walked toward a large shed next to the kettles of boiling water.

Inside, a complex apparatus of pedals, bars, ropes, cogs, and slender buckets poured water into a large elevated vat. The ropes holding the buckets descended into and rose up from a dark tunnel that led directly to an underground cistern or stream. Bowmark considered how high the mesa was and marveled at how much rock had been chipped away to make this well. Montee showed Bowmark how to strap his feet to the pedals and hold the bars, and then he strapped himself into the other tread mill. The shadowy stone room filled with the creaks of machinery and splashes. Working the mill took effort, but not so much that Bowmark could not talk.

"I notice that everyone, save you, has their left ear cut at least twice. Why is that?"

Montee wrinkled his nose. "Because I am not a criminal."

Bowmark pedaled a few steps. "I don't see the net that gathers those facts."

Montee snorted. "In Megaloth, every conviction merits a cut in the left ear."

Bowmark paused briefly. "So then, Larkum is . . ."

"A thief, a mangler, a breaker, and an inciter."

Bowmark trod for several breaths before saying, "It seems we have come to the wrong place."

"The stripes on yer back say otherwise."

Bowmark frowned a moment. "Ah. Those. I'd forgotten about my scars there. My crime was defending myself in a public place at Bysea. And interrupting a judge's supper." They trod some more. "Why are you here?"

"Me? Mmm." The apparatus creaked. "Normally we don't discuss this with degenerates. But ye're unusual, so ye I'll tell. This could be the place we wake up."

Creak. Splash. Creak. Splash.

"Wake up. Does it offend to ask for explanation?"

Montee wiggled the tips of his fingers. "When one of us wakes, all of us will wake. Then we will be out of yer nightmare."

"Mine?"

"Someone's. Each time I touch the Capacity Stone, I feel that at any moment I will wake."

"So then." Bowmark sipped lukewarm water from the jug set by his hand. "Scolla has ordered me to leave the Stone alone."

Now Montee paused. "Ye take orders from a spitter?"

"His advice kept me alive. I can't take your Stone to my island. I must learn how to fight without whatever the Stone gives you."

"Mm."

"So, how long have you been here?"

"Perhaps a year. I came with Larkum to help found the Gathering."

Bowmark sucked air through his teeth, hissing. Did he dare ask? If the previous inhabitants had been slaughtered by the Gathering, Larkum might not want him asking questions about the history of this place. "What was here before?"

"Bare rock."

"I doubt that. I know what it takes to cut and lay this much rock."

"The Capacity Stone gives incredible strength."

What had Scolla delivered him to? *Creak. Splash. Creak. Splash.*

"Montee, am I going to be allowed to leave?"

He wiggled his fingertips. "Perhaps."

"Perhaps." Bowmark sighed. "Fumes." He pedaled. "Who are we hiding from?"

"Megaloth. More to the point, the band of border patrol known as the Crimson Cohort."

Bowmark blinked away tears. After Sunrise had read about the Crimson Cohort—a group of warrior women—in the Atlas, he had said he wanted to wrestle one.

Then they talked about the daily life at the Gathering, required chores, and Larkum's rules, or rather, rule: Everyone should do as he said. Montee assured Bowmark that Larkum was fair, for a degenerate criminal. Why were the Crimson Cohort searching for the Gathering? Because the men had stolen the Capacity Stone from the Crimson Cohort and broken their spell of slavery.

By the time two candles had passed, Bowmark had learned about horrendous Megaloth justice. Magical pedestals distributed along the Frontier each had a peg for the Stone. When Stone and pedestal were matched, whoever touched the Stone could thereafter never travel more than a hundred kilms from the pedestal. The Megaloth Empire had only one Stone, but many pedestals, and used them as invisible cages. Criminals and their families were forcibly moved to the Frontier, subjected to the leash of the Stone, then sentenced to work the farms and keep watch for the encroaching ungols. But they were not allowed weapons, but rather forced to rely on the communication network to call for aid. The Crimson Cohort patrolled the borders, but they couldn't be everywhere at once. Entire families and farms were routinely torched or torn to shreds by ungols riding bears, buffaluks, and leapers. The Capacity Stone, when removed from the pedestal, strengthened the women of the Crimson Cohort.

When Bowmark stepped off the apparatus, he felt as invigorated as he always did after a good workout. His legs hurt, but in a different way than the saddle inflicted. He followed Montee into the sunlight and blinked until his eyes had adjusted. Twenty men sat in a double circle around the white Capacity Stone, which was set on a sharpened stick that protruded from the top of a tripod of bound reeds. Montee nudged him and nodded toward the tripod. "That's nae a magic pylon as the empire uses. So we strengthen ourselves rather than enslave ourselves. Someday I'll wake up by using that Stone."

Bowmark examined the Capacity Stone more closely. It was more like a chunky triangular bracelet than a stone. At one angle it seemed like opaque white marble, but at another like translucent glass. The etched patterns reminded Bowmark of those on his magical staff. Montee ambled off to the showers. The men sat perfectly still in their tan robes, hands resting quietly on knees. Larkum, the master of the gathering, rose silently, stepped to the pylon and placed his hands on the stone. glowed and changed from white to blue. Ecstasy suffused his face. When he let go the stone returned to marble-white.

Larkum walked up to Bowmark and said calmly, "Attack me."

Bowmark hesitated, the command so at odds with the tone of voice, that he wondered if he had heard correctly. He crouched into a wrestler's stance, elbows up, hands out.

Larkum did not move. "I mean for you to attack me with a knife."

Bowmark straightened and pulled a knife from his waistband. "Do you want me to try to wound you, or kill you, or what?"

Larkum continued calmly, "You may try to kill me. You won't succeed." He raised his relaxed hands to his center.

Bowmark held the knife in his right hand and scribed lazy circles in the air as he considered. He stepped sideways, nearly into Larkum, and swiftly slid the knife across his torso.

But Larkum had stepped sidewise also and blocked Bowmark's thrust, grabbed his wrist, and pulled him forward as his elbow smashed into Bowmark's jaw. Larkum trapped his knife arm as he shoved Bowmark's chin back. Bowmark tried to grab Larkum's neck as Larkum's leg swung around his, and they teetered for a moment before falling, Larkum atop Bowmark, and his elbow onto Bowmark's stomach. Bowmark punched him in the head. Larkum set his knee on Bowmark's arm, seized throat and squeezed.

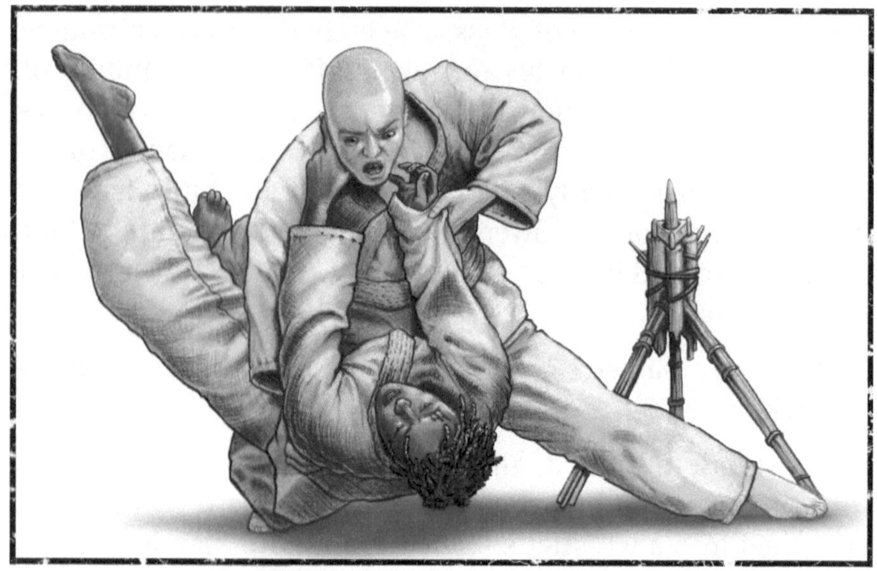

The throat squeeze seemed redundant to Bowmark as his paralyzed muscles could not draw air. Black splats burst on his vision. He snaked his arm under Larkum's and grabbed his shoulder for leverage to bend Larkum's arm. His arm bent, but Larkum did not lose his hold. Bowmark bucked. He grabbed Larkum's ear. Larkum smashed the side of his head onto Bowmark's nose. Sparkles radiated in waves. He bucked again as his vision failed. He turned the knife around in his trapped hand, but before he could do more than touch the tip against Larkum's thigh, Larkum wrenched his arm straighter. Bowmark pushed weakly against Larkum's weight hen passed out.

Consciousness returned a few moments later as air poured into his tortured chest.

Larkum gazed at him mildly as he stood, straightening his robe.

Bowmark gasped. "I want to learn that maneuver. And one for a man with a spear."

Larkum smiled. "Good instincts. Does not give up. Good strength. But Fulcrum Technique takes more than that. Do two more hours on the buckets."

Bowmark's head throbbed. His throat ached. He rolled over, practiced breathing, and rose slowly. As he dragged himself to the buckets, behind him Larkum added, "Good attitude."

This initiation would kill him. Bowmark strapped his feet onto the pedals. He wiped off the blood under his nose with the back of his hand and then palpated the back of his head. A painful lump grew there. His ribs had a variety of complaints as well, though, thank Giver, his liver seemed fine, so far. Who know what would break inside if Larkum kept dropping on him?

A young man with wan skin redolent of soap strapped in beside Bowmark. His lobed ear was slit twice. After grunting that his name was Narich, he pedaled in silence for a candle.

Bowmark needed to think about something beside his growing fatigue. "I came here because I was told this was a school. How many other people came thinking this was a school?"

Narich shrugged. "Me 'n eight more to start. But oncen you touch that stone, you don' want to go back. Peaceful here."

"Has anybody left?"

"Mm. Sure-sure. But you don' want to go the way he went. Nopps, he tried to take over and challenged the old man. Got spitter food beat out of him. Larkum told him he couldn't touch the Stone for a month. That night Nopps jumped offen the edge."

"You're sure he wasn't pushed?"

"Sure-sure. Fuzzballs saw him."

"So you say you and others came to learn to fight. But now I've been given the impression this is supposed to be some kind of rebellion against the Megaloth Empire. How are fewer than a hundred men with nothing but knives and bare hands supposed to defeat an empire?"

"Larkum says when we're ready we'll spread out to the southern frontier to secretly teach the convicts and their families Fulcrum Technique. Since they've not got weapons they'll need to know how to disarm them who do. With the frontier in rebellion, the empire loses a lotta their food. Then the rebellion spreads. You not from the south, are ya?"

Bowmark's shoulder ached where he had hit the ground. "No. I'm from an island, far from here. So far even the seafolk don't know where it is."

That sated Narich's curiosity. He spent the rest of the time telling Bowmark about every food stall he had ever robbed.

When they were done with their two hours of hauling up water, Larkum again challenged Bowmark. The moves were different; the result was the same.

Bowmark blinked up at Larkum and rasped, "That, too, I want to learn." *Two* ways to defeat a man with a knife. Not only might he kill RaiseHim, he might live through the proving! The hope of survival blossomed in his heart.

"Mm. Do you know you can surrender before you pass out?"

"If I surrender before my enemy, I'll be swimming in lava with a spear in my gut. One of us must die. It is so written."

"Mm." Larkum reached down a hand to help up Bowmark. "You ready for another round of buckets?"

Bowmark rubbed his painful throat. "If that will help me learn this fulcrum technique."

Larkum laughed heartily. "Nah-nah. Showers, kitchen, and rest for you. Your lessons start on the morn." With good cheer he whacked Bowmark on his bruised back. At first, Bowmark thought he was being attacked, but everybody stayed calm, so the blow might be how Megalothi encouraged each other. Whatever it was, it was one custom he was not taking home.

After a glorious shower and a solitary supper of tarts, nuts, and bread slathered with herbs and honey, Bowmark walked through dusk to his dark room. He lowered himself to the floor and carefully leaned against the rough wall. In the dim light, movement slowly resolved itself into Scolla exercising the female spitter's arms.

Scolla glanced at him, then whined, "You are weeping."

"Not so," rasped Bowmark. His whole face wanted to scrunch in pain. On the morrow he would likely not be able to talk or eat. "My eyes are leaking because they are tired and full of dust. My whole body is tired."

"I smell much bruising on you."

"Truth." He breathed heavily, inhaling the ginger scent of spitter, rock, and salve. "I do not know for certain yet, but I think we may be trapped here."

"Zzz. You mean you think *you* may be trapped here. I am free."

Bowmark's jaw hurt far too much for him to clench it. "Scolla. There are times I don't like you."

"Tonight, I will research escape paths for you."

"So then. Thank you. Though I do need to stay long enough to learn these fighting techniques. I do not know how long that will take." He considered how long it took him to learn to wrestle, juggle, throw knives, and the many other martial arts he must know. Slowly, he rolled out a blanket and lowered himself onto it by degrees. "Did you know the Stone was used to keep defenseless people in constant danger of ungol attack?"

"Sss. Then it is the same as the one stolen from the Crimson Cohort. Sst. We should leave soon. The Crimson Cohort are searching for it. They are incensed. Ss ss ss ss. Swear to me you will not touch that Stone."

Bowmark could swear to nothing. He fell asleep.

In the morning his legs were so sore that Bowmark considered walking on his hands to the group of men seated around the Capacity Stone. Rather than moving at all he squeezed his eyes shut hard. Scolla had not lowered the leather door, neither when he left nor when he returned, so cold dew weighted their blankets.

Montee stepped into the room and laid upon the floor a folded tan uniform and a cup of hot choca.

"Th-th-thank you."

Montee smiled with closed lips, hiding his sharpened teeth. "Don't delay or ye'll regret." He turned to join the others.

Bowmark seared his tongue as he gulped the choca. Despite the sensation that he had torn most of his muscles and broken some bones, he pulled on the loose trousers and long open shirt that was tied together with a long belt. The fabric was rougher than his fine linen and covered with poorly stitched repairs and dark stains he assumed was blood. After tying the belt in his best imitation of what he saw on the others, he minced to the circle of men sitting on chilled stone. Their frosted breath briefly clouded the air as they chanted softly.

The men finished their recitations and visits to the Capacity Stone. It flared a different color for each person who touched it, always returning to white. When they rose, Larkum told him, "You, sit. Watch. There will be a test."

Bowmark smiled grimly and shivered. Of course, there would be a test. He was a stranger. Likely the first wrong response would cause his death. Couldn't he learn whatever he was going to learn here somewhere else?

The men did a variety of exercises, stretches, and gymnastics. Under his loose uniform, Bowmark tensed, relaxed, and flexed his muscles, attempting to gain some warmth. He felt proud of himself for not screaming as he flexed torn muscles.

Then the men paired off. "Ha!" they shouted as their hands and feet and bodies whirled in intricate dances of attack and defense. "Ha!—Ha!"

Larkum walked away, came back with a box, and lifted the lid. Each of the men picked a knife. They chose new partners and resumed their combats. Larkum tilted the box in front of Bowmark.

Bowmark chose a knife and felt its edge. "This is sharp!"

"Sure-sure. Makes us pay attention."

The blade did make Bowmark pay attention.

A half candle later, sweat dripped from everyone's chins and elbows. Blood spattered a few robes. Larkum called the men to chores, some to water mill, some to laundry, many to construction and the digging of an escape tunnel in Larkum's cell, some to sweeping or washing, and some to kitchen duty. The ones who had been cut touched the Capacity Stone again.

Larkum wiped his sleeve across his face before settling beside Bowmark. "What did you see?"

"What I saw was not wrestling nor boxing. Somehow your people have learned how to deflect another's power, um, charge. You take. You take an attack and spin it to a harmless direction, or, or—" Bowmark inhaled deeply and motioned with his hands. "You use the enemy's own strength to defeat him."

Larkum arched his eyebrows. "Very good. What you describe is the act of creating and utilizing fulcrums. You shall be a delight to teach. Now, touch the Stone and join the mushroom detail."

Bowmark said cautiously, "Give me pardon. I will not touch the Stone."

Larkum frowned briefly. "I'm not telling you to do this for you to gain strength or nimbleness, though both would increase. Touching it will speed the healing of your bruises. It will help you to learn faster."

"Give me pardon. Please. I must not." Bowmark averted his eyes. These people liked to sit and stand more closely than he was comfortable with. They also stared into each other's eyes aggressively and spoke rapidly and loudly.

"Mm. Your pain, not mine."

In truth it was. Bowmark unfolded slowly. A muscular man missing three fingers named Nooker led Bowmark, laden with buckets of water, across the springy reeds to the mini-mesa dripping with bean plants. When Bowmark glanced at his hand, the man growled, "I'm not a-gonna tell you." They watered the beans and took the empty buckets to the corral. Neither Bowmark nor his goatish were glad to see each other. They entered the caves lining the small arena that had been converted into a corral. Nooker lit a candle, and they gazed upon piles of dung crowned with mushrooms.

Bowmark knelt, astonished. "I've never seen anything like this."

"You've not had mushrooms afore?"

"I've picked them off logs." He pulled up a red ball and sniffed it. "The largest animal we have is the pig. We use its manure for the grain terraces." Dad had made Sunrise and him carry plenty of bucket loads to those terraces. Sunrise would have loved these caves. Limestone caverns were much smoother, larger, and lighter than the few lava tubes they had explored. Sunrise would have loved the bridges and spires too. He would have been excited to see these new fighting techniques. Fumes and ash, he would have loved this whole adventure.

Nooker boomed, "Picking mushrooms is not a death penalty. Best not have Larkum see you so dissatisfied with your chores."

Bowmark tried to smile, but his face could not accomplish the deed. "No. No. I am only remembering what an enemy did to my brother . . . and me." He plucked a handful of mushrooms and tossed them into a bucket.

"Forget the past. Ignore the future. Attend to the present. Recite that with me as you work."

An echo whispered back their words as they gathered. How could Bowmark forget the sight, the feel of his spear piercing Sunrise's chest? How could he ignore the future when his coming challenge to the usurper RaiseHim was why he had come here?

With buckets full and hands stinking of manure, they trotted back to the communal kitchen, where Nooker taught Bowmark how to clean and slice most of the mushrooms onto netting to dry, and the rest into a large pot of stew. They carried water to more of the small mesas atop spires,

1. Training Plaza
2. Larkum's Quarters
3. Pumphouse & distillery
4. Showers
5. Bowmark's Quarters
6. Gate
7. Flanking Balcony
8. Entrance Watchtower
9. Gourd Tower
10. Plumeria Tower
11. Lentil Tower
12. Edamame Tower
13. Severe Watchtower
14. Carrot Tower

and then the manure to tiny caverns chipped into the larger spires. Spent mushroom compost was carried and spread over the gardens. Most of the day being spent on these dirty, stinking chores reminded Bowmark of his time in High Harbor mucking stalls and weeding the orange rice fields. How was it that his memories of these things were happy now?

Shower, lunch, chanting around the stone in the windless, hot arena. His instruction began, without knives, and though he hit the ground time and time again, he broke nothing but his pride and skin. Larkum told him how to move energy within his body and how to project force and how to mentalize. Much of his instruction seemed many words about nothing, but listening let him practice his patience as well as rest.

The days fell into a rhythm with the only variety being his chores. Sometimes he scrubbed the arena; sometimes he chiseled on the escape tunnel Every day he spent two candles bringing up water. He learned about who despised whom, why nearly all despised Montee, and how Larkum's strong arm kept animosity under control. He learned to ignore who went into whose cell at night. Every day he learned a new move or combination of Fulcrum Technique. Bowmark learned five ways to take or neutralize a spear, six ways to deflect a knife attack, and how to recognize an enemy's stance along with the proper counter stance.

Every day he said, "No," to Larkum's urging that he touch the stone, and every night he said, "No," to Scolla, who urged him to leave the Gathering now. He felt torn on the issue. The sooner he reached home the sooner his brother and father could be safe. But the longer he stayed, learning this fighting technique, the more likely it was that he could defeat RaiseHim. Returning only to die on the end of a spear would help no one, and it would waste the death of his best friend as well as consign his family to death. No, as painful as it might be, the wiser course was to train for as long as it took to be confident in success.

After Scolla left for a night of food procurement, Bowmark would add a few sentences to his journey book and practice with the staffshifter, magic rope, and lightball. While he could not take his magic items onto the Disc, they might help him survive the journey home.

If he could show the protocol officer the stripes on his back and persuade her that they represented the Bysea treasure of peaceful streets, he could have three treasures. With Scolla, four. No, he only had two he could depend on the officer accepting. Giver, eight more to find. Couldn't the Fulcrum Technique be considered a treasure?

The last thing he would do before huddling in his blankets each night was hold PledgeKept's crude wooden Giver's Hand medallion and ask to be guided safely home and to be given the chance to defeat RaiseHim despite the unsettling feelings he had about killing another man.

After curling up on his hard bed, he would try to not think about Sunrise, Moongleam, Father, Spearmark, and that night in the treasure room. He never succeeded.

As the days passed, Bowmark's understanding of combat grew as well as his knowledge of the area. After a month he was trusted to patrol the vicinity with a partner. The Gathering was ever vigilant for the day the Crimson Cohort might find them. They had detailed maps of the region and kept continual watch over every possible entrance to their remote canyon. Bowmark learned most of the patrol routes, water sources, dangerous wildlife, and colluding goatish herders.

Every so often a new recruit or two would show up. All had scarred ears that marked them criminals of the Megaloth

Empire. They were given a different welcome than Bowmark had. They acted as though they had been recruited beforehand. Bowmark wondered how much political power Larkum had outside this small community. Besides his physical prowess, Larkum held some strange sway over the men that made them incredibly loyal to him.

Bowmark recognized some of the leadership qualities his father had demonstrated, but Larkum was also seen as a kind of holy man whose wisdom and plans for overthrowing an empire inspired an awe that Bowmark had never seen before. As though a priest, protocol officer, and king were all rolled into one. Bowmark had never wanted the responsibility of kingship, let alone that of spiritual leader. He could not imagine how any man could carry such weight honorably. But Larkum never seemed to lord his power over others except during training, where his ruthlessness was couched in the context of education.

Could Larkum truly have the good of these men at heart? Or did he lead because he liked the feeling? The thought haunted Bowmark. If by some miracle, he could fulfill his mission and depose RaiseHim, what kind of leader would he be?

The days began to grow shorter, which Bowmark found deeply disturbing. How could the sun change its course and speed so drastically? This and many other unsettling thoughts were easier to avoid when he was introduced to muscle building exercises: lifting heavy iron bars, chains, and stones. A man with massive muscles named Harker taught him the proper forms for lifting the weights, and Bowmark delighted in learning how to isolate and strengthen specific muscle groups. In turn he taught those who were interested new cliff climbing techniques, acrobatics and how to juggle.

He learned what the season called autumn was in this land, and then the one called winter. Bowmark hated those seasons. But his skills continued to improve, his muscles grew, and he gained more confidence that he would not waste Sunrise's death. Soon after the days began to lengthen again, Bowmark was able to disarm and defeat all but three of the other trainees. If he could disarm Larkum, Bowmark knew he could defeat RaiseHim. That goal consumed him, driving his exercises, drills, chores, and thoughts.

SURPRISE IS WORTH 100 WARRIORS

~ CRIMSON PLATOON TRAINING MANUAL

Fog enveloped the mesa, sharpening sounds and muffling vision. The low cloud slicked the stone with a film of water. Beads of water spangled Larkum's eyebrows as he stood before Bowmark and tilted the box toward him. "Time for knife practice."

As Bowmark reached into the box, someone tugged on his robe.

Scolla whined in Zledek, "I hear a messenger fly. Get the honey to attract it."

Bowmark replied in Zledek. "I'm in the middle of a lesson. You have five of them. Why do you need more?"

Larkum glared at Bowmark with raised eyebrows.

He told him in Common, "He keeps these bugs as pets. He wants me to catch him another one."

"What kind of bugs?"

"Ah, messenger flies."

Larkum looked alarmed. "If you have honey, catch it!"

Bowmark ran to his cell and retrieved Scolla's ceramic vial of honey. He returned, unstopped the cork, then held up the opened vial, waving the honey about to scatter the scent. After a few moments, he, too, could hear the tiny buzz of a messenger fly in flight.

Three of the gold insects materialized through the fog. One flew straight to the honey. One flew a tiny loop before resuming its flight. One wavered in its flight path. Its long thin body supported by four furiously beating wings.

A man named Shadim whipped off his tunic and used it to bat down the looping bug. He stomped on it.

Bowmark cupped a hand over the bug on the vial of honey and crouched to present it to Scolla.

Scolla took vial and bug and raised them to his ear. The bright insect buzzed in a staccato pattern.

The men gathered around to watch. Some of them started to speak, but Larkum abruptly motioned them to be quiet.

Bowmark watched, puzzled, as the insect buzzed on. Save the melodic chirping of a lizard, silence as thick as the fog wrapped them.

Finally, Scolla turned and tugged at Bowmark's leg. "We are leaving now," he hissed in Zledek.

"Why?" Bowmark asked.

"What?" Larkum asked.

"Sss. The Crimson Cohort are moving up the Severe Valley." Scolla scratched his shoulders with his claws.

Bowmark could not understand the non sequitur. "How do you know that?"

Scolla hissed and held up the bug. "The messenger told me."

Bowmark stared openmouthed, then exclaimed, "Messenger flies are called messenger flies because they carry *messages*!"

Men watched him blankly.

Bowmark explained. "We have a small black bird we call a checkerking because of the way it hops through the brush. It isn't a playing piece, nor does it play checkers." They still gazed at him. "I never asked why messenger flies were so named."

Impatiently, Larkum said, "What did your spitter say?"

"*Scolla* said the Crimson Cohort are moving up Severe Valley. He wants us to leave now. Are we in Severe Valley?"

"Mm. We're in a tributary to it. A well-hidden one." Larkum glared at Scolla. "Bowmark. Crush the bugs you have."

Scolla hissed.

"Give—give me pardon. The bugs are not mine to give or kill."

Larkum's hand shot out and grabbed Bowmark's throat. "Did I order you to argue with me? Could be you're not a spy; could be your talking spitter is."

Bowmark kept his hands down and stammered past the pain and pressure. "S-Scolla's lived the past three decades in Discoria and—and—"

All the men drew closer to watch.

Larkum roared, "Discoria has an alliance with Megaloth!"

Bowmark choked out, "Spitters don't bother with human affairs."

Larkum pulled Bowmark's face close to his.

Montee raised his voice. "He believes he's telling the truth."

Larkum did not turn from staring into Bowmark's eyes but produced a knife from his sleeve and held it at the ready. "Do *you* believe he's telling the truth?"

Montee bared his sharpened teeth. "I've never heard otherwise."

Larkum slowly moved the blade toward Bowmark's jugular. Bowmark's breath grew ragged. Could he disarm and subdue Larkum now? His heart beat fast. The sound of many shuffling uniforms tore both men's eyes away from each other and toward the group. Several men who had worked long hours with Bowmark were now standing, eyes squinting, their posture unsure.

Larkum's eyes darted between them, calculating. A few heart beats later he shoved Bowmark away. "You had so much promise. You could have helped us write history. But you only care to serve your spitter god. Go! Take your dung-eater with you."

Bowmark staggered back. Fury burned his veins. He fought the desire to leap on Larkum and pummel him senseless. Mentally rehearsing one of the morning mantras, "The sun rises and sets without my consent, but I control myself," he turned and strode back to his cell where he jerked his bedding up and rolled it into an awkward bundle, stuffing as many of his meager belongings as he could into his backpack.

Behind him, Montee said, "Ye smell angry."

"That's surprising. What do I have to be angry about?" He shoved his magic things into their places on his belt.

"I don't know. Ye're leaving alive after a long visit. Ye learned how to disarm a man with a spear and knife. That is what ye wanted."

"I didn't want to be tossed out like moldy bread. I'm a king! He—" Bowmark spun to face a wall and press his forehead and forearms against the cool stone. He forced himself to calm down. After he had slowed his breathing, he picked up his backpack and faced the mountainfolk. "You're right. I wanted to learn more before I left, but it's more important to survive and go back to my duty." He swung the backpack over his shoulder. "Montee, why don't you come with me? We could practice together, and I could pay you well."

Montee's violet eyes shifted. "The Stone is here."

Bowmark scooped up the saddle that was propped against the wall by the door. "I *hate* that Stone. It's made a slave of you. It makes a slave of everyone."

Bowmark's first shocking memory of a slave auction in Discoria burned before his eyes. He relived his helpless despair at witnessing a cruel system he had no control over.

"The only difference between you and those poor slave farmers on the rontier is that you volunteered to be a slave." He pushed past him. Scolla scrambled about placing his medicines and books in neat pockets of the saddle bags.

Bowmark couldn't carry everything in one load. "Scolla, wait here. I'll retrieve the goatish and be right back."

Montee caught up with Bowmark and walked beside him. "My regret is there aren't millions of Capacity Stones so that everyone might have one."

"You know, spitters hate such magic stones."

"I did not know that."

"I think I understand why now. It's evil. It shouldn't be used by anyone."

Bowmark walked lightly across the giant reed stem that bridged the fortress and first spire, followed by Montee. Bowmark tried to ignore the crowd that gathered. "So, what if the Stone doesn't help you to wake up? What happens after years of touching the Stone three or four times a day?"

"No one knows."

"The Crimson Cohort don't know?" Bowmark stepped over a slick spot on one of the shorter reeds.

"Each woman will serve only three years before she returns to Megaloth to retire in glory."

Why only women in the Cohort and not men? Different people, different customs, but a custom like this was nonsense. "Everyone here except Larkum treats you like a dirt-eater. Are you sure you want to stay?"

Montee laughed. "I survived before ye came. I'll survive after ye leave. As long as Larkum needs my nose, they'll nae harm me."

Fog still hid the fifty-stride drop below them while they trotted from spire to spire. Knowing the area well, Bowmark located the goatish herder quickly. Montee held the reins as Bowmark cinched the saddle. He gave the goatish herder a pearl and thanked the young man for his service. The mountainfolk said, "I wish yer spitter was staying long enough to teach me the messenger fly language. No one here knows it. But so goes life. Farewell and stay safe."

All the goatishes jerked their heads up and stared toward the ortress though all they could see were the walls of the hollow. Their noses twitched.

"Aren't you coming back with me to get the rest of the baggage?" Bowmark asked.

"I'm on far watch. I have some cliffs to climb. Mm. Wait a moment." Montee stuck a finger into a tiny pocket on his flap. "Here. Show this to the next mountainfolk ye meet. Tell them I'm still here and that I'm still well. Ye can also tell them that I thought ye were a decent degenerate." He dropped a tiny, pointed ivory object into Bowmark's palm.

Bowmark studied the ivory. "It looks like . . . a sharpened baby tooth?"

"One of mine, yea."

"I thought we were friends. I show this to a mountainfolk and they'll think I killed a baby to steal his teeth."

"It is my gift to ye to cause remembrance if I should die before I wake. My name, which ye tell no one except another mountainfolk, is Squall upon the Water on a Late Moon Day."

Bowmark closed his hand around it. "Thank you. I will keep this in my friendship box from Rolocton."

When he arrived back at his cell, Bowmark saw that Scolla had already wrapped the female spitter and lined up their saddle bags. Bowmark scooped up most of the bags and the female, still comatose after all these months. Wasn't she a lost cause by now? On the way out, he passed the men who had resumed practicing. They seemed calm for a people whose enemy approached. If only he had the Atlas to check the area. For all he knew, the Severe Valley could be thousands of ropes long, and there could be a thousand hidden tributaries.

Loaded down with their supplies and the female spitter, Bowmark took the reed bridges slowly. Scolla scuttled over them effortlessly.

When he finished loading the female spitter and the rest of the bags on the goatish, Bowmark suddenly remembered that he was still wearing the attire that The Gathering had provided him.

"Scolla, hold the reins. I will feel like a thief if I take these clothes."

Scolla whined impatiently. "No one will notice or care about those rags. We must make haste!"

"I'll notice. I will not sacrifice my dignity to that… man. It will only take a moment. I've got my other clothes here in my backpack." Bowmark bounded back to the fortress.

He was untying his belt when he heard, or felt through his feet, the breaking of rock. He dashed out of his cell and shouted at the nearest sparring pair. "Did you hear that? Is someone working in the escape tunnel?"

The two men stopped and listened. One shook his head. On the far side of the arena, Larkum let go of the man he was positioning and headed toward Bowmark.

Bowmark hastily retrieved his backpack, pulling his Gathering tunic back on. It had been a mistake to come back here.

Larkum intercepted him. "What mischief are you making now?"

Bowmark kept his gaze around his feet. "None. I did not want to leave with your uniform."

Larkum sneered. "Take it and go! I consider it a small price to pay to be rid of your insolence. But what nonsense are you speaking to my men on your way out?"

Bowmark clinched his jaw. "I made a mistake. I thought I heard rock fall in the tunnel. I spoke before I remembered that no one is working there at this time. I am sorry I interrupted your lesson." *You son of a slug!*

"Mm. You have sharper ears than the rest of us. And we've almost reached breakthrough. Stren! Foli! Go check on the status of the tunnel. *You*, go off!"

Bowmark hunched his shoulders. Apparently Scolla was right about the clothing. "That I will."

Larkum returned to his circle of students.

Bowmark stood, thinking, and held PledgeKept's Giver's-Hand medallion. *Ah, Sunrise, the Atlas did not begin to tell the wonders of this world.* How would Sunrise have found a way to laugh at Larkum and thus stay happy?

While training in the Gathering, he had managed to escape for brief times the mental four-room prison of Sunrise's death, MoonGleam's hatred, Father with a knife pressed against his throat, and the shapes of women that made his days and nights miserable. For that he did feel gratitude.

After he had calmed himself again, he headed for the gate, passing near the Capacity Stone on its tripod. He felt a surge of hatred toward the object and all it represented. Larkum stopped his instruction to watch Bowmark.

A shrill whistle echoed in the stone fortress. A ball trailing dark yellow smoke and a rotten egg stench rolled between Larkum and Bowmark. The ball exploded with a great light and cruel bang.

Bowmark fell back, too late covering his pained ears. A black spot obscured his vision and so he saw only bits of what happened next. Women with red helmets, streaming white braids, and opaque white skin ran screaming from the doorway of Larkum's cell.

Nooker hauled Bowmark up and shouted in his face, "You traitor!"

The women in front knelt and readied bows. Women standing behind them brandished spears.

Bowmark tried to pull away from Nooker, who suddenly grunted and collapsed on him. An arrowhead protruded from the man's chest. They both fell down.

Larkum kicked an archer in the head and began an intricate dance of defense with another woman in blood red leather holding a spear. Men and women shouted as though from far away. Everyone moved too fast for Bowmark to follow.

He crawled toward the nearest cover to take refuge until his vision cleared. It was the Capacity Stone tripod. His eardrums felt as though arrows pierced them. Crimson Cohort! These were the Crimson Cohort. They had come for the Capacity Stone. They intended to enslave people like the slaves he had seen in Discoria. No, these women should not have that power. But did he owe any loyalty to The Gathering? Should he stay and fight with them? To what end? Larkum simply used the stone to enslave people in a different way. But neither could he leave the stone to be used by the Megaloth Empire to enslave families. He could not save the slaves in Discoria. But if neither The Gathering nor Megaloth had this stone, he *could* save countless others from slavery. His conscience presented him with only one option.

His fingers moved up the wooden stand until he felt the Stone. He seized the white bracelet and slipped over his hand. A green hue danced across the surface of the magical relic. A cold shock rippled up his arm, filled his lungs, accelerated his heart and fizzed in his brain. The pain in his ears fled, and he could hear and locate the breathing of every person in the fortress and the peeps of every lizard behind a wall. His eyes cleared so that he saw every grain of grit on his arm. Strength surged through each fiber of every muscle. Exultation coursed through his veins. *So this is waking up!*

He rolled to a stand and ran with ease toward the gate. An arrow clanked against the cooking pot on his back. He zipped across the reed, skidded to a stop, and strained to lift the end of the reed out of its bracket. Two women leaped onto the reed bridge. "Go back!"

They continued to walk, less sure than he had been, with their arms held out for balance. The one in front stopped to draw an arrow.

Bowmark dropped the end. The reed bounced on the edge of the bracket, then on the side of the spire, and then led the women in a plunge into the ferny tops of growing reeds at the base of the mesa.

Bowmark sat, his elation turned to grief. He had just killed women! He looked up in time to duck a spear. Guilt gripped his throat as he sped across the bridges and into the grotto where his goatish and Scolla waited.

He bounded onto the goatish, which responded to his rush with a gallop up the ravine to where the cliff split two ways. Bowmark tried to urge his beast the way he had come to the Gathering. The goatish flung itself into the other ravine, clattering down the narrow path for five ropes before the animal stopped, panting and drooling. The goatish refused to move farther until Bowmark vaulted off and kicked its rear. Then the beast ran two ropes with Bowmark chasing it. Kicking the idiot beast again simply made the goatish kick back. Bowmark grabbed the reins and pulled his mount until he came to a slope where he could climb to the top of the broken land and see the geography. The goatish had led them into a dead end.

He stood, staring at the maze of cracks and ravines and canyons until a figure in red popped up from a ravine two ropes back. She spotted him and blew a high-pitched horn before he could drop out of sight. *Fumes!* He skidded down the slope and grabbed the goatish's reins.

The goatish finally trotted, perhaps to keep its head from being wrenched off its neck. Bowmark leapt upon it and they jumped down narrow, boulder-strewn trails until they came to the dead end. They faced a lake surrounded by sheer cliffs. A crack in the cliff on the other side fed the lake with rushing water. Hope slipped from him. No—he need not surrender. He had the magic cord. There would be difficulties, but he could pull the goatish up to that ravine on the other side of the lake.

He didn't know if goatishes would go into water or even if they could swim, but the beast followed him. The lake was deeper than he had hoped, and soon he was paddling next to the goatish. Scolla emitted a high whine as the water lapped against the sides of the saddle.

Bowmark studied the cliffs and lake again. He had passed here several times before to collect berries, but never ventured farther. This time he noticed a depression, a dimple in the water. What would cause that? A sinkhole!

A quick glance at the retreating cliff showed they were drifting toward the whirlpool. Shoving at the beast's neck while kicking against the now discernible current, Bowmark tried to push his goatish and the spitters toward the cliff.

Scolla threw off his blanket and screamed, "What's wrong, what?"

"Scolla! We've fallen into a current. We're being chased by warriors. What do you think is wrong?"

"There is more! I see it on your face!"

"Don't bother me now." The goatish refused to turn. The beast stupidly continued to paddle directly toward the dimple. Bowmark could not kick harder than he already had. The water shoved his legs and torso, and the goatish pulled on his arms. He grabbed the beast's twisty horn and hauled back to no effect. "You're stew!" he shouted.

"What's wrong, what?"

He tried to shove the goatish's head under water.

"What are you doing, what? I can't swim! The female will drown!" Scolla grabbed his arm.

"Stop it! Ow! Puncturing me isn't going to help."

The current quickened.

Gut churning, Bowmark shouted, "Scolla! Where does this lake drain to?"

Now Scolla saw the funnel. "No! Quite no! Bad idea! We shall drown!"

They swooped around the funnel, slid in and spun.

Bowmark cupped his hand over the female's nostrils. "Hold your breath!"

"Nooooo!"

The sinkhole sucked them under.

A FEW TRIBUTARY COMMUNITIES WALLED THEMSELVES
OFF FROM THE IMPENDING DANGER. BUT THE WALLS
ALSO BLOCKED EASY TRADE ROUTES.
AND SO THE TOWNS WITHERED.
                              ~THE OUTER TERRITORIES
                               OF THE MEGOLOTHI EMPIRE
                               BY CALUS THE CARTOGRAPHER

A roaring confusion clutched and churned them as Bowmark hung on like a limpet to the saddle handle with one hand and covered the female spitter's face with the other. One foot scraped stone. They were flung into an eager current that swept them into total darkness, shoved them beyond the possibility of resistance, and batted them into a cold, echoing hollow.

Bowmark sucked in damp air as they sped through an unfathomed space. The goatish groaned. Scolla screamed, "You have killed us! Why? Why?"

"Shh. Listen." In the pitch black Bowmark felt the back of the saddle to ensure that the female spitter was still securely fastened and above water. He maneuvered the goatish so that the beast led their race. Better the stupid beast hit a wall than him. Why wasn't he freezing to death? The Stone! His plan had been to keep it from the Crimson Cohort, but now that he had the Capacity Stone, he could surely defeat RaiseHim. Montee was right. This Stone was a marvel.

"Why do they pursue us, why?" Scolla whimpered. "No. Why do they pursue you, why? Humans do not bother with us. The Crimson Cohort are not raiders after loot."

"Shh."

Echoes drew closer.

"Scolla, float here—"

"We don't float!" he shrieked.

"I meant hang onto the saddle such that only your head is above water. And the lady's. Here. No, stay lower. Scolla! Listen to me. If the roof is low, the goatish can protect us, but only if we're lower than—Hold your breath!"

The goatish's horn crunched into the limestone roof.

Bowmark pulled Scolla into the water. The body of the goatish scraped along the low roof. The goatish squealed, then snorted water. They went under. Only his breath-holding practice as a child diving for mollusks kept Bowmark alive until they emerged into another dark cavern. The walls sounded close. Perhaps they were in a tunnel instead of a cavern. They plunged on without pause. Again the roof descended and shoved them under.

They shot into a fern-lined well of green shade clinging to the undercut walls. Just as rapidly, they were sucked under again.

They popped up in a twisty ravine where cracks in the high crust above them let in rays to sparkle on algae-padded rocks. Swift lizards darted in and out of the columns of light.

The goatish groaned. Startled insects fell from the walls, flared as their wings spread in the shafts of light, then winked out as they glided into dark moss.

Scolla climbed up Bowmark's back and whined, "Stop us before we are dashed to bloody parts."

Bowmark considered. Would his magic cord adhere to slimy rock? Scolla was gripping Bowmark's dreadlocks like reins, his fast, ragged breathing hot in his ear.

The sawtooth roof dropped to within a few hand-widths of their heads. They plunged into darkness. The current jostled them between boulders. His knee bashed against one.

Bowmark tightened his hold. If he combined the lightball, the cord, and his staff, he would be able to do . . . what? But he was being flung about too roughly to attempt retrieving his magic things. He needed both hands to stay upright and keep the spitters above water. Frigid water slapped his face.

"Stop us!" Scolla shrieked.

"I'm trying!"

The goatish slammed its head into a boulder and went limp.

"Scolla, I'm going to need you to let go of me for a—"

"We can't swim!"

"I know you can't swim! You can hang on to the saddle!"

A standing wave boosted them up, then flung them down. The underground river straightened and sped up. Only the occasional small, glowing cricket relieved the darkness.

"Stop us!"

"I can't do that until I get my magic things. I need to submerge my head to reach the sack with the light and rope. Ow! Scolla! I can't do it if I'm bleeding to death!"

"You have killed us!"

Something scaly brushed Bowmark's foot. He yipped and curled into a ball.

"Whatwhatwhat?"

"Scolla! Silence!"

Icy air whooshed by.

Think: one quiet goatish, one hysterical spitter, half the supplies inaccessible as long as Scolla kept a death grip on his head. Going somewhere unknown fast. "Scolla, listen to me. What can you see ahead of us?"

"The goatish."

"Ahead of the goatish!"

"Even I cannot see through a goatish."

"So then. So then. If you won't get back in the saddle, climb up a bit higher."

"The ceiling will rip off my head!" Scolla shouted.

Bowmark raised an arm. "It's higher than I can reach." A point of stone scraped across the side of his hand. "Down!" Ashes ashes ashes. "I need that light!" Without waiting for argument, Bowmark bent forward, and wrestled his hand into his belt bag. Without both hands holding on, he was pulled under. When his head broke water, Scolla screamed curses at him in Zledek. Scolla's claws perforated his shoulder. He fumbled in the bag until he grasped the ball of light, withdrew it, and held it on the side of the goatish.

He wished he hadn't. Cave fangs lined the roof as far as he could see. Some nearly touched the surface of the river. They were careering through an enormous spiked gullet.

The body of the goatish smacked into a fang. The tip snapped off and nearly crushed Bowmark's head.

Scolla wailed once, then whispered, "We are dead."

Quite likely, but, by Giver's Hand, he was a king's son and he would not drown in this black tunnel without resistance. Kicking and shoving, he steered their bulky goatish past most of the fangs. They thudded into a thin rock that swirled them about. For several terrifying moments, their bodies preceded and protected that of the goatish.

Scolla curled into a silent ball as Bowmark tried to think how his staffshifter and cord could help. He could likely catch hold of a fang in a thicker part, but to what end? The only exits were fore and aft. Hanging on to a tunnel fang to be buffeted by the current was counterproductive, like catching a sea snake: much work for loss. Even with the Stone, he could not imagine pulling themselves along the wall against this fierce current.

The ceiling slowly rose, and the fangs retreated. The company bobbled over some shallow falls. They shot through the darkness like a tiny comet in an immense night.

Scolla's ears flicked. Bowmark listened, and presently he heard a vibration, a far off, indecipherable roar.

Sliding past gnarled columns of stone, they arrowed toward the increasing noise. The shadows cast by the lightball lost their crispness.

Bowmark's stiffened fingers poked the lightball back into the bag. A wan light delineated the slumped boulders guarding the river. He pulled out the magic cord, thinking that they might be able to leave the river here and find an exit that would not kill them.

Too late.

They swirled around a bend to face an irregular opening to the sky filled with the mist from the roaring waterfall their river dashed over. They spurted through into free-fall.

Bowmark maneuvered the goatish under them while falling through a confusion of spray and light. They smashed into a roiling pool and were instantly sucked under and pinned to the scoured floor. His breath had been jarred from him, but Bowmark had consciousness enough to know they would be trapped by the fall's vortex if he could not push free. He gripped the back of the saddle with one hand and flailed his other until he found the female spitter. Tearing at the webbing, he grabbed her. Scolla clung to his sleeve. He released the goatish and tucked a spitter under each arm. He thrashed his feet, touching the bottom several times without securing a hold. They were swept up, then shoved down again. For an everlasting moment they were pinned to the rock tumble.

Bowmark shoved off. Despite being pounded by the body of the goatish, he kept his footing long enough to push away from the vortex. He kicked toward the shore. When his knee hit the shingle, he stood, coughing in the drifting sheets of mist, then waded onto land. Hope of help flared briefly at the sight of several buildings clustered near the water's edge. But gaping holes in the walls that loomed over piles of mossy bricks and shingles signaled that the town was abandoned. Another large stone and metal structure clung to the cliff wall next to the waterfall. The remains of a huge steel waterwheel, grown over with dripping moss creaked mournfully.

Scolla unfolded and shrieked, "See to the lady! Has she drowned, has she?"

Bowmark dropped to his knees, his muscles burning. He grabbed two of the female spitter's feet and upended her. Water trickled through her nose slits. She sneezed five times.

Scolla shouted, "Check her for broken bones."

Bowmark laid her on the damp gravel and weeds to squeeze her arms, legs, and torso. Tezledeks had a vertical rib cage, and he did not know their anatomy well enough to discern any breakage. Scolla laid his ear on her chest to listen to her heartbeat and breath.

Scolla sat back to squeak, "I cannot check for internal injuries." Then he sneezed out water.

Bowmark grabbed Scolla's feet and flipped him over. Scolla screamed as water bubbled through his nose slits. Bowmark laid him beside the female and turned to view the churning pool.

Wavering mist obscured everything. A dark object, the goatish, appeared and disappeared as the vortex rolled the goatish up and down. How was he to retrieve that?

The magic cord tangled around his forearm. He smiled. "Loath to lose me, are you?" He slid off the cord and hurled most of it toward the goatish. "Cord, stick!" The sudden jerk nearly pulled him into the maelstrom. Digging his heels into the scree, he hauled. The weight and all the forces on the goatish resisted.

Behind him, Scolla whimpered. Bowmark had to suppress a surge of disgust. Such a coward. He continued to pull. A sudden release let him splash back on his rear onto the sharp gravel. Wincing, he stood and pulled in the head of the goatish. He spit on the head, threw it downstream, and tried again. This time he waited until the body was nearly at the crest of its cycling before he tugged heartily. The body skipped across the pond. In addition to its head, the goatish was missing a leg.

Bowmark could not muster the slightest feeling of pity for the beast as he dragged the body up to the shore.

Heavy brush and a ruined wall on the riverbank confined them to the shore, a wet, silty, rocky border between river and land. Mist from the waterfall drifted over them, and yet Bowmark did not feel cold. Did the Stone also protect against cold?

He first searched for the bag of food. A hunger he could not understand had seized him. The crackers had turned to mush. He had scooped in only a mouthful when Scolla whined frantically, "There go the children!"

Bowmark snapped up and scanned the shore, but he could see no children on its gleaming boulders.

"In the river. Look!"

Bowmark turned and saw, amid the seethe and roar, three of the bags skipping rapidly downstream.

No help for it. He grabbed the spitters, plopped them onto the body of the goatish, and dragged all into the current.

Holding the body in front of himself, he kicked mightily, but the distance between them and the bags widened. He flung the magic cord at Scolla. "Use this to catch them."

Huddled on the goatish carcass, with one arm around the female, Scolla whined, "I cannot."

"Fumes!" Bowmark shouted, kicking harder instead of beating the stupid spitter. "How many times have I told you that if you bothered to exercise you wouldn't be such a weakling?"

"Quite too many," Scolla muttered. "We prefer to exercise our intelligence."

I hate Scolla; I hate Scolla; I hate Scolla, became Bowmark's mental rhythm as he kicked.

Ahead, a ruined foot bridge stretched across part of the river. A bag snagged on ivy that dangled from it. The two other bags tugged on the first until they separated. Just before Bowmark reached the snagged bag, the foliage broke off.

Bowmark propped himself on the goatish and tried to grab the bag. He caught only brambles. The second attempt succeeded. That bag held most of the rumsha treasures and a sack of nuts.

Bowmark handed the bag to Scolla who grasped it with vibrating toes. "What are you doing?"

"Shivering. I am cold."

"I've never seen you shiver before. Should we pull over and start a fire?"

"We must not lose the children."

"Do eggs drown?"

Wheeze. "After a day in water, yes."

"Then, then, your people have experimented on your children?"

"Sss. Quite no, no, no. As have humans, tezledeks have survived floods in our history. We have recorded the results."

For the next candle they flowed past tumbles of rock and sparsely grassed fields with occasional clusters of abandoned houses grown over with ivy and whipcord trees. They startled a family of four legged, thin speckled creatures that jumped impossibly far, and glided in the shadow of red-streaked stone arches.

A surprised garloon stared at them with brown eyes, then hooted in derision. Bowmark quickly looked away so that he would not provoke him.

"He doesn't think much of our boat, Scolla." Single, bad; group, good. But the garloon wasn't chasing them. A small mercy of the Giver.

Scolla only wheezed as he shivered.

The river rushed into a canyon and slapped against a giant brick wall that stretched from the highest point on one side of the river valley to a high point on the other. Water funneled around foundation blocks and through metal bars at the base.

Bowmark stopped paddling. Now what? Then he saw a gap with several missing bars. Paddling towards it, he pressed down on Scolla. Scolla hissed.

Bowmark let up. "Fine, then whack your head."

Scolla uncovered his eyes and saw the approaching wall. He squealed and flattened himself a moment before the river shoved them through the low arch between corroded metal bars.

Strong eddies on the other side of the wall pulled them out of the main current. The bags nestled in some overhanging shrubs.

Bowmark recognized the shrubs and their tiny edible plums. He wrestled the goatish carcass over, grabbed the bags, and dragged all up the riverbank to a fairly flat spot. He charged back to the shrubs, and, with fingers spread wide, raked plums into his mouth. He scarcely took time to spit out the pits before inhaling another mouthful.

Scolla wheezed faintly. "We need a fire."

Bowmark swallowed. "So start one."

"I cannot."

Bowmark stripped the bushes before returning to the wheezing Scolla and paralyzed female. "You could have gathered kindling." He growled as he flipped the goatish body over and found the saddle bag with the flint, oil, and waxy accelerator.

Eddies had deposited a variety of river drift. Bowmark gathered some of the bark and branches, ate some water beetles, and made two piles, one for warming themselves, and one for drying their blankets. The strong noon sun lifted a mist from the goatish. Bowmark frowned at the body until he realized he was looking at supper.

He stuffed the accelerator under the drier logs and poured oil over both. "Scolla, fetch me the skinning knife." He showered sparks on the accelerator until the wax popped into flame.

"I cannot. You need to make a bed of dry grass near the fire for the lady." Scolla wheezed loudly.

"Again, you think I'm your servant. Move your lazy belly and do it yourself." He moved to the second pile of wood. "I'm so hungry I could eat even you. Raw. Help me get some food." The fire started. Rummaging through the bags, he found the packet of smoked fish. He crammed them into his mouth, hoping he wouldn't starve to death before they reached his stomach. He fumed that he hadn't had the time to pack foodstuffs for his departure.

When he turned to Scolla, the spitter held only a few blades of the scanty grass, and still sat where Bowmark had deposited him, staring hopelessly at the female.

"So then," Bowmark grumped.

"Pleazzzzz," Scolla wheezed. "Help her."

Some waterroot trees clustered a short walk away. Bowmark trotted there to strip off a blanketful of leaves. There, he chewed on a smooth-skinned caterpillar, but the insect tasted so foul, he nearly lost his fish. As he knelt by the sparkling river to rinse out his mouth, Scolla screamed.

Bowmark raced back. Scolla huddled in the same spot. Jerking about, trying to see the attacker, he scooped up his staffshifter and shouted, "Where is it? Where?"

"I called, zzz, for help. Zzz. If any, zzz, People hear, sh, sh, they will. Come qui—quickly."

Bowmark put his staffshifter back in its sheath. "You might have done that sooner. You might have warned me."

"My blood is, zzz, frozen. My thoughts, zzz, are slow."

"So I observe." After retrieving the leaves and dutifully arranging the female on them, Bowmark got out his largest knife and eviscerated the goatish. From the intestines he squeezed out some turds that he tossed to Scolla. As he spitted the liver and arranged the pieces over the fire, he said, "You aren't usually this useless."

Scolla's ears lifted briefly from his eyes. "I do not, zzz, usually, zzz, have a broken arm."

"What?"

"And toes."

"Scolla!" Bowmark dropped pieces of liver on a hot rock where they sputtered. "Why didn't you say something sooner?" He knelt by the hunched spitter.

"There were, shhzz, priorities."

"It might be too late to set your arm properly. This could hurt you for the rest of your life."

"Next. Hhh. Teach me. How to eat mold."

"No need for sarcasm." Bowmark hurried over with the bag of medicines. Some of the clay containers had broken, strewing multicolored pastes.

Scolla groaned. The pain alleviator had washed away. The soporific had been diluted, but it was otherwise untainted. That he sucked up. Gasping, he gave the now nervous Bowmark instructions. He screamed when Bowmark pulled his arm to straighten the bone but slept through the binding of the arm to sticks and the wrapping of his stubby toes on one foot to immobilize them.

Bowmark sat on his heels and studied the two sleeping spitters. *Now it's my turn to play the nurse. But first, I need to eat.*

One consumed goatish later, Scolla woke up under a blanket with a hot sun overhead and Bowmark drinking from a dented pan. He whimpered. "I had hoped I would sleep. Perhaps the medication has lost its efficacy."

Bowmark stood over him, suppressing his urge to laugh. "Ho, but you did sleep. For two days." He handed the spitter his eyeshields, then awkwardly helped place them properly.

For two days Bowmark had cooked the goatish, scavenged a nearby ruined farmstead, exercised the female's limbs and changed her position, and watched the sun cross the sky. The boredom had been excruciating. Maybe they could finally do something now that the spitter had waked.

Bowmark admired the Capacity Stone on his wrist again. The third treasure. No one in StoneGrove would ever touch this but himself.

With great care, Scolla sat up. The effort seemed to exhaust him. "I do not understand."

Bowmark poured a bowl of cleverstick leaf tea for him. "Hmm?" The sweet smoke of burning loveweed joined the steam before breezing away.

"You are more sensitive to cold than I am. Yet you endured the hours in the cold river as if the trial was nothing."

"That was a journey I don't wish to repeat." Understatement. Maybe Sunrise would have delighted in the trip.

"Quite no and no." He slowly scanned the camp. "Did anyone come?"

"One of the tezledeks? No."

They listened to a lizard singing in the triplethorn bush and the river riffling over some small rapids downstream.

"Where is the goatish, where?"

"I'm surprised you don't remember. The goatish died. I ate it."

"Scolla's ears flicked. "All?"

"Not the hide. And I gave you the turds, see there?"

"It is not possible for one man to eat an entire goatish."

"I took two days to do it. I ate some lizard and some plums also. Game seems to be scarce around here."

Scolla clicked his teeth. "Something here is awry."

Bowmark stood up and backed away. "Nothing is awry. You have had an itch about my eating since we met. Why do you think I'm a pervert when I eat?"

"We eat but, aah, once a night." Scolla picked up his braced arm and, wincing, shifted his arm to his lap.

"Considering what you eat, I'm not surprised. Quit scratching me about it. I work hard. Harker taught me that to build and maintain these strong muscles I must eat more meat than normal. You remember Harker. The student with arms as thick as my legs. I wonder if he survived the Crimson Cohort. Anyway, I need these muscles to kill RaiseHim. So I need to eat."

"Not a whole goatish."

Bowmark flung out his arms. "You won't quit. Why don't you feed your lady and go back to sleep? I need to finish the travois."

"What do you wear on your arm, what? It is not a gratitude gift."

The Stone flashed as Bowmark turned his arm. "With this Capacity Stone, I can easily defeat RaiseHim."

Scolla's high voice rose to a squeak. "Take it off! Now!"

"No. I won't. How do you think I stayed warm and strong in the river?"

"Always a price must be paid. How long have you worn it, how long?"

"Since I snatched it from the Crimson Cohort. They won't be able to enslave anyone now."

Scolla squealed, "That is why we are pursued! We would not have ended in the river if you had left it! I would not have broken bones. The goatish would still be alive. You have stolen us disaster!"

Bowmark shrugged. "I'm going fishing. You take care of the lady. Tomorrow morning, we head for the coast. I'm ready to go home." He caught up his fishing gear and stalked off.

Scolla wailed, then screamed the distress call. No one came.

THE FAILURE OF AN INDIVIDUAL INFECTS THEIR ENTIRE HOUSE.
THE FAILURE OF A HOUSE INFECTS A CITY.
THE FAILURE OF A CITY INFECTS THE EMPIRE

~ CRIMSON PLATOON TRAINING MANUAL

The sun shone through a high haze. The smell of fried fish still lingered as Bowmark arranged their goods on the travois he had built by dismantling the unnecessary parts of the saddle. Dragging the bare ends of sticks on the ground dissatisfied him, but he could not think of a solution. The Sea Predators made a little use of pulleys, wheels, and wheelbarrows, however they had no wagons. He had no experience with the making of wheels. The occasional farmer sometimes built travoises to help haul loads of hay, and so he was familiar with the concept. Since the angle of the rear stowage of the saddle was different, he repurposed some of the padding to be pillows for the spitters.

He and Scolla studied the regional map he had procured in Jukalog, but could not discern where they were. The canyon country they were in lacked most of the detail and precision of the coastal maps.

Scolla whined again. "Leave the Capacity Stone for the Crimson Cohort. In the history we know, no one has touched the Stone for more than a few minutes a day. We do not know how it will affect you when you wear it for so long."

"The effect is I feel great. If you keep complaining, I'll leave without you. I don't think I need you anymore." He didn't. Once he reached the coast, he was sailing home, ten treasures or no ten treasures. The important thing was killing RaiseHim. The thought brought a grim smile.

"Our agreement!"

"Truth. As bad a bargain as I have ever made. Let's go."

He hoisted the spitters onto the travois and picked up the poles. Since rivers run to the sea, he had decided to follow the river for as long as it stayed above ground. However, he had pulled only half a rope when Scolla screamed, "Enough! Enough!"

Bowmark dropped the travois and picked up Scolla. The spitter was damp with a reeking, brown, sticky fluid.

After being set down, Scolla wheezed for a moment before saying, "I cannot tolerate any more jostling. The pain, zzz, is overwhelming. Take us by river."

"I don't trust the river. It's too fast. Only the Giver knows when it would drag us under again." He wiped his palms against a tuft of dry grass. "What is this goo?"

Scolla sighed. His head lolled. "Inflammation byproducts."

Leaving the spitter here where there was no game, and therefore no dung, nor any tezledeks, would likely be a death sentence. The spitter was annoying but not worth killing. Bowmark sighed.

The next day, Bowmark poled a makeshift raft along the edge of the river. It was simply the remains of the saddle lashed to several large sticks. It shamed him how ugly his craft was, but he refused to spend more time on its construction. A bourgeoning sense of haste made him loath to lose another moment away from StoneGrove. He fantasized about all the ways he could disarm, humiliate and kill RaiseHim.

Near noon, an odd sight immobilized Bowmark. He stared for several moments, then poled the raft half onto land and trotted over to a bone-white, hollowed tree skeleton. Branches radiated around a central hole that resembled a screaming animalistic head. Sight, touch, and the dry click when he tapped the different pieces together told him that the tree skeleton truly was bone. Bone! On the ground a handful of variously shaped animal skeletons with shreds of scales or dried hide on them dotted the ground. What kind of tree grew bones? Back on the raft, he shook Scolla awake.

"I need you to explain this to me."

"Leave me alone."

"I think you really need to see this. I don't know why, but this tree frightens me."

Scolla lifted his blanket to peer at the dirty white structure. He froze, then whimpered, "Snickering Doom."

"What? What is that thing?"

Scolla groaned. "This will hurt me, but we must leave the river and head southwest as fast as possible." He groaned again. "Perhaps it is time for me to swim. We have fled the daggertooth to fall into a grunger pit."

"I touched that whatever-it-is without harm."

"That mother tree is dead. We must leave before the sidj find us."

"Then." Bowmark pushed the raft.

"No! Heed me. We must leave the river."

"But it's the fastest way to travel."

"Not from this valley. Fetch the map."

Bowmark complied resentfully.

Scolla's claws tapped out routes on the stiff, wax-coated page. "The river runs the whole length of the Valley of the Sidj until it hits these mountains and becomes the Dismal Sea in the north. Only miniscule things that love salt bracken water live in it. By great Fortune, this valley is encompassed by mountain ranges that the mother trees cannot surmount. The only way out is south."

"Uh, Scolla. The page is blank where you're pointing."

"The valley of the sidj is not well known. But I know we must cut across the valley to this guarded pass."

"Why guarded if the trees can't climb?"

"The mother trees cannot once they have rooted. The sidj can."

"Wait, wait." Bowmark pointed to the bottom of the map. "That puts us on a road to Megaloth. I don't want to go there. They would seize my Stone."

Scolla carefully picked up his broken arm and gently laid it across his torso. "It is the only way out of the valley. And Megaloth City is the easiest place to gain the treasures you require."

"I don't require anything but the shortest way home. And the chance to kill RaiseHim, the protocol officer, and everyone else in the plot."

Scolla clicked his teeth. "Yes, and so it is that Megaloth is the shortest way home. When we were at Jukalog I ordered your canoe to be delivered to the Megaloth east bay. It is there waiting for you."

"Oh right! More herding! How shall I thank you for stealing my boat and forcing me hither and thither? I have never been so close to leaving you behind."

Head and shoulders slumped, Scolla traced invisible patterns on the sticks that braced his arm. A fly landed on the map, crawled a bit, and flew away. He said quietly, "Of all places on this wide world, I would that I not die *here*. Even if I do not die from a sidj murdering me, if one finds my body, I shall be fed to a mother tree."

A thread of Bowmark's fraying patience snapped. "Once you're dead, you won't care. What difference does it make who eats you?"

"With the sidj, every difference." His ears flopped as he gazed at the paralyzed spitter. "You are not from here, so you do not understand the horror. Since I must beg, I do beg of you: Please, if either of us die in this valley, please weight our bodies and throw us into deep water where fish will eat us."

"That is a Sea Predator honor I can grant you."

Scolla whispered, "Thank you."

"Now honor *me* and tell me why."

Scolla squirmed in the hot sunlight. "Do you understand genetics, do you?"

"What is a genetic?"

Scolla sighed and wheezed. "When you were born, parts of you appeared like your mother; parts of you appeared like your father."

Bowmark swallowed his anger at this rudeness. He nearly growled, "My mother was faithful, truth."

Scolla cocked his head. "I did not imply else."

Bowmark breathed carefully and reminded himself: different people, different rules.

Using his lecture voice, Scolla said, "This is true of nearly all that walk upon the world. The sidj are horribly different. Tch. Tch. Tch. The mobile sidj are like you in that they can eat a fish or a goatish and in the morning wake nowise different."

"How long is this explanation going to take? I'm hungry."

"Sss! The sidj are born—The sidj are grown—The sidj develop on the tips of the mother tree's branches. Indeed, they are conscious for some time before they break off. The, zzz, developing sidj use that time to listen to the mobile sidj and learn."

"What does this have to do with my mother's faithfulness?"

"Nothing. Pay attention. When they break off the tree, they can walk already, if they have legs, and they start to work. The armless ones carry loads. The legless ones chip flint for spearheads or sharpen the birthpod strut scythes. The tiny ones hunt gophers in their holes or dig up worms. Those with fingers weave tool belts. Those with scoops dig."

"Wait, uh, what? Are the sidj all cripples? I thought you were talking about how children resemble parents."

"The sidj resemble what the mother tree eats."

Bowmark recoiled. "No. Not possible. Why do you tell me such a lie? Ah! Ah, I know. You intend to trick me into going to Megaloth City."

Scolla shook his head. "I do not care where you go after we leave this vile place. You pick the destination."

"You seem sincere."

"Zzz. Pay attention. The sidj cycle begins with one, maybe two starving mother trees in the entire valley. With so few sidj, there is little hunting pressure. Grazers and their predators wander down from the mountains. Idiotic humans who refuse to remember what happened two decades before, move to the bluestone mines."

"What—"

"Bluestone is ground to a fine powder and used as a brilliant, permanent pigment in an expensive paint. Do not interrupt. The valley fills with game. The well-fed sidj give the meat of predators to the mother tree. She grows more and more sidj who feed the tree more and more meat.

"The mother tree sprouts mobile trees. The mobile tree breaks off and runs away on root pads. About half the sidj tribe follow the new tree and try to direct it to a fertile spot. The new mother tree runs for one or two days without pause. When the new tree does stop, its root pads force themselves into the ground, and the new mother tree never moves again."

"How—"

"The mobile sidj throw gobbets of flesh into the central hole at the top of the tree. Stop interrupting. Now the sidj feed the tree both predators and grazers so they can exploit all the food sources of the valley. The new mother tree sprouts more trees and sidj. Some have horns. Some have multiple legs. Some, some, and some. There is a fantastic mutation rate. The ones that are born useless are eaten by the mobile sidj. If a great hunter dies, he is fed to the mother tree.

"The best catch is any type of people: garloon, human, dractil, seafolk. Zzz, I forgot seafolks are a variant of human, zzz, tezledeks. If any of these peoples are fed to a tree, the subsequent sidj gain more speech and cunning. The sidj multiply, spread, and fill the valley. All the animals are consumed. The bluestone miners are consumed. When nothing else is left in the valley, the tribes fall on each other until there are only one or two trees remaining that have not starved to death."

Bowmark frowned and pulled on a lock of his hair that was becoming too matted. "So, how. How do I tell I'm looking at a sidj, and not you or whatever it resembles?"

"They, zzz, retain a certain sidjness. Most peoples' eyes are set within a bony cage. The eyes of the sidj protrude and are more mobile, much like that of some types of lizards. Their eyes never change. They have antennae. They are usually bone white. They travel in packs of ten to thirty."

Now Bowmark hissed. "Ten to thirty. So." He scanned the horizon. The skeleton shapes littering the ground had all been different from each other. "They are about your size on average."

Scolla wheezed, "Normally there are a few much smaller. Some are somewhat larger. A very few are larger than you."

"So, then. You've persuaded me. Where's the pass?"

Scolla awkwardly maneuvered the map about with his uninjured hand as he scanned from it to the far blur of mountains. Finally, he tapped a page. "I believe we are here. The Forbidden Pass is there."

Now Bowmark looked from the map to the distance. His fingers traced the ranges surrounding the blank valley. "We came in at . . . Barrelung Falls? And floated down, I can't read this. Ah, Hopeless River."

"Sshhh. I should have known when we came to the wall. Snickering Doom. That wall was built to keep the sidj confined to this valley."

"Oh yes, the wall! I could climb it." Then Bowmark remembered the overhanging rim of the cliffs and wall. He might be able to climb by himself, but there would be no way to bring the spitters along. "No. Never mind."

Bowmark squinted as his gaze swept the land and he calculated. "Given the terrain and my need to drag everything; I think we are facing a week-long journey. Maybe more."

Scolla passed his hand back and forth over his broken arm while extruding his sticky black rope, thereby adhering the arm firmly to his trunk. "Give me the sleeping powder." When Bowmark did so, he adhered the container to the hollow of his shoulder.

Would they have been better off if he had left the Capacity Stone behind? He rubbed it and studied the sparkle within. It alternated pulsing from translucent white to brilliant green and cast a glow over his skin. No, he needed this. The Stone was the key to his victory. He tried to articulate to himself how and why, but the words did not form. Nevertheless he knew. Somehow he knew.

Bowmark pulled the broken saddle-turned-travois off the makeshift raft and prepared to drag the spitters for over a thousand ropes.

The next day, the sky was obscured slightly by a high haze and hot air hugging the ground. Bowmark stopped jogging. An unease prompted him to scan the undulations of terrain about him, every copse of sparsely leafed trees, and every pile of naked rocks. The eerie quiet that held only the scrape of pole against stone and dirt had surrounded him ever since he left the river. Why this silence bothered him so, he could not say until he came across a slaughter site. Green and black flies rose and fell in swarms on discarded hide, turds, and cracked bones with the marrow sucked out. There was very little blood spatter. *What's here for the flies to eat?* He had no sooner had the thought than the flies decided he was their next meal.

He outran most of the biting insects and slapped the rest. His retreat left him in a copse of scraggly trees. At first he approached with trepidation, worrying that these could be Mother Trees. But closer inspection revealed they were mere wood. This was fortuitous because he needed to see more than he could while dragging a travois. The tallest tree had thorns large and sparse enough that he could easily avoid them. He climbed until the trunk dipped under his weight. There, heading away from the slaughter site, a faint black blur with ragged edges sometimes detached and split into single dots. The speed at which they moved impressed him.

The fly bites stung as he shifted to scan increasingly rocky ground around him. There, behind him, a blur with different proportions seemed to be following their pole tracks. "Fumes and ashes," he breathed.

Then battled within him the desire to abandon the spitters and the duty to hold to his promise. He decided to keep hauling the increasingly sticky spitters until either they died, or until protecting them meant his death.

Back at the travois, he gritted his teeth as he studied the lumps under the blanket. They no longer smelled of ginger, but rather stank of decay. Perhaps they had already died? No such luck. He could hear their gentle wheezing. Grimly, he picked up the end of the travois and trotted toward the far-off mountain range.

Hunger gnawed at his stomach and weakened his thighs, but he pushed ahead, snatching insects that rose from his footsteps. His efforts left shards of chitin stuck between his teeth, and wing dust coating his tongue. The thought of his flesh feeding the intelligence of motley, mutated tree slaves kept his feet moving. Sweat runneled the dust on his face and chest. He swerved and stopped only when he saw early plums. That none of the other bushes and trees bore fruit or nuts yet offended him. Fruit-bearing plants on his island sensibly bore all year long.

At dusk, he climbed another tree and saw his trackers had camped within a circle of fires. They were closer. No help for it. He had to rest. He drank the last of the water and slumped beside the travois.

The next day was worse. At dusk his pursuers were camping close enough that the following day would see them overtaking him. Exhaustion pinned him to the ground, but hunger refused to let him sleep. He spent the night staring at the stars and rummaging through useless ambush plans.

That next morning, Scolla informed him that hoisting the spitters into a tree would not protect them from sidj, as most of them were able to climb. With deep aggravation, Bowmark grabbed the travois, and began the final leg of this hopeless race.

Five candles later, he topped a rise, staggered a bit, and dropped the travois to take a breath. The muscles in his arms and back burned and twitched. He stood crouched with his hands on his knees and blew hard through a throat that ached with thirst.

His pursuers jogged over a hill that was only three gullies behind him. Not sidj! A diminished company of chalk white women with bows and spears, wearing dark red leather armor, jogged in disciplined ranks.

Bowmark snatched the travois and skittered down the rise. He heaved the travois onto his back, so the ends of the poles lifted off the ground, and he waddled left to the far side of a rock pile. The travois thumped back to the ground. He had not the strength to wholly carry the sticks save for a few moments. Maybe losing the track would confuse his pursuers enough that he could—he could what? Giver knew.

He ran with the travois bucking and prancing behind him. Rounding a thick copse he ran smack into a sidj.

Nearly forty of them lay napping, most with belly to air, and a few butchered a handful of small, furry animals. The sidj Bowmark had knocked over scrambled upright in an unnaturally fast and jerky manner. It had two legs, but three arms, and stood as tall as Bowmark's waist. Dried blood was spattered around its dingy white maw and chest. Bowmark and the little monster with protruding eyes and a serrated beak stared at each other in shock. Tarnished and bloodied wooden hand scythes and knives lay strewn across the trampled grass.

The sidj snarled and vibrated its fringed antenna.

Bowmark kicked the thing in the face. "AAAAAAAAA!" The sidj arced through the air like a child's ball. Bowmark screamed and sprinted through the camp over the sidj too small or too slow to evade him.

The sidj tumbled in confusion.

"AAAAAAAAAA!" Bowmark charged through the site. The travois broke some sidj limbs. The creatures scrambled for their weapons. A sidj as tall as Bowmark stumbled to its feet. He swerved around the monster. A dust cloud roiled up behind him. Howls of pain and howls of excitement mingled in his wake.

Now was the time to dump the spitters and run unimpeded, but his hands would not let go of the poles.

Women's screams joined the howling. Weapons clashed.

Bowmark dared not look back as he plunged ahead. He pulled and pulled and pulled, then was surprised to find himself face down in the dirt. How?

Listening intently, he lifted his head. He heard nothing save the wheezing of the spitters. The travois lay across his back and legs. He flexed each limb with deliberation. Nothing broken. His right foot was caught in a tangle of wiry vines. When he drew his foot in, the tangle gave way and filled the air with the smell of mud.

Mud!

Bowmark threw off the travois. Dizzy and shaking he slowly stood, craning his head to see behind him. No movement. He had tripped on the banks of a streamlet, a shining thread bubbling through the roots of sedges and forbs.

Bowmark ripped out plants to form a tiny pool that gradually filled with silty water. Something moved in the mud and he snatched up a soft-skinned creature that wriggled until he whacked it against a rock. He slurped the animal down whole, gagging on the tail. Probing brought forth a few grubs.

During his tenth time of sucking the pool dry, a honeybee bobbed on a sedge blossom near his nose. When the insect flew off, he followed it to a copse and a hollow log filled with buzzing.

A heavy rock tossed from high in a tree smashed the log. Grub-filled honeycombs splattered across the grove. Frenzied bees shot about, searching for a foe to sting. They did not notice the mud-coated man far above them. Confused by their utter ruin, they did not follow the metal claws that slowly drew chunks of the comb away.

Bowmark ate comb, honey, grubs, mutualists, and parasites all. His vision cleared, and euphoria rushed in. Strength flooded his limbs. Ha! He had escaped both sidj and the Crimson Cohort. Thinking of the sidj made his hair rise. Dried mud flaked and broke off as he rubbed his arms. So many shapes, so many ways to appear evil.

He again flung the magic cord, staffshifter gripping one end of the cord in its metal snake fist, over the limb directly above the shattered log. He drew up more honeycomb which he jammed into a bag. When he started scraping up more chunks of punky wood than honey, he reattached everything to his person and settled back against the trunk to wait for the bees to carry their queen elsewhere.

Belatedly, he realized he should have been scanning the area. He needed to add hunger to the list of things that make you forget to think. Holding as still as possible, he slowly studied the land below and about him.

A flash caught his eye. He turned only his head and saw a female soldier tearing apart the supplies on his travois. One. His eyes flicked back and forth. Only one. How had she not seen him? She upended the bag with fire materials and sent them bouncing over the rock and dust.

He had to get to her before she discovered his tracks to the tree. To stay unseen meant he would need to descend the tree on the broken log side, into the whirling cloud of furious bees. *Hot lava, but this will hurt.* He crept down, buzzing gently, hoping to calm the small warriors. Then he stepped on some.

Their crushed bodies exuded an odor that told the others to attack. The stings burnt like molten iron droplets. He covered his eyes with one hand and peered one-eyed through a slight gap between two fingers as he crawled away to the brush lining the streamlet. His concentration on crawling unseen to the woman helped defer some of the pain. After an interminably long time, the surviving honeybees streamed back to the broken log.

He finally crept close enough that he could hear her muttering fiercely while throwing his things against a boulder. "Moldy man! Rot him!"

He crawled closer.

Her head jerked up and her nostrils flared.

Bowmark hurled his cord. "Rope, stick!"

She spun toward him, flung up her arms, and fell under the tangle of rope.

Now he could pull the stingers from his skin.

His tiny pool had filled again, and he used the water to wash off most of the layers of mud while the Warrior Woman cursed him. "You creeping crud! You mildewed rag!"

The search for the salve took a long time. She watched with squinted eyes and set, red-stained lips as Bowmark gathered his strewn supplies.

Scolla moaned. The woman had placed him with his arm at an awkward angle.

Bowmark hastily set him in a comfortable position on the travois.

The woman strained at the rope and spat. "One admirable thing about you—you take good care of your parents!"

He placed the female spitter and tied down several bags.

"Now that I know your stench, you'll be easy to track."

He covered the spitters with a tattered blanket and tied down some more bags.

"You killed my entire company! You killed my best friend!"

Bowmark stopped and swallowed hard. His vision blurred. He blinked back clarity and picked up the woman's backpack and loose weapons.

"There's no name evil enough for the human who allies himself with the sidj."

He poked through her backpack and pulled out a water skin he set aside and several strips of pemmican he hesitated over. Then he ate them.

"What kind of monster doesn't care when he condemns thousands of people to death?" the woman demanded.

Bowmark slowed his chewing and examined the woman trussed in the dirt. She had several shocking red gashes in her opaque white skin. Her thickly muscled limbs indicated that she practiced the lifting of weights. Sweat and dust had made her white hair dingy, shaved on the sides, and braided in many strands that wove through a beautifully formed metal headdress. Reddened eyes lined with dark soot glared at him. Silvery gray irises made her gaze intense. He swallowed, and said, "Enslaver, how do you say such?"

"Enslaver? We create order. We enforce the law. We only enslave criminals."

"And their innocent families."

"Those families are not innocent. Nor are you. Thousands of the poor in Megaloth will starve because of you stealing the Capacity Stone." She glared at him with startling disdain.

"I only take away your power to enslave," Bowmark said.

"How do you think we protect the farms on the ungol Frontier?"

"You train the farmers how to fight, and arm them?"

"You fool! We don't arm criminals! Defense is *our* job! *We* protect the food that feeds Megaloth. *We*, the Crimson Cohort. Know this, son of dung-eaters, we will retrieve the Stone, with or without your arm attached to it! We will not let the ungols rule our fields."

Bowmark adjusted the Stone on his wrist, then pulled out some rope and stood twisting it, reluctant to do what came next. His vow to Sunrise to not waste his death steeled him. He turned to kneel beside her.

Her breathing accelerated. She strained uselessly against the magic cord.

His hands trembled as he removed two large knives that were sheathed on her forearms, then he tied her hands together and lashed her forearms up to her elbows. He turned one of her knives around, curious at the instrument. It had a knife edge and point on a disproportionately large hilt. And there, a small button. Like his staff shifter. Was this a magical weapon as well? After some fiddling, the weapon telescoped to three times its original length when whipped quickly. He could not figure out how to collapse it back down without risking injury, but determined that it was not magical, simply a marvelous mechanical design like the spyglass he had seen earlier.

The woman cried out, tears pooling in her eyes. "Do you leave me for the sidj to throw into their vile trees?"

He tied her ankles. "I'll leave you water there, and your sword . . . things, on the other side of those rocks. When you free yourself, go home. Don't follow me."

The woman looked around desperately, her face turning from worry to despair.

She breathed as deeply as her bindings would let her, and softened her voice. "Listen. What is your name?"

"Why would I tell you that?"

"I understand. Please listen to me. My name is Lilk, of the Adamantine House. If I return without the Stone I might as well slit my own throat. I have so vowed. And you… you… sir. You are being manipulated by the Stone. It changes people. It causes men to go insane. This is why only women are sanctioned to use it for combat. Please. Please think about your behavior. Has it changed since you've worn it?"

Bowmark's hand almost reached a knife. His emotions were sloshing from grief to intense anger to regret to desire to despair. His hand returned to the Stone, and he had to force his trembling fingers back to the task of tying.

Lilk continued, pleading. "My mother killed herself because the Stone was lost under her watch. Our entire house is disgraced. I am here to restore our honor."

Bowmark jerked at a knot. The emotions were coalescing into a deep misery and puzzlement at how he had arrived here. "Your honor is not worth more than the life of your friend or yourself." His own words sounded hollow and weak, as if spoken by someone else.

Her voice hardened again. "My entire house must kill themselves if I do not succeed. More blood on your hands because of your selfishness."

Bowmark pulled Lilk's face up to his and shouted, "I did not kill my friend—you did! You would use this Stone for slavery! I will use it for liberation! You live by stupid rules! Stupid laws! Stupid protocol! Change your rules or die! You choose!"

He blinked. He had said something wrong. "I mean—I. I need to change my people's rules." He lowered her. "Rope, come."

The magic cord slithered into his hands leaving her bound with the rest of his tattered jute rope. "Don't follow me." He fled to the travois and picked up the handles. "Leave me alone."

He ran away as she screamed, "Murderer!" after him.

UNQUENCHABLE ANGER. PARANOIA. RECKLESS RAGE.
THE STONE INFECTS MEN.
THUS THE BURDEN FALLS UPON THE ELITE WOMEN.

~ CRIMSON PLATOON TRAINING MANUAL

That night, Bowmark sat with his arms around his legs and his chin on his knee. High clouds dimly streaked the greater moon. The boulders released the day's heat against his back.

Groggy Scolla stumbled around the travois and whimpered. He thrust a box toward Bowmark. "The lid is broken. My ointment is missing. What happened, what?"

Bowmark rubbed the Stone. The bee stings were mere annoyances now. His various scrapes had nearly healed, or at least *seemed* that way. Still, he felt somehow brittle. Would the people of Megaloth truly starve without their slaves? *If so, they deserve to.* Bowmark raised his head a thumb-width. "Scolla, come touch the Capacity Stone. It can heal your arm."

"Quite no. I tell you again, leave it where the Megalothi will find it."

"Do you like to live in pain?" Bowmark asked.

"The Stone is dangerous. Do you not see how you have changed, do you not?"

"So you tell me over and over. If you won't be healed, go away and leave me alone."

"Another bottle is cracked. What happened, what?"

"A Crimson Cohort woman threw our stuff around. I stopped her. Some things were broken. That's all."

Scolla squealed, "Sss! You had the chance to give it back! They shall pursue you forever!"

Bowmark dragged a blanket over his head to shut out the stupid spitter and mused hopelessly about lovely, red stained lips.

The land had wrinkled into gullies and long, erose ridges of rock. Bowmark could not find a route that did not jolt Scolla mercilessly. The spitter hissed constantly, yet refused to take any of the sleeping powder. The cool morning had evaporated into a burning afternoon in which all the water had been drunk and the early grasses had already turned brown and crackled underfoot.

Bowmark paused to wipe sweat from his forehead before it could trickle into his eyes. He despised Scolla's stubby legs that dictated the spitter must be a passenger and not someone who could help haul. He detested where he was, for he needed to be home to kill RaiseHim and the other royal conspirators. He had compiled a growing list of those he would personally execute when he returned. He resented this stony valley empty of game, greens, and fruit. He abhorred this land filled with nightmare sidj he must continually watch for. He hated the promise he had made to Scolla to keep him from being eaten by the sidj. He resented the dirt that caked his scalp. He loathed the stupid goatish who had put him here.

Wiping his face again, he stared at the far-away, jagged wall of mountains before him, then slapped a stingfly.

A sudden push from behind knocked him headfirst into the gully. Scolla tumbled after and rolled over his head. Dazed, Bowmark looked up. Scolla threw sleeping powder in his face.

A persistent pain in his back nudged Bowmark awake. Nausea gripped his empty stomach. Foulness coated his tongue. He blinked one eye. His head lay on his torn blue shirt. He reached up to rub his headache.

The Stone! The Capacity Stone was gone!

Shaking, he pushed himself upright. "Where is it?"

Scolla waddled into view. "Zzz. You may thank me, young human, for I have saved your life."

Bowmark had trouble focusing. He felt brittle and horribly hollow. "What? The Stone. Where?"

"Zzz. I knew the Crimson Cohort would pursue us to the end of the world."

Bowmark coughed. Every time he coughed pain stabbed in his back. Clumsily, he reached behind and fingered a wound tied with thread. When he brought his hand back, dried flakes of blood hung on his fingertips.

"The arrow did not fully penetrate your backpack, sss, and knocked us down, by great Fortune, into this ravine."

"Fortune?" His brain buzzed. Had he heard correctly?

"Zzz yes. I knew we would be hidden for some moments."

"You. You put me to sleep."

"Yes. Zzz zzz. I pulled the arrow out of your backpack and bit it in half. I then bit a hole in your back."

"You *bit* me?"

"I smeared blood on the back half of the arrow and inserted it in the hole. I hid the front half under me."

"You *bit* me?"

"Necessity for ruse. A warrior of the Crimson Cohort came with swords to kill you. When she pulled out the arrow, she thought it had broken off inside you. You did not move. She thought you were already dead, so she grabbed the Stone, kicked your head, and ran away. Shh."

"You *bit* me! *Did I taste good?*"

"Zzz zzz zzz. No. Too raw."

Bowmark threw himself at Scolla to throttle him. "*You gave away my stone!*"

Scolla gasped. "I saved your life."

Bowmark squeezed.

Scolla swelled up, clawed his arms and kicked.

Bowmark screamed from pain and fury as he squeezed tighter.

Scolla ripped deep furrows through his tunic sleeves and into Bowmark's forearms.

Bowmark dropped him and fumbled for his staffshifter.

Squealing, Scolla deflated and scrambled up the gully bank.

"*You stole my stone!*" *Zip!* The snake claws smashed into the thin soil.

Scolla scuttled toward a crevice in a tumble of jagged stone.

The blood pumping from his arms slicked the staffshifter, spattering the ground and Bowmark's legs. "*I need that stone!*" *Zip!* The staffshifter's outstretched claw pierced through one of Scolla's upper ears, pinning him to a rock. Bowmark's free hand formed a fist.

Scolla tore free and slipped into the crevice.

Bowmark shoved the staffshifter into the crack, scraping and rattling against its sides, but not feeling the soft resistance of flesh. The spitter had gone too deep. "Come out and face me like a man, you coward, you thief, you sludge!"

He peered into the crevice. On instinct he drew his head back as an ill-smelling black blob shot out of the crack.

He dropped to his knees and strained to pull away the boulders he could not have moved in his full strength.

Vision narrowed to what his hands touched. Using his staffshifter as a lever also failed to budge the natural fortress. *Ashes!*

He stood too quickly, staggered with dizziness, grabbed the boulder, and pounded on it with his fists. "Kratchnak! Maybe I can't get you; but I can get your lady!" He slid down the bank to the travois and threw back the blanket covering the female. His hands fumbled for the staffshifter he had left at the boulder pile.

He pulled a knife from his waistband and dropped it because he needed a larger one, the one in his boot seam.

"Do not harm her," whined Scolla.

Turning was problematic, but Bowmark accomplished it after two false starts. Part of him remarked that he was losing too much blood. The rest of him only wanted revenge. "Why not? I'm tired of dragging her. She's just dead weight! Why shouldn't she go forth and *be* dead?"

Scolla came close to stand on the edge of the bank. "She has but barely begun her life. Do not take it away."

"*You took away my stone!*" The knife slipped in his hand.

Scolla flung his hands in front of himself. "Please! I say please! Please!"

"Please won't bring back my Stone!" He blinked away dust that fizzed on his eyeballs. "You betrayed me. You—" His knees wandered away from the rest of his body until he fell on them. He flung the knife, but where it went, he could not see. What he did see was the sleeping powder vial still adhered to Scolla's shoulder. The traitor had tricked him! He reached for Scolla but grasped a rock. His elbows hit the ground. He toppled onto his back. "Scorch you, Scolla!" he mumbled hoarsely. "Scorch you!" His hands could no longer grip, nor could his eyes stay open. His consciousness flittered away.

We're so glad you read this book. If you liked the adventure, it would be kind of you to leave a review somewhere so other people can discover this book. It also helps greatly if you ask your local library to order a copy of the book.

Josh Foreman has worked in the video game industry for decades. Artist and designer, he's worked on such games as Descent 3, Guild Wars, Ori And The Will Of The Wisps & Blankos Block Party. Josh is also known for his sculpture tutorials on YouTube. He does other stuff, too. For instance, he keeps an entire stable of trolls well-fed. Don't get him started on talking about videogame cutscenes.

Josh is happy to receive comments, corrections, and adulation at www.breathoflifedev.com or his YouTube channel www.youtube.com/scrybe.

Rose Foreman was born and things progressed from there. After gaining a degree in Clinical Lab Technology, she swam in the South China Sea, the Atlantic Ocean, and the YMCA. She has climbed Mt. Fuji, Mt. St. Helens, and viewed Mt. Denali. She has raised and released five children. (including Josh Foreman). Cyborg (cochlear implant) and avid gardener, she enjoys collaborating with her oldest son on stories set on Talifar. Don't get her started on talking about Rwanda.

Now turn the page to read the first chapter of

Scarred King III

TALES OF TALIFAR

THE SCARRED KING III

PROVING

One rock dug into Bowmark's shoulder, and another lower down on his back, where muscles spasmed around the pebble. Bowmark tried to shift, but he could move nothing except his dry lips and desiccated tongue. He meditated on those two points of pain, for no other thoughts entered his mental blankness. His throat hurt. An illness? Had he been screaming?

The rocks poked. Hunger twisted his stomach. A sound of movement reached his ears, yet he himself was not moving. If he concentrated, he could move his hands a bit. His fingers probed strands crossing his legs.

After more concentration, he half-opened one gunk-encrusted eye. Slanted sunlight. Dusk, or dawn? Strands crossed his face and held down his shoulders, but exhaustion held him down more thoroughly than the spitter rope did. He rubbed his dry tongue against his dry lips.

A black spitter, with one of his long arms bound by sticks and bandages, and wearing pin-holed goggles waddled over and looked down at him. "You should be dead!" he hissed in Zledek. His bat wing-shaped ears trembled. His hands flared wide. His wrinkled skin smoothed as he swelled, and spines popped out. Even though he was only the size of a two-year-old human, from the ground he appeared huge.

Bowmark blinked his one open eye and tried to think. His arms began to sting and then burn ferociously. "Water."

"Sss. Our water is gone. Pay attention. You should be dead!" He brought Bowmark's biggest boot knife into view and lowered its point to within a thumb-width of Bowmark's eye.

"Scolla?"

"I shall now tell you what you must do, or you die."

Bowmark had trouble focusing on anything but the knife point near his eye.

"From this time to forever, you shall do what I tell you without hesitation. Never again will you disobey me. Never, or you shall die."

Memory rushed in. "Scolla!" he rasped. "By His Hand! Did I hurt you?"

Scolla hissed and leaned closer. "You tried to kill me after I saved your life! Quite *yes* you hurt me!" A tear in one of his upper ear lobes was crusted with blood.

Shame burned his mind. Bowmark had put that tear in Scolla's ear. "And—and—and the lady? Did—did I hurt her?"

"Not directly. However, she and I are starving in this blighted land."

Scolla drove the knife into a nearby desiccated animal carcass with startling violence. "We starve because of your rashness. You have damaged us and our mission with your stupidity."

Bowmark's throat ached with more than desiccation. "I threatened a helpless, harmless woman. How could—how could—I am become RaiseHim."

"Next command. Never call me friend. I do not like what you do to your friends."

"I can't go back if I'm a bigger monster than RaiseHim. I have failed Sunrise. I have failed Father. Why? Why did I attack you?"

"Because you are a faithless human. I shall never trust you again."

"How do I live with myself? I want to tell you I am sorry, because I am. I am sorry. But—but regret does nothing. I can't make this right."

"No. You cannot."

"Scolla, please. Please. The jugular, the vein on side of my neck. Slice it, and I'll never hurt anyone again."

Scolla said slowly and distinctly, "I cannot walk out of this valley before the Sidj catch us."

Bowmark tried to swallow. "So. So I need to carry you out."

"Yess."

With rocks boring into his back, his intestines knotting up in pain, and the memory of his insane rage searing his mind's eye, Bowmark could not think coherently. One mercy: His arms had quit burning. Now they felt cold, as did his feet. "Sco—" He closed his eye. Forming words required inordinate concentration. "Then you need to release me."

"What will you do, what?"

He didn't know. He didn't know what he was anymore. The cold and numbness spread.

"Human, answer me."

He had. His lungs seemed reluctant to inflate. His heart stumbled. "I'm sorry," he breathed. He felt claws and finger pads touching his face. "I will fail you, too. Again." And he wouldn't even be with Sunrise. Where would His Hand throw him?

"Stupid human! Rouse yourself."

"Cold. Dying."

"You are always cold."

Not when he wore the Capacity Stone. Then, he was always warm. Bowmark felt, as though through padding, Scolla laying his head and ear against his chest.

"You are cold. Your heart is slowing."

No one to bury him decently in water. He would be tree food. *Scorch my life.*

Clawed fingers spread his mouth open to dribble in honey. Salivary glands stung. He choked weakly, and then appetite took over. He sucked down honey, comb, and grubs faster than Scolla could stuff them in. Somewhere during his slurping and chewing, Scolla ate the extrusions that had held Bowmark. Gratefully, Bowmark rolled onto his side and gnawed on the hide bag to extract every last flek of honey, which had ended long before his hunger had. Finally, he croaked, "More."

"There is no more."

Trembling, Bowmark planned out his movements a long time before attempting them. Three efforts brought him to his hands and knees. The gouges on his arms had been sewn, not with Scolla's usual neat, tight stitching, but with large, careless loops. Because Scolla had sewed one handed or because he was angry? "I feel terrible."

"As do I. Stand or die."

Bowmark sat back on his legs to look straight at the spitter's shades. Behind Scolla, mountain peaks glowed with the light of the rising sun. How was he going to pull the spitters to safety with Scolla telling him to die at every step? "I detest being threatened."

Flicking his ears in dismissal, Scolla said, "In this I do not threaten. I only state a fact. Also," he wriggled the knife out of the carcass, "you have threatened me innumerable times. You have tried to kill me twice. I have guided you, healed you, and protected you. Still you seek my harm. I shudder to think that I allowed a vicious animal to say he is the same as me. Henceforth, you call me Master."

Helpless rage burned the backs of Bowmark's gritty eyes. Yet the spitter spoke truth. He spoke truth. Bowmark's shoulders sagged. One hot tear scalded his right eye. "So."

"So stand."

With much swaying and stumbling, Bowmark stood and gripped the travois. He needed only to reach Forbidden Pass. Then he could step off a cliff.

Editing and Story Development Assistance:

Kim O'Hara, Bloo, Jeff Gerke, Frank Foreman

Science Advisors:

Domika Clarke, Ian Dwyer, Rose Gallo

(If you are a scientist and would like to advise us on future work please email us at BreathOfLifeDev@gmail.com)

Beta Readers:

A.J. Bakke (also the longest and best Patron), AJ Scudiere, Brian Schaab, Damon Rath, Isla Rose, Jennifer Hoffman, Juls Finney, Kessandra Pendragon, Lucas Michalczyk, (Also a great help with the blurb!) Michael McClelland, Nicole Stufflebeam, Sigrid Sol Karll, Kessie Carroll

Constant Companions during development streams and Discord:

Chris Thompson-Peat (AKA Fizzmatix) who has been a good friend and collaborator with both tech and art.

Endivies who gives wonderful real-time feedback during visual development streams and continually pushes for boopable noses.

GarThor, Orztirr, Demithyle and all the others who bring good positive vibes to the Discord.

Miscellaneous Shoutouts:

Chris Elliot, long time friend and creative encourager.

Kirill Federspiel, long time friend and philosophical/ artistic inspirer.

Neil @ Real Terrain Hobbies who gave an unprompted shoutout to Scarred King 1 on his amazing YouTube channel, and provider of terrain inspiration.

And a huge thanks to all the Patrons and Guild Wars fans who have supported us over the years!